HARD FALL

A Lucy Guardino FBI
Thriller

D1214888

SPECIAL EDITION: INCLUDES
FREE BONUS NOVELLA,
AFTER SHOCK

CJ LYONS

AFTER SHOCK

A Lucy Guardino FBI Thriller Novella

CJ Lyons

EDGY READS

Never surrender, never quit the fight.
~Francis Guardino

CHAPTER 1

LUCY GUARDINO HEAVED her body free from the black pit that had been her prison, her bloody handprints a stark contrast to the snow. She rolled over, faceup. The sky was growing dark. Not the complete absence of light that had drowned her when she'd been trapped belowground. Rather, the twilight of a winter's night. A scarlet ribbon of light clung to the hills in the distance, the last remnant of sun that this day would see.

She closed her eyes and rubbed the skin on her neck left raw by the rope. Home. She wanted to go home. To be with Nick and Megan.

How long? How long since her captor had left her? How much time did she have? Snow numbing her body through her wet clothes, her breath coming in shallow gasps, she tried to quiet her thoughts enough to perform the simple calculation.

January. Sun set around five. He'd said his deadline was seven. But how long had it taken her to free herself?

How long since he'd left?

How much time did her family have before he killed them?

A bird screeched, shattering the quiet. Lucy opened her eyes. Some kind of owl. Bad omen. Her throat clenched against unbidden laughter, choking it to silence. Even the slight attempt at making a sound burned, her throat scraped raw from almost choking to death down below.

But she hadn't choked to death. Hadn't drowned either. She'd escaped.

Her body shook with cold—all she wore were slacks, a silk blouse, and a thin suit jacket. She was soaked through. But she was alive.

He hadn't intended that. He thought she'd die down in that pit.

Which meant he wasn't infallible. He made mistakes.

The biggest one was threatening her family. Nick. Megan. She had to save them.

Get up! In her mind, her voice was loud, not to be ignored. The barn. She had to make it across the field to the barn. It would be warm there—and she was cold, so very cold. Maybe there'd be a phone. A car. Weapons.

The dog. Panic danced with pain, centered on her left ankle and foot. For a second she couldn't breathe, terror throttling her—as effective as the rope had been earlier. Red spots swirled through her vision and refused to vanish even after she closed her eyes. Oh hell, how could she have forgotten the dog? It would scent her blood, stalk her, finish the job it had begun.

Nick. Megan. Their names were a tonic, easing the turmoil. Thinking of them, she could breathe again. She could put aside the pain—no worse than the pain when she'd had Megan, too late for an epidural. What a blessing that pain had been. So very worth it.

Taking control of her breathing, focusing on nothing except her family, Lucy climbed to her feet. *Oh God, it hurts, it hurts so bad. Breathe,* she told herself. *Just breathe. Nick and Megan are depending on you. You're the only one who can save them.*

The pain inched away, waiting for the chance to ambush her again with her next step. She clenched her fists, refusing to lose her momentum. This time she was ready. She took a short hobble-step, balancing on her left toes only long enough to swing her right foot forward.

She staggered across the snow-covered field, leaving a trail of blood behind her. Each step thundered as her left foot touched the ground no matter how briefly. Twice the pain overtook her, forcing her to stop, losing precious time.

Through the haze of misery, she saw Nick's face, the special smile he reserved for their private moments, coaxing her forward. Megan's laugh swirled around her, buoying Lucy up against the tide of pain, and she was able to start moving again.

She breathed through the agony, clinging to thoughts of her family, and the barn—a large metal Quonset-hut structure a hundred yards away—slowly grew closer.

The evening was silent. No distant lights or rumble of cars. Just the whispered sigh of wind through the trees that surrounded the field and the rasp of Lucy's breathing. She wrapped her arms around her chest, trying to generate some heat. Her right hand clasped Megan's bracelet—it had saved her life. She couldn't wait to see Megan, to tell her how her gift had saved them all.

She imagined her daughter's arms—and Nick's as well—hugging her tight, so tight. They'd be all right, she vowed. He wasn't going to harm them. Not tonight. Not ever.

Not while she still drew breath.

She blinked and realized she'd made it. She was at the Quonset-hut barn with its large sliding door, built for farm machinery like combines and tractors. There was a smaller, man-sized door beside the larger one. She reached for the latch but stopped.

Light edged its way around the door. More than light. Sound. The rustle of someone moving around inside.

He was in there. She could end this here and now. Finish it before he ever had a chance to get near her family.

Or should she run? Shape she was in, injured, weak, cold, no weapon—how could she take him on?

She glanced around, hating how much effort it took to force a clear thought through the cold that muddled her mind. The sun was gone, vanished behind the hills to the west, but it wasn't completely dark, thanks to the twilight glow offered by the snow. Across the fields there was nothing except trees.

She had no idea what lay beyond the barn. Perhaps escape. Perhaps her captor's accomplices.

Perhaps the dog.

That made up her mind. She couldn't face that beast again.

Lucy's hand tightened on the latch. He'd made his final mistake, letting her live.

———◦———

THEN
JANUARY 21, 7:34 A.M.

"MEGAN! DON'T MAKE your dad late." Lucy called up the stairs from the kitchen as she munched on a piece of peanut-butter toast, holding the toast with one hand and unplugging her cell phone from its charger with the other. "Not if you want time to stop by the vet's and see if Zeke's feeling better."

Their orange tabby swirled between her legs, leaving marmalade streaks of hair on Lucy's black slacks as he meowed, pining for his missing canine companion. Lucy would never admit it to anyone, but she missed the exuberant puppy as well.

Zeke, Megan's Australian shepherd, had gotten sick yesterday, with vomiting and diarrhea so bad Lucy and Megan had rushed him to the vet. Poor thing was going through a stage where he ate anything—who knew what tasty treat he'd found while in the backyard. Seeing Megan so upset, in tears as they'd left Zeke with the veterinarian, was exactly the reason Lucy hadn't wanted any pets in the first place.

It was one of the few times she and Nick had actually fought—and that she'd lost. They'd only been in Pittsburgh a few months, and she was just getting her feet under her in her new job leading the FBI's Sexual Assault Felony Enforcement task force. Nick had his new psychology practice. Megan was juggling school and soccer and making friends. It couldn't have been a worse time to take on the added responsibilities that came with an animal.

So, of course, they'd ended up with two, a dog and a cat, in the space of a week. She still wasn't sure how that'd happened—blamed it on the mild concussion she'd suffered at the time.

Nick bounded through the door to the garage, accompanied by the noise of his Explorer idling. "Megan!" he shouted up the steps.

"I told you I have to cover group tonight, right?" he asked Lucy, stealing a bite from the opposite side of the piece of toast in her mouth while she freed her hands to slip into her suit jacket and smooth stray crumbs from her blouse. She wiped peanut butter from his lip, snagged a quick kiss. Peanut butter and mouthwash, not the best combo.

"Mom's coming to sit, since I have no clue how long this snoozefest in Harrisburg is going to last." Her appointment to the Governor's Task Force on Violent Crime Prevention was meant to be an honor, but so far the monthly meetings had been more about placing blame and whining about budget cuts, and less about taking action. Exactly the kind of meetings she despised.

Megan clomped down the steps, her school bag slung over her shoulder, gym bag with her karate gear in hand. "Why is Grams coming to babysit?" she asked, rushing past Nick and Lucy as if they were the ones dawdling. "You said I could go to the movies with Emma after karate, remember?"

Lucy glanced at Nick, rolling her eyes out of sight of Megan. Ever since she'd turned thirteen Megan seemed to think her parents were addled old folk she could outwit with fast talk and misdirection. Sad thing was, given Lucy and Nick's busy work schedules, Megan's tactics too often worked. "Nice try, but no."

"Mom—"

Nick intervened. "You're not old enough for an R-rated movie."

"But Emma's parents—"

"Aren't the puritanical monsters we are. I know, I know." Lucy ruffled Megan's dark curls, which matched her own, and hugged her daughter, despite Megan's protests. "Besides, it's a school night."

Megan squirmed free. "I don't need a babysitter. I'm thirteen. I should be babysitting other kids."

"We know that. But—" Lucy looked to Nick for help. How to explain that her anxiety had nothing to do with Megan and everything to do with the outside world and the people who inhabited it? Psychopaths like the Zapata drug cartel thugs who'd tried to burn down half of Pittsburgh last Christmas.

"But we would feel better having another adult here with you," Nick said, emphasizing the "another."

Nice touch, Lucy thought. It helped having a clinical psychologist to share the load when negotiating with a teenager.

Although lately it felt like much of Megan's behavior was less about rebellion and more about reestablishing balance to her world. A suspicion confirmed when instead of pulling away from her mother, Megan reached out a hand to stroke the braided black Paracord bracelet she'd given Lucy for Christmas. Megan had made it herself, incorporating a secret touch: the clasp concealed a handcuff key. Something that would have come in handy a few months ago when a serial killer had taken Lucy hostage.

Lucy hated that her daughter thought that way. Hated that she had to. She wore the bracelet every day, not because her duties as supervisory special agent in charge of the FBI's Sexual Assault Felony Enforcement squad put her in danger—ninety-nine percent of her time at work was spent behind a desk fighting terminal boredom, not violent felons. She wore it because she wanted Megan to feel secure. "Besides, your grandmother hasn't seen you in a week. It'll give you two time to catch up."

Since Megan knew exactly how to shamelessly manipulate her maternal grandmother into doing almost anything, she smiled and nodded. "So it'd be okay if Grams took Emma and me to the movie instead of Emma's big sister, right?"

"Wrong," Nick and Lucy chorused.

Megan just grinned. Then her expression turned mournful. "Does Zeke really have to stay another night at the vet's? He's going to be okay, right?"

"Dr. Rouff said he'd be fine," Lucy answered. "She's only keeping him as a precaution."

Really? Nick mouthed. She gave him a small nod as she hugged Megan goodbye, glad that she'd found time to call the vet already this morning. Just like she'd found time to schedule quick trips home during the day yesterday to check on Zeke when he first started acting sluggish and then got sick. Not because she really cared about the rambunctious puppy who was as likely to eat her shoes as his dog food. No, of course not. It was Megan she was worried about.

"You don't fool me, you old softy," Nick whispered as he grabbed Lucy around the waist for another kiss. "You are devoted to that puppy."

Lucy squinched her nose at him. "Hush. You'll blow my image as a kick-ass federal agent. It's the only way I get any respect around here."

Nick chuckled, shaking his head. "Yeah, right."

"Come on, Dad. We're late." Megan waved goodbye and ran out with Nick on her heels.

The door slammed shut behind them. For one rare moment the old Victorian fell silent. Then the heat clicked on, old pipes creaking in protest as steam rattled through them. Lucy glanced around the kitchen with its bright-yellow paint and busy-family-on-the-run-Post-it–note decor. She slid her service weapon into the front pocket of her bag for the long drive to Harrisburg, slipped her backup Glock into its ankle holster, grabbed her travel mug of coffee, and headed out the front door.

Lucy always parked her Subaru nose-out in the driveway, since the garage was crammed full of bikes and other junk, leaving only room for one car. Plus she had to leave in the middle of the night more often than Nick—at least she used to. Now that his patient load at the VA's PTSD clinic was climbing, it was a fifty-fifty toss-up who would be called out into the dark hours.

Nick had scraped her Impreza clear of the few inches of overnight snow and started the engine so it would be toasty warm for her. Fifteen years of marriage and he still remembered the little things.

As she walked out to her car, double-checking her bag to make sure she had the files she needed, she reminded herself to try to think of something special to surprise him. Maybe for Valentine's Day she'd kidnap him, take him to a fancy hotel for the night, no phones allowed except to call room service. They could go dancing—Nick loved to dance, and he was good at it. A skill learned growing up in Virginia with its tradition of cotillions, not to mention three sisters to squire to parties.

Smiling at the image of Nick's arms wrapped tight around her, guiding her across a dance floor, she'd reached the hemlocks flanking the driveway when movement came from the shadows.

Lucy spun to face the threat, but she was too late. A man's arm wrapped around her throat.

CHAPTER 2

Now
5:07 p.m.

LUCY EDGED THE barn's door open the slightest crack, straining to see where the man was. Surprise was her only weapon.

The hinges let loose with a creak that split the night. She stepped back, positioning herself behind the door, and held her breath. Maybe he was too far away to hear.

Footfalls sounded. Close, very close. The light inside the barn went out. Lucy braced herself, ready to pounce, knowing she'd only have one chance at this. But there was nowhere to run, nowhere to hide—not moving as slow as she was.

Somewhere inside her a stray spark of warmth gave her strength as she waited in the frigid night air. With it came Nick's voice, chiding her for never being willing to back down from a fight.

"You can't always win by outstubborning everyone else," he'd said.

They'd both laughed, knowing perfectly well that that was how Lucy *always* won. She never surrendered, never gave up . . . a trait that had caused more than her fair share of problems both at work and at home.

Nick. She blinked hard, willing him back to the shadows of her mind. Focus, she had to focus. Time this just right.

The door swung open. A man's hand holding a semiautomatic pistol slid into sight. Lucy shoved her entire weight against the door, slamming it shut on his wrist.

The hard edge of the metal door hit him just below the thumb, where it was most vulnerable. He cried out, tried to jerk his arm back inside. Keeping her weight on the door, pinning his hand, she wrenched the weapon from his grasp.

She fumbled the gun between her frozen, numb fingers. Finally got a solid grip on it. Felt so much better having a weapon.

Time to finish this.

Lucy released her weight from the door and threw it open, raising the pistol at the man caught inside the barn. In his effort to pull his hand free, he'd pivoted so that his back was to her, and the darkness almost engulfed him.

"FBI! Hands where I can see them," she commanded. It felt like she was shouting, but her voice barely scratched above a whisper. An aftereffect of almost strangling down in that damn pit. Still loud enough that the man complied—that's what was important.

"On the ground," she ordered, entering the barn, leaving the door open and keeping her distance so he couldn't rush her. Dim twilight edged through the door, barely enough to make out the strangely shaped shadows of farm machines and the silhouette of the man in front of her.

He stood only six feet away, too close for comfort, but she couldn't risk losing him to the blackness that crowded the rest of the barn. Any farther in and she wouldn't be able to see her own hands holding her weapon, much less her captive.

"I said, get down on the ground," she repeated when he didn't comply. Her voice was swallowed by the darkness, a faint ghost of her usual tone of command.

She reached behind her, fingers brushing the steel wall, searching for the light switch. The barn was warmer than outside, but not by much, making her glad the man still had his back to her and couldn't see the chills shaking her aim.

"You're dead," he said in a snarl that she wasn't sure was a promise or a threat. Didn't matter as long as she was the one with the gun.

She felt a switch and flicked it. The outside light above the door behind her came on. Not much help. Instead of black-on-black darkness, now she could make out grey shadows maybe ten feet inside the door. The farm equipment took on the shape of prehistoric monsters, all claws and straggly arms and squat bodies.

The man made his move, pivoting and lunging at her weapon hand. Lucy rolled with his weight, using her hip to send him up and over, down to the floor. His hand closed over hers, both of them clenching the pistol as he kicked her right foot out from under her and pulled her down on top of him.

Her weight crashed down onto her injured foot. Pain

19

screamed through her. The fight was surreal: arms and legs flailing in shadows, occasionally crossing the sliver of light coming through the door, then vanishing into darkness once again. He grabbed her hair, pounded her face into the cement floor, releasing a gush of blood from her nose. She shot an elbow so hard into his neck that his head whipped back and sent a bunch of hoes and rakes and shovels that had been leaning against the wall clattering to the floor.

Finally, the man caught her from behind in a bear hug, both hands now on top of hers, wrapped around the gun. Her free arm was trapped between his arm and his body as he leaned his weight back, hauling her with him, the pistol rising until she aimed at the ceiling. He braced Lucy's arm against the floor and squirreled his finger around the trigger, pinching her finger as he pulled over and over again.

The sound of gunshots hammered through the space, echoing and reverberating. Hot brass flew from the semiautomatic, pinging against the concrete floor, searing Lucy's hand. One casing tumbled into her jacket, hot against her cold body.

The magazine emptied, and the slide flew back, pinching the man's hand above hers. The pistol was now useless except as a blunt instrument. The man relaxed his grip, and Lucy took advantage, rolling her weight in the opposite direction and twisting, aiming an elbow to his armpit as she scrambled for one of the garden tools.

The air smelled of gunpowder and hay. Lucy's breath came in jagged rasps, each one burning her already raw throat. She shook away any feeling that could distract her, intent on piercing the shadows and delivering the next blow. The man was taller, bigger, stronger, less exhausted—all he had to do was wear her down. Which meant she had to strike, and strike fast.

She grabbed a rake near its working end and aimed it like a claw at his face. The movement broke her free of his stranglehold. She kept rolling onto her feet. Big mistake—she'd forgotten about her left foot. Riding the wave of pain, she planted her foot, braced herself with the rake, and aimed a kick to his solar plexus that had him clutching his gut.

She hopped back, all her weight now on her good leg, groping behind her to lean against the wall and try another kick. Too late, too slow. He was climbing to his feet, half turned away from her, hands lowered as he hauled in a breath.

Lucy took advantage of his pause and swung the rake at his throat, ready to follow up with a jab to his solar plexus. He saw the movement and grabbed the rake from her, sending her flying face-first into the wall, striking a metal circuit breaker box hard enough that the crash rang through the space. Fresh pain brought tears to her eyes as the bones in her nose crunched.

Before she could recover, he grabbed her from behind. She launched her right fist back into his groin, throwing all her weight into it.

"Bitch," he gasped as he released her. She spun around. He was breathing hard, but it was from pain, not exhaustion. She was down to her last reserves of energy.

Lucy had to end this. Now. As he straightened, she pushed off with her good foot, put her head down, and rushed him. She plowed into him, spinning him off balance so that he faced away from her, and shoved him into the side of a large piece of equipment that sat against the opposite wall. Its shadow suggested that it was big and heavy enough to do some damage.

Something at the base of the machine must have caught the man's foot, because he suddenly flipped forward, flying from her grasp. His scream echoed louder than the gunshots. There was a sickening thud of metal meeting flesh, and his scream died.

Lucy couldn't stop her momentum, crashing into him from behind, cringing at the feel of unrelenting metal crunching into the man, her weight pushing his body deeper into the maw of the machinery.

She twisted away, flailing her arms against a darkness so complete she could barely make out the man's silhouette; the machine had swallowed him. Her hand brushed a horizontal metal bar, then hit a sharp curved blade longer than the spread of her fingers.

She hobbled away, panting. The man didn't move, didn't make a noise. The smell of blood and the sour spray of stomach acid filled the air.

She backed against the wall, hitting the edge of the large sliding door, and finally found the lights. Flicking them on, three bare bulbs hanging from the curved ceiling twenty feet overhead, she was greeted by a macabre melding of man and machine: A huge combine, painted a cheerful spring green. In front of it, several rows of blades, deadly daggers arranged a few inches apart. Impaled on them, one row spiked through his face, a second through his belly, was the man, his blood pooling at his feet.

———◆———

THEN

10:24 A.M.

LUCY WOKE, MIRED in the cotton-packed grogginess of whatever drugs they'd given her. They? He? No, surely there'd been more than one? The void in her memory blindsided her. Terror lanced through her, starting in her gut, then spreading cold throughout her body.

She fought through the haze. Remembered Nick and Megan leaving, walking to her car—then nothing. It took her a minute to connect her senses to her limbs. Weapon—where was her weapon?

Not at her hip. Her feet were bare—socks and boots and backup piece missing.

She pried her eyes open. At least she thought she did. The blackness was so complete that she couldn't tell which way was up. The vertigo triggered a bout of nausea, and she closed her eyes again, focused on her breathing until it passed.

Her hands were bound behind her with zip ties, the plastic cutting into her skin. *Tight. Very tight.* She grabbed hold of that stray thought racing past, thankful to have one clear thing to concentrate on. Forced her muddied mind to repeat it, seeking truth behind it.

The zip ties were tight. Very tight. Ahh . . . yes. That was actually good—most people didn't realize the tighter they were, the more easily zip ties could be broken when stressed in the right way.

One clear thought led to another as she piecemealed her existence here and now into something she could make sense of. She lay on concrete. Cold. Roughly finished. Basement? Cellar? There was no light, not the faintest crack coming from a window or door. No sounds of the outside world, nor of the inside of a house.

A silence so deep it produced its own echo.

Which meant she was alone. No backup. No one to call for help. No one.

Her body shook with the cold, and she forced herself to return to her inventory. In addition to her weapons, they'd taken her jacket, her belt, her boots and socks, and all her jewelry, including her wedding ring and Megan's bracelet. Left her in her slacks and blouse—thin protection against the cold, but a comfort nonetheless. They needed her alive and unharmed . . . for now.

A quick list of possibilities filled her mind. There was Morgan Ames, the teenage psychopath, daughter of the serial killer Lucy had captured. But Morgan and Lucy had reached a tentative détente, thanks to Nick. Lucy let Nick counsel Morgan and keep tabs on her while Morgan stayed away from Megan.

So, not Morgan. Her father reaching out from prison? Maybe, but he had enough on his hands with his trial date approaching. The Zapatas, the drug cartel that had attacked Pittsburgh?

Maybe. A definite maybe. Because of Lucy, one of their favorite sons was dead, not to mention a huge distribution pipeline destroyed. Grabbing a federal agent from her own driveway? That had cartel written all over it.

Then why sedate her? Why not just throw her in a car, torture her in some spectacular way destined to go viral on YouTube, and dump her body as a warning?

Not that it might not still come to that . . .The chill of terror returned, her entire body shaking as she fought to push back images of what the Zapatas had done south of the border.

But this felt too . . . civilized? Too meticulous, too elaborate for the Zapatas.

Which brought her back to why? If she understood what they wanted, she could find a way out of this. Who were they? What did they want? Why her?

Without answers, she was helpless.

Before she could roll onto her feet to start exploring her prison and search for escape routes, a man's voice rang out from above.

"The bureau's official policy is no negotiating with terrorists," he said in a calm tone. He wasn't speaking loudly, but the room's strange acoustics made his voice reverberate as if attacking her from all sides. "You need to know two things about me, Special Agent Guardino. First, I'm not a terrorist. And second, this is not a negotiation."

She twisted her body, searching for the source of the voice. Impenetrable blackness greeted her from every direction.

"At seven o'clock—that's in eight hours and thirty-two minutes—your family will either be alive or at least one of them will die cursing your name. Who lives and who dies? That is the last choice you will ever make. Because you will die here today. That I promise."

It was difficult to understand his words, the way his voice echoed and boomed. But as she analyzed the sound, she realized that the space was smaller than she'd thought. And that the voice came from a speaker—there was a faint hum underlying everything he said.

So. He wasn't in here with her. More the pity—a hostage might come in handy when she broke free.

"Who are you?" she shouted, wincing as her own voice bounced back at her. She shuffled her body across the floor, assessing the dimensions of her prison. It only took two moves to find a wall.

"Names are unimportant. What you need to know is that I'm a man of my word and I've done this before. Believe me when I tell you I know the outcome of our little encounter here today. I've already won. There is nothing for me to lose. But there is everything for you to lose. If I need to, I will kill every person you have ever loved. You will listen to their screams, watch them die, and you will be helpless to do anything about it."

Like hell, she thought, bracing herself against the wall. More concrete. Smooth, not cinder block. She pushed herself to a standing position and started to work on the zip ties.

He continued, "It won't come to that. It never does. Your only hope, your family's only hope, is for you to realize I'm telling the truth and give me what I want. You have eight hours and thirty-one minutes left."

There was a faint click, and he was gone. Leaving Lucy in the dark, no idea where she was, no idea who he was, and no idea what the hell he wanted from her.

CHAPTER 3

LUCY SMEARED THE back of her hand against her smashed lip, mixing her own blood with the dead man's.

It was good to finally have light so she could assess her situation. Make sense of it, make a plan. Why did that simple thought seem to take minutes to process?

Cold wind gusting through the barn door left her shivering. It didn't help that she was soaked through and barefoot. Even if she found her boots, she couldn't put them back on, not with one foot swollen and bleeding, bones crunching every time she placed her weight on it. She needed a doctor's attention, probably even a surgeon's, but she couldn't waste time on a distraction like a broken foot; there was too much at stake. Too much she had to take care of before she could take care of herself.

Like saving her family.

She retrieved the rake and gripped its handle, bracing her weight against it, taking the pressure off her foot. Didn't stop the pain. Her body felt like a firing range target after a SWAT team drill: a scattershot of holes and gashes and ragged tears.

Each beat of her heart throbbed through her entire being, pinpointing an assortment of injuries: Knuckles scraped raw. One hand not working quite right. Probably more broken bones. It was hard to breathe with her nose dripping mucus and blood.

Her throat felt swollen to the point that each gasp threatened to strangle her and finish the job the man facedown at her feet had begun. He'd promised that by seven o'clock someone would be dead.

And he'd said he was a man of his word.

What time was it now? Panic surged through her, but she forced herself to take things one step at a time. First, a way to warn her family.

She stared down at the man she'd killed. Grunting with pain, the rake wavering as she balanced it against the concrete floor, she awkwardly searched his pockets with one hand. Contaminating the crime scene. She knew better.

As an FBI supervisory special agent, she'd be called upon to describe and defend each blow of the encounter. It wasn't often an FBI agent was forced to kill a man in close-quarters combat. The brass, the lawyers, the shrinks—they would all be dissecting every second, every decision she made, every step she took today. God, the press—they'd have a field day.

"You sonofabitch," she muttered, long past caring that there was no one alive to hear her. Once again her voice surprised her, emerging as a thin whisper, barely audible even here in the still and quiet barn. It hurt to speak, but no more than any of her other injuries. "Give me something. Car keys, a phone—"

Nothing.

She cursed and straightened, her bad foot throbbing. Red flashes strobed into her vision with each heartbeat. He had to have a phone.

His vehicle. He must have left it in his vehicle.

The cavernous barn was filled with large equipment: the combine, a smaller tractor, various blades and attachments. The door at the opposite end seemed miles away, but she had no choice. There was no phone here inside, nothing to help her reach her family.

As she limped toward the door, shivering at even the thought of returning outside to the cold, anxiety pounded through her, driving her despite the pain. Had he kept his word? Sent his men after Nick? Or had he betrayed her and sent them after Megan? Maybe her mother?

No way of knowing.

She was damned if he had, damned if he hadn't. At least, either way, he was still dead.

She didn't even know his name. A weak rumble of laughter shook her. She clutched the rake tighter, bracing her body with it. Couldn't risk falling. Might never get back up again.

The thought brought more impotent laughter mixed with tears. The sound was sharp, raspy, no louder than a whisper. Yet, despite the pain from her bruised vocal cords, she couldn't stop.

Hysteria. Shock. Not to mention a healthy dose of awe.

Who in their right mind would have predicted that a Pittsburgh soccer mom, an FBI agent with a job meant to keep her chained to a desk, a woman barely five foot five, would have ended her day killing a man with her bare hands?

Sure as hell was the last thing on Lucy's mind when she got up this morning.

———•◦•———

THEN
10:52 A.M.

LUCY SHIVERED IN the absolute darkness of the prison her kidnapper had left her in. It had been a long time since Lucy had done any tactical training involving close-quarters combat or skills like breaking free from zip ties. Her job as head of the Sexual Assault Felony Enforcement Squad required a different set of talents: managing a multiagency, multidisciplinary task force, investigating cases no one else wanted and playing diplomat to local, state, and fellow federal law enforcement agencies.

Now that ninety percent of the Bureau's resources were dedicated to counterterrorism and financial crimes, the rest of the Pittsburgh field office had dubbed her tiny corner of the building the Island of Misfit Boys. Catching terrorists was so much sexier than chasing pedophiles and serial rapists, but Lucy wouldn't have it any other way. Her people were twice as dedicated and ten times as determined as any other squad in the Bureau. They might not make headlines, but they saved lives.

Despite the long hours at the desk required by her position, Lucy made sure she stayed in shape and kept up with the latest tactics. At least she hoped she had, seeing as her life now depended on it.

Nausea roiled through her gut. Not just *her* life. Maybe her family's as well.

No. She couldn't think that way. If her kidnapper had Nick or Megan, he would have shown her proof, used it against her. Which meant they were safe. For now. Her only job was to get the hell out of here and keep them that way.

The tight restraints had left her hands numb. Lucy raised them as high as she could and brought her bound wrists down hard against her tailbone. Nothing. This had definitely been easier to do when she was a few years younger.

She shifted position, bracing herself against the wall. The disembodied man—oh, how would she love to disembody him for real—had threatened her family. She allowed her rage, her sense of violation, her fear to flow through her, tightened her muscles and strained her shoulders to raise her arms higher, and brought them down in one quick snapping motion.

The blow rocked through her as the zip ties broke. Free now to explore her prison, she began by walking the perimeter.

The walls and floor were all poured concrete. The ceiling was high overhead, beyond her reach. From the way sound echoed, she guessed it was concrete as well. She was against a short wall, only about four feet long. If she stood in the center and stretched her arms, she could touch both sides. The corner was a tightly formed ninety degrees, no sign of light or any crack or seam.

She explored the wall with her hands. Above her, as far as she could reach, her fingertips brushed the edge of a pipe. Not metal. PVC. Maybe three or four inches in diameter, judging from the curve. Too small to escape through if she could climb her way up there.

The pipe frightened her more than the darkness. She couldn't hear any sounds coming through it, couldn't see any light edging its way inside.

Was she buried underground? She shook away the panic that came with the thought and kept following her hands as she blindly felt her way along the walls of her prison.

The long wall was only eight feet—nothing on it that she could feel. Another short wall. Another PVC pipe, again above her head, midway along the wall, same as the first.

An almost-forgotten memory sucker-punched her as she imagined how her prison appeared in daylight. Four by eight by at least seven or eight feet high. Poured concrete. Pipes on two sides.

A small cry eluded her control, and she slumped against the final, featureless wall. The echo of her tiny sound of terror pummeled her, and she put her fist into her mouth, biting off any further sounds.

It was her childhood nightmare come to life.

Every neighborhood had its haunted house—the place kids told horror stories about, trying to spook each other with dares to trespass, test their courage. Growing up, Lucy's neighborhood had been no different, only the tragedy that echoed into her and her friends' lives was all too real: a toddler had wandered into a septic tank with an open lid and drowned.

For weeks, Lucy had had night terrors: swimming and smothering in raw sewage like quicksand, pulling her down, down . . .

Panic drove her pulse into a gallop so strong she felt it in her fingertips. Her breathing quickened as well, then she clamped her throat shut, holding it in. Feeling the burn of her lungs fighting for release.

Was that how it would feel? How much air did she have? Even if she found the overhead hatch, could somehow reach it, even if she got the hatch open, would she find anything except a wall of dirt or more concrete trapping her inside?

Surrendering to the need to inhale, she smashed her palm against the nearest wall. A septic tank. Where better to bury someone alive?

Lucy's childhood nightmare. *How could he have known?*

He didn't, she told herself, pushing away from the walls to explore the floor between them. He couldn't have. A buried septic tank was simply the perfect place to stash someone you don't want anyone to see or hear.

And what better way to dispose of a body?

The man had promised she would die. He just hadn't said how long it would take.

CHAPTER 4

THE BARN STANK of diesel and dried grass. And now death. A simple metal Quonset hut, designed to house tractors and equipment and combine attachments like the one with the wickedly sharp blades. The one with the man's body facedown, impaled against its blades.

Using the rake as a makeshift crutch and bracing herself against the galvanized-steel exterior wall, Lucy hobbled toward the front door. As she made her slow, ungainly progress, she passed the open door she'd entered through, taking one last look outside, across the snow, at the place where she should have died.

The glare of the light above the door made her trail of blood appear black against the white. Empty field—no help there. In fact the only tracks were her bloody footsteps, the man's boot prints, and the tracks of a large dog.

Christ, the dog. Where was the dog?

Terror gripped her, and she stopped. The rake shook in her hand. She didn't—she couldn't—face the dog. Not again. Her stomach rebelled, and if she'd had anything to vomit, it would have come up. Ignoring the pain, she forced her body to keep moving.

But that didn't stop her from holding her breath, listening hard for the soft thud of the dog's footfalls, the gleeful wheeze of its breathing when it caught sight of its prey, the whoosh of its rush through the air as it prepared to pounce.

She turned her back on the field and the pit beneath it. She needed to get to her family. Now. Before time ran out.

Seven o'clock. He'd said she had until seven. What time was it now?

Her foot brushed against a stray piece of equipment, and she gasped, the pain so swift and overwhelming she almost dropped the rake.

"No time," she muttered, the thought of Nick and Megan a lifeline leading her from the pain. She resumed her circuit of the barn.

Her grip on the rake was weakening, fingers past burning to numb. Only good thing about the cold was that her feet were also numb, as long as she kept weight off her mangled left foot. The threat of the dog was a constant worry, but she'd seen no sign of it while she was dealing with its owner.

Dealing with. She made a choking noise, swallowing blood and finding a loose tooth with the tip of her tongue. Be honest, Lucy. *Killing* its owner.

She'd killed before—been forced to during the Zapata cartel's attack on Pittsburgh last Christmas. But that was at a distance, through the scope of a long gun. Nothing like what she'd done tonight.

The man's final shriek tore through her memory, jarring her. She froze, imagining he wasn't dead, had somehow pushed himself free of the combine blades and now followed her, intent on finishing what he'd started. Killing her. And her family.

If her captor had lied, if he'd been working alone, then she could relax. After all, he was dead, which meant no one left to threaten her loved ones.

If he was working alone. He'd made a big show of sending texts and talking about others taking orders from him, spoke of coordinating everyone to get everything done by seven o'clock, but she'd seen in him an hubris that matched that of the child predators she hunted. Men ensconced in worlds of their own creation, worlds where they held all the power, didn't easily delegate to others. Wouldn't risk losing control over any aspect of their lives.

Her instincts said he was working alone. But she couldn't risk her family on a gut feeling. She needed to *know* they were safe.

She reached the front wall of the barn, tugged the door open, and was rewarded with the sight of a Jeep Grand Cherokee. She would have shouted for joy if she could've still felt her lips. Victory, though, quickly turned to ash.

The dog, a large Rottweiler, trained to kill, was in the Jeep's rear compartment, kenneled inside a crate. It saw her—or smelled her blood, tasted a second chance to finish what its master had started—and began to bark and lunge against the steel walls that trapped it beyond the reach of its prey.

She hated the dog, but she couldn't waste time dealing with it, as long as it was locked up, safely out of her way. She had to overcome a bigger obstacle: the dead man didn't have car keys on him.

She limped to the SUV and opened the door. Climbing inside brought new waves of pain—pulling her weight up onto the seat, twisting to raise her left foot inside, setting it down again as gently as possible. By the time she finished, her jaw was clenched so tight it felt like hot needles driving into her eardrums. Didn't help that the dog, which outweighed Lucy, was throwing its weight back and forth, rocking the Jeep as it howled for release.

The Jeep was an older model. No nav system, no OnStar, no phone. At least not within eyesight.

But—thank you, Lord!—the man had left his keys dangling from the ignition. Guess he didn't think killing her would take him more than a few minutes. For some reason, the thought made her want to howl in concert with the damn dog.

Her fingers trembling, she turned the key, holding her breath, expecting this to be some kind of trick, a trap.

The dash lit up with bright lights, the radio startling her as it belted Christian death metal, joining with the dog's howls to create a bone-jarring cacophony. But all of her attention was on the dashboard clock.

5:37 it read in blood-red digits.

Lucy added her own whoop of joy to the noise filling the Jeep. Time. She still had time.

If her captor was a man of his word.

She rammed the vehicle into drive, and sped down the dirt lane. Leaving behind the barn and the man she'd killed, she pushed the accelerator, skidding out onto the paved road the farm lane intersected, without even checking for oncoming traffic.

The dog protested from the rear, where its crate shifted and tilted, then thumped back down. She stabbed the radio off, needing all her energy to block out the pain and figure out where the hell she was.

There was no traffic. The road was two lanes, blacktop, twisting and winding with trees on one side and barren fields on the other. No lights, no signs of civilization.

Then she spotted a road sign. Route 51. So close to home. She could have died—body never to be found—and she would have been just a few miles from home. She forced the thought aside. She had to get home, to save Nick and Megan. . .

No. She shook her head, her brain foggy with pain and adrenaline. No. She didn't know for sure where Nick or Megan were, much less who her captor had targeted.

A phone. She needed to reach a phone.

The January night was clear, stars cascading across the sky. They'd bought their Christmas tree from a farm not far from here, she remembered. Nick dunked homemade doughnuts into hot cider at the farmer's stand while she and Megan slurped hot cocoa topped with dabs of marshmallow whip.

She stomped her good foot onto the accelerator, the wind shaking the Jeep. Up ahead a familiar red-and-yellow sign lit up the night, obscuring the stars. Sheetz. A roadside mecca for weary travelers throughout Pennsylvania, promising hot coffee and clean restrooms, but most importantly to Lucy, a phone. She could get help to Nick and Megan.

An eighteen-wheeler coming from the other direction suddenly cut her off, turning left into the Sheetz parking lot ahead of her.

Didn't the idiot driver see her? There was no room to maneuver around the tractor-trailer. She slammed on the brakes, kicking her useless left foot and sending pain howling through her body.

The dog's barking grew frantic, competing with the screech of the tires. The Jeep wobbled and lurched as she yanked the wheel, spotting a narrow opening between the truck's front bumper and the guardrail leading into the convenience store's parking lot. The trucker finally spotted her, hitting his brakes and twisting the wheel until he almost jackknifed.

The Jeep's center of gravity was too high. It finally surrendered, toppling over the guardrail.

Lucy wrenched the wheel. The seat belt and air bags did their job—her body hurled in first one direction, then slapped back against her seat. *No, no, no,* her voice screamed inside her head. This couldn't be happening. She didn't have time . . .

The Jeep skidded to a stop, resting on its passenger side. Lucy hung from the seat belt, her body trying to fall into the other seat against the door that was now the floor of the vehicle.

Other than a slap from the air bag deploying and more muscles wrenched in unnatural directions, Lucy wasn't hurt. She clawed the remnants of the air bag away. The dog whimpered.

She twisted in her seat and tried to push her door open. It didn't move. The sound of the dog's claws skittering against glass echoed through the suddenly quiet vehicle. Had the kennel broken open? She strained to turn to see into the rear.

Was the damn dog clawing its way over the seat even now, ready to finish the job it had started earlier, eager to tear her apart? This time it wouldn't stop at her foot and ankle. It would go for the jugular.

She rammed her weight against the door. Still nothing. Even if she did get it open, it was going to be almost impossible to climb out on her own, not fighting gravity and with her smashed-up foot.

She didn't care. She didn't have time for impossible. Not if she was going to save her family.

———•———

THEN
1 1:1 1 A.M.

SHE WAS IN a shitload of trouble, Lucy decided, as she paced the interior of her concrete prison. *Literally.*

She hugged her arms around herself, cursing the fact that she'd dressed in a thin silk blouse for the meeting in Harrisburg rather than her usual layers of fleece. Maybe she'd freeze to death.

Not a bad way to go. She forced the renegade thought aside. No one was dying. Not today. Not with her family in this guy's sights.

Besides, the concrete and dirt she was buried in made for decent insulation. Despite the snow and frigid temperatures outside, she was cold but not freezing.

How much air did she have? She stopped, doing some quick calculations in the impenetrable black . . . No,

AFTER SHOCK

air wouldn't be a problem, not as long as the outlet pipes
were open.

Easy to seal them off, the pessimistic voice continued,
cataloguing the number of ways Lucy's kidnapper could
kill her. *Or hook them up to a vehicle's exhaust pipe, pump carbon
monoxide down here. Or fill the place with water—then it'd be a
toss-up between drowning and hypothermia.*

Or just leave me here to starve.

No, she'd die of thirst first. Didn't matter.

"Not. Going. To. Happen." Lucy's voice ricocheted
from wall to wall, surrounding her with the affirmation,
driving her doubts away. For now.

He was probably listening. Maybe even watching if he
had concealed a thermal-imaging camera in one of the
pipes or on the ceiling.

Lucy didn't care. She wasn't playing by his rules. Not
with her family's lives at stake.

She continued her exploration of her dungeon. She
walked the perimeter again, fingertips touching the outer
concrete wall, feet sweeping the ground invisible to her in
the dark, searching for anything hidden there. Halfway
down the length of the tank, her toe brushed something
hard and sharp.

Lucy stopped. She abandoned the anchor of the wall
and stooped to feel what her foot had struck. A cinder
block. In the center of the floor.

It was just an ordinary cinder block. No hidden
compartments with a stash of weapons, a cell phone or
radio. Nothing that could help her. It was really too
heavy to use as a weapon, but if she had to she would.

She sat on it, face turned up, pondering the blackness
above her. There was only one reason why her captor

would have left it here.

He'd needed a way to climb out.

Lucy jumped up and balanced on the side of the block. Hard to do in the dark, with nothing to orient her. She wobbled and caught herself with one palm pressed against the wall, the other raised overhead.

Found nothing. Just more empty blackness.

She stepped down, sat on the block again. At five foot five, she should have felt it if the ceiling were seven feet high . . . Yeah, sixty-five inches plus another sixteen or so of arm reach, plus the eight inches of the cinder block . . . She had to do the math twice to be sure, but seven feet was eighty-four inches, and she should have more than cleared that.

Okay, maybe the septic tank was eight feet tall. Made more sense—if her guy was at least six feet tall, he could probably have made it out of a seven-foot container without the block. But at eight feet, he'd need a few extra inches, give him leverage to boost the lid open.

When she was a kid, she'd seen two kinds of lids on tanks like these. Big, thick concrete plugs—no way he'd use that, not until he was certain he was finished with her—and slimmer metal or resin hatches that resembled manhole covers. It'd have to be one of those, something he could open from either side.

If he could do it, so could she. Only she'd need more than a few inches to reach it.

She stood the cinder block on its short side, doubling its height. The floor was level enough that it didn't wobble too much. But climbing onto the tiny platform wasn't easy, even with the walls to brace against. She balanced both feet on the eight-inch square and stretched . . .

Twice she ended up falling on her ass, once she caught herself before falling but skinned her shin on the edge of the block, and finally, breathing slow, concentrating on her feet planted just so, raising her hands bit by bit over her head . . . she found the ceiling.

The small victory thrilled through her. She had enough room to plant her palms flat with a bend in her elbow—good, she'd need the extra leverage once she found the hatch.

It couldn't be far. Even if the block had slid to the side after he pushed off it to climb out, the hatch had to be near the center of the tank. Her fingers swept through the darkness. She forced herself to look straight ahead—couldn't see anything above her anyway, and tilting her face up was messing with her precarious balance.

She found two breaks in the flawless concrete: large eyehooks screwed into the concrete about six inches from each other. Stretched her fingers a few inches more and caught the lip of a round structure.

She'd found her escape route.

CHAPTER 5

GRAVITY ALWAYS WINS, Lucy's father had told her when he'd taught her how to ride a bike. He'd said it with a smile as he helped her up off the pavement and back onto her two-wheeler. Dad didn't believe in training wheels, he believed in finding your own way, always getting up no matter how many times you fell.

Never surrender, never quit the fight. Lucy had adopted his motto for her own after he died of lung cancer when she was twelve—fighting until his very last breath.

He hadn't told her gravity was also a bitch—she'd figured that out herself over the years. And right now that bitch stood between Lucy and her family's safety.

She released a scream born of frustration and pain. Or tried to. The only noise she could make with her swollen vocal cords was a muffled whoosh. But the dog's howling from the back of the Jeep more than made up for it.

A man's face appeared at the windshield. Followed quickly by two more men—both teenagers, one wearing a Sheetz uniform. "You okay?"

"Break the glass," she ordered. It emerged as a whisper. She wasn't even sure he'd heard her over the noise of the truck idling a dozen feet away. "Get me out of here."

They turned away, talking among themselves.

One of them, probably the truck driver, older and stouter than the two boys, climbed up to yank on the driver's side door. He got it open, the entire vehicle shaking and shuddering. Cold air rushed inside, chilling parts of Lucy's body that had finally just thawed.

The clock on the dashboard blinked and changed its reading. 6:01. No time to waste.

The dog snarled and growled at the man. His eyes went wide as he looked behind Lucy to the rear compartment. "That dog safe?"

"No. He's not." She felt like snarling herself. It took all her strength to twist her head to look at him, given that she was hanging on her side, only the seat belt digging into her flesh to keep her from falling. "I'm FBI Special Agent Lucy Guardino. I need to use your phone."

Damn, she could barely hear herself. The harder she tried to shout or yell, the more muffled her voice.

"You hurt? Look pretty banged up. What's all that blood on your shirt?"

"Just give me the damn phone!"

"Hold on, the rescue squad's on their way." He vanished from sight.

"I don't need the rescue squad, I need a phone," she

cried out in frustration. The last words vanished into the night, inaudible gasps mingled with tears.

At least he left the door open so she could freeze to death. She'd just have to get out of here herself. She grabbed the edge of the doorframe with her good hand and gritted her teeth. This was going to hurt like hell.

She unbuckled her seat belt, letting gravity have its way with her. Bracing her good foot against the center console, she pushed her shoulders and head through the door.

Plan worked too well. She hadn't realized the Jeep wasn't only resting on its passenger side, it also was lying on an incline angled back end down. First rule of close-quarters combat: wherever the head goes, the body follows.

Gravity, the fickle bitch, knew that rule all too well. As soon as Lucy's shoulders cleared the car, she slid headfirst out and over the side, landing in a wave of pain so intense everything went black.

———◆———

THEN
1 1:43 A.M.

LUCY SCRAMBLED BACK down to the floor of the concrete tank and carefully repositioned the cinder block directly beneath the hatch. She climbed back up, found the septic tank's lid again and explored it with her fingers.

It felt like resin—good, it wouldn't be as heavy as a metal cover. No hinges on this side; it appeared to rely on gravity to keep it in place. Gravity and anything her captor had placed on top of the tank. For all she knew there could be a dozen feet of dirt or several inches of concrete sealing her inside. .

No, she thought with determination. He wasn't done with her yet, so he wouldn't have cut off any chance of his reaching her. She hoped.

She pushed against one edge of the cover. Was rewarded as it gave way. A thrill of anticipation fueled her efforts, and she pushed harder. All she needed was to lift the cover above the rim so she could slide it aside.

It can't be this easy. The devil's advocate inside her head sounded a warning. *It must be a trap, some kind of trick.*

Lucy ignored the voice, excited as she tilted the cover up far enough to catch on the top of the tank, releasing a narrow crescent of light into her prison.

She shifted her fingers to the opposite side of the hatch, sliding them into the small gap she'd created, and pushed the cover away from the opening. A few minutes later she was staring into the pale winter sun almost directly overhead. The blue sky surrounding it and cotton-puff clouds floating past were welcome sights.

Okay, now for the fun. Time to see if all those Pilates and core workouts were worth it. She reached through the opening and grabbed onto the rim. It was about two feet wide, plenty of room. Abandoning the security of the cinder block, she swung her legs up to brace against the nearest wall. Then she pulled with her arms as she pushed with her legs, leveraging herself up and out of the black pit.

Sweat covered her, leaving her instantly chilled by the colder temperatures outside. She rolled onto the septic tank's concrete roof and took a moment to blink at the sky, listen to the birds in the distance, and breathe in the crisp, sharp scent of winter.

A shiver rocked her to her feet as she took in her surroundings. She stood in the middle of an empty snow-covered field. Trees surrounded the field on all sides, the closest at least a quarter mile away. The only sign of civilization, other than the septic tank, was a Quonset hut-style barn about a hundred yards away. The barn was large enough to block any view beyond it, but she guessed that out of her sight, on the far side, there would be a road or some kind of drive leading up to it. Which meant civilization.

Her suit jacket lay crumbled at the edge of the packed snow surrounding the buried septic tank. No signs of her parka or bag, but below the jacket she found her socks jumbled up with Megan's Paracord bracelet. She sat, put the jacket on, shoved Megan's bracelet into a pocket, then worked the socks on to her numb feet. Immediately felt better.

She took a step into the snow where the sun glinted off something bright. Her wedding ring, which she slipped on with a kiss to the cold gold—her good-luck ritual—but no signs of her necklace or earrings or boots. No bag, no watch, no phone, no belt, no weapons.

She pictured her takedown—at least how she imagined it had happened. Grab her, inject her with fast-acting sedative, remove any weapons, restrain her, dump her in the trunk of her own car. Less than two minutes' work if you knew what you were doing.

Drive the car to a place where it wouldn't be found, exchange it for another vehicle, drive here.

Yes, there were the tire tracks in the snow leading

from the barn to the buried tank. Looked like an SUV or truck. Boot prints and snow packed down—where he must have dumped her while he removed the restraints and did a more thorough search, taking her jewelry, jacket, and socks before replacing the restraints and lowering her into the pit.

Those eyehooks secured to the tank's ceiling—crude pulley system? Maybe it was just one man behind this after all.

She catalogued all the evidence in her mind's eye, but her feet were already protesting the cold, so she sped up to a jog, heading toward the barn. Rolling hills filled the horizon, no signs of a cell tower, no sounds of traffic or civilization. The barn and whatever lay beyond it were her only hope.

A phone. All she needed was a working phone. She had to call Walden, her second-in-command. He'd take it from there. Walden, a wizard of efficiency, would mobilize the local police and get her family into a secure location.

Once they were safe, she could put her energy into finding her captor or captors and figuring out what the hell this was all about. She smiled at the thought, the fresh air and taste of freedom exhilarating. Man of his word, her ass. He dared threaten her family? When she got her hands on him . . .

Her fantasy was interrupted by barking. She spun, trying to place the sound, fantasizing for one brief moment that it was Megan's puppy, Zeke. Then another thought clicked. Zeke wasn't sick; he'd probably been poisoned by her captor. Clearing the way for the attack on her this morning.

The dog barked again. Dogs came with owners, and owners came with cell phones—or vehicles.

Hope fueled her pulse, and she ran faster. She'd escaped her prison, thwarted her captor, would save her family, and then catch the bastard. Be home for dinner early, if she was lucky.

The dog's barking faded into the distance before Lucy could pinpoint its location. It could have belonged to her captor, she knew that, but she was totally exposed and vulnerable here in the field, so she had no choice but to head to the barn.

Besides, if he had a dog keeping guard on her prison, wouldn't he have left it chained near the entrance to the septic tank? Prevent her from escaping in the first place?

Nothing her captor had done made sense. Despite Lucy's joy at escaping, that realization was an itch she couldn't scratch, irritating every nerve ending and leaving the hair at the back of her neck standing upright.

Or maybe that was the cold. Her entire body burned with it, her steps faltering despite her urgency. The barn waited patiently, its galvanized-steel surface a solid, dull presence that promised salvation.

She was only twenty yards from it, close enough to make out its large sliding door and the patches of rust hugging the curve of its roof. The wind was in her face, but she felt, more than heard, a rush coming from behind her.

Just as she turned to look over her shoulder, a large brown dog, mouth bared to reveal all of its teeth, pounced.

CHAPTER 6

LUCY WAS DYING. It was taking much too long, this shredding of body and soul, pain ripping through her from every direction, tearing at her mind, raging through her limbs.

Should never have fought so hard to escape, a contrarian voice echoed through her brain. *Drowning or hanging would have been much faster and less painful.*

Something tugged at her mauled foot and ankle. Despite the blaze of pain, all she felt was cold.

That's what you get, the voice continued. *Just because you can never take the easy way out. Now it's too late. Might as well just give up, let go . . . stop fighting.*

Cold, she was so cold. Letting go would be so easy . . .

Never quit the fight. Her father had lived by those words—died by them as well. Lucy remembered how his death had devastated her mother. The void it had left in her life—she'd been Megan's age.

Megan. Her brain stuttered for one infinite moment, putting a face to the name. More than a face, everything.

The smell of No More Tears shampoo, the sting of being on the receiving end of a well-rehearsed adolescent eye roll, the pain of every scrape, bruise, illness, vaccine shot . . . everything that was her daughter flooded through Lucy.

With Megan came Nick. God, Nick . . . What had she done? He would approve, she knew, he would forgive her, but how could she have sent that monster after him?

What choice did she have? At least Nick had a fighting chance. More than Lucy's mother or Megan.

She'd killed one of her captors, but who knew how many might still be out there? She had to help her family. Had to reach them. Or at least be at their side to fight. She couldn't abandon them, couldn't give up, had to save them.

Pain like lightning shot through the frozen numbness that gripped her body and mind. Lucy's eyes popped open as she flailed her arms, trying to lunge at an unseen force. Strong hands and stronger bands crisscrossing her chest held her down. Her foot and ankle raged with fire, pain so intense she struggled to hold onto consciousness, her vision blazing black and red and white. The wailing shriek of a wild animal howled in time with the pulses of agony.

"Stop!" she cried out, not knowing who or what she was fighting against. Her voice emerged fainter than a whisper. "How long?"

"Easy now," a man's voice, calm, authoritative, told her. A paramedic. Trying to help. "What's your name?"

"Phone. Get me a phone." Lucy strained to be heard.

"Don't worry, sweetheart. We'll take good care of you. Are you allergic to anything?"

Lucy shook her head, but large foam blocks held it still. The paramedic adjusted a stiff plastic collar around her neck. It held her chin up and rubbed against her already raw jaw. Time, what time was it?

"I need a phone."

He was close enough to hear that. "We'll get you one as soon as we can. Any medical problems?"

"No. Get me a phone."

He turned away, leaving her powerless, strapped to a board. "Splint in place?"

"Good to go."

"On three."

Lucy was jerked off the ground. The medic's face came into sight, then bounced away again. More men, two near her head, one at her feet. She tried to sit up, but the straps circled her chest and belly as well as her arms and legs. Trapped, she was trapped.

"Let me go, I need to go." She wanted to shout, thought she was shouting—how else to get their attention over the roar of pain and the beast howling in harmony? But instead her voice emerged thinner than the night wind. "Let me go."

A bump as they set her down, her foot jostling, releasing another lightning strike. A gasp tore from her.

"We'll get you something for that in just a minute, sweetheart," the man nearest her head assured her. "Just got to get you into the ambulance and call med control."

"Phone," she begged. "There's no time." Her voice barely reached her own ears.

The man gave no sign of hearing her. He was busy looking over his shoulder, talking to someone Lucy couldn't see. It was so hard to think with all this damn noise inside and outside her head. She had to focus. She needed to . . . Someone needed her, she wasn't supposed to be here, she needed to . . .

"Give me a phone!" She mustered every bit of energy. "Now."

They bounced her into the back of an ambulance, one of the men jumping up inside with her, her words swallowed by the noise of the engine and a beeping by her side. One of the doors at her feet slammed shut. The other started to close, then swung open again, another man sticking his head inside.

"That's Lloyd Cramer's Jeep," he said, his voice loud enough to make Lucy close her eyes in an attempt to lessen the blow. "And one of his damn dogs in the back. Any sign of him?"

"Nope. Just her. No ID. Must be in the Jeep."

Lucy opened her eyes to tell them who she was. Her vision swam, and nausea made her swallow twice before she could find her voice. It still wasn't normal, every word scraped out in a harsh whisper. "I'm Lucy Guardino. FBI. I need a phone."

The door slammed shut before she could finish. The man beside her was leaning over, talking to the driver beyond her vision. If he'd heard her, he gave no sign of it.

Then they were moving, siren wailing, the man busy talking on a radio, reaching across Lucy, adjusting IV tubing running into her arm, inflating the blood-pressure cuff until it felt like a tourniquet, touching her foot and releasing another wave of pain, clamping an oxygen mask over her face, further muffling her attempts to make herself heard.

It was as if he were everywhere at once, the way he

used the tight confines of the ambulance, moving with ease like a sailor accustomed to choppy waters. He never stopped, seemed to always have something more to attend to, even once brushing her hair out of her eyes so she could see.

Time, she had no time. How long had she been out? She couldn't move her eyes far enough to see if there was a clock, and the medic moved too fast for her to see his watch. How much time was left before her captor's deadline? Seven o'clock. She had to reach her family before seven.

Lucy fought to speak, to tell him about Nick and Megan and the man out there, hunting for them. She wanted to beg for his help, for a phone, for just one call to send help, but the toll of her injuries and the exhaustion that flowed through her now that adrenaline had evaporated made it impossible for her to form the words coherently in her mind, much less push them past her bruised vocal cords and out her lips.

No words escaped as she fought the pain and lost. Her eyes fluttered shut once more, her only cry for help the release of a single tear.

———◆———

THEN
1 1:57 A.M.

THE COPPER TASTE of terror filled Lucy's mouth as the

world around her slowed into a multisensory freeze frame. The air billowed with smoke from the dog's hot breath. This beast was nothing like Megan's playful puppy. This was a killer, its eyes wild and furious.

Snow crunched beneath its paws as it launched itself at her. Lucy's heart raced so fast the beats blurred into a blitz that thrummed through her entire body.

She pivoted to present a smaller target. Powered an elbow into the dog's rib cage. Their momentum threw them to the ground. The dog's teeth snapped in the air beside her ear as she ducked her head down, protecting her neck, relying on primal instincts to keep her alive. Saliva sprayed her as claws dug into her back, ripping through her jacket.

Survival lay in not giving the animal time to clamp its powerful jaws on her. Lucy twisted her body beneath the dog's weight, struggling to protect her head while also aiming blows at the dog's vulnerable spots. It shook off another elbow to its rib cage and snarled as her fingers impacted its eyes. Then she landed a hard knee to its genitals, followed by another kick as she threw the dog off her.

It howled in fury. She scrambled to her feet. Her breath came in gasps. The entire universe had shrunk to a small circle, target-sized: Lucy and the dog. The beast outweighed her, was more powerful. She couldn't win this fight, leaving flight as her only option. No way she could outrun the animal, not for long, but if she could find a weapon, reach the shelter of the barn . . . She'd just planted her right foot when pain tore through her left calf as the dog clamped down with its teeth.

Lucy kicked with all her might. The dog's grip

loosened enough for her to slide her calf free, but then it regained a purchase, biting down hard on her foot where it met her ankle. She felt the crunch of bones giving way, the pain so sudden and shocking she fell facedown into the snow.

Lucy cried out in anguish as the animal dragged her closer. She clawed at the ground, found nothing but snow, twisted her body face up, fighting to sit up and strike at the animal.

The dog held on, not releasing her no matter how she struggled, its baleful gaze fixed upon her, unblinking. Then it tore at her leg with its front claws, her blood billowing into the air, spraying the snow crimson.

Suddenly the blue sky was blotted out by shadow, followed by a man's smiling face.

"Hold," he told the dog. The dog stopped clawing at Lucy but held onto her mangled leg, its jaws a pair of vise-grips. "Good dog." He crouched down beside Lucy.

"Who are you?" Lucy gasped. "What do you want?"

The man was dressed in khakis and a fleece jacket. He had brown hair, brown eyes, nothing to distinguish him at all except his smile. It was a smile in name only: lips curled in the right direction, a few teeth showing, eyes wrinkled in delight. But unlike most smiles, it didn't promise pleasure or happiness. Instead, it was filled with false regret. As if Lucy were a wayward child who'd broken the rules and now faced punishment.

"Who I am is of no consequence." His voice was as devoid of true emotion as his smile. "What I want is for you to understand the futility of your position. I told you there was no way out. I promised you that you would die here. I'm a man of my word. Now do you believe me?"

"Call off your dog."

In answer, the man hit Lucy in the face with a closed fist. The blow was lessened by his position, crouching, balanced on his toes in the snow, but it was still strong enough to send her sprawling to the side, fresh pain exploding in her ankle as her body twisted against the fulcrum of the large dog holding her leg fast in place. She landed facedown, the air knocked out of her, snow filling her nostrils and scratching against her eyes. Before she could move, the man wrenched both her arms behind her and handcuffed her—real handcuffs this time, not plastic zip ties.

The whole thing was a setup, she realized, trying to think clearly through the pain. Designed to do what? Distract her? Demoralize her?

"What do you want?" She hated that the words came out more like a plea than a demand. Sucked in her breath, fought to regain her composure.

"Release," he said. The pressure on her foot vanished—he was talking to the dog, not her.

He hauled her to her feet. She wobbled, unable to place her weight on her left foot as waves of agony swamped her. Nausea overcame her and she fell to the ground, vomiting.

The man stood and watched. The dog sat and watched, panting, its breath billowing in the cold air.

Once Lucy's stomach was empty and the dry heaves had passed, she turned her face, wiped it in the snow, took in a mouthful and spat it out again. The frozen crystals felt good, offering a numb escape from the pain.

A short-lived respite. When he saw she had nothing left to throw up, the man jerked her up once more. Lucy made her body go limp. She wasn't going back down into that black pit, not again. Even with the dog, even with the snow and cold, even with no one to hear her or see her or help, she'd rather die out here in the light than go back to the septic tank.

His answer was to haul her up and shove her forward another step, forcing her weight onto her injured foot. Then he kicked her leg out from under her, toppling her back to the ground. Lightning blazed through her, shattering her thoughts, making it impossible to feel, hear, see anything but pain. The dog sprang forward, excited by the sudden movement. It nosed Lucy's injured foot, its hot saliva mixing with her blood.

"Still some fight left." He pursed his lips and made a disappointed noise. "Okay then. Your choice. I warned you what would happen if you didn't believe me. You just signed a death warrant. Who's going to die, Lucy? Your husband, your daughter, or your mother?"

CHAPTER 7

Now
6:22 P.M.

RIDING FLAT ON her back strapped to a board, unable to even turn her head, was making Lucy carsick. The bright overhead light of the ambulance was impossible to avoid, so she kept her eyes shut, which helped the nausea but made her feel as if she were floating, somewhere outside her body.

"Crank up the heat," the paramedic called to the driver. "She's still hypothermic."

"It's up," the driver yelled back. "Why's she so cold? Wasn't outside that long."

"I don't know. She's soaking wet and has some injuries that don't add up. Like that foot—I never saw a foot and ankle that mangled from getting caught under a brake pedal."

"We're only ten out from the hospital."

They hit a bump, sending a jolt of pain through Lucy's body. It was sharp, yet nowhere near as intense as it had been before. She was so cold. Made it hard to concentrate on anything, including the pain.

She remembered the last time she'd been in an ambulance. Right after she'd first moved to Pittsburgh. She'd gotten a few bumps and bruises, and a piece of metal had sliced into her back. Nothing a few stitches hadn't taken care of, yet some people at the office had been upset when she returned to work after leaving the ER. Muttered about her trying to be some kind of superwoman.

Which surprised the hell out of her, since at the time she was searching for a girl kidnapped by a serial killer. If it had been their daughter, wouldn't they have wanted her back on the job?

Funny. Maybe it was because she was a woman. After all, the same people hadn't said anything about Taylor, a junior agent on her squad, coming back to work after breaking his arm that same day. They'd cheered him.

At the time she'd been irritated by any distraction from finding the girl. But later when she had time to think about it and talk it over with Nick, she'd felt sorry for them. People like that, they just kept their heads down, clocked in, clocked out, and went on their dreary way.

Those people—the ones who couldn't understand why she did what she did—they never would have climbed out of that hole in the ground today. Not even once, much less twice.

They didn't realize it had nothing to do with physical strength. It went deeper than that, this need, this hunger, this drive to never give up on anything or anyone—not even herself. Thank God she had it, whatever it was, because without it her family might die.

Her eyes snapped open, squinting against the bright light. What time was it? Nick. Megan. Her mom. She had to warn them.

"Phone," she pleaded once again. But her voice was even softer than before. Her mouth was parched by the oxygen blowing in—it tasted sweet, like when she'd blown up a bunch of balloons for Megan's birthday party. She licked her lips and tried again. "Phone. I need a phone."

The paramedic leaned over her, shielding her from the light. "I know you're cold," he said, misunderstanding her muffled whisper. He tucked a foil blanket closer around her body. "Hang on, we're almost there."

She tried to shake her head no, but he'd already turned away and the cervical collar and restraints holding her in place on the backboard prevented her from even that small movement.

Inside her head she screamed in frustration, but the only noise she could actually make escaped as a defeated whimper.

———•———

THEN
12:19 P.M.

LUCY STOPPED STRUGGLING and lay back in the snow. She stared at the man, focusing all her energy on him. What did he want? The thought reverberated through her. He'd threatened her family again. This time he sounded serious—too damn serious.

62

"I'll do whatever you want." She forced her voice to stay level and calm, a promise, not a plea. "Just tell me what you want."

It took a moment, but finally he nodded. "Fine. Let's start by getting you back inside your lovely accommodations."

The pit. Her prison. No. She remembered his earlier promise. Her coffin.

With her leg out of commission, the dog waiting to pounce, and the man with unknown weapons or accomplices to back up his threats, what choice did she have? Besides, she'd escaped once; she could do it again.

She hoped.

This time he helped her to her feet and let her lean on him to protect her injured foot. They performed a bizarre three-legged walk back to the opening of the septic tank. The dog followed alongside, occasionally turning its head to fix Lucy with a menacing glare, but otherwise keeping its distance.

The man sat Lucy down near the opening to the pit and rummaged through a backpack. She fantasized about pushing him down into the tank, making another run for it, but he was never close enough. And of course there was the damn dog.

The man glanced over his shoulder at her, a twisted smile on his face, and Lucy knew he'd put his back to her to see if she'd succumb to temptation and try something. More mind games. She was sick of them.

"Remember that DC journalist who vanished a few years ago? The one investigating the senator?" he asked with a grin. Just two folks, making casual conversation, his posture said. "All they found was his Mini Cooper parked by a lake. Three years and no trace."

He held a climbing rope loosely in his hands, turned to face her. "That was me. It's what I do. Make people vanish. Forever."

She tried to tune him out and use her precious time above ground to analyze her surroundings. The man and dog had come from the opposite direction—their path cut across the far edge of the field from a thick stand of pines and hemlocks.

Strange place to park a vehicle—the trees stretched as far as she could see. Maybe a logging road? Then she spotted the binoculars inside the man's pack. Bastard. He'd watched her escape—probably via a camera concealed inside one of the pipes. Waited for her. Just to set the dog loose and bring her down.

Games. That's what this man lived for. No matter what he told her, she needed to remember that this was all just a game to him. Stimulation, adrenaline, a sense of power, control . . . that's what fed him. He enjoyed competition—as long as he won.

She hid her smile. She might not know what the man wanted, but she knew what he needed: victory. To be the victor. She would use that.

"You have a decision to make, Lucy," he said. "Think of all the questions your disappearance will leave. No closure, not for your family. How many hours, how many years will they spend searching, wondering? Maybe I could drop a few hints—a secret bank account, evidence of an affair—"

Lucy jerked at that, unable to stop the movement. No way would Nick ever believe she'd been unfaithful. Never. But just raising the question, how painful—and he'd never have an answer. And Megan. What would happen to Megan?

Nick would do a great job raising her alone—he had more maternal instincts than Lucy. Something she always felt guilty about. And they'd have each other.

She blinked, stared into the sun. No. She couldn't give up, couldn't think like that. She was going to get out of this. She wasn't going to let this anonymous SOB take her family from her. No way in hell.

The man uncoiled the length of climbing rope and wrapped it around her chest and beneath her arms. She heard the click of a carabiner, then he leaned into the opening to the pit and worked the rope through the hooks in the ceiling.

It took him awhile to lower her into the tank, but he didn't seem to mind. She thought of the time and effort he was taking. Protecting her leg—the leg that he'd caused to be injured in the first place. Trying to buy her trust? Keeping her emotionally off balance, more likely.

She sat in the shadows on the concrete floor, unable to see him even when she craned her neck far enough back to view the opening. He hadn't sealed her in again, but he hadn't joined her either. Was he sending the dog down, locking that beast in with her?

The thought brought more fear than she wanted to acknowledge. Not just fear of the animal, fear of her absolute lack of control. Feeling powerless was a mere eyelash away from feeling hopeless, and she couldn't afford to go there. She needed to keep hold of hope, no matter how desperate. Without it, she was doomed—and he was still a threat to her family.

The fact that he hadn't replaced the lid, the sunlight

that shone down through the narrow opening, the sound of the birds in the distance—these all kept her hope alive.

Then a shadow blocked the light. He lowered himself into the pit, thudding to a landing behind her. His hands came down on her shoulders. "Shall we get started?"

No, she wanted to scream. But she kept silent and still. Waiting. It was his game, his move.

"Do you have any idea how special you are?" he asked. "You see," he said as if she'd answered him, "I have a friend who discovered a vulnerability in the Department of Justice's security software. Actually, there are quite a number of vulnerabilities, which is why the FBI built an entire center in West Virginia devoted to creating a new and improved system, complete with Nextgen biometric security."

She wished she could see him. Faces told so much more of the story than a voice in the dark.

"So here I am with a back door into the old DOJ network, and there you guys are, ready to move everything into the cyber equivalent of Fort Knox. Which means I need to move fast. Find someone with high enough clearance to access the mainframe so my friend can perform his magic.

"We started with hundreds of potential candidates. Winnowed them out. They had to be from a field office in a city large enough that if they went missing for a few hours no one would notice, yet small enough that we'd be able to breach their security. Had to have administrative privileges on the computer system. They had to be vulnerable. Married. Preferably a woman. With a husband, child, mother to protect. Young enough that they'd be eager to live, experienced enough that they'd know when to cut their losses."

His voice dropped with an edge of excitement, almost sexual. "And then we found you, Lucy. What a treasure trove you turned out to be. All those news stories on you, including photos of your husband and a glimpse of your daughter. Your dear mother living close-by, all alone in the house you grew up in. Not to mention how lucrative the job became once I dangled your name in the right circles.

"Let's see." His voice up ticked, and she knew he was counting on his fingers. "My original clients are paying five million to have a back door into the new database. A few mob guys ponied up another two million to gain access to the confidential informant list as well as the undercover database.

"Then came the Zapatas. Do you have any idea how much those people hate you for what you did, destroying their North American operations last month? Not to mention killing their favorite son. Ten million if you die quickly, twenty if I take my time."

He paused, let that sink in. Lucy honed in on his voice, searching for any change in his breathing or pitch that would indicate he was bluffing. She didn't hear any. He was telling the truth.

"Hope you don't think me greedy." He ruffled her hair with his fingers, knelt behind her, and placed his mouth right next to her ear. "But I'm planning to take my time."

CHAPTER 8

Now
6:31 p.m.

"FORTY-YEAR-OLD female, restrained driver, rollover MVA," the medic called out as they wheeled Lucy into the ER's trauma room. He'd added two years to her age, but that didn't even bother her. All she wanted was for everyone to stop talking long enough to hear her and get her a goddamned phone.

Her fear had been replaced by frustration, which had morphed into fury. Bad enough to be hauled from one place to another like a loaf of bread, but to be tied down and ignored?

Another lift and bump as the medic finished his report and they moved her onto the hospital's stretcher. Men and women appeared and disappeared in her vision as they cut off her clothing, replaced the medics' monitor leads, adjusted her oxygen mask, checked her vitals, started another IV and drew blood, listened to her heart and lungs, ran cold jelly and an ultrasound over her belly, took X-rays of her neck and chest and foot, all the while poking and prodding every inch of her body.

There had to be a clock in the room, but she couldn't see it from her position, restrained to the backboard. What time was it?

The doctors and nurses talked above her and around her, their words sounding like some kind of strange foreign tongue as they circled her captive body like sharks in a feeding frenzy. She thought she had a chance to make herself heard when one of them bent to shine a light in her eyes, but then his partner called to him from the foot of the bed and he was gone.

"Hey, did you see this?" one of the doctors said, his voice tight with excitement. He stood at her foot, and she braced herself against the pain that his touch was about to bring. "Open metatarsal fractures, ankle and calf basically shredded. Thought this was an MVA?"

"There are ligature marks on her wrists and neck," a woman's voice said from beyond Lucy's vision.

"Let's call Three Rivers about that foot—it's going to take a vascular repair. We might have to LifeFlight her over there," an older man said as he examined Lucy's foot, releasing a fresh wave of anguish. The machine monitoring her heart rate sang out in a staccato beat. "No. Wait. Are those tooth marks?"

As they talked *about* her instead of *to* her, Lucy was busy working one hand free of the Velcro restraints. The nurses had replaced her clothing with a hospital gown and had her warming under heat lamps. As she thawed, she felt more of the aches and pains that barraged her body, but her focus also returned.

Once her hand was free, she watched for the next

person to come close. It was a woman in scrubs. As she reached to adjust Lucy's IV, Lucy snaked her fingers around the woman's wrist and squeezed hard.

"Give me a phone," she said, the words scraping raw against her vocal cords.

The woman patted her arm as if Lucy were a child. But she did lean forward to listen. "What happened to you, honey? It's okay. You're safe here."

Before Lucy could answer, the two men abandoned their examination of her foot and approached the head of the bed from the opposite side.

"C-spine clear?" a man asked someone across the room.

"Looks good."

The sound of Velcro ripping filled Lucy's ears as the cervical collar and restraints were removed from her head. The man pushed his fingers against her neck bones. "Anything hurt?"

"No," Lucy said, trying to crane her head free so she could read the clock she'd glimpsed on the wall beyond him. What time was it?

He frowned, but the nurse repeated for her. "She says no."

He released his grip on her head, and finally she could turn far enough to see the clock. 6:47. Still time, but not much. She needed to contact Walden, get him to send local police to protect her family. Now.

Both men leaned forward, hovering just above Lucy's face. One of them removed the damn oxygen mask. "Okay then, what happened?"

Finally, someone to listen to her. Lucy mustered every ounce of command presence and forced it all into her shredded voice. "I'm an FBI agent. Get me a phone. Time's running out."

The nurse's eyes went wide. She jerked back, and Lucy thought maybe she was reaching for a phone, but the older man said, "First, I need to know if a dog is responsible for your ankle and foot injuries."

Lucy nodded. "Forget the dog. Lives are at stake. I need to warn them."

"How long ago did the dog attack you?"

Who the hell cared? She needed to get help to Nick and Megan, warn the FBI about the attack on their computers. "People will die if you don't get me a phone. Now."

Her voice was fading, but something in her face must have convinced the nurse, who said, "Let me grab my cell for you."

"How long?" the man repeated.

Lucy shrugged, regretted the movement. Did they have any idea how painful lying on a slab of wood felt after being banged up? "Don't know."

She'd escaped the septic tank the first time a few hours after the man had taken her, but she'd been knocked out part of that time . . . The sun had been almost directly overhead—she remembered that—before the dog . . . She flinched at the memory of the pain. "Around noon. I think."

She pivoted away from the doctors, ignoring the pain that lanced through her leg with the movement. Glanced at the clock. 6:49.

"Get me the phone. Or call the FBI office. Please, you don't understand—time is running out." Her voice faded before she could finish.

Didn't matter, the doctors had turned their backs to her, eyeing the X-rays once again. "Damn. That's way too long. Open fracture, contaminated, dog bite . . ."

The younger man moved back down to her foot, pressed one finger against it for a long moment, then released it. "Delayed cap refill, circulation's compromised. She'll probably lose it."

"Still, we should let the surgeons decide," the older man said.

"I'll give them a call, see if they want to transfer her to Three Rivers." Three Rivers Medical Center was one of Pittsburgh's major trauma centers. Sounded like this small community hospital wasn't equipped to deal with her injuries—least of her worries.

The second hand on the clock wouldn't stop its relentless movement. 6:50.

"Forget the foot," Lucy tried to shout. She pulled herself up to a sitting position and immediately wished she hadn't. Her vision blurred with a wave of dizziness, but she had their attention again. Where the hell was the woman who'd promised the phone? "I need the FBI. Now."

Before the men could answer, the woman returned—along with a sheriff's deputy. Relief surged through Lucy. She just needed to hold on for another minute or two, long enough to get word out to her team. They'd take care of Nick and her family.

She turned to the deputy. His expression was dour. No surprise. Locals didn't like messing with anything federal—and she knew right now she didn't look like any FBI agent they'd seen before. Didn't matter. As long as he listened and called Walden. Walden would take it from there.

"This the woman who crashed Lloyd Cramer's Jeep?" he asked.

"She says she's an FBI agent," the nurse said.

"You see any ID?" Before anyone could answer, he handcuffed Lucy's wrist to the bed rail.

Lucy jerked against the restraints in surprise. "Take these off."

"Whoever she is, I'm not taking any chances," the deputy said. "And there won't be any phone calls until we get to the bottom of this."

"Bottom of what?" the younger doctor asked.

"Bottom of whoever killed Lloyd. I just found his body back at his barn. Someone skewered his face on a combine blade."

———◆———

THEN

2:31 P.M.

THE MAN WAS silent, giving Lucy plenty of time to think. He wanted her to imagine all the myriad ways he could torture her before killing her, taking his time, keeping her alive until she begged for release.

Hell with that.

She wasn't playing by his rules. Or his timeline. She knew how this would end.

She also knew how to save her family.

Who cared about the database of pedophiles and predators? She'd caught them before, she'd catch them again—or someone would.

She gave him the damn password.

Behind her, he stirred in surprise. She almost smiled. "What was that?"

She repeated the string of numbers and letters. They were easy to remember: the date and abbreviation of the city where Megan had been conceived. Something no one except her would know—and maybe Nick, but he was awful with dates. "It's the passcode."

His breath echoed through the dark chamber. Then silence.

Suddenly he was right behind her, his arms snaking through hers to pull her body upright, pressed against his. Her left foot hit the floor with the unexpected movement. She gasped in pain.

But not much fear. Now that he had what he wanted, he'd kill her. But her family would live. There was nothing for him to gain by hurting them—a sociopath like him, it was all about getting what he wanted. And she'd given it to him.

Time to die.

She waited, limp in his arms, balancing her weight on her good foot. Knife to the throat? Gunshot to the head? No, he was greedy, he'd take it slow. Didn't really matter. He might have gotten what he wanted, but so had she. He thought she'd given up, that he'd won. Wrong. She'd won: her family was safe.

He slid one hand free, palm beneath her left breast, against her heart. Nothing sexual about his touch, more clinical. His arms were well muscled, not straining as he supported her weight. His breath came in slow, hot waves, brushing the top of her head as he effortlessly held her in place.

Then he dropped her. Pain screamed through her foot. She choked back her shriek, but couldn't stop the whimper that emerged.

"You disappoint me, Lucy." His voice was smooth, a stiletto that cut through her calm. "Don't waste my time. We only have until seven."

He'd mentioned that deadline earlier. What happened at seven?

"I gave you what you wanted," she protested.

"I told you what would happen if you disappointed me. I told you I'm a man of my word." He sounded betrayed.

She struggled to get beyond the pain reverberating through her body. Shifted her weight away from her injured foot. Then froze as he leveraged his booted foot against her bloody one. He didn't press down. Just held it there, a silent threat.

"Do you think I'm stupid?" he demanded. "I study my subjects, know everything about them. I know the wrong passcode will lock the system down, send a security alert. And I know you, Lucy. The way you saved all those children from the hospital bombing. How you never give up on a victim, even tracking that serial killer years after everyone thought he was dead."

He let up on her foot. She leaned away, bracing herself, knowing he was toying with her.

"You're smarter than any serial killer," she said, trying an appeal to his vanity. "I knew better than to resist. The password is the correct one. I would never try to trick you, not with my family's lives at stake."

He crouched behind her, his arms stroking her shoulders and arms, tracing the lines of her body in the darkness. She shivered, straining to anticipate his next tactic. How could she convince him that he had won?

"No," he finally said, his hand caressing her injured foot. His touch was gentle, barely brushing the torn skin and mangled bones beneath it. Still more than enough to send a shock wave of pain through her body. "You would never give up this easily."

He stood once more, stepping back, abandoning her on the floor. A bright light seared through the darkness—his phone a few feet in front of her. A slide show of images played across it. Her mother. Nick. Megan.

"No," she gasped. "I gave you what you wanted. Please, no."

"I told you what would happen if you disappointed me, Lucy." His tone was fatherly, chiding a wayward child. "I'm a man of my word."

The images rotated like a roulette wheel.

"Your choice, Lucy. Which one will die?"

CHAPTER 9

"I'LL NEED ALL her possessions and clothes bagged for evidence," the deputy told the ER staff. Lucy rattled the handcuffs to get his attention.

"FBI," she mouthed, cursing her stolen voice. But there was still hope. If she could get him to call the FBI, they'd verify who she was—it would take longer than calling Walden directly, but she'd have to risk it. What choice did she have?

"I'll call them and get the detectives down here to do an interview," he told her. His expression was strained: a simple MVA turned into a homicide investigation was less than routine for a weeknight's patrol. It was clear he was trying to do everything by the book, but Lucy needed him to throw the book out.

She rattled the cuffs again. The deputy bent close. "The man?" she whispered. "Cramer?"

"If you are who you say you are, then you know I can't question you until you've been read your rights and the doctors clear you. And if you aren't, well, we'll just wait for the detectives. Nothing's getting thrown out on a technicality, not on my watch."

Lucy shook her head, frustrated that he didn't understand. She took a breath, trying to bolster her voice. Decided to go ahead and play the role of the victim, hoping he'd respond better than he had to her earlier demands. "He threatened my family. Please. Check on them."

The more she tried to talk, the more it felt like she was being choked all over again.

He gave her one of those single-jerk-of-the-chin cop nods that could mean yes or could mean no, turned to speak into his radio, then left to join the doctors just outside the open door to the room, beyond her hearing.

She lay back on the stretcher and closed her eyes, blocking out the light blaring down into her face, distancing herself from the pain.

She glanced at the clock. Panic ripped through her, twisting her gut.

7:00. Time was up.

If she was wrong and the man who'd kidnapped her hadn't been working alone, then his partners could be anywhere. He'd left her to die in the pit hours ago. Plenty of time for his accomplices to find her family and infiltrate the FBI's computer system with her passcode.

Nick could already be dead. Her stomach clenched, and for a moment she couldn't breathe. Fear had a stranglehold on her chest. Her heart thudded so hard and fast it set off the alarm on the monitor behind her.

"Are you okay?" a nurse asked.

Lucy opened her eyes and nodded. The nurse didn't

see the lie; she was busy checking her vitals on the monitor.

How long since the man had left her to die in the tank? No, that wasn't the right question. The right question was: where had he gone first?

If what he'd told her was the truth, then he'd need a computer that was part of a law enforcement network, tied to the National Crime Information Center and with admin privileges. It didn't have to be an FBI or DOJ computer, but it needed to be more than a mobile data terminal like what the deputy had in his vehicle. No way would the man be able to physically breach the FBI's field office in Pittsburgh. But a computer at a police station would work.

Her gaze centered on the deputy. He still hovered near the door, frowning, one hand on his weapon, as he talked to her doctors. Why hadn't he already called the FBI? Why hadn't he asked more questions? Miranda be damned. She was a federal agent, a man was dead, you'd think he'd want to know something here and now rather than waiting for a detective.

Maybe he was working with her captor. Or maybe her captor was law enforcement. He'd said he had a schedule to meet. Seven o'clock. Maybe it was a work schedule, starting a shift that would give him access to the computer and, through it, the DOJ database?

Or maybe the deputy was just an unimaginative cop, content to do his business without getting involved in federal messes best left to the brass and detectives. Her mind whirled with suspicions and second guesses.

It didn't matter. She needed a phone—one call to Walden, to make sure her family was safe, and she could relax, let the doctors do their work, and let the rest sort itself out.

She glanced at the nurse. She'd been sympathetic, she'd come so close to giving Lucy a phone. A phone that Lucy saw was still in the pocket of the nurse's lab coat. She just needed to get her alone for a minute.

Lucy tapped on the bed rail with the handcuff and nodded to the nurse when she turned around. "Need to pee," she whispered.

"They're talking to the surgeons at Three Rivers about LifeFlighting you there—it's the best hope for your leg. The deputy is trying to figure out what to do with you if they do. Either way, you need surgery. They'll put a catheter in there."

Lucy shook her head. "Can't hold it."

The nurse nodded, patted her shoulder, and went to join the men. One of the doctors left, and the other shrugged at the nurse before following him from the room. Lucy hoped that shrug didn't mean they wanted the nurse to put the catheter in here, or worse, a bedpan—her best bet was if the nurse took her to use a restroom.

The nurse kept talking to the deputy, giving Lucy time to sit back up and assess her situation. Naked except for a hospital gown, her left foot swathed in bandages and an ACE wrap holding a splint in place, another splint on her left hand . . . not much in the way of assets. She didn't even have Megan's bracelet any longer—it, along with everything else she'd worn, was now in brown paper bags in the hands of the deputy.

She glanced at her left hand. Her wedding ring was gone—she vaguely recalled the younger doctor cutting it off during the frenzy of her arrival. Because of the way her hand and fingers had swollen. Boxer's fracture, he'd said.

Her lucky charm. She couldn't stop staring at her naked ring finger, barely visible beyond the edge of the splint. For some reason losing her ring made her even more fearful that something terrible had happened to Nick. Magical thinking, he often chided her—usually with a laugh that his über-rational wife could be so superstitious.

Superstition or not, the panic was real enough. She needed to get out of here. Now.

The nurse left and returned a minute later with a wheelchair.

"It's not like she's going anywhere. Not with that foot," she said to the deputy as she transferred the bag of IV fluids to a pole attached to the back of the wheelchair. Lucy couldn't help but think that pole would make a good weapon. "And the bathroom is right there." She nodded to a door on the opposite side of the room.

The deputy went to check it out himself, ensuring there were no weapons and no means for Lucy to escape. At least that's what she'd be looking for if she were in his shoes.

"Okay, okay," he told the nurse. "By the time you're back, hopefully the supervisor will be here. I have a call in to the FBI about her. They're going to call back." The deputy sounded irritated that Lucy was still his burden to bear, but at least he had contacted the Bureau—or claimed he had. He unlocked Lucy's handcuffs and returned them to his duty belt.

"My family?" she asked.

"The person I spoke with at the FBI said once they verified your identity, they'd send someone out."

Lucy shook her head. That would take too long. Why couldn't he understand that they were out of time? "Call Don Burroughs. Detective, Major Crimes, Pittsburgh Police. Ask him to send someone. Now."

That earned her another scowl, but it seemed like he was thawing, actually beginning to believe. "You better not be yanking my chain, lady——"

"I'm not."

"All right." He turned to the nurse. "I'll be right outside." Glared at Lucy. "Making *another* call."

The nurse lowered the bed rail and helped Lucy swing her legs over the side. Her left foot felt like a deadweight, tugging at her body as if trying to escape.

"You okay?" the nurse asked. Lucy nodded, and the nurse guided her into a standing position, braced against the bed, her injured foot off the floor. Then the nurse added a second hospital gown, draping it from back to front, returning to Lucy a small amount of dignity, before sliding the wheelchair into place behind her.

Lucy slumped into the chair and let the nurse lift her leg onto the padded footrest. The exertion had left her drenched with sweat and feeling flushed. Hard to believe that a short while ago she'd been freezing.

The nurse pushed her into the small restroom. Before she could help Lucy up onto the toilet, Lucy made a grab for the nurse's phone.

She snagged it from the nurse's pocket, but her movement was clumsy, lacking the finesse she needed to hide it. The nurse whirled. "What do you think you're doing?"

————◆————

THEN
3:12 P.M.

HE STOPPED THE slide show on Megan's image. Lucy sat up straight, gaze lasered in on her daughter's photo. She was not going to let this man hurt her family. Not an option.

She was going to kill him. Lucy had no idea how, but the thought brought with it a certainty that dulled all pain.

He sensed her shift in mood. His foot stomped down on hers. Her shriek echoed through the space for what felt like hours. By the time the sounds died, she was facedown on the floor, barely able to breathe, the cold concrete freezing her tears.

"I gave you what you wanted," she pled. "Do whatever you want with me, leave my family alone." Her words emerged in a fever-rush of anguish and fear.

Then she saw. Instead of focusing on the big picture of how to save her family, she needed to answer the smaller question: what did he want, right here, right now?

He wanted the pain to distract her. No. More than that, he wanted it to break her. Wanted her to surrender to it. To him.

He wanted to emerge from here the victor.

As much as she wanted the pain to stop, she realized she could use it.

"Please," she begged, no longer fighting the tears.

She watched his face in the dim light, trying to read his expression. His eyes widened slightly, just for a moment, and his lips curled in a genuine smile. Finally, a glimpse of the true monster—he enjoyed her pain, but even more, he relished her loss of control.

Now she knew what the beast fed on. Just had to figure out how to keep him happy long enough for her to kill him.

He crouched down beside her again. "Megan's the easy choice," he said in a conversational tone. He softly stroked her hair away from her eyes. "After all, Nick can always have more kids. Let's see . . . she's in English now. That gives my guys time to grab her when classes change in nine minutes."

"No." Lucy had to fight to keep the anger from her voice, to reveal only her pain. "Please. No."

Her entire body shook—cold and pain and adrenaline taking their toll. She lay on her back in the growing shadows that filled the pit, the cerulean sky dancing at the edge of her vision. Freedom. She couldn't let it distract her, had to think only of keeping this madman happy.

"You're right. Best to save Megan for last. Besides, she's easy to get to. Any time." He pursed his lips as if concentrating, consulted his phone once more. "Let's see. Your mom's at a planning committee for the church bazaar. And then she'll be meeting her gentleman friend, Charlie, for an early-bird dinner and bowling. Did she tell you, she bowled a one-eighty last week?"

Lucy let the shakes devour her body, released herself to her tears. Snot poured from her nose, and she turned her face into her shoulder to wipe it clean. Closed her eyes for an instant, hiding her triumph.

Bastard wasn't all-seeing, all-powerful. He didn't know her mom had canceled her plans with Charlie to babysit Megan tonight. Her mom wouldn't be anywhere near her own home this afternoon; she'd be coming into the city to Lucy's house. Could she take the chance, send him to Mom's house?

No. Too risky—he obviously had someone following her. They'd know when she left for Lucy's place.

"Not your mom?" His tone was a strange mix of surprise and pleasure. "I'd actually thought you would have chosen her. She's old, already had her chance at a family, happiness. So it's Nick? Really?"

Nick. Yes. He was at the VA today instead of his private office. He'd be surrounded all day, and into the night since he had group. Protected by his patients, soldiers—young, fit, ready for action.

"Lucy? I need to know. Who do you want me to kill? Is it Nick? Megan? Or your mom?" The man sounded impatient, as if Lucy had been dawdling for no good reason.

Lucy rolled her face back up to the thin slice of sky, keeping her expression blank. Stray tears coated her eyelashes, coloring the world with rainbows as she blinked. Her face was numb, her body numb, and she used that to her advantage.

He leaned forward, his face blocking the sky, creating her world. Master of the universe.

For now. Bastard.

She buried her fury beneath the numbness. "Please. I gave you what you wanted. That's the real code. I promise." She was sobbing again, tears warming her frozen skin. "It's the day Megan was conceived. How could I make that up?" Again, the glint of satisfaction in his eyes. Good.

His gaze searched hers. Then he abruptly stood, towering over her. "Answer me, Lucy." He planted his booted foot over her injured one and shifted his weight down.

The blissful numbness vanished in a tsunami of pain, swamping all conscious thought. Lucy couldn't restrain her scream. It echoed through the small space, escaped into the empty sky so far overhead, then disappeared.

"Who's it going to be, Lucy? Who's going to die?"

He applied more pressure to her ankle. Lucy's body jackknifed upright, her shoulders straining against the handcuffs as another shriek escaped. He removed his boot. Her pants leg was shredded, the black fabric looking like soot caught in a mass of blood and mangled tissue. Nothing remained of her sock, and she swore she saw the glint of bone in the ugly gaping wound that extended from her shin down to her foot.

All this filled her vision in the time it took for her scream to consume all the breath in her body. She fell back, gasping.

He raised his boot high, ready to stomp down with all his weight.

"No!" she cried. "Nick! Take Nick."

CHAPTER 10

LUCY CLOSED HER fist around the phone, but the nurse easily wrested it away. "Please. I need to talk to the FBI." The nurse looked at her skeptically. "Deputy Renfew said he'd already called."

"And is waiting to hear back from the duty agent. My family is in danger. They may not have time."

The nurse squinted at Lucy, then the door, and finally nodded. "But I'll dial, and we keep it on speaker."

Lucy gave her Walden's direct number. When he answered, the nurse took over. "This is Mary Townsend, a nurse in the ER at Riverside Community Hospital. To whom am I speaking?"

"FBI Special Agent Isaac Walden. What do you need?"

Never had Lucy been so relieved to hear Walden's deep, soothing tones. She reached for the phone but the nurse held it away from her. "Do you work with a Lucy

Guardino?"

"Yes. She's my boss. Supervisory special agent in charge of our Sexual Assault Felony Enforcement squad. Why?" Concern edged his voice. "Has something happened?"

"Could you please describe her?"

Lucy rolled her eyes. She didn't have time for this nonsense. Walden responded with a thumbnail description of her, enough to satisfy the nurse, who finally handed Lucy the phone. Lucy held it close to her lips, straining to raise her voice loud enough to carry through the airwaves.

"Find Nick and Megan," she said. "And secure my mother—she should be at my house with Megan. Nick's at the VA. This morning I was abducted, and the man threatened my family. He has my administrator database code, so call Taylor and have him run a security sweep of the system and alert Clarksburg and Quantico." Her voice faded to a thin, raspy whisper.

"Are you safe now?" Walden asked.

"Yes." Lucy could barely manage the single syllable.

The nurse interrupted. "She has several fractures and severe damage to her left foot and ankle. The doctors are talking to Three Rivers about a transfer to get her to the surgical specialists she needs to save her leg."

Lucy grabbed the phone back. "Get my family to safety."

"On it," he assured her. "Can you describe any of the subjects?"

"I—" She paused, realizing that the nurse was listening to an admission of guilt. What the hell, it was self-defense, pure and simple. "I killed the man I saw.

During my escape. A county deputy, Renfew, ID'd him as Lloyd Cramer. I don't know how many accomplices he has."

"Got it. Let me check on your family and tag this deputy as well as Taylor. I'll call you back soon as I have answers." He hung up.

Lucy sagged back in the chair, still gripping the phone like it was a lifeline. "One more call?" she asked the nurse in a meek tone. "My husband. Please?"

Walden had suitably impressed the nurse, who nodded. "Of course. No problem. I'm going to see if they're transferring you or not. Agent Guardino." She added the last in a tone of respect.

Lucy couldn't care less about the title or her medical care. All she cared about was reaching Nick. She called his cell, holding her breath until he answered. "Callahan here."

She couldn't respond right away: her heart felt as if it had leapt into her throat, swelling with gratitude. Nick was alive. He was okay.

"Hello?" he repeated, his Virginia accent leaking through. "Anybody there?"

"It's me," she said. "Lucy," she added, in case her hoarse whisper wasn't clear.

"Lucy, what's wrong?"

"Where's Megan? Have you seen or spoken with her or my mom?"

"There's a story." Country-western music in the background. He was in his car—the only place he listened to that radio station. "She conned your mother into letting her and Emma get a ride after karate from Emma's older sister. Only instead of going to Emma's house, they went to check on Zeke at the vet's. And then Emma and her sister left Megan there while they went to that damn movie."

Megan was alone? Panic parched her mouth. Before she was able to form any words, Nick continued, "Just picked up the little rug rat and we're on our way home to have dinner with your mom. Say hi, Megan. It will be the last time you get to use a phone for a long, long time."

"Mom." Megan's voice carried through, lighting Lucy's heart with a joyous fire. "Tell Dad he's overreacting. I didn't mean to lie, not really. But I knew you didn't want me going to the movie, and I really, really wanted to see Zeke, make sure he was okay. And I asked Grams for permission—well, kind of—so there's no reason to ground me."

"We'll see about that," Nick said. "Anyway, what's up? Your voice sounds funny—don't tell me you got into a shouting match with those bozos in Harrisburg. Hey, Walden's on the other line."

Lucy chose her words carefully, not sure if Megan could hear her. "Nick. Don't go home. I never made it to Harrisburg. A man threatened me as well as my family—"

"Are you okay?" His voice changed, became razor sharp.

"I'm fine. I had a little accident. They brought me to Riverside Community."

"We're on our way. What about your mother? She's waiting at the house."

"Walden's sending someone. He'll arrange an escort for you as well."

"Why? Thanks to Megan's escapades, no one could possibly know where we are, and if you're safe at the hospital, then we will be as well. I'll call Walden back, tell him to have your mom brought there."

Great. Just what she didn't need: explaining the events of the day to her mother. But he was right. There was no way her captor's accomplices could know where she was—hell, they probably didn't even know he was dead yet. With her family safe and Walden on the job, she could finally relax.

She glanced at her mangled leg. Thought about the kind of person who would turn a beautiful animal into a vicious killing machine. Decided he'd gotten what he deserved back in that barn. "Is Megan's puppy okay?"

Nick's laughter was better than any pain medicine the doctors had. "You big softy. Yes, he's fine. The vet said we can bring him home tomorrow."

Exhaustion washed over her, pulling her under like a riptide. "Okay. Good. I'll see you soon."

"Love you, Lucy-loo," he whispered before hanging up.

"Love you, too," she replied, even though the line had already gone dead.

———◆———

THEN
3:53 P.M.

HER SCREAM DIED, burying Nick's name in silence. Dear Lord, what had she done?

Sobs shook her—real tears beyond her control. Nick would be okay, she promised herself. He could take care of himself, he was safe at the VA, he'd be all right.

Lies to dull the real pain.

The man grunted in satisfaction, made a show of sending a text on his phone before pocketing it, then circled behind her, embracing her once more, his lips close to her ear as he whispered, "Nick it is."

He slid the rope that circled her chest out from under her arms, transforming it into a noose around her neck. "Get up, Lucy. Your work isn't done."

The noose suspended from the overhead eyehooks was just tight enough to remind her how easy it would be to die: all she had to do was lean her weight forward. A few minutes later, it would all be over. If he hurt her family, she might consider that option. But only as a last resort—she wasn't giving up the fight. Not yet.

"What more do you want?" she asked from her position sitting on the floor.

Instead of answering, he pulled her to her feet and lifted her back up onto the cinder block. Gone was the gentleness he'd shown when he lowered her into the pit earlier. Now he handled her as if she were less than human, an inconvenient object to be dealt with.

She fought to find her balance on the cinder block. Keeping her good foot planted and allowing her injured one to dangle was almost as painful as bracing both feet on the narrow square. Suddenly the rope around her neck yanked taut. Her body jerked up, handcuffed arms arcing behind her.

The cinder block wobbled beneath her, her foot slipped, and the noose tightened, digging into her neck. She gasped for air, could barely make a sound.

"Whoops, not yet," he muttered. He repositioned her foot on the cinder block, then dug a finger between the rope and her skin, loosening it enough that she could breathe.

Lucy blinked against the wave of anxiety that swamped her as she hauled in one lungful of air after another, hyperventilating, rejoicing in the simple act of breathing.

"Okay then," he said in a calm tone that made her wish for just one chance to wrap her hands around his throat as tight as the noose he'd forced on her. "Guess I'll be going."

He used a corner of the cinder block to boost himself up to the opening above them, almost knocking Lucy off-balance once more. The noose tightened, but not enough to cut off her air. She fought to regain her footing on the block as he swung free of the pit.

To her surprise, he didn't close the lid immediately. A few minutes after he left, water gushed from one of the pipes, flowing so hard and fast its spray quickly soaked her.

"What are you doing?" she shouted into the rapidly growing darkness, straining to be heard. "I gave you what you wanted!"

His laughter echoed from above, waning sunlight shimmering blood red from the water filling the tank. Then he appeared once more. "I'm going to check out the code you gave me. If you told me the truth, I won't be back. The Mexicans will have to be happy watching you either drown or hang yourself.

"But," he turned the simple word into a dire warning, "if you've tried to double-cross me, then I will return. Before the tank fills. And I'll bring your daughter with me. You might want to stick around for that—if you lied and I get back and you've killed yourself, I'm giving her to the Mexicans."

"No. You said I could choose. Leave Megan alone. I told you the truth. The code works. I promise." The rope around her neck made it hard to scream loud enough for her voice to carry above the sound of the rushing water. Not to mention the pain shooting through her as she struggled to keep her balance with the water surging against the cinder block. It took all her will power and concentration to keep enough of her weight on the block to prevent the water from pushing it away.

"I sure hope so, Lucy. For Megan's sake. But either way, Nick dies. Like I said. I'm a man of my word." He slid the lid closed, leaving her alone in the black emptiness of the tank.

Lucy didn't waste time or energy. She focused her entire being into moving her handcuffed hands into the jacket pocket where Megan's bracelet lay. On that and not losing her footing on the damn cinder block. Hard to do between the gushing water below and her entire body suspended from the noose, shaking above.

Finally, her fingers grasped the bracelet. She twisted the Paracord until she had a firm grip on the handcuff key concealed in the clasp. She had to bend her wrist and contort her arms to get the key into the lock.

Just as she flexed her wrists far enough to turn the key, the cinder block wobbled an inch too far and toppled, leaving her body dangling from the noose. The rope cut into the flesh around her neck, cutting off her air. She kept working the key; it was her only hope.

Her entire weight pulled against the noose strangling her. Her vision flared red against the blackness surrounding her. But she managed to keep control of her fingers long enough to turn the key. The click she'd been waiting for resonated through her entire body.

She fumbled one hand free and pried her fingers beneath the noose. Gasping for air, each breath burning her throat, she clung to the rope. Without the cinder block, she'd have to use the rope and the wall for leverage—not easy with one leg out of commission, but it was the only way.

Lucy gritted her teeth and pushed her leg against the wall to lift her weight enough so she could pull the rope loose and free her head from the noose. Then she dropped to the floor, landing on her good foot and hanging onto the rope with one hand. Using the other to find the cinder block and set it back upright, she took a deep breath and gathered her strength for the climb out.

The water was already up to her ankles, but that was the least of her worries. If he was monitoring the camera—she assumed it was positioned in the other pipe, the one that didn't have water flowing through it—then this might be an even shorter escape than her earlier one.

And the dog? What if the dog was waiting up there for her?

She grabbed the rope and pulled up her good leg to stand on the cinder block. Dog or no dog, killer or no killer, she was Nick's only hope.

She'd be damned if she'd let anything stop her from saving him and Megan.

CHAPTER 11

THE NURSE RETURNED just as Lucy was wiping her tears of relief with the sleeve of her gown. "Everything okay?"

Lucy sniffed and smiled. "Yes. My family's safe. They're on their way."

"Great." The nurse pushed Lucy's chair back into the trauma bay. She grabbed a warm blanket from a steel cabinet and tucked it around Lucy's lap. She didn't ask for the cell phone back; Lucy hung onto it, hoping that Nick or Walden would call and update her.

"Let's get a move on," the waiting doctor said.

"Where?" Lucy asked.

"The surgeons at Three Rivers want an MRI. We only have one tech this time of night, but I told them this is a priority." The doctor barely made eye contact as he spoke, standing over Lucy and looking down on her. It made her neck hurt to look up at him, so Lucy didn't bother.

"I'm not leaving until my family gets here."

"We'll send the scan to Three Rivers by computer. They'll decide whether or not to LifeFlight you." He spoke as if what she wanted were irrelevant.

"My family can drive me. Silly to waste a helicopter trip." Lucy wasn't arguing just to be a contrarian, although she definitely enjoyed pissing off the arrogant doctor. Driving this time of night—especially with Walden escorting them—would only take ten or fifteen minutes longer than flying.

The main reason was that Nick and Megan couldn't come with her on a helicopter. And once she had them here, safely in her arms, there was no way in hell she was letting them go again. Or her mother.

She picked up the cell phone the nurse had lent her. Better warn Mom that the police were stopping by the house and Walden was coming to pick her up. Mom liked Walden, but she did not like being ordered around or rushed. Thankfully, Walden was less likely to annoy her than Lucy would have if she'd been able to go herself.

"The tech's doing a CAT scan now," the doctor said to the nurse. "Can you get her down to MRI and prep her?" His tone made it clear that he was past ready to get this difficult patient out of his ER and into the hands of someone else.

"No problem."

Lucy dialed her mom's cell. No answer. Probably didn't even have it with her. She left a message on the voice mail just in case.

The nurse pushed her toward the hall. The deputy waited there, looking a bit abashed—he'd spoken with Walden, no doubt. Lucy met his gaze, held her wrists up to ask if he was going to use handcuffs, and he shook his head and turned to lead them through the ER, hand on the butt of his gun as if expecting an ambush from the snotty-nosed kids slumped in chairs in the waiting room or the old man wheezing as he pushed an IV pole down the hall.

Lucy tried her home phone. No answer. Maybe the police had escorted her mom out of the residence while they cleared it and checked for danger? A thin hum of anxiety vibrated through her. Her captor had said he was going after Nick. Mom should have been safe at Lucy's house.

If her captor was a man of his word.

"We're shorthanded," the nurse prattled as they rolled down the corridor. "Flu and RSV hitting hard, not to mention that stomach bug. I think the radiology tech is doing a belly CT, but hopefully we won't have to wait too long." They reached an elevator bank, where several visitors stood waiting.

Lucy barely saw them as she stabbed the phone, calling Walden this time.

The deputy commandeered the first elevator that arrived and shooed the visitors away. "What floor?"

"Basement," the nurse answered. "The MRI's one of the older ones. Only thing down there. Except the morgue."

Idiot, Lucy berated herself as she waited for Walden to pick up. What the hell had she been thinking? Believing for an instant that the psycho who'd taken and tortured her would ever keep his word? Fear and guilt collided. Walden finally answered but was cut off almost immediately as the call was dropped.

"You won't get any reception," the nurse said, sliding the phone from Lucy's hand and pocketing it. "Can't have it near the MRI battery, anyway."

The elevator doors opened and they entered a dimly lit hall. It smelled less hospital and more moldy basement. The tiny squeak from the chair's wheels on the dingy linoleum echoed and bounced from the exposed pipes overhead. The walls were cinder block, painted an institutional pale green meant to be calming but that reminded Lucy of baby puke.

Which made her think of Megan. Wished she'd had time to talk to her. But they'd be here soon—it was only a fifteen-minute drive.

But what about Mom? "Is there another phone I can use?" she asked the nurse. "I really need to check in with my family."

They reached the far end of the corridor, where the MRI suite was. The deputy opened the door to a waiting area, took a look inside, saw the room was empty, held the door as the nurse pushed Lucy inside, then closed the door to stand guard outside.

A row of chairs stood along the near wall. The far wall had several curtained changing areas. A reception desk, empty except for a phone and a computer terminal, guarded a large solid door leading to the MRI examination area. On the wall behind the desk was an emergency call button with a small intercom speaker.

"You can use the phone as soon as we get you prepped," the nurse told her.

"How long will this take?"

"Thirty-forty minutes." The nurse scrutinized the bag of IV fluid hanging from the pole extending up from the back of the chair. "All done. That's your first dose of antibiotic." With swift fingers, she detached the tubing from the IV, leaving Lucy's hands free. "Your vitals have been fine, and they have a special monitor of their own for the scanner." She removed the sticky monitor leads from Lucy's chest and unhooked her from the portable monitor that hung from the back of the chair.

"Okay, now I need you to answer this questionnaire." She took a clipboard from a hook on the wall. "You work on that while I go check on the tech." She nodded to the large red-and-white sign on the opposite wall, warning about the MRI's powerful magnet. "Don't skip any questions. We don't want any surprises. I once had a patient who forgot about a dental bridge—not a pretty sight."

Lucy nodded and took the pen she offered. The nurse left, and Lucy began the slow process of wheeling the chair with her one good hand, ignoring the questionnaire, to head to the desk where the phone was. To her surprise, the deputy entered and moved to stand in front of her, thumbs hooked into his duty belt, fingers stretched along the wide belt buckle.

"You know officer safety comes first," he said. His way of apologizing.

"Of course," she answered. He'd done everything by the book. Wasn't anyone's fault that the book didn't cover situations like this.

"And after finding Lloyd like that . . ." His voice trailed off. "You sure he's the one did this to you? Sure doesn't sound like him. No history of violence. Bit of a prepper type, keeps to himself, except for his dogs of course. Trains them and rents them out as guard dogs.

Loves those animals more than most humans."

A sudden thought speared through Lucy, distracting her from her mission to get to the phone. No. She couldn't have—but the barn had been dark, she'd never gotten a good look at man's face, just the faintest impression as they'd struggled. "Photo?"

"Of Lloyd Cramer?" He pulled a driver's license encased in an evidence bag from his pocket, held it in front of her. "This is him."

Brown hair. Brown eyes. Lucy hunched over the photo, studying it for clues, her stomach revolting as her fingers gripped the plastic bag so tight it almost slipped through them. This was not her man—not the man who'd kidnapped her.

The man was still out there. Her family was still in danger.

She'd killed the wrong man.

CHAPTER 12

FOR A LONG moment, the only sound in the room was the buzz and crackle of the fluorescent lights. Lucy tried to gather her thoughts. Had she killed an innocent man? No, he had a gun, had attacked her . . . Farmers carry guns. She was on his land, hiding in the dark . . . No, the dog was his. He had to be working with the man who'd taken her.

The man who was still out there. Her family wasn't safe yet.

The phone on the desk rang, the shrill noise jump-starting Lucy's attention. She thrust her fear aside as the deputy answered. "Yeah, she's right here." He wheeled her to the desk and handed her the receiver. "It's Special Agent Walden."

Walden. The man had impeccable timing. "There's definitely one subject still out there," she said. "Where are you?"

"I'm on my way to Riverside." His voice sounded distant, heavy.

"Is my mother with you?"

A pause. "Lucy, I need you to wait at the hospital. Don't leave until I get there."

"Why? What happened?" Fear clenched her heart so tight she couldn't breathe. "Are Nick and Megan okay?" Then she realized he hadn't answered her original question. "Walden, let me speak to my mom."

"I can't. Lucy—"

She knew that tone. Had used it herself when preparing victims for bad news. The worst possible kind of news. "No. No, it can't be. He said—"

The man had said he'd go after one of her family. A man of his word.

Suddenly the deputy and everything else in the room seemed very far away as Lucy's world collapsed. Not her mother . . . Denial, always the first instinct. No protection against the truth revealed by Walden's silence.

Finally, Lucy found her voice again. "What happened?"

"The locals I sent to your house found her. She's on her way to Three Rivers."

Relief rushed over her. "She's alive. What did he do to her?"

Bastard must have gone straight to her home after leaving Lucy in the pit. Maybe seven o'clock wasn't a deadline but the time when his window of opportunity opened. Her mind picked at the tiny details, refusing to recognize the gruesome truth. Her mother injured, her home a crime scene . . . and all of it her fault.

Lucy closed her eyes, tried to see her mother's face.

She couldn't. Her entire body was awash in cold, more numb than it had been when she climbed from the pit into the snow. She swallowed twice before she could force any words out. "How bad?"

He hesitated, and she knew it was worse than she'd dared think.

"Don't make me imagine it, Walden."

They both knew the things Lucy had seen in the course of her work. The stuff of nightmares. The truth could only be a tonic to whatever horrors her fear and imagination could conjure.

"A knife," Walden finally said. "He used a knife."

Christ. The phone slipped from Lucy's grasp. She fumbled for it on her lap.

"She was unconscious but still had a pulse," Walden continued. "But the medics—"

"She's not going to die." In Lucy's head the words translated to an anguished plea: she *couldn't* die. Not her mother. Not because of Lucy.

"Nick? Megan?" Lucy asked, both hands awkwardly gripping the phone. *Please, God . . .* She couldn't finish the silent prayer, too fearful it might not be answered.

"Just got off the phone with Nick. They were pulling into the Riverside parking lot. I told him to find you and stay there. I'm only a few minutes out, and the county is sending more men as well. I was just calling to make sure you were still there. I'll alert hospital security as soon as I hang up."

His voice, calmly delineating the mundane tasks associated with protecting her and her family, helped to keep her focused. It didn't stop the roiling in her gut or the chills that had suddenly overtaken her, but if Nick and Megan were safe, nothing else mattered. Except . . . Mom . . . No, she still couldn't quite make that fact feel real. Her mother. She clutched at the blanket over her chest with the fingers of her left hand, twisting it into a tight ball wedged against her splint. Not Mom. No. She was going to be all right. She had to be.

A knock came at the door, and the deputy answered. Nick and Megan?

"Talk later," she mumbled into the phone, then hung up. With her good hand, she turned the wheelchair around to face the door. Saw the deputy standing, relaxed. Couldn't see who he was speaking to but heard the words "FBI."

The deputy backed up, holding the door open for the people outside. Lucy straightened, anxious to see Nick and Megan but also haunted by the bad news she'd have to share with them.

The door clicked shut, and the deputy turned to her, leaving his back to the newcomer. A man in a conservative dark suit. Brown hair, brown eyes. Six feet. Caucasian.

Her captor.

Lucy's warning emerged in a rasp, too late to help. The gunshot was a mere muffled pop that would never make it past the thick walls of the MRI suite. The deputy's eyes went wide then he slumped to the ground, a gaping bloody hole in the base of his skull.

"Nice to see you again, Lucy." The man stepped over the deputy's corpse. "Well, maybe not for you."

He glanced at his watch. "Good thing I was just down the road at the technical college. Remember the campus safety initiative you spearheaded? Hooking up all the local colleges with the NCIC and the Uniform Crime Reporting databases so serial rapists could be identified and caught sooner? Can't tell you how helpful the folks over there were. So ready to help an FBI agent chasing a sexual predator."

He slid a black leather wallet from his pocket and flipped it open like an actor on TV. Lucy's stolen credentials. He'd been following a timetable, not a deadline. Seven p.m. Perfect time to find a small campus security office understaffed as the long twelve-hour night shift arrived.

She had given him what he wanted, leaving him enough time to visit her home and find her mother first. Anger tunneled her vision, and she forced herself to breathe deep, clear it. She needed to find a way to stop him. Now.

Nick and Megan are on their way. The words hammered through her mind. One way or the other, the man couldn't be here when they arrived. Her heart pounded at the thought of what "the other" option might entail.

What choice did she have? Trapped in a wheelchair. No way could she reach the phone or emergency call button behind her before he struck. Anyway, did she really want to call civilians here, risk their lives? Bad enough her own mother had been hurt because of her.

"Why are you here?" she asked, hoping his answer might provide her a way out of this.

He smiled. That same half-joking, half-leering smile he'd given her out in the field after he'd sicced the dog on her. "You saw my face. Can't have you live to tell anyone. Besides, I promised you that you would die today." He flashed a wink at her. "I'm a man of my word."

She had a hard time finding enough spit to swallow. Gave up and simply nodded. Sat up straight and tall in the chair. She needed this to happen now, before Nick and Megan arrived. "Get it over with."

His smile widened, but he didn't shoot. Instead, he lowered his weapon and kicked the guard's body to the wall behind the door. "Don't you want to say good-bye to your family first?"

He opened the door and gestured outside. "You can come in now."

Lucy's blood turned to ice, horror freezing her from the inside out as Megan rushed in, followed by Nick.

CHAPTER 13

MEGAN ONLY HAD eyes for her mom as she raced through the room, falling into a half crouch beside the chair to hug Lucy fiercely. "Mom, are you okay? What happened?"

Lucy didn't answer; she just held on, wrapping her arms around Megan—splint be damned—as if she could stop any bullets aimed at her daughter. But it was Nick she was worried about.

After fifteen years of marriage, some of her habits had rubbed off on him. Including how she entered a room. Just as she would have, Nick paused, assessing the situation in two blinks. Cataloguing her injuries. Catching the warning in her eyes. Seeing the dead deputy half-hidden behind the open door.

He was torn between running inside to protect her and Megan, fleeing to get them help, and attacking the man behind him. The tug-of-war ended with Nick awkwardly pivoting, fist raised, only to be met by a pistol in his face.

The man chuckled, jerked his chin to invite Nick all the way inside, then closed the door and locked it. "Figured you'd want a little privacy for our family reunion."

"Who are you?" Nick asked. There was a dangerous edge to his voice and his fists were still clenched. Lucy saw his struggle as he forced his emotions aside and tried to negotiate. "What do you want?"

The man was having none of it. He glanced past Nick to Lucy. "Does he really think I'm going to fall for any of his shrink BS?"

"He doesn't know you like I do," she answered. Her voice was getting stronger—driven by desperation or simply a sign that the swelling was beginning to ease, she wasn't sure. Good thing, though, because her voice and her knowledge of this man were their only weapons.

"Guess we'll have to change that." Before Lucy could protest, the man raised his pistol.

For a heartbeat she thought he was going to shoot Nick like he had the deputy, but at the last minute, the man instead struck him on the side of the head with a blow so forceful Nick fell to the floor. Then he kicked Nick in his stomach.

"Dad!" Megan screamed, but Lucy held her tight, forcing her face into Lucy's shoulder.

"Don't look," she whispered.

Nick groaned, doubled up in pain, hands up to protect his head, blood seeping through his fingers.

The man nudged Nick with his shoe. "Getting the picture, doc? Oh, and by the way, your taste in music sucks. How can you listen to that wailing and whining country crap?"

Another piece of the puzzle. The man couldn't track Nick or Megan by their phones—they both had units secured by FBI software. He must have placed a tracker and bug inside Nick's car.

Lucy squeezed Megan tighter. She ran her fingers through Megan's hair and rubbed her shoulder, brushing the IV pole on the back of the chair. She remembered how the nurse had placed the metal rod into its housing, tightening it with a simple collar screw. Hope flared through Lucy as she stretched her fingers to try to loosen the screw.

Megan placed a hand over hers. "He'll see. Let me." She breathed the words into Lucy's ear.

"Everything's going to be okay, Megan," Lucy said, patting Megan's back. "Now, get behind me."

Megan obeyed, moving to crouch behind Lucy's chair. The man shook his head at them. "Shouldn't make promises you can't keep, Lucy."

She didn't. Not ever. "Let them go. The police are on their way."

"You telling me what to do?" The silence between them filled with hostility. She had one chance to play this right—play him right—and save her family.

"No. Of course not. I'm giving you information. You're a smart man. Leave now and you can slip away. The police will never find you."

"You know this is all your fault, right?" he said. "You chose this path. From the moment you decided you were better than the rest of us, that you were a hero."

The vision of the man she'd killed filled her mind.

"I'm no hero."

"No. You're not. It's time your family knew that." He pulled out his phone. "I'm going to play our conversation for Nick and Megan. Let Nick hear how you chose him to die. How you sent me to kill him."

She remained silent, knowing anything she said would make it worse. Nick would understand.

"And Megan. How about if I show her what I did to your mother? What *you* let happen, Lucy. After you disobeyed me and went after my man. Actions have consequences, Lucy."

"Grams?" Megan said, her voice a strange combination of fury and worry. "Don't you dare hurt my grandmother!"

"Poor girl," he said. "If she lives through the night, she's going to need some serious counseling. Oh, that reminds me, you really should keep your knives sharpened. They were so dull. Caused much more pain than necessary—something else you're to blame for."

Lucy bit the inside of her cheek to avoid screaming in frustration. "You're right. It's all my fault."

"Trying to manipulate me again, Lucy? You know that won't work. I'm in control here. I've always been in control. I'm the one with the power."

"I know that. How could I not? You hold my family's lives in your hands." She couldn't risk glancing down at Nick, had to keep the killer's gaze locked on her, but in the edge of her peripheral vision she saw Nick slowly stretch his body. Preparing to strike. "If you wait for the police, no one will get out alive."

"Including your family." His gaze dared her to say the words, make them fact.

"Including my family."

What was Megan doing back there? It shouldn't take this long to loosen the screw. She still wasn't sure how Megan would get the IV pole to Lucy when the time was right. Timing. It all depended on split-second timing.

"Everyone you love will die because of you, Lucy. Because you thought you were smarter, better than me. Because you dared to think you could win."

"But I'm not. Not smarter, not better, not going to win. We both know that. And you can prove it. Take control of the situation. Leave now before the police get here." Her words came through clenched jaws. She held her breath, hoping he didn't see the flaw in her argument—it would only take a few seconds for him to kill Nick and Megan before escaping. But she was counting on his need to see their pain—her pain. To see her crushed, totally surrendering.

To emerge the victor.

She almost had him when a pounding sounded on the door. "Open up. FBI!"

The man whirled in anger, aiming his weapon first at Nick, then at Megan, who ducked down behind Lucy. Lucy pushed herself out of the chair and stood, blocking the man's line of fire. From the corner of her eye, she saw that the light on the intercom beside Megan was now blinking red. Ahh . . . smart girl.

The man said nothing, but his gaze filled with venom. He placed a foot on Nick's throat and aimed once more at him. Then he cocked one eyebrow, daring Lucy to make a move. She stood, unsteady, weight on one foot.

Lucy ended the silence, unable to bear it anymore. "Take me hostage. Leave them."

She had to get him out of here before he realized there was no escape. Given the basement's layout, stepping out into the hall would be stepping into what SWAT guys called the fatal funnel. "You don't have much time. They won't negotiate for long."

"No. I don't have much time." His tone had changed. Less rushed. Lower, restrained . . . in control. Shit. He'd made a decision, and it wasn't the one she wanted. "Neither do you. We'll finish this. Now. Together."

CHAPTER 14

"WHO DIES FIRST?" the man asked. Only a few feet separated him from Lucy but the way she was tottering, pain spiking through her leg, she knew she'd never reach him. Not in time. "Your choice, Lucy."

Nick looked up from his position on the floor. Met her eyes. Smiled. Then scissored his legs to kick the man's feet out from under him. The gun went off, a bullet striking one of the chairs against the far wall. The man landed on one knee, aiming at Nick.

A blur of motion came from beside Lucy as Megan slid the IV pole free. She ran forward, using it like one of her karate staffs, darting to strike the man's wrist, then whipping the pole back, swinging it into the man's face. The man dropped the gun. Nick scrambled to grab it.

Nick leapt to his feet, holding the pistol, hauling Megan back as she aimed yet another blow on the downed man. Megan's hair had fallen into her face, and when she brushed it back, her expression was fury personified.

Lucy hadn't moved. "Megan, get behind me," she ordered. Nick gave Megan a quick hug, and Megan backed up a few steps, standing between Lucy and the man on the ground and still holding the pole like a club.

The door burst open, and Walden rushed inside, accompanied by a sheriff's deputy. The deputy whirled on Nick, but Walden stopped him. "He's one of ours."

The deputy knelt to secure the killer whose eye was already swollen shut and wrist bent at an unnatural angle. Megan was stronger than she looked—but Lucy knew that already.

Lucy reached for Megan, who was trembling from head to toe. Hugged her hard from behind. "Nick, take her out of here."

Nick gave the weapon to Walden, hauled in a breath, eyes wide, as he turned to Lucy. But he wrapped an arm around Megan, carefully steering her around the fallen deputy and as far away as possible from the man on the floor.

"Walden—" She didn't have to say anything more. He nodded and joined Nick and Megan, escorting them out of the room.

"I made a mistake," the man on the floor said, his voice muffled as the deputy pushed his head down to search him.

"You made a huge mistake," Lucy agreed, most of her mind mentally mapping Nick and Megan's exit to safety. Adrenaline jangled her nerves. All she could see was the man's gun aimed at Nick, then at Megan as Megan swung the pole. A split second either way . . . She turned her head away, swallowing hard against acid that filled her throat as her gut clenched with fear. She'd almost lost them.

"I chose the wrong victim," the man said. Why the hell wouldn't he just shut up?

"You chose the wrong family." She sank down into the wheelchair, hoping he didn't see that she simply didn't have any strength left to stand.

She wished the deputy would hurry and take this filth from her sight so she could get out of here and be with Nick and Megan. She still had to tell them about her mother. Needed to find out if her mother was okay.

Exhaustion tempted her. Her eyes were so heavy, her energy gone. She kicked her bad leg against the chair, using the pain to keep her alert. Couldn't relax. Not until she made it to Three Rivers and her mom.

"*Your* family. They don't make you vulnerable or weak." He craned his head up to meet her gaze.

God, she was tired. So very tired. She didn't have patience for his games. "No. They don't. They give me strength."

"They're why you never lost hope. Why I couldn't break you."

He had. Deep inside, she knew he had. She wasn't sure if that fracture could ever be healed. But she wouldn't give him the satisfaction of knowing. The deputy hauled him to his feet as she said, "No. You couldn't."

A security guard appeared in the doorway, holding a pistol. He holstered it and joined the deputy to remove the man. The man acted as if they weren't there, as if no one existed except him and Lucy. He twisted within his captors' grips to look over his shoulder at her. Then he smiled. "Thanks for the fun, Lucy. You were the best ever."

Startled, she glanced up at his words. His expression wasn't of a man defeated. Rather of a man who'd just won, big-time.

As the two men escorting him separated to fit their threesome through the door, the killer abruptly dropped his weight, pivoted to push the deputy away, and grabbed the security guard's weapon with his restrained hands. Then he vanished into the hallway.

Where Nick and Megan were. Terror propelled Lucy back onto her feet as the two men raced after him, leaving her hobbling behind. The sound of gunshots...Oh God, oh God . . .

"Nick! Megan!" she screamed, but the gunfire drowned her out.

Finally, there was silence. Somehow she'd made it to the doorway, but now she wasn't sure if she could bear to see what was on the other side. She lurched into the hallway.

The security guard was down, the deputy standing over him. Beyond them the man in the suit sat slumped, back against the wall, his white shirt now peppered with blood. More blood gushed from his mouth, and his face was slack, eyes dull. He still gripped the stolen pistol, held awkwardly to one side of his body in his handcuffed hands.

Walden approached him, weapon drawn. He kicked away the man's pistol and checked his pulse. "He's gone."

The dead man had chosen his own way out, kept control of his destiny, just like he said he would.

She couldn't see Nick or Megan. Had he destroyed what was left of her family during his suicide-by-cop?

Using the wall for support, she limped down the hall.

"Nick? Megan?" She could barely say their names. Her heart was already shredded, caught between hope and despair. She couldn't tear her gaze away from the dead man. The man with all the answers.

She spotted movement at the end of the hallway. A door opening. Nick and Megan. Running toward her. Safe and whole and alive.

The pain in her foot vanished as she lunged forward, pulling them into her arms.

She had no idea how much time passed before the medical people arrived. "Guess we'll get that MRI at Three Rivers," the nurse said. Lucy's gaze caught on the dead man, now surrounded by police officers.

She didn't even know his name. She didn't care.

Just as Nick was helping her back into the wheelchair, Walden reappeared, clenching his phone in his hand. He met her eyes, shaking his head sorrowfully.

A howl of anguish escaped her as Lucy realized the price she'd paid for surviving.

EPILOGUE

"DO YOU UNDERSTAND what I've explained to you about the complications of the procedure, Mrs. Guardino?" The vascular surgeon at Three Rivers Medical Center wielded a clipboard filled with consent forms. "Animal maulings aren't like normal injuries. We're dealing with nerve damage, crush injuries, infection, necrotic tissue. There's a good chance we won't be able to save the leg. And, even if we do, it's questionable how much function you'll regain."

Nick watched as Lucy stared listlessly at the forms. She wore a patient gown as well as an assortment of bandages, splints, and dressings. She lay on a stretcher, and her left leg was propped up on a foam triangle, strapped into place, a thin layer of gauze hiding the ugly mass of swollen and dead tissue. IV tubing bristled from her right shoulder, where they'd inserted a special line that fed into her heart to give her fluids and antibiotics.

Medication that was probably too late to save her foot, but that could still save her life.

She finally answered the surgeon. "You're saying I won't be taking my husband dancing." Then she laughed. A hollow sound, it thudded against the tile walls and made the seasoned trauma doctor flinch.

Nick didn't blame him. Ever since Walden had told them about Lucy's mother dying, it was as if his vibrant wife who never surrendered to anything had been lost to pain and exhaustion and grief. Not to mention the haze of drugs.

At least he hoped he could blame the drugs for most of it. They'd wear off in time. The rest . . .

She signed the form the surgeon held for her, her signature a random scribble, not at all her usual confident loops and spirals.

Nick couldn't help but wonder if Lucy would ever be herself again. A flutter of fear beat against his chest wall as he held his wife's hand and she didn't return his loving grasp.

Back at the other hospital, he'd been torn between leaving Megan with Walden and staying with Lucy. It was the type of decision Lucy made every day, but he'd felt lost, overwhelmed. Until Walden rescued him by declaring the case a matter of national security, thus federal jurisdiction, and bringing both Nick and Megan here to Three Rivers to be with Lucy.

Only Lucy wasn't here. Not really. Sometime after that man had died, after she'd seen her daughter forced to defend them all, Lucy—*his* Lucy, the fierce warrior filled with passion and compassion—she'd vanished, leaving behind this empty shell of a woman.

The surgeon also seemed to realize Lucy wasn't herself, even though he'd only met her a few hours ago. He turned his clipboard toward Nick. "Perhaps you should give consent as well, Mr. Guardino."

"It's Callahan," Nick corrected. "Dr. Callahan, in fact." He sounded like an ass, saying that, didn't know why he did, except he desperately needed to regain some control over this nightmare, over his life.

"Oh, you're a medical doctor?"

Nick took the clipboard and pen. "No. PhD. Psychology." He scrawled his name. Signing consent for the surgeon to cut off part of his wife's body.

The forms completed, the surgeon lost interest. "A nurse will be in to take her to the OR in a few minutes." He left them.

Nick had never felt more alone. Standing beside his wife, holding her limp hand, waiting for this all to be over. Would it ever be over?

During their fifteen years of marriage, he'd seen Lucy through every possible emotional storm: passion about a case, frustration at the system, anger when justice wasn't served. He'd seen her exhausted, in despair, even frightened.

He'd never seen her surrender. Not like this. Vacant, drained. Defeated.

"It's going to be okay," he murmured into her hair as he kissed her forehead, avoiding the staples holding together one of her many lacerations.

No response.

He was thankful the hospital staff hadn't let Megan into the pre-op area. His stomach knotted at the thought of her seeing her mother like this. Hell, he wasn't sure *he* could bear to see Lucy like this.

"Lucy, really. I promise. It will be okay." He squeezed her hand again, his wedding band rubbing against the empty spot where hers should be. Would they ever get it back? Or would it be forever entombed in the bowels of some evidence locker? "You know me. I never make a promise I can't keep."

He squeezed harder. So hard it had to be painful. She didn't answer, didn't meet his gaze.

The nurse came. "It's time. You can wait in the family area outside the OR."

"No. I'll go with you as far as I can." Nick couldn't bear letting go of Lucy, not one instant before he had to. Together they rolled her stretcher down the hall until they came to a set of double doors leading into the operating suite.

"I'm sorry," the nurse said. "This is as far as you can go. You need to say good-bye now."

Nick reached across Lucy's body to embrace her, his tears wetting her cheeks as he kissed her. Her lips were cold, her face slack.

"I'll be right here," he promised. "Both Megan and I will be here when you wake up."

She blinked at Megan's name. Finally nodded. Squeezed his hand. "Remember what you promised," she whispered, her voice low, so low he could barely make out her words. "Don't forget."

He kissed her again, hope rekindled by the tiny spark that had returned to her. "I won't. It will all be okay. I know it will. You're strong, Lucy. The strongest person I know. You'll make it through this—*we'll* make it through this. I promise."

Her eyes slid closed as if she were too weary to keep them open. But she nodded again. "I believe you. I love you, Nick. And Megan. More than anything."

"I know. We know." He gave her hand one final squeeze as the nurse opened the door and pushed her through to the other side, to the sterile area where ordinary men like Nick were forbidden.

Suddenly it occurred to him that their entire marriage had been like that. Lucy crossing each day into a strange world filled with violence and evil and chaos. A world ordinary people lived their ordinary lives hoping they never had to acknowledge even existed—along with their need for people like Lucy. Men and women strong enough to enter that world and save them.

Now it was Nick's turn to save Lucy—and Megan as well. His entire family was at risk, contaminated by the evil that had escaped from Lucy's world into theirs.

Part of him was angry, wanting to blame Lucy for tonight's bloodshed. If she wasn't the fierce, passionate warrior she was, this would have never happened.

He held onto that pain, using it to fuel the fire he'd need to get through this. Because he'd promised Lucy they would get through this. Because everything that happened to their family was as much his fault as hers.

When he'd first met her, he knew who she was, what she was, and he'd fallen hopelessly in love with her and everything she stood for. Part of him felt a coward that he could never fight on the front lines like she did—part of him felt relieved that because of people like her, he didn't have to.

Nick gripped the railing that ran along the wall, head bowed, fighting to regain some sure footing amid the emotional turmoil engulfing him. Mostly, being with Lucy made him strive to be a better man, to find the courage to change the lives around him just as she did.

When he looked up, Lucy was gone and the doors had closed. He stared at them for a long moment, feeling lost and alone. Then he drew in a deep breath, chasing away ghosts of fear to focus on the one thing he was certain of: Lucy would survive.

With that thought as his anchor, he went in search of the family area, his mind already spinning with ideas, ways to help both his daughter and wife—and himself. Names of counselors he trusted, victim advocates, child psych specialists, patients he'd worked with, soldiers who would understand what Lucy was going through better than he could...

He was not about to let the darkness claim his family. Never. He'd promised Lucy.

And Nick was a man of his word.

HARD FALL

A Lucy Guardino FBI Thriller

CJ Lyons

EDGY READS

PROLOGUE

———————

UNTIL FIFTY-EIGHT days ago, Lucy Guardino never dreamed you could have a panic attack in your sleep.

It was the dog. Always the damn dog.

Haunting her day and night.

Lucy jerked upright, fingers clutching her throat, fighting to loosen a rope that was no longer there. She couldn't breathe, was suffocating, terror throttling her as effectively as the real noose had.

Her heart beat so loud and hard it ricocheted through her body. Her gasps filled the darkness surrounding her, red streaks blazing through her vision, the pressure on her chest, pressure around her throat so tight... she was dying.

The damn dog would finally get what it'd wanted all along.

Lucy reached for her weapon. Her gun, where was her gun? Her hand flailed, hit the back of a couch. Awareness crept into the darkness. *Her* couch. The movement shook the blanket from her body and her left foot thudded to the ground.

Pain shrieked through her, slapping her fully awake.

She wasn't choking to death, the pain reminded her. Wasn't dying.

That'd been fifty-eight days ago. This was now. Her new reality.

Thanks to the damn dog.

She blinked, the room slowly coming into focus. The old steamer trunk they used for a coffee table. A fireplace, its mantel filled with family photos. The overstuffed chair from her mom's house, now angled beside the bay window—her daughter Megan's new favorite place to sit and pretend Lucy didn't exist.

The way the shadows fell across the wing-backed chair, for a second, she thought she saw her mother sitting there, watching over her as she slept. Like she had when Lucy was a kid, after her father died.

I'm so sorry, Mom. Guilt settled like a rock in her stomach. She wished for tears to blink back, but she had none left. What good were tears, anyway? They couldn't bring her mom back.

Her living room. In her house. The room where her mother had been killed by the man sent to kill Lucy. No wonder Lucy felt compelled to haunt it night after night.

Couldn't change the past, just as she couldn't save her mother. But she had been able to save her husband and daughter. She tugged the blanket closer to her body, her heart thudding against the T-shirt she'd worn to bed. Nick? Safe and sound asleep upstairs in their bed. Wasn't that why she'd crept down here to the couch, so her night terrors wouldn't disturb him? One of them deserved a good night's sleep.

She leaned forward, bent over her ankle and massaged the nooks and crannies of scar tissue and missing muscle. Felt the alien bumps and knobs left behind by the surgeons with their plates and screws. Her ankle and foot now had more hardware than an erector set. The dog's handiwork.

The dog was dead. Not by Lucy's hand. It had been trained to kill—had done its best on her. Animal control had no choice. It had died peacefully in its sleep.

The man who'd turned a beautiful animal into a raging killing machine, he'd died as well. By Lucy's hand. Not so peacefully and wide awake. *His* screams never haunted Lucy.

She shook away memories from fifty-eight days ago. Focused on the simple, undeniable fact her life centered on: her family was safe.

The pain in her leg subsided to its usual dull roar. Unlike the blinding blaze when the dog first mauled her ankle, the pain now danced across a spectrum. From the spiking intensity of infrared blasts to tooth-rattling ultraviolet electrical shockwaves, less intense but more unnerving. A rainbow of agony.

Although her bones had mended nicely, apparently nerves heal more slowly. The doctors said it might take years—or never. And while they were healing—or not— the electricity racing along their synapses erratically causing random impulses the brain interpreted as pain.

Leaving Lucy with a choice: a life of painkillers, popping pills to numb her body and mind or a life of pain.

She couldn't live without her job and when your job is an FBI Supervisory Special Agent leading a team of armed men and women, you can't do that job while taking narcotics, so Lucy chose the pain. Treated it as she would any other suspect—observing, analyzing, predicting what it would do next, and preparing against it.

So far the pain was winning, able to sneak past her defenses, blindside her. Not for long. Because tomorrow—she glanced at the railroad clock on the wall, her eyes now adjusted to the dim light, 3:14 a.m.—no, today, today was the day she returned to work.

Fifty-nine days ago, she'd almost lost everything. Now she was taking it all back.

She pushed herself upright, reached for the cane propped against the couch, and grit her teeth against the purple haze of pins and needles as her foot brushed against the oak floorboards. Took one step, then another toward the bedroom upstairs where her husband slept.

Pain or no pain, panic or no panic, no way in hell was Lucy letting anything keep her from doing her job. From healing her family. From getting her life back.

Starting today.

CHAPTER 1

Friday, 9:46 am

LUCY'S FIRST INDICATION that this day wouldn't be going as planned came when she entered Pittsburgh's Federal Building and was stopped by security.

The Federal Protective Service guard, one she didn't recognize, snapped to attention when Lucy swiped her employee ID at the turnstile and an alarm sounded. "Ma'am, step back, please."

"I think it's expired." She hobbled to one side so she didn't block anyone else and cursed herself for forgetting to check the date on her ID. Thankfully, she'd left plenty of time before she was due to meet with Isaac Walden, second-in-command of her Sexual Assault Felony Enforcement squad. She gestured to the cane. "I've been on medical leave."

The guard didn't relax his attitude. Instead, he nodded to one of his comrades at the security desk who came out from behind it to stand a few feet from Lucy, covering his partner. She almost laughed at the thought that she might be a threat to anyone—but forced herself not to. FPS guards were not known for their sense of humor.

Ever since the Zapata cartel had burned down a sizable chunk of the city last Christmas, security throughout Pittsburgh had been high.

No one was more paranoid than here at the Southside Federal Building where the Joint Counterterrorism Task Force was housed as well as several sensitive investigative units including High Tech Computer Crimes and Innocent Images. The FBI, DEA, ICE, ATF, US Marshals, and now Homeland Security Investigations all had a presence. One stop shopping for any wannabe terrorist trying to make his bones.

"The badge, ma'am."

Lucy handed the first guard her building pass. He passed it to the second, who relayed it to the main security desk for validation.

"I have my credentials," Lucy offered, keeping her hands at her sides, making no threatening movements.

The guard responded by sliding his right hand to the butt of his weapon, his left hand raised, palm forward in the universal gesture for "freeze right there."

The second guard returned and handed her a temporary ID. "I've been instructed to escort you, Supervisory Special Agent Guardino. Do you have any weapons with you?"

"Of course I have weapons." Why would he even ask? Federal agents were mandated to carry both on and off duty. "And I don't need an escort."

"Sorry, ma'am. Orders. Please remove all weapons

prior to passing through the body scanner. We'll need to examine the cane as well."

She frowned at him. Agents didn't pass through the scanner, only civilians. Was there a reason for their extra precautions? "Are we on alert?"

Neither answered her, focusing on her movements as she removed the forty caliber Glock from her belt holster and her backup weapon from her bag and carefully placed them, as well as her bag and cane, on the table beside the body scanner. The first guard checked her belongings while Lucy stepped into the scanner and raised her hands.

She grit her teeth. The cane helped her balance and eased the pressure on her left ankle until the nerves finished healing. She could walk without it—well, hobble would be more like it—but only with a lot of pain and effort. Better get used to it, she told herself as the machine whirled around her. She wouldn't be using the cane forever—couldn't if she wanted to pass her physical fitness assessment and return to full active duty.

The guard gestured for her to step free of the machine. "Stand here, please. Legs spread wide."

Shit. The brace. Overtop her left sock she wore a plastic ankle-foot-orthotic brace or AFO that kept her toes from dragging on the ground. She winced as the guard patted down her leg. "That's an ankle brace prescribed by my physician. I was injured in the line of duty two months ago."

He didn't look up as he rolled her pants leg high enough to examine the form-fitting plastic and its Velcro straps. Finally he nodded and stood. "This way, ma'am."

Lucy collected her belongings and followed the guard

onto the elevators. To her surprise he hit the button for the top floor.

"No, ma'am," the guard said when she reached to hit the correct button. "My instructions are to escort you directly to Administration."

Admin? That usually meant a summons from the Special Agent in Charge. She couldn't remember the last time she'd spoken to Markel—but he had sent flowers while she was in the hospital. Or his secretary had. She probably was supposed to send a thank you note or something. She sucked at office politics.

As they rode in silence, an impulse to jab the button for the floor where her team and office were instead of riding to the top made her smile. What would the earnest guard do? Shoot her?

She'd like to see him try. Probably he'd just shout, "Ma'am, stop, ma'am." Well, she was losing her patience with all the damn ma'am-ing and searching and escorting as if she were a civilian.

The doors slid open and Lucy strode out, ignoring the guard she left in her wake. He hurried to pass her and lead the way—not difficult given her slower pace with the cane—but she felt a smug ray of satisfaction warm her from the inside out. Petty, she knew, but she'd take any opportunity to feel back in control.

They reached the Special Agent in Charge's suite, but her escort led her past it to the Assistant Special Agent in Charge, John Greally's office. John was a friend. They'd partnered in the field when Lucy was still in training, and their daughters went to school together. What was going on? He never asked her to come up to his office; John preferred a more casual and hands-on approach to supervising—something Lucy herself tried to emulate. If he had something to say, he would have come to her, not the other way around.

Lucy glanced at the secretary sitting at the desk, guarding the ASAC's door. She was someone new; Lucy didn't recognize her. No answers there.

"They're waiting," the secretary said, nodding to the door behind her.

They? Lucy wondered. The guard stood aside, allowing Lucy room to enter alone.

It always disoriented her when she entered Greally's office because the space was the antithesis of the man. The office was Spartan, no clutter, not even a calendar in sight. Just a large, modern-style desk with a sophisticated computer set up and a single photo of his family. Two not-so-comfortable appearing chairs waited in front of the desk. The obligatory photos of the president, Attorney General, and Director lined the walls.

Typical generic administration office. No signs of Greally's personality. The father who cheered and whistled at his daughter's school plays. The boss who came down to gossip with Lucy's squad and steal coffee from her private stash.

Or the friend who'd brought his work with him to the hospital so Nick could spend a few hours home with Megan.

This was the office of an Assistant Special Agent in Charge, an administrator. Not the real John Greally.

Who at the moment was nowhere to be seen. Instead, a woman hovered in the back corner, staring out the window with its view of the Steeler's practice field. "Do you know when Greally will be back?" Lucy asked her.

The woman glanced over her shoulder at Lucy. Seemed especially interested in her cane. She twisted her mouth and slowly turned to face Lucy. "He'll be joining us shortly, Special Agent Guardino."

Most folks around here called her Lucy. She preferred it that way. "I'm sorry, have we met?"

"No," the woman, a blond in her thirties said, clipping the syllable short. "But we've spoken on the phone and you've ignored several appointments I scheduled."

Right. Who could forget a voice more irritating than pepper spray? "Ah...Ms. Carroll from Employee Assistance. I explained over the phone that I won't be requiring your services. I'm returning to duty. Before my sixty days of medical leave is up—as you can see."

Because of the hazardous nature of the job, the FBI provided excellent health and disability benefits. Benefits Lucy was determined not to make further use of. It might take her a while to get back to full active duty, but she was determined to get there, leading her team from the front lines, just as she had fifty-nine days ago.

Carroll's smirk made Lucy itch to look over her shoulder, check her back for an ambush.

Lucy went on the offensive. "I brought my doctor's release for limited duty, my range qualification on both my service weapons, passed my psych eval, and a drug test showing that I've been off all narcotics for weeks." Nineteen days to be exact. Her doctor told her it was too soon, but she was afraid that once she was placed on disability, it would be far too easy for administrative busybodies like Carroll to bench her with a medical pension rather than accommodate her return to modified duty.

She pulled the file from her bag and offered it to Carroll.

"I'm afraid none of that matters, Agent Guardino," Carroll said, making no move to accept the paperwork. "If you'd bothered to consult with me—"

"All due respect, Ms. Carroll, but this has nothing to do with you. I've been cleared for modified duty. All that's left is for me to speak with my supervisor about my squad's open cases." The administrator might be queen bee of her little cubicle hive, but Lucy had faced down serial killers, a vicious drug cartel, and even a psychotic bomber holding a hospital hostage. She turned the full weight of her glare onto the Employee Assistance functionary. Carroll looked away first.

Before Lucy could savor her victory, minor as it might be, the side door opened and Greally rushed in. "Lucy, you're here," he exclaimed, folding her into a bear hug. "Security screwed up, they were supposed to have your pass waiting." He handed her a new badge. Then he spotted Carroll standing behind his desk and his demeanor shifted from friend back to boss. "Why don't you both take a seat? And I gather these are for me?"

He slid the file from Lucy's hand and moved around behind his desk, displacing Carroll. She approached the chair but waited for Lucy to sit down first. Greally also sat, putting him and Lucy on an even level, but Carroll remained standing. Not hard to read the nonverbal power play there. Lucy shared a half-smile with Greally and was relieved when he returned it, obviously thinking the same thing.

"Did you go over Lucy's options with her?" he asked

Carroll.

"Option. Singular. At least according to the new personnel directives." Carroll crossed her arms over her chest. "I'm afraid Supervisory Special Agent Guardino wasn't very receptive."

"You're talking about me walking out with a medical pension. Quitting. For good. Of course I'm not receptive."

Carroll stared down at Lucy. Lucy kept her focus on Greally. He broke the silence, clearing his throat. "Ms. Carroll, give us the room, if you please."

Carroll sniffed, nodded, and walked out, back stiff, heels thudding against the institutional carpet. She didn't quite slam the door behind her, but it definitely closed with a pissed-off exclamation mark.

"Sorry to have wasted her time," Lucy said, edging forward in her seat. "I'll go catch up with my team and their open cases."

"I wish it were that simple," Greally said, his expression turning serious. "A lot has happened since you left," he began. "With the new director in DC and his mandate to turn the Bureau into the world's best counterterrorism investigative organization—"

She'd seen the new director's press conferences on CNN. Typical DC political posturing.

"We're already devoting ninety percent of our manpower and resources to counterterrorism. And Homeland Security Investigations was created to cover that territory, so why the pissing match? Ask me, we should be headed back to the reason why we were created in the first place: fighting crime." Whoops. She hadn't really meant to say that aloud. Two months off work and her diplomatic skills were rusty. Didn't matter;

Greally had heard it all from her before.

Then the meaning behind his words sank in. Greally had warned her weeks ago that with a new Director came changes, but she'd never dreamed...She swallowed against the metallic taste that filled her mouth. "My team?"

"The Sexual Assault Felony Enforcement squads were experimental to start with," he reminded her. "The new director is dissolving the program."

"That's ridiculous. Our unit alone has cleared over three hundred cases."

"The director is giving ICE control of the online child pornography mandate since they already have the Innocent Images program. They'll continue to coordinate with local law enforcement and the non-government organizations in the coalition you created."

Just like that. The team, their entire reason for being—gone. Vanished in a political Ping-Pong game.

"My people? Walden? Taylor?"

Greally kept his face neutral—obviously this wasn't the first of these kinds of conversations he'd had recently. But damn it, this was her team they were talking about.

"Reassigned. Taylor went back to computer crimes two weeks ago—the SAC felt he was much too valuable to be in the field." Never mind that Taylor had originally left his job as an analyst with the High Tech Computer Crimes squad to endure the rigors of the FBI Academy because his dream was to be a Special Agent in the field.

Greally continued. "Come Monday, Walden will report to the bank robbery desk." Because the FDIC insured most bank deposits, the FBI was required to be involved in bank robberies, but local law enforcement usually handled all the heavy lifting, so it was more a question of shuffling files than real investigation.

"Did he choose that or did you?" she asked, not bothering to filter the bitterness from her tone.

He jerked his chin up at that, accepting her challenge. "He did. He only has three years before he has his thirty in, said it was easy time."

"That doesn't sound like the Walden I know." Except...it kind of did. Walden had been working crimes against children longer than any of them. The kind of cases that tended to consume most investigators, burn them out fast.

"I didn't tell you earlier because, up until this morning, I was still fighting to keep you on board as a task force coordinator or the like. Even the SAC tried, but Washington isn't buying it."

Lucy's chin sunk to her chest. The past two months only two things had kept her going: the fact that her family was safe and she had her job to return to. Without her job, what was she?

She knew the question was cliché, but that didn't help her find an answer.

Greally stood and came around the desk to take the chair beside her. Back to being her friend instead of her boss. "Look, I know this isn't easy. Believe me, your squad isn't the only one being overhauled. We've been mandated to cut eight percent of our workforce. But you have options, Lucy."

He glanced at the folder on his desk. "You can take a medical pension. I've read the reports. The doctors hold out very little hope that you'll ever return to full active duty."

"I've the right to a modified duty assignment." They both knew it wasn't about her rights. This was about her family. Every few years she'd had to uproot her family, move to a new city, a new position. The one thing she hated about the paramilitary organization that was the FBI. Being promoted to lead the SAFE squad was supposed to end that.

Only she hadn't counted on what had happened two months ago or on the political upheaval that came with a new director.

"There's so much more you could be doing outside the Bureau," he said.

Lucy shook off the idea of leaving the Bureau. "No. What are my choices if I decide to stay?"

He frowned. "Not many if you're restricted from the field. Maybe reviewing complaints for Employee Assistance—"

She scoffed at that. "You mean working for Carroll? No way. There's got to be something else."

"Not unless you'd consider moving. Maybe back to Quantico?"

"No. We can't. Megan—" Lucy couldn't leave Pittsburgh. Not after Nick had worked so hard to build his psychology practice. He couldn't abandon his patients. And Megan. Lucy didn't understand why, but Megan wouldn't even consider moving out of their house after Lucy's mom had been killed there. Lucy couldn't upset what little stability and security Megan had, not now.

He frowned. "Then OPR. They're always looking."

OPR. Office of Professional Responsibility. The Bureau's equivalent of Internal Affairs—policing their own.

"I'm not sure they'd consider you," he continued. "You haven't exactly made many friends over there these past few years."

Especially not two months ago. When she'd been forced to betray the FBI in order to save her family.

"Would you have done anything different, John?" she asked. "If it'd been Natalie and Kate they threatened?"

He glanced at his desk and the photo of his family. Shook his head. "I don't think anyone faults you for what you did, Lucy. But that doesn't make it the right thing, either. At least not in the mind of the Bureau."

One thing the Bureau hated: contradiction. Like an agent being forced to choose between the job and her family's lives. Doing the right thing didn't always mean following regulations.

"When do you need to know?" she asked, masking her exhaustion. And her day hadn't even started yet.

"Take the weekend."

She planted her cane and heaved her weight up out of the seat—sitting felt good but getting up always hurt like a sonofabitch.

Greally stood as well. "Lucy, I've been fighting like hell to make this all go away, wanted you to come back, everything the way it was."

Her body felt heavy, reluctant to move. To leave the one place she'd felt most at home, to leave the people she considered family, to leave the job she loved and felt was her destiny.

"I'm sorry," he repeated.

She nodded and shuffled out the door, wondering if she'd ever find her way back again.

CHAPTER 2

LUCY LEFT, GREALLY'S new secretary's stare following her as she limped down to the elevator. More than the front office staff watching her, she felt as if the entire building was judging. They all knew what she'd done two months ago.

To them, she'd betrayed the unspoken code, putting her family's lives before the Bureau. Something the administrators and agents who worked OPR would never understand, or if they ever had, they'd forgotten once they moved into their sterile office suites here on the top floor. To them, Lucy was an incalculable risk, a wildcard. Family didn't fit into the FBI's Bible of operating procedures.

This was why she loved working down in the bowels of the building, side by side with men and women who really understood their mission. It had nothing to do with whatever the current administration wrote up in fancy press releases and everything to do with protecting and serving the innocent, anyway they could.

She forced herself to limp a little less, placing more

pressure on her bad leg, and instead of stopping and waiting for the elevator, enduring their stares, she continued to the stairwell. Stairs were the bane of Lucy's new existence. Because of the damaged nerves, she could no longer tell when her foot was firmly planted on the ground, and so she had to look down, watching each step. Plus, it was difficult to maneuver the cane, so she usually ended up with more of her weight falling on her bad leg.

But the world was built full of stairs, just as it was full of assholes like Carroll, so Lucy grit through the pain and made her way down to the floor that housed her office. At least for the next three days.

Her new ID got her through the locked doors that stood between the unsecured common areas and the wing where criminal activity—like analyzing illegal pornography in order to identify victims and perpetrators—occurred.

Lucy gazed out at the once wide-open space now transformed into a cubicle farm. "What the hell?"

Her question was answered by a barrage of pistol fire—Nerf pistols equipped with harmless foam bullets. Taylor popped up from behind one of the cubicle walls, his forever bed-head hair and blue eyes peeking over the top.

"Hold fire," he shouted, giving a pretty good impression of the range master at Quantico.

He stood up, forsaking the cover of the cubicle wall, and the pistol-wielding shooters turned their aim onto him. None of them had hit Lucy, but somehow they all nailed Taylor right in the face. Which told Lucy a lot about the shooters: her adorable analysts from the High Tech Computer Crime section. Geeks and proud of it.

They'd been even more proud when Taylor, one of their own, became a full-fledged Special Agent, gun and all.

"Sorry, Lucy," Taylor said, dodging friendly fire as he skirted the cubicle maze to join her. "We're working on modeling a fire fight where a Fish and Game officer was caught between Border Patrol and some traffickers. Guess we got a little carried away."

"What's with the new decor?" she gestured to the cubicles. They made the space seem small and crowded, not at all conducive to the collaborative atmosphere she'd fostered.

"SAC insisted. Said we were wasting too much time working together, so now, we're each assigned a separate, private workspace. First thing he made me do when he put me in charge." He frowned at the memory then smiled impishly. "Of course, I told him each work station would need to be fully equipped and got a thirty percent increase in my equipment budget."

"Which you have spent wisely, I see." She nodded to the bright pink pistol dangling from his hand. Taylor, a thirty-five-year-old wiz kid and certified genius, was irrepressible—not even the new administration would be able to shackle his enthusiasm.

"Where's Walden?" she asked, looking around the maze of cubicles for her second in command.

"Waiting in your office." Taylor glanced over his shoulder and dropped his voice. "With a case."

One of the techs called him away. Lucy made her way around the cubicles. When the squad had originally been established, the floor plans called for a large executive corner office but no private conference area. An oversight she'd corrected by shoving her desk into the back corner to make room for a conference table and chairs.

The two interior walls were glass, enabling her to see that seated around the table were Walden as well as a man and woman with their backs to Lucy. Walden was a decade older than she, a solemn black man, but with a surprising sense of humor that showed itself at unexpected times. Good money that he was the one who'd outfitted the High Tech Crimes guys with their pistols and ammo.

She was lucky to have him as her second in command; their strengths and weaknesses nicely complemented each other. In addition to the trio at the table, prowling the area around her desk was a thirty-something man who would have been at home on the Steeler's offensive line.

Oshiro. What was a US Deputy Marshal from the Fugitive Apprehension Strike Team doing here?

Before she made it to the door, Oshiro swung his shaved head her way, spotted her, and with a grace and speed that defied the laws of physics for such a large man, rushed out and had her in a crushing hug.

"Sweet Lucy Mae! How are you?" He raised her off her feet with the hug but deposited her oh-so-gently back down so that only the slightest twinge of pain rang out from her foot.

"Little Timmy Oshiro." She couldn't help but smile. Oshiro had the reputation as one of the toughest bad-ass deputies the Marshal's Service had ever produced—even the hot-shot Homeland Security guys moved out of his way when he came barreling down a hall—but he didn't intimidate her. She'd seen firsthand how gentle and kind he could be with her victims. That more than made up for any other shortcomings. "How's the only federal agent in Western Pennsylvania who's been hauled in front of OPR more than I have?"

His grin would have scared little kids into eating their broccoli. "Actually, I think you're one up on me there." He jerked his chin toward her leg. "Guess they didn't charge you with treason like the rumors said."

"They tried." Tried to charge her with several offenses, mainly for the crime of surviving the attack on her and her family. To save her family, she'd been forced to give her FBI administrative password to her attacker. That security breach could have been disastrous for the DOJ, but thanks to Lucy escaping and Taylor's computer wizardry, they'd not only caught everyone involved, they'd been able to expose and repair a hidden security flaw in the DOJ computer system.

Unfortunately, not before the man sent after Lucy had gone to Lucy's home and found her mother there. A few hours difference and the man would have found Megan home as well. That thought was what kept Lucy up at night...until she finally would drift to sleep, only to wake in terror, panicked that she hadn't reached her family in time, that she'd lost them all.

Lucy glanced down at her foot. If you did the math, her ordeal translated to a win for the good guys. Except Lucy had almost lost her leg, her daughter had been traumatized, and her mother had been killed.

Oshiro gave her another hug, this one less effusive and more consoling. "Sorry. Heard about your mom. You doing okay?"

She nodded, then looked up to meet his gaze. "Just

want to get back to work. Of course, that was before I learned I don't have a job any more."

His smile returned, this time revealing his teeth. Some said Oshiro resembled a hyena. They were wrong. Mako shark would be more like it. Once he was committed to something or someone, nothing could force him from his path. A lot like Lucy that way. "Wanna go out with a bang? I have the perfect case."

CHAPTER 3

"WANT TO TELL me why you've brought two civilians into my squad?" Lucy asked, glancing through the glass walls into her office. This was a secure area. Civilians never came here.

"Technically," Oshiro drawled, "only one and half civilians. The man is Seth Bernhart."

"The Assistant US Attorney?" Lucy squinted at the back of the man's head. "I thought he quit a few years back?"

Oshiro frowned, turned her so their backs were to her office. "Burned out was more like it. Was working in Atlanta doing some of the initial Innocent Image prosecutions."

Innocent Images was federal law enforcement's intensive effort to identify the victims and perpetrators in child pornography. Because of the sheer volume of images, early on, before computer algorithms were created to help ease some of the burden, it required being closeted in a small, dark room, scanning pornography over and over for clues, hours on end.

It messed with a lot of law enforcement officers' heads, even after mandatory counseling and periodic psych evals were begun.

"Walden worked Innocent Images in Atlanta before he came here," Lucy remembered.

"He and Bernhart worked together. Most prosecutors never want to see the evidence, say they need to compartmentalize, focus on the trial. Not Bernhart. He was the young hotshot newbie headed for the fast track to DC, wanted his fingers in every pie when it came to his cases. Then he got in over his head with one case and it swallowed him whole."

Now it was all making sense. "June Unknown. Everyone was obsessed with that one, even Walden."

They both knew Isaac Walden was the most levelheaded agent around. Nothing upset the man's equanimity—at least not since Lucy had met him two years ago when she came to start the Pittsburgh SAFE squad. But he never talked about his time in Atlanta. She'd thought it was because his wife died there—a sudden stroke on Thanksgiving eve four years ago while Walden was working late at the office.

"Bernhart left the US Attorney's Office after he prosecuted several of the men who had June Unknown's images," she continued. June Unknown was the reason why the SAFE squads were created, in the hopes that a multi-agency, multi-jurisdictional approach to child molestation and other sexual felonies would be more fruitful in capturing the worst of the worst.

Lucy's squad had more than proven successful. Too successful, maybe, as other agencies such as ICE began to shoulder some of the burden, using the tactics and strategies she and her team had developed. "The actual perpetrator was never arrested, right?"

"Never found. But there's more to it than that. A lot more." He glanced over her shoulder into her office. "Want to hear it from him?"

"You know they're pushing me out, shutting us down. If we can't close this case—" It was bad enough leaving all their other open cases for local law enforcement or other agencies to take over. But one that Walden was personally involved with? She couldn't let him down.

Then she nodded to herself. Walden. Clever man. That was the point. He knew she'd never let him down, knew she needed something to focus on, maybe even thought this case was big enough to save the squad from the budget axe.

It wasn't, of course. But Walden also knew that Lucy specialized in finding ways around the rules.

Oshiro clamped one of his beefy hands down on her shoulder. Just hard enough to get her attention. "This isn't about you or your squad, Guardino. This is about saving a life. More than one. You up for it? Or were you planning to sit around twiddling your thumbs until the brass kicks you to the curb?"

He was half-joking, half-serious. Which pissed her off. She shrugged his hand away and stalked past him to her office door.

Behind her she heard him murmur, "That's my Lucy Mae."

Irritated—with his heavy-handed tactics, Oshiro really belonged more in feudal Japan than on the streets of Pittsburgh—she pushed the door open so hard it slammed against the wall behind it.

Bernhart and the woman sitting beside him both jumped. He came out of his chair, angling his body to shield her.

Who was this damsel in distress? she wondered, even as she regarded the former Assistant US Attorney. She'd last seen him at the San Diego Conference on Child Maltreatment a few years back, giving a report on his new tactics of using civil reparation suits against pedophiles and how they could help law enforcement and prosecutors obtain confessions. Then, he'd appeared young, cocky, handsome. A crusader whose passion was contagious.

The man before her now still had that same fire blazing in his eyes but his features, always angular—hawkish, she'd heard a defense attorney describe him, although that might have been more about his prosecutorial style—were gaunt, as if he'd lost more weight than he could spare.

He nodded to her and slid back into his seat, and Lucy got her first good look at the woman. She was in her mid-twenties, long blond hair pulled back in a ponytail that made her appear waifish. No makeup, simple green jersey dress, and matching cardigan. But her eyes—there was nothing young or innocent about them. Pale blue, they looked washed-out, as if they'd seen too much.

Haunted. Lucy had seen that same expression on so many victims she'd lost count.

Walden stepped forward to make introductions. "Supervisory Special Agent Lucy Guardino. You already know Seth Bernhart. And this," he indicated the blonde, "is June Bernhart, aka, June Unknown."

The Girl Who Never Was: Memoirs of a Survivor
by June Unknown

What Happened in the Mall the Day I was Born for the Second Time

I WAS BORN in a mall on a rainy day in June. I know it was raining because while I was in the back of the van, I heard it thrumm-thrumming on the roof. And then when we got to the mall, even though Daddy parked between some Dumpsters near a rear entrance before he opened the van's door and lifted me out, a few drops splashed against my skin.

I'd seen and heard rain, but never felt it before. Rain was like biting into an apple—a red one, not the hard green ones—crisp and clean with promise.

Daddy had me dress up that morning, told me not to get dirty, so he carried me across the black pavement, shiny slick with water, his feet splish-splashing. Then he opened a door and we were inside, the rain and outside smells—so many, so different than home!—locked away behind us.

He set me down, adjusted my skirt and collar, grimaced at my hair, which had curled loose from its ribbon during the long, long ride in the van, then twisted his face in the look he sometimes got when I didn't perform as expected for the camera and he'd have to do it all over again, but then shrugged. "It'll do."

I knew better than to say anything—he hadn't asked me a question. Baby Girls should be seen and not heard. That was the rule.

He took my hand and dragged me down an empty hall with ugly lights that hurt my eyes and hard floors that made each step feel like a slap. My shoes pinched—I'd grown too much since last time I wore them for a Dress Up, but that usually didn't matter since when we played Dress Up at home, I never was walking anywhere.

The hallway was different than the hallway at home. That hall goes from the front door—which I never go near, it's a No Touch—past the living room and dining room back to the kitchen.

The hallway now, walking down it with my toes pinched together and Daddy tugging my hand, was all brown and gray, and worst of all, noisy. Like there was a big TV blaring at the end of it where the bright light gets even brighter and I wanted to close my eyes and cover my ears. I wished Daddy had never brought me here. I didn't know what a mall was and suddenly with all the noise and lights and smells, I didn't want to. I wanted to go home.

A weird feeling filled my stomach—like I'm hungry, which I was because Daddy ate breakfast but didn't feed me any; he did that sometimes when he said I looked fat or if he was afraid I'd throw up during a performance—but this feeling didn't stay in my stomach. Instead, it dragged me down from the inside out, just like how I felt when Daddy got upset because I'd been a Bad Girl and I was waiting to see what he's going "to just have to do about it."

I think back but couldn't remember being a Bad Girl. I'd been a Good Girl, honest. I wanted to tell Daddy, but I couldn't say anything because he hadn't asked me, so I dragged my feet and squeezed his hand and looked up at him, hoping he'd look down and give me one of his smiles. I lived for Daddy's smile, the one that made it all the way to his eyes and wrinkled his face. I'd skip breakfast, lunch, and dinner, wear pinchy shoes, play Dress Up, or other game he wanted to see him smile at me like that.

He didn't smile. He didn't even look at me. Just yanked my arm. Hard. Rushing me down the hall to the noise and light. Then I saw people. Strangers like the ones on TV. They were walking past the opening at the end of the long hall and I couldn't see to the end of the space past them.

I felt like throwing up. Dizzy, off-balance. I'd never been around any real life people except for Daddy. I was scared, wanted to run, but he crushed my hand in his.

We reached the end of the hall. The ceiling stopped here and beyond it there was a big space, like outside, but when I twisted my neck to look way, way up, I saw another ceiling, this one filled with curvy windows high up, higher than the trees in our yard, higher than the mountains beyond them, I think.

People, lots of people, too many, moving too fast, too close. I could smell them, all different smells, sharp and fake, churning together. The taste of their smells made me gag.

The noise hurt my ears. It slammed at me so hard I closed my eyes, squeezed them hard, wishing it would go away, and when I open them again, I'd be home, safe in bed with Daddy.

He shook me. Hard. I opened my eyes. Daddy crouched down, his face twisted. Time to shape up, Baby Girl, that look said. So I did. I stood tall, chest thrust out, arms folded behind my back, smile for the camera on my face.

"See that table?" Daddy pointed out into the open area, the place that made me feel dizzy and scared. I looked past the people to see bright-colored lights and windows surrounding the space, and in the center there was a bunch of little round tables. I smelled food— burnt sugar, meat roasting, spices I don't recognize— and my stomach growled.

But Daddy had asked a question. Did I see the table? I looked again, made sure I was telling him true. There, the one with no people at it, back in the corner near a trashcan. "Yes, Daddy."

He handed me a coloring book and crayons—brand new!—and twisted me so I was facing away from him and toward the wide open space and the strange people and the table.

"You're going to sit there and color. You will not

leave until a man comes and tells you to draw a picture of a green elephant. Then you will go with him and do what he says. Understand?"

No. But no was never the right answer. I wanted to ask so much more, but Baby Girls are to be seen and not heard, so I can't.

"Yes, Daddy."

He stood behind me, his head over my shoulder so he could make sure I was looking at the right table. I felt his breath on my cheek, smell his smell—pancakes and syrup—and I wasn't sure why, but tears spilled from my eyes and everything went blurry as I blinked them back.

Baby Girls don't cry. Not unless Daddy said it was okay.

He gave me a little shove from behind and pushed me forward out of the shelter of the hallway into the space. I moved a few steps—Daddy said to, so I have to—but slowly, hoping he won't notice me being Bad, I inched my head back so I can look over my shoulder.

He's gone.

The people terrified me, some of them coming so close I could touch them. I'd never touched anyone except Daddy, never in my whole life. And no one has ever touched me except him.

No one had ever talked to me either. When I was little, I used to think the people inside the TV were talking to me, but Daddy said to stop being stupid, so I did.

I reached the table. Climb onto the seat. The top of the table was sticky and there was a dirty napkin stained with ketchup. I didn't want my new coloring book to get dirty too, so I tried to clean it up before I set my book down. I can't throw the napkin away because Daddy said to sit and color and not leave.

So I did. For a long, long time. So long that I wet my pants and my mouth was dry and my stomach knotted with fear and hunger and missing Daddy and wondering who the green elephant man was—will he take me back home to Daddy? I wanted Daddy. I hated this place. I wanted to be home, I wanted these people to all go away, I wanted to use the toilet, I wanted to get clean, I wanted the noise to stop, I wanted my Daddy...

Then the lights go dim. There was the rattle of metal and I looked up to see people pulling down gates over the food places. A few of them stare at me.

While I sat and colored—I'd filled in all the pictures and drawn a bunch of my own in the spaces in between—people had come and tried to talk to me, but none of them were the green elephant man, so I said nothing, just sat and colored like Daddy told me to.

Now two more people walked over to me. Policemen, like on TV. They walked different than the other people. One a man, one a woman. I blinked and stared up at the man, hoping he was the green elephant man, and if he was, that he'd take me back home to Daddy.

He talked a lot. So did the woman. But no green elephant. So I sit and color like Daddy told me to, even though I had to pee and I was afraid I'd wet my pants again and I didn't want to do that in front of the police.

Police shoot you and yell and put handcuffs on you. I'd seen it on TV.

Daddy said to be a Good Girl, so I tried really, really hard.

But they grabbed me up and no matter how I kicked and screamed, they didn't listen, they just took me away, away from the table Daddy told me to sit at, away from the green elephant man I was supposed to listen to, away from home, away from Daddy.

That day was the last time I ever saw him.

CHAPTER 4

LUCY WOBBLED A bit on her cane, searching for a comfortable position. Walden noticed and stepped forward, sliding a chair out for her at the conference table. They both knew she'd come back to work too soon, just as they both knew she couldn't stay away another minute. She remained standing, assessing their civilian guests.

June Unknown. Every law enforcement officer working crimes against children knew her story. Nightmare was more like it. Abandoned at a mall when she was nine or ten—no one knew her true age. Just as no one knew her true name or where she came from or how long the man called Daddy had held her captive.

Hell, back then, when they first found her, they didn't even know about the pornography. Daddy didn't release that out into the pedophile community, once again selling June's innocence to the highest bidders, until after she was discovered at the mall. Given that the images were later found piecemeal and out of order, mixed in with tens of thousands of other images, no one pervert owning the entire collection chronicling June's childhood on one computer, it had taken law enforcement almost a decade to identify the girl in the Baby Girl collection of images as the girl found in a mall without a name.

"June *Bernhart?*" Lucy's gaze was on Seth as she asked the question.

"We became involved and were married after I left the US Attorney's Office. Obviously, it's not public knowledge," Seth answered. Seth's voice was one of his best weapons—sure to mesmerize juries and the media. Combined with his distinguished looks and obvious passion for his cases, he could easily have left government service for a seven-figure income doing on-air commentary for TV.

Instead, he'd quit to represent a single client in expensive civil cases mired with jurisdiction and procedural pitfalls. A single client who was his wife. Talk about career suicide.

Lucy pivoted to stare at June. The younger woman met Lucy's gaze without flinching, the most relaxed person in the room despite being the center of scrutiny.

Seth cleared his voice and laid his hand over June's on the table, giving her a quick, reassuring squeeze. Lucy carefully lowered herself into the chair and drew in her breath. This woman before her, she was why Lucy did her job—why she was compelled to return to work, no matter the cost. It wasn't sexy work, didn't grab front-page headlines like tracking terrorists, but it was important work.

She might only have three days left before her squad was officially terminated, but damn it, she was not going to deny a victim like June Unknown any assistance she could offer. "What can I do for you?"

June opened her mouth, but Seth patted her hand and spoke. "You know the civil suits I've been pursuing on behalf of June?"

"Asking for reparations from anyone found guilty of possessing her images. My understanding is that it might go all the way to the Supreme Court."

"The lower courts have upheld the findings in our favor for the most part. So far we've sued eighty-three defendants and won judgments adding up to over ten million dollars." He paused. Not for breath, rather for dramatic effect. "But that's eighty-three defendants out of fourteen hundred twenty-seven convicted of possessing images from the Baby Girl collection—not to mention the untold tens of thousands more who have yet to be brought to justice."

Lucy raised a palm. "You're preaching to the choir. We know how rampant the problem is."

So of course the powers that be were eliminating the SAFE program, she didn't add, focusing on Seth and June.

"It's not about the money. Our hope is that if the Supreme Court upholds our verdicts, this strategy of pursuing civil reparations might become a useful weapon for law enforcement to threaten defendants with during plea bargain agreements. In other words, what June and I are doing is important not just to victims, but also prosecutors and law enforcement officers. Not to mention the legislation it might spawn to further protect victims' rights."

"I don't understand," Lucy said, trying to curb her

impatience. "Are you here because of one of your civil suits?"

June planted both her palms on the tabletop and shifted in her seat as if uncomfortable. "We're here because you and your team might be able to stop the child predators from killing the case before it ever goes to the Supreme Court."

"How so?" Lucy asked.

"There have been threats. Against June's life," Oshiro put in from where he'd planted himself near the door. "At the last trial, they also threatened the judge, so the Marshals got involved. But they've smartened up. This time it's only June they're targeting, and since it's a civil proceeding, we can't offer her protection. Not officially, at any rate."

"But Oshiro here," Seth nodded toward the big man, "gave us some names—retired agents. Even with their protection, even living like fugitives, the bastards still found us." Bitter anger colored his voice.

June pushed to her feet, obviously impatient with all the rhetoric, revealing her extremely pregnant belly for the first time. "It's not just me they're threatening. This time they want our baby."

The Girl Who Never Was: Memoirs of a Survivor
by June Unknown

How I Got My New Last First Name

IT WAS THE social worker who gave me my name.

"Jane Doe is no name for a girl her age," she told the doctor and a policeman—this one different from the first two; he wore a suit and wouldn't look at me.

I was sitting on the floor in the corner of a small room that smelled like Daddy does after he comes back from running. Looking up at the adults sitting at the table and standing above me made me feel tiny, like if I squeezed myself small enough, I could escape through a crack in the wall and run home to Daddy.

But Daddy had left me. I didn't know where home was. The green elephant man never came—maybe he knew where Daddy was.

Daddy told me to sit and wait, and I'd disobeyed. I was a Bad Girl, and we'd just have to do something about that, but sitting here cold and shivering, and my stomach strangling—it was so twisted—and my hair and face sticky with tears and snot, and my fingernails torn from clawing at the grate in the car they locked me in when they took me from the mall...what was I going to do?

Follow Daddy's rules. Baby Girls are to be seen and not heard. I hadn't said a word.

Do as you're told. No one had told me to do anything, except the policeman who kept yelling "Stop fighting!" when he and his partner put me in their car. And then the doctor who took my Dress Up clothes and touched me all over and took pictures, but his camera wasn't anything like Daddy's. He said to hold still. So I did.

"We need a name for our report," the new policeman said.

There was a nurse. She lied. Told me everything would be okay. It wasn't. I was a Bad Girl. I hadn't stayed and waited like Daddy told me to, and now I didn't know what was going to happen. I didn't like her. Nurse Liar.

"She's got to have a name," Nurse Liar said. "She's at least eight or nine years old." She kept touching me, patting my hair, helping me on with the new clothes they gave me, squeezing my arm. I didn't like her touching me. Nobody touched me but Daddy. That was the way it should be.

"Maybe older," the doctor said. He was an old man with a beard that hid his face. "I'd guess ten From the X-rays. The radiologist can tell better."

Social Worker—I kind of liked her. She looked me in the eye and had hair that was red, almost as bright as the leaves on the sugar maple in our backyard when the weather got cold. I always tried to make that color red with my crayons and paints, but never got it right. Not shiny and bright like her hair. She bent down so her face was the same level as mine. "Please, honey. You're safe here. We're not going to hurt you. Just tell us your name so we can find your mommy and daddy."

That got my attention. I don't have a mommy—not sure I ever did. I never met a woman (outside of the ones on TV) before. But if she could find Daddy, then I could go home, that was a good reason to break a rule, right? And she'd almost asked a question—I was supposed to answer if Daddy asked me a question, so maybe it was okay to answer her? All I had to do was give her my name.

"Baby Girl," I answered.

Everyone went quiet and stared at me. I focused all my attention on Social Worker. She was the one who said she could find Daddy for me.

"Your full name, honey. What's your first and last name?"

I stared at her blankly. Do people have names at first and then make new ones? Daddy only gave me one name. Maybe I'm not old enough to have a last one?

She tried again. "How about your parents? What are their names?"

That one was easy. "Daddy."

There. I'd answered her questions. She said that was what she needed to find my daddy. I folded my arms across my chest and stared at the wall, painting a picture on it with my mind since they took my crayons and coloring book away. And I waited for her to go get Daddy.

Instead, she stood and huddled with the others. I caught a few words. Most of them I didn't understand. "Severely traumatized." "Prolonged captivity." "NCMEC." "Long-term care and placement." "What's the date?" "How's that for a name? Better than Jane Doe?"

That's when they erased my first name, Baby Girl, and gave me my last name: June Forth.

Then they took me away again and I was lost, Daddy nowhere to be found. I did my best to be a Good Girl and said nothing, not even when they asked questions. Daddy always said never talk to strangers, never trust anyone, that he was the only one I should listen to and obey.

He was right. I never felt scared with Daddy. He took care of me; he loved me.

These people, these strangers, I didn't know why they wanted to hurt me, why they wouldn't let me go home to Daddy, but I couldn't trust them.

They didn't love me. Not like Daddy.

CHAPTER 5

———— ∼ ————

LUCY STARED AT the pregnant woman. Below the table top, out of sight of the men, her hand clenched the cane so tightly sweat dripped down its aluminum casing. She was angry. At her damn foot trying to distract her with its never-ending Morse code drumming. At the Bureau with their cost-cutting strategies.

Most of all, at the men who treated women and children as disposable objects, used for their pleasure and profit, then discarded.

Men like June's father. He'd used her for his sexual depravities since she was an infant. Raised her to obey him, taught her that pleasing him was her only reason for living. Then, when she'd grown too old, sold her to another pervert.

Investigators working the case over the past fourteen years since June had been found had an abundance of theories—all which led to more unanswered questions. Like what happened to her mother? Had June's father killed her or had June been stolen from her? Was he even her biological father or was being "Daddy" part of his twisted fantasy? Had he done this before or since? Where was the man who he'd sold June to? Arrested? Detained? Or just cold feet?

Their working hypothesis was that the man who called himself "Daddy" worked in IT or software development. All of the images of June, including the ones dating back to when she was an infant, remained untraceable to any originating computer or ISP address. Even after hundreds—thousands—of man-hours working the case, Daddy remained a mystery.

But those man-hours had eventually, nine years after she'd been left in that mall, identified June as the subject of the Baby Girl photos and videos. Thanks to the work of Isaac Walden and Seth Bernhart.

Lucy knew how much this case meant to Walden. No way in hell would she let him down. "Tell me about these threats."

June paced the small area between the table and Lucy's desk, knuckles pressed against the small of her back. She glanced at Seth, obviously giving him permission in the shorthand body language of married couples. Seth slid a photo from his pocket and set it on the table between him and Lucy.

It was an ultrasound. Of a baby.

"That's my latest ultrasound," June said. "Taken two weeks ago." Her voice cut off abruptly. Lucy glanced over her shoulder at the pregnant woman, but June had turned her back on everyone to stare out the window behind the desk.

There wasn't much to see except a glimpse of the Steeler's training field. And the row of plants that had wilted in Lucy's absence.

"Yesterday," Seth took over for June. He slid another sheet of paper onto the table. "This was posted on *Backlist*." A *Craig's List* type of site that had been tied to human trafficking, murder for hire, and other criminal activity.

The paper was a screenshot of an ad. It included the same ultrasound image with a caption: *Looking forward to adding my Baby Girl's baby girl to my collection! Daddy.*

The Girl Who Never Was: Memoirs of a Survivor
by June Unknown

The Knock on My Door that Changed Everything

I DIDN'T MAKE it past my first year of art school. Away from home for the first time, living on my own, surrounded by men—you can probably guess why.

Dr. Helen, my foster mom, had taught me how to appropriately interact with guys, at least enough to get me through adolescence, but she'd died of a heart attack the summer before I started college and now she was gone.

I tried to keep her words alive in my memory, but they were soon overridden by anxiety and a need to seek comfort the only way I'd ever learned how: in the arms of a man. The girls my age avoided me, sensing I only pretended to be like them. The guys my age quickly figured out I was an easy mark, passive, willing to do anything they wanted—a cheap date, they thought.

But my needs went much deeper and I began to

turn to the older men on campus: my professors, the TAs, even the doctor who ran the student health clinic and the campus minister. No one was off-limits if I thought they could give me what I craved: the security I'd felt as a child when it was just me and Daddy.

Ten months later, I was miserable. Every relationship, whether a one-night stand or a month-long fling, had ended the same way: with them walking out and me feeling dirty, wretched, and alone. It didn't help that every single man told me it was my fault, blamed me for starting things, seducing them.

They were the innocent pawns and I was some kind of manipulative schemer out to ruin their lives with my clinginess and neediness.

It was during that year that I, for the first time in years, began to have flashes of memory. Me and Daddy. The way he smelled when he wrapped his arms around me at night. The rough scrape of his beard stubble against my skin. The smiles I'd work so very hard to earn.

I thought maybe I was going mad. I ran away from school and used the inheritance Helen had left me to flee to her cottage in the Lowcountry of South Carolina. She used to take me there for vacation and I'd fallen in love with the quiet of life on the water, the color and light blossoming on my palette and in my paintings. Now that she was dead, leaving me as her only family—how pathetic was that, a woman with no family trying to raise a girl with no concept of family?— the cottage was mine.

There, busy painting, alone, I felt almost at peace.

Until one day there was a knock on the door.

At first I didn't hear it, I was so enmeshed in creating the exact pale yellow of the sky at dawn that morning, but it came again, louder this time, jolting me from a cloud of pigment. My mind still filled with sunlight and dawn mist, I stumbled to the door and opened it without thought.

Two men stood there. A white man with dark, wavy hair, wearing a dark-colored suit that was already wrinkling from the heat and humidity. With him was a black man in his forties wearing slacks and a polo shirt along with a pistol at his waist.

"This is FBI Special Agent Isaac Walden." The first man made introductions. His voice was as warm as that elusive morning sunlight I'd been struggling to capture. Reassuring beyond his years—he wasn't that much older than I was. It made me forget my original intention of making an excuse and shutting the door. Instead, I leaned toward him, anxious to hear more. "I'm Assistant US Attorney Seth Bernhart. Are you June Forth?"

They held up IDs and I nodded numbly as I examined them. It's funny what goes through your mind when something totally unexpected happens. I'm not sure why, but my first thought wasn't of Daddy— rather it was of my mother, a woman I'd never met, at least I never remembered meeting.

I didn't even know what mothers were until I figured it out for myself watching TV—I was old enough to know better than to ask, even when Daddy gave me permission to speak. Somehow I knew any talk of mothers would make him angry at me for being a Bad Girl.

Yet, now, in this moment, facing these men, I blurted out, "You found her. You found my mother."

The two men glanced at each other. Seth—somehow in my mind he was already Seth, especially after my words turned his expression sorrowful, his shoulders drooping as if I'd given him an extra burden to carry. "No. We're here to talk about the man who raised you when you were young. Could we come inside?"

And that was the start of it. We sat at my kitchen table drinking sweet tea, me apologizing for the mess since there were half-finished paintings and sketching materials covering every surface. No one except Helen had ever been inside the cottage with me before and I had no idea how to play hostess to men like these.

They were uncomfortable, stiff at first, skirting around the issue of Daddy, but Helen had prepared me well. I knew someday this would happen: men in suits wanting to know the details.

More than that, they had pictures. And videos. From the time I was a baby to when I was ten and he left me at the mall.

Said thanks to new computer technology they'd finally figured out that the girl abandoned in the mall that June day was the same girl in those images. Me.

I was nineteen and knew enough to understand exactly what they were saying. I wasn't even surprised, thanks to Helen. But I was curious.

"Why?" I asked. "Why come to me now? After all this time?"

The black man remained silent as he had for most of the conversation. But Seth leaned forward, his gaze meeting mine, seeing my agitation, and silently asking permission. Then he placed his hand over mine. It felt good. Warm. Protective. Like I was a part of something bigger than just me alone.

If I was honest with myself, I would have realized that it felt a lot like being with Daddy.

"Because," he said, his voice low and soothing, yet still filled with power, "if you're willing, if you're strong enough to face the men who have entertained themselves by collecting your images all these years, I'd like to put you on the witness stand."

I frowned. Even Helen had never been able to help me sort out my feelings about the possibility that Daddy had shared his pictures and films with strangers. Daddy loved me and that was a fact. It was also a fact that he'd been a bad man. Evil some people would have called him.

But I could never think of him that way—not even now, knowing the truth that I'd never understood as a child.

"Me? Testify? I don't know those men." It wasn't the going to court that had my mind whirling; it was the thought that being in court, in front of the TV cameras and sketch artists and reporters, that maybe Daddy would see.

Maybe he would find me after all these years.

I took a sip of tea but couldn't taste it. How did I feel about that? About Daddy coming back into my life? I had no idea. Fear. Excitement. Dread. Ecstasy. Anger.

None of Dr. Helen's names for emotions fit. Not a single one. They all pinched like those too-small shoes Daddy had dressed me in that last day.

"I've already gotten my convictions," Seth was saying. "What I want is for you to go on record, explaining how much damage they've done to you. How your life is changed because of what your father did. How the fact that men like him gain pleasure from looking at those images of you has forever impacted you."

"What good would that do?"

"It will help me to convince the judge to give them the maximum sentence. So they can't ever hurt another child again."

I almost said no. I wanted to say no. The last thing I ever, ever wanted to do was to face the men who had seen the intimate moments Daddy and I shared. I was old enough, nineteen, to understand how awful it was—the things in those pictures and videos. But no amount of time could ever make me hate Daddy. He didn't do anything to me; we'd done things together. He loved me the only way he could.

But those men, the strangers who paid to see what should have been private between me and Daddy?

Those men I hated. The word for my emotions came and it fit, along with more. Those men, prying into private moments, stealing bits and pieces of my life, they were the ones who made me feel ashamed, dirty. They deserved to be punished.

"Would it really make a difference?" I asked, my voice sounding as soft and uncertain as a child's.

Seth squeezed my hand. I felt safe with him. He would protect me.

"Yes," he said. "I think it will. I think together we might be able to make a huge difference."

He had me at "together."

"I'll do it."

CHAPTER 6

LUCY FOCUSED ON the ultrasound images in front of her. The baby's face was tilted toward the viewer, her perfect features seeming to smile out from the womb. Innocence defined.

She barricaded her emotions and focused on the immediate threat. Which meant getting answers Oshiro and Bernhart might not be forthcoming with if June remained. "Walden, could you grab Taylor so the two of you can go over June's recent movements? Online and off. We need to know how someone could access her ultrasound."

Seth leaned forward. "We never shared our copy with anyone. It had to come from the medical center's files."

"Don't worry. Taylor will track it down." Walden took his cue, escorting June from the room. She didn't protest, but Seth did, half rising from his seat, his gaze following them through the glass walls of Lucy's office. "But—"

To Lucy's surprise, Oshiro also pivoted his bulk, ready to follow June and Walden.

"Sit down," she ordered the Deputy Marshal.

His expression could have toppled an oak tree, but Lucy deflected it with a raised eyebrow and glare of her own. "Want to tell me why a Deputy US Marshal on the Fugitive Apprehension Strike Team is pulling protective duty on a witness in a civil trial beyond his jurisdiction?"

Seth shifted in his seat but Oshiro remained impassive. "Taking vacation. Boss has no say who I spend it with."

Okay. So it was going to be one of *those* situations. No wonder they'd come to her—going off the DOJ's roadmap was a talent Lucy had reluctantly embraced over her sixteen-year career with the Bureau. And with her squad already on the chopping block, she had nothing to lose.

She turned her attention to Seth. "Yesterday you learned of this threat, called Oshiro, he takes a sudden vacation, and you and June come up to Pittsburgh from DC so he can protect June until the Supreme Court arguments?"

He shook his head. "Until the baby is born. And after if we don't find the bastard by then."

A father protecting his wife and child. She didn't blame him. She'd do the same. Had done the same two months ago.

She waited and he continued. "This case could be a game changer in the fight against child predators. But nothing is more important than my family. I don't care what it takes. We need to stop this SOB before he can hurt June or the baby."

"Why Oshiro?" she asked. The two men glanced at each other.

Oshiro didn't squirm but he did seem uncomfortable—first time she'd ever seen that kind of flinch, as microscopic and fleeting as it was, from the inscrutable deputy. "Because I'm the guy who could've caught June's father, but didn't."

Bernhart leaned forward, his face earnest. "You don't know that. Besides, it was fourteen years ago."

"The bastard who bought her from her so-called Daddy got away back then because I was too young and stupid and cocky to imagine the idiot I'd stopped for running a stop sign was anything other than the mild-mannered suck up he'd seemed. It was my first year on the job, working a rural township PD. Stupid, rookie mistake. I never ran the guy through NCIC, too eager to get on with 'real' policing. Never knew until too late that he was wanted for possession of child pornography. If I had hauled him in, Mr. Green Elephant, maybe I could have gotten the real identity and location of June's Daddy and we wouldn't be here today."

It was the longest speech Lucy had ever heard Oshiro make. "I don't understand. You discovered his identity but he's never been questioned?"

Oshiro didn't meet her gaze. "The township I was working in was forty-some miles away from the mall where they found June later that night. And once she was in Children and Youth's custody and they pieced together what had happened to her, it was days later that they released her photo to the press, searching for her family."

"So what made you think you had stopped the man

Daddy sold her to?"

He hauled in a breath, shifted his weight, then finally looked her in the eye. "I stopped the guy, he apologized, handed me his ID and registration, was so polite. Looked like some college professor or something. But on his front seat, next to him, there was this eight-by-ten photo of a little girl. He saw me looking at it and gave me a story about how it was his daughter's school photo and he'd promised her he'd get it framed as a birthday present for his wife, but he'd forgotten and the frame store was closing and that's why he was in such a hurry."

"You let him go," Lucy said.

"I let him go. Then I see June's photo at roll call a few days later...but it was too late."

"By the time the State Police pieced everything together, he was dead," Seth explained. "Murdered."

Daddy cleaning up his tracks. Quietly, efficiently. No wonder he'd been able to elude investigators for all this time.

"I doubt if Green Elephant Man would have given us Daddy anyway," Seth said in a quiet tone Lucy knew was aimed at assuaging Oshiro's guilt. From the way Oshiro studied the floor, she doubted it helped. "Not like anyone else we've caught, not even the guys we've sued have been able to provide any useful intel on Daddy. And if we had caught Green Elephant Man sooner, what would have changed? June still would have ended up in foster care. Her pictures would still be out there. Only thing different is that we would have linked her to the Baby Girl collection too soon for her to be able to testify or bring the civil suits—she would have been too young. And maybe she and I would have never met."

Both men fell silent, each staring at the ultrasound lying on the table between them.

Lucy brought them back to the here and now. "What makes you think it's June's father behind this? Why not some other pedophile determined to stop the civil suits, using her father's name to frighten her?"

"What does it matter?" Oshiro said. "A threat is a threat."

"I'm not saying you're wrong. I just wanted to know if you have any more evidence." Playing devil's advocate, searching for holes in a case theory was something Lucy did with her team all the time. It kept them on their toes, prevented tunnel vision that might blind them to other possible investigatory avenues.

"You mean other than his boasting in public?" Seth asked, tapping the print out of the *Backlist* ad.

"Take a step back. The man who called himself Daddy and created the Baby Girl collection was obsessed with June. There's a good chance he's still just as obsessed with her as he was back then."

Oshiro made a noise that translated to, "duh."

Lucy pivoted the ad so it was face up before the two men. "He may still want her, but he definitely does not want to share her like he did when he released the Baby Girl collection."

"I don't understand," Seth said, pulling the ad closer and scrutinizing it.

"I have no idea if the threats during the earlier court proceedings came from Daddy, but I'm fairly certain this one does."

"Right," Oshiro said. "So we're on the same page."

"No. I'm saying you need to look at the bigger

picture. Witnesses like June have their identities protected by the court."

"Of course," Seth said. "That's why the lawsuit only uses her first name."

"But I think June's pregnancy and the fact that her first name is not very common allowed someone to learn her real identity. After all, how many pregnant women would be coming and going from courthouses during the same time as June's testimony? Any casual surveillance would easily identify her after a few appearances."

Seth frowned. "So that means it isn't Daddy after her, it could be anyone? But you said—"

"I said it could have been anyone threatening her *earlier*. But this," she nodded to the ad, "this came from the man so obsessed with her that he isn't willing to share her or her baby with his fellow pedophiles. We may have other threats to deal with in the long haul, but this immediate threat, this is from June's father. And it's bigger than that."

Seth shook his head. "I don't understand."

Oshiro pulled the photocopy up to his face, comparing it with the real ultrasound. Then he nodded as he saw what Lucy had spotted earlier. "He's not just threatening her. He's staking his claim."

"Exactly. Which is why he removed any identifying info from the ultrasound image in the ad. Daddy is a legend among child pornographers. If he emerges from the shadows after not being heard from for fourteen years, you can bet they'll listen and obey."

"Wait." Oshiro frowned, all the skin on his shaven head wrinkling into furrows. "That means he could call on them for help. He could have a freaking army of perverts at his command, watching and waiting for the right time to grab June and her baby."

Lucy nodded. "Which means it's not only about finding Daddy—it's about protecting June from an anonymous army commanded by a man techno-savvy enough to hack into a medical center's protected database."

Seth pushed to his feet, leaning his weight forward onto the tabletop. "We need to do both. Oshiro, you take June, hide her, keep her safe. And you," he directed a laser-sharp gaze at Lucy, "you and I are going to find this bastard, hunt him down, and make him call off his dogs. And I don't care how the hell we do it."

CHAPTER 7

OF COURSE, IT never was as simple as that—a fact that Seth Bernhart, as a former AUSA, should have known. It worried Lucy that he'd allowed his emotions to get the better of him. She could understand why, with his family involved, but it made her leery. Would he be less of an asset to protecting June and more of a liability?

Oshiro picked up on her feelings. After she sent Seth out to work with Taylor and Walden, the Deputy Marshal lingered behind, just long enough to meet her gaze. "Don't worry about Bernhart," he grumbled. "He's solid."

Then he was gone to commandeer a cubicle and arrange for a safe house for June. Lucy stared through the glass walls of her office, watching body language tell a story as Taylor coaxed a smile from June while they worked at searching her online footprint for any signs of a security breach. Walden looked over from his own workstation, his chair pushed uncomfortably far from his desk as he positioned himself between June and the door, playing the role of protector.

Seth hovered behind June, one hand on her shoulder, leaning between her and Taylor as he added his own details to the database Taylor was constructing. But it was June who Lucy focused on. She'd survived, not just Daddy's abuse but also the trauma of entering a world she was wholly unprepared for. Despite all that, she'd found the courage to stand up and try to make a difference.

Lucy glanced at her desk littered with a backlog of memos and office detritus. Meeting someone like June put things in perspective.

The child predator known as Daddy had gone undetected for over two decades—in fact, if he hadn't released the Baby Girl collection and made the mistake of selling June when she grew too old for his preferential needs, he might never have gotten onto their radar at all.

How many more men like him were out there? It was a question she asked herself so often that she'd worn the edges off like a worry stone, no longer charging her with anxiety and anger, but rather simply leaving her exhausted and feeling older than someone still a year shy of forty should.

Avoiding her desk with its overflowing in-box, she turned to her window garden. From the water sitting in the saucers, it was clear her bromeliads and orchids had suffered from too much attention rather than neglect. The thought brought a smile as she pictured each of her team members wandering in here on some random pretense to care for her plants while she was gone.

Why had Daddy kept Baby Girl alive? she wondered as she examined the plants, seeing if she could salvage any. Why sell her instead of killing her? Did he need money so badly that it out-weighed the risk? But the Baby Girl collection of videos and images should have easily netted him six to seven figures.

Maybe he had feelings for Baby Girl in his own warped way? After all, it had only been the two of them for almost ten years. Could she even be his biological child? Had Daddy grown too attached, unable to destroy the evidence that was his Baby Girl?

Huge, huge risk. Born of sentiment? Hubris? Greed? Or simple naiveté?

Her cell phone rang. Nick, calling to check on her between patients.

For a fleeting moment, she was tempted to ignore his call, let it go to voice mail. Not because she resented the intrusion—far from it—but because sooner or later they'd need to address her future here at the Bureau, or lack there of.

She sank into her desk chair, her ankle thanking her with a sigh of relief, and answered.

"How's it going?" Nick asked.

"Good," she lied. He didn't answer right away, so she amended it to, "Fine." Still he waited—he knew her much too well. "Okay. The foot hurts like a sonofabitch and it's the least of my worries."

She gave him a quick rundown of the imminent demise of her squad and the decision she faced. "So what do you think? Can you see me sitting at home watching soap operas and eating bonbons?"

"As if." The sound of his office chair squeaking as he leaned back emphasized his words. "We've talked about this. I'm fine with anything you want to do, as long as—"

"Megan," she interrupted him. "We need to put her first. She'll never let us move." Not that Megan had spoken to Lucy about it. Any time Lucy or Nick broached the issue, Megan left the room, refusing to discuss why she was so adamant about staying in the house where her grandmother had died.

They'd talked to the trauma counselor about it, but she didn't have any answers, either.

Lucy hesitated, hating what it might do to her already shaky relationship with Megan if she and Nick forced the issue. "Unless maybe this is an opportunity. Do you think it's a good thing for her to leave, start fresh?"

"Don't go putting this on me." His voice held a subtle tone of warning.

"You're right. We need to decide together. But I'm not sure if even bringing it up is going to upset her. She's so volatile—I'm never sure if she's going to lash out at me or give me the cold shoulder." Of course, she couldn't really blame Megan. The one and only thing they seemed to agree on was that it was Lucy's fault that her mother had gotten killed.

The logic was irrefutable. If Lucy was a "normal" mom instead of an FBI agent, her family would never have been targeted. Who could argue with that?

"It'd be worse to hide anything from her," Nick said. "The trauma counselor thinks Megan's processing her grief in a very mature manner for a thirteen-year-old. I have to say, I agree. When I was driving her to school this morning, she told me that since you were going back to work and would be too busy, she's taking charge of Sunday dinner."

Lucy was glad he couldn't see her wince. Her mom

usually hosted Sunday dinners, the table laden with all her most treasured family recipes—recipes Lucy, whose idea of cooking was pushing a button on a microwave, had never mastered. Loss swept through her, leaving her cold despite the sunshine streaming through the window.

"One more thing to blame on me and my job," Lucy noted.

"Not true." Typical Nick. He'd never let her get away with feeling sorry for herself. "She's trying to help, Lucy. She needs to do something to fill the void left by—"

"Nick. She won't even talk to me, not about anything important, can barely look at me. And when she does, the look on her face—" Lucy broke off. It wasn't just the pain she saw in Megan; it was the reason behind it.

If Lucy hadn't been working late that day two months ago, her mom wouldn't have been at their home to babysit Megan. It was only sheer luck that Megan hadn't gone home right away after her karate class that had saved her from being there when the killer struck. Every time Lucy looked at Megan, it wasn't just her mother's loss she felt, it was the enormity of how easily Megan could also have been killed.

"Nick." She swiveled her chair so her back was to the glass windows of her office, her voice barely above a whisper. "I don't know what to do. Was I wrong to come back to work?" It certainly felt so, the way the administrative Fates had conspired against her. "But quitting, what would that teach Megan? That her mom is scared? Too weak to keep fighting the bad guys? Wouldn't she feel even less safe?"

They'd had this conversation dozens of times over the past few weeks as Lucy pushed through her rehab in order to return to duty. Being an FBI agent, doing what she did—it truly was who she was, but Lucy was prepared to sacrifice it if it meant helping her daughter heal.

But of course nothing was ever that easy. Even Nick, with his years of experience working with PTSD patients, didn't have the answer.

"I wish I knew," he said. "All we can do is take it one day at a time."

She was glad he couldn't see her eyes roll. One day at a time was the mantra the trauma counselor used at every visit. Lucy wanted to do something, anything, fix things. How long could she face yet another "one day" waiting for time to work some miracle of healing?

"I told Megan we'd go out to your mom's house," Nick continued. "Collect the recipes and pans and stuff. Maybe this afternoon? Might be a good time for you two to forge some kind of détente."

Lucy swallowed her sigh before the phone could send it to Nick. "I'm not sure. Work."

There was a long pause. Too long.

"Sounds like you already decided to stay with the Bureau. Even if it means accepting a position you'd despise." His Virginia accent sharpened. Megan wasn't the only one dealing with the trauma of what had happened two months ago.

"It's not like that. Walden asked me to look into a new case." They both knew Walden never asked anything for himself. She gave Nick a brief overview. "And we only have three days to find this guy before the Bureau shuts us down for good."

"Anything I can help with?" Nick's expertise was in

trauma, which made him particularly astute when teasing through victims' profiles.

Lucy filled him in on her thoughts about June's threats and the man or men behind them.

"You know this isn't new behavior, right?" he asked when she finished.

"What isn't?"

"There's no way a man with that level of obsession didn't keep track of June after he left her at the mall. What happened to the Green Elephant Man?"

"ID'd as a guy living in…" she glanced at her notes, "Pine Grove Mills. About forty miles away from where June was left. But by the time they got to him, he was gone."

"So they never found him to question him?"

"Oh they found him. Three months later his decomposed body was discovered at Black Moshanon State Park. He'd been shot."

"See. Your guy, this Daddy character, was tying up loose ends. Compulsive and obsessive—on an emotional level. Control, that's what he wants. Absolute control."

"Maybe why his tastes skew so young. But then why let June out of his control at all? Why not kill her outright? Solves all his problems."

"I'll bet she was his first. But not his last. And he's been tracking her all this time."

"But now she finally poses a threat to him, so he's going on the offensive?" That didn't feel quite right.

"No. I think now she finally has something he wants. Her child."

Lucy leaned back in her chair, the mid-day sun warming her face. "Sometimes I worry about how easy it is for us to think like these sick, twisted creeps."

Nick's sigh resonated through the phone. "So do I. Another thing to keep in mind when you make your decision." A chime sounded—his next patient arriving. "Gotta go. Love you."

Her decision. Letting her know he'd support her, whatever she decided. But also a warning that he and Megan would be the ones who had to live with her choice.

Shit. How screwed up was she that she'd rather focus on worming her way into the mind of an obsessive child predator than deal with her own future?

CHAPTER 8

SPECIAL AGENT ISAAC Walden swiveled his chair so that he could look past June and the others to keep an eye on Lucy. So typical, the stubborn way she limped around her office, checking her plants before finally allowing herself the comfort of sitting down. Lucy never took the easy way out, whether it was standing up for a victim, chasing a target, or acknowledging that her body needed more time to heal.

In so many of their cases, time was the enemy. And Lucy refused to surrender.

Should he tell her that time was also running out for Seth? No. Not his secret to share.

He glanced at the former prosecutor. Close examination revealed the ravages of the fight he was losing. Thinning hair; sagging, sallow skin; an unhealthy, yellow-green pallor. According to the doctors, Seth should have been dead and buried weeks ago, but the man was as stubborn as Lucy, refusing to slow down until he was certain that June and her unborn child were provided for. Family first, that was what was keeping Seth alive.

A sigh rippled through him as he watched Seth sooth June's hair, steadying her with a hand on her shoulder. She covered his hand with her own, an unconscious gesture of intimacy that reminded Walden of his own wife. Five years this Thanksgiving he'd lost her, but not a day went by that he didn't feel her presence with him. Her voice chiding or coaxing him on dark days when all he wanted was to stay in bed, the glint of her smile in every pretty girl he passed, the ghost of her warm touch when he returned home at the end of the day as if his apartment weren't cold and empty.

"We need a money trail," Walden mused. June and Seth glanced over at him; Taylor's rapid-fire typing didn't falter. The kid was annoying that way, able to multi-task and handle several lines of thought simultaneously.

"Good thought," Taylor said. "I already applied for a warrant for the ad—even on *Backlist*, ads have to be paid for. Funny that. The guy could have posted on a dozen DarkNet forums anonymously and for free. If all he wanted was to stake a claim, declare his intentions to his fellow pedophiles, why go public?"

"He wanted our attention," Seth said.

"He wanted *your* attention," Walden corrected. "You've been chasing this Daddy creep for years. Maybe you're getting close?"

Seth shook his head mournfully. "Not that I know of. But we did submit filings for a new batch of civil suits right before June went in for that ultrasound. Maybe he's connected to one of those cases?"

"You're suing men who have already been convicted of possessing the Baby Girl images, so I doubt it. The investigators would have already combed through their lives."

"Maybe he's worried one of those men could lead us back to him?" June asked. "Maybe that's your money trail? Who they bought the images from."

Walden beamed at her. She'd come so very far from the girl he'd met four years ago. That girl would have never spoken up when surrounded by three men. She would have sat quietly, waiting for their instructions.

"Good thought," he said, although he was certain the original investigations covered it. Although they didn't have his secret weapon: Taylor and his team of cybersleuths. "Seth, can you forward me the criminal case numbers? We'll start combing through the evidence, see if anything was missed."

"That's going to take time."

"My guys are pretty fast," Taylor said. Not boasting, simply stating a fact. "And now that I have the hospital database hack, they can eliminate potential subjects who don't have the skill set necessary."

"Wait, you already figured out how he broke into the hospital records?" Seth asked.

Taylor leaned back, finally giving his keyboard a rest. "Well, yeah. You said time was of the essence."

"Kid, you're a genius," Walden proclaimed. From the maze of cubicles, the other cybertechs laughed, several launching Nerf bullets and arrows at Taylor who ducked and grinned. "How about I treat you to lunch?"

Seth frowned at that, glancing at Oshiro, who was working the phone at the desk opposite. The US Marshal radiated the same intense energy as Lucy, not sitting as he spoke, instead doing a two-step shuffle, pacing the narrow space behind the desk chair.

"You didn't tell anyone you were leaving DC." Walden understood why Seth was so over-protective of June, but with Oshiro on the job, she was in good hands. "No one knows you're here."

"I know. But—"

June's stomach growled, interrupting whatever worry Seth was about to voice. They all glanced at her, Walden chuckling and Seth with an indulgent grin.

"Guess the kid's made her position clear," Walden said.

Oshiro hung up and turned to them. "I've set up a bunch of dummy purchases in the DC area in case anyone's following your credit cards and booked you into a vacant grad student apartment here. Last place anyone would look for a pregnant woman and a former US Attorney."

"How'd you find a vacant student apartment in the middle of the semester?" Taylor asked.

"Didn't. Called a friend's kid and offered him a free week in a four-star hotel with all the room service and pay-for-view he could want. He's dropping off his keys in an hour—said to excuse the mess and you might want to wash the sheets."

Walden stood, clapping his hands together. "Lunch. I'm treating. Hofbräuhaus." Maybe this detail wouldn't be as difficult as he'd thought. Between Oshiro handling protection and Taylor's geeks tracking their subject, he and Lucy might have little to do except file the paperwork.

If this was going to be the last SAFE case, not a bad way to go. Especially after they nailed Daddy once and for all.

CHAPTER 9

—∿—

BY THE TIME Walden knocked on her door to tell Lucy that they were headed over to the Hofbräuhaus, she was engrossed in her second reading of the Baby Girl case files. The first time through, she'd been looking at the big picture of the events leading up to where they were today.

Now she was combing for clues. If they could identify and locate the man known as Daddy, they could end this.

"Did you realize he didn't actually put the Baby Girl images up for sale until after the incident at the mall?" she asked as she rubbed her eyes. She should use reading glasses for working at the computer but hated the way they pinched her nose.

"Yes. I figured he thought it was less risky that way, disseminating them after she's gone."

"I'm not sure. Seems to me, if he was ready to auction her off, he could have gotten more money for her by putting those up first." She frowned. Felt like she was close to understanding something important about how Daddy's mind worked.

"But he made a ton of money from the images—why bother selling her at all? Why not just destroy the evidence?"

Lucy rolled her shoulders. "He's been so careful, covering his tracks all these years. Selling June and releasing her images might be the only two mistakes he's made."

"Not much to go on—at least not for the past decade we've been hunting him."

"Are you really going to take a job with the Bank squad?"

Her abrupt change of topic didn't faze him—Walden was not easily fazed, period. "I think I'm due for a little peace and quiet. Something in short supply around here."

He was talking about what happened two months ago. She sighed. Couldn't everyone move on past that so things could get back to normal?

Except she had no clue what normal meant any longer. Just that it was going to be damned hard to return to anything remotely resembling it without Walden there acting as her counterweight.

"Are you coming to lunch?"

"I'll meet you there," she said, barely glancing up from the computer monitor.

"Sure?" He turned the affirmation into a question.

Lucy jerked her head up. "I can manage driving myself a few blocks. I just want to finish catching up." She hadn't been involved first hand, didn't have the intimate knowledge of the case that Walden, Oshiro, and Seth Bernhart had. Plus, she could sense there were patterns here, swirling just beneath the surface of all the random facts.

He met her gaze and nodded slowly. "Have a care, Lucy. This case will swallow you whole."

"Then why'd you bring it to me?" Especially now, she didn't add.

"Seemed a no-brainer when Seth called me yesterday. Right place, right time, right investigator." Lucy wondered if he meant himself or her. Didn't matter, she was in it now and wasn't about to be a liability, even if she was on modified duty.

She waved him away. "Order the *Jagerschnitzel* for me. I'll be there in twenty."

"You better. I'm not going to let good food get cold and go to waste."

He left and she turned back to the case files. They had Walden's investigative magic all over them.

It wasn't often that they were able to identify a victim of child porn, not with images found randomly on computers all over the world and dating back a decade. Hell, they hadn't even realized the collection *was* a collection of the same girl's images, not until Walden pieced it all together.

She imagined Walden, hunched over a computer in a dark room, spending his days and nights, hundreds of man-hours, examining frame-by-frame, pixel-by-pixel, the worst kind of horrific images. Four years ago, when he worked the Baby Girl case, he'd just lost his wife. He should have been lost in mourning—Lord knew she would have been if she lost Nick.

Instead, he'd poured his heart and soul and grief into saving one little girl.

New technology had helped to locate computers with the Baby Girl images but it had been a quirk of nature that had led Walden—and later, Seth Bernhart, the AUSA in charge of prosecuting the subjects who'd possessed the images—to June.

A birthmark. Not very large, just big enough and distinct enough to show up with image enhancement. They'd known the images were all taken in the same location, but they hadn't been able to prove they were all of the same girl—not as if they were time-stamped and not every subject had possessed the entire collection, so they found them randomly and out of order—until Walden followed the birthmark as it slowly grew with her.

Walden used the National Center for Missing and Exploited Children's database, thinking best-case scenario, he'd find a missing person's report or worst case, a Jane Doe autopsy report. Instead, he discovered a Jane Doe *found* report. From almost a decade before.

And then, with the help of Children and Youth, he and Bernhart had tracked June. Too late to save her, but in time to help them maybe save others with Bernhart's legal strategy.

When Lucy looked up, it was almost two o'clock— forty minutes since the others left for lunch. She grabbed her cane and bag and left her office, hoping Walden had ordered for her.

She was surprised to see Taylor still there, hunched over his keyboard, his face scrunched in concentration, resembling a toddler putting together a puzzle for the first time. As she watched, two of the High Tech Crimes guys were crouched low, trying to sneak up behind him, Nerf submachine guns at the ready.

Taylor's fingers barely broke their rhythm as he pulled a lever beside his computer, unleashing a catapult filled with Ping-Pong balls at one would-be assassin and, using the reflection in the computer monitor to aim, shot the other one with his pink pistol, firing over his shoulder.

"Awg…" Both techs moaned in fake dying agony as they writhed on the floor.

Then Taylor caught sight of Lucy. She was smiling but he spun in his chair, suddenly serious. Not because of her, she realized. Because of the damn cane.

"Clean that up," he ordered the techs. "Someone could slip and fall."

They scrambled to clear a path for Lucy, mumbling, "Sorry, boss." She wasn't sure if the words were for her or Taylor.

She crossed to his workstation without incident. "Thought you went to lunch with everyone else."

"No." His gaze slid back to his monitor with its lines of code. "This medical records hack…it's…poetic."

"Right." She knew better than to question his sense of cyber-esthetics, or to interrupt him when he was in the middle of analyzing code. "Want me to bring you back something?"

"Walden's got my order. I think I'm close to isolating his signature—"

Lucy left him to his cyberprowling and took the elevator down to the garage. She hated elevators so it was almost as much punishment as the stairs, but she was already exhausted and hungry and needed to conserve her energy. She was ready for another of the anti-inflammatory pills the doctors had prescribed—ibuprofen on steroids, he'd described it—but they ripped her stomach apart so she could only take them with food.

Her foot and ankle—hell the whole damn leg, not to

mention her back spasming from holding her body so stiffly—throbbed with the force of a sledgehammer. She opened the door of her Subaru Forrester and carefully shifted her weight onto the driver's seat. Before her injury she never would have imagined how complicated the mechanics of getting into and out of a vehicle could be. After she'd come home from the rehab hospital, she'd tried riding in Nick's Explorer, but it was too high to climb, forcing her to always put weight on her injured foot.

She'd needed a new car anyway, thought she'd just get another Impreza like her old one. She'd loved that car, the way it could out-accelerate just about anything on the road, especially around the twisty switchback mountain roads. But it was too low-slung. So she'd sacrificed both her five-speed manual transmission and her sports car for the SUV. She had to admit she did like riding up higher and she'd been able to adjust the seat and steering wheel so that it was as close to comfortable as any vehicle could get with her foot howling with each pothole, sharp turn, or sudden stop.

Thankfully the Hofbräuhaus was a straight shot down Carson from the Federal Building. And no potholes.

She pulled alongside the Cheesecake Factory, hoping to find a parking space. The Hofbräuhaus was directly in front of her. Beside it was the terraced amphitheater where summer concerts were held. The concrete steps that served as seating also led down the steep hill to the Heritage Trail that ran alongside the river and the boat landing. On both sides of the steps were zigzagged handicapped-accessible ramps and there were large concrete planters with small trees and shrubs scattered throughout the plaza.

No joy with parking, she'd have to circle around the block or hit the garage on Carson. As she pulled up to the stop sign on Water Street and signaled her turn, a group of people emerged from the Hofbräuhaus across the street. June and the others.

Seth had his arm around June's waist but he was in earnest conversation with Oshiro. June tilted her head up, her gaze searching the clear blue sky, hair ruffling with the March wind. There was supposed to be a storm front moving in later today but right now the sun was shining. June broke away from the men, her fingers trailing down Seth's arm, squeezing his hand before wandering off to perch against a nearby planter. She closed her eyes and stretched her body, basking, as if she hadn't seen sunlight in ages.

Seth and Oshiro continued their conversation, bodies angled toward each other, shoulders and heads hunched like football players huddled together on fourth and long. Walden spotted Lucy and sprinted across the street, coming around to her driver's side window. In his hand was a plastic bag, hopefully brimming with food for her and Taylor.

She rolled down her window. It was breezy, in the fifties—not bad for a Pittsburgh March. Walden leaned in. "Knew you wouldn't make it. Don't worry, I have you covered." He raised the bag, releasing the enticing aroma of *Jagerschnitzel* into the Forrester.

"Thanks. I lost track of—" Motion from the group across the street caught her attention. No. Not the men standing at the curb waiting for Walden to return with the car. Rather a motorcyclist speeding down Water

Street. The street was clear of traffic, yet he swerved directly at Seth and Oshiro. "What the——"

Before she could finish her thought, the motorcyclist raised a hand and aimed a gun at Oshiro and Seth Bernhart.

CHAPTER 10

—~~~—

WALDEN DROPPED THE food and sprinted across the
street as Lucy shouted a warning to Seth. Oshiro spotted
the weapon and spun to push Seth down. The gun went
off.

The motorcycle jumped the curb, ramming Oshiro,
the largest target, knocking his feet out from under him
and toppling him into Seth as he fell. With both men
down, the motorcycle, a large, wide-based Harley,
screeched as it changed trajectory. The cyclist wore a
visor, darkened to hide his face so it was impossible to get
a look at him.

Lucy gunned the engine, swerving the SUV to stay
out of Walden's line of fire as he aimed his weapon at the
motorcyclist. There was no clear shot because June was
too close, pinned between the six-foot-wide concrete
planter and the motorcycle.

The shooter saw his chance to grab a human shield,
hauling June across the body of the motorcycle. At the

sight of Walden standing in the road, aiming his pistol, a motorist on Water Street slammed his brakes. The car's fender clipped Walden, spinning him around and sending him sprawling to the ground.

Lucy only had time for a quick glance in the mirror to check on Walden as she twisted the steering wheel—couldn't ram the motorcycle and risk injuring June, but maybe she could get in front of him, block his escape on Water Street.

The motorcyclist had another plan altogether. Instead of veering back onto the street to make his escape, he swerved down the nearest ramp leading past the amphitheater and to the river.

Oshiro struggled to get up, blood covering his face and something obviously wrong with his arm. Seth crawled out from under him, calling June's name.

Lucy scanned the terrain in front of her. No way would the Forrester fit on the handicapped ramps and the steps were too steep. But adjacent to the plaza was an undeveloped parcel of land covered in dirt and weeds, surrounded only by a plastic mesh snow fence. She pressed down on the accelerator, twisted the steering wheel, and sent the SUV flying over the curb and through the fence.

Mud and decapitated plants churned the air as she raced through the lot, dragging stray lengths of bright orange plastic fencing material behind her. She aimed for the corner of the lot that overlooked the trail leading to the river, praying her memory was correct. If it was, then the slope of the trail meant the paved path lay only six to eight feet below the parcel she was speeding across—the SUV could make that drop as long as it didn't roll over.

Of course, even if she was right and the pavement was only a few feet below her, not the twenty-some feet it was on the opposite side of the plaza, then she still had one more problem—how to turn the SUV to stay on the path without it sliding down the hill and into the river.

Already planning her trajectory, she angled the Forrester and tried to gauge a speed fast enough to make the leap but slow enough to maintain control. Beside her, she spotted the helmet of the motorcyclist as he zigzagged down the ramp. The sharp turns and June's struggles had slowed him down. Good, she could still beat him to the riverside path. He must be planning to take it downriver to make his escape.

Or maybe he had a boat waiting at the landing? But that meant accomplices and planning—could they have put this all into motion during the hour June and the others had been inside having lunch?

The ground sped past too fast for her to finish her thoughts. She was out of time and flying through the air, her height enough to spy the dark waters of the Monongahela beyond the large concrete wall that suddenly appeared in front of her. Damn, she knew she'd forgotten something. Guess that solved the whole "what was going to stop her from driving into the river" problem.

Now it was a "how was she going to keep from slamming into a concrete wall when she finished flying off the side of the slope and hit the ground" problem.

The Girl Who Never Was: Memoirs of a Survivor
by June Unknown

Why Your Real World Wasn't Ever Mine

EVER SINCE THAT night in the mall, just about every adult I met who knew my truth acted like they'd rescued me.

Hellhole. Prison. Dungeon. That's what they called my home.

To me it was the world for the first ten years of my life. And for the next nine years, I tried desperately to go back—at first literally, and then when I understood that was a lost cause, figuratively.

I hated this "real" world. Everything moved too fast, sounded so loud I'd be exhausted from my constant startles and jerks. Space made no sense and I got sick every time I rode in a car or elevator.

And the people. So many people. Strangers, all of them, yet they crowded against me, sometimes touching me, talking at me with words I didn't understand, asking me things I didn't know how to answer. Often they'd just stare at me with the look Daddy used to get when I was a Bad Girl and disappointed him, made him re-do a picture or video or just didn't act like a Good Girl should.

Daddy would usually just shrug and ruffle his fingers through my hair, tell me "It's okay, Baby Girl," (unless I was really, really Bad, but I don't like to remember those times). Not these people. They'd get that look, frown, then talk above me, over my head to whatever adult was around as if I wasn't even there.

But they'd never leave me alone.

And there were so many rules I didn't know about and no one told me. Like wearing Dress Up clothes all day and night. All those buttons and zippers and laces and layers—inside out, backward, I had no clue what to do with them all. When it was time for Dress Up, Daddy always dressed me, gentle pushes, arms up, turn around, hold still, there you go, beautiful.

Here, all I got were yelling and spankings and laughed at.

Clothes were just the start. Social Worker and the grownups in the houses I went to—a new one over and over with new daddies and mommies and sometimes other kids, they were the worst, knew I didn't belong and made me pay for it every minute—they all talked to me about Good Touch and Bad Touch, but when you have no idea of the difference between private and public, and the only touch you've ever had came served with declarations of love, I didn't understand.

Just like I didn't understand about closing the door when using the toilet or being in there alone—I hated being alone almost as much as I hated being with these noisy, smelly people—or taking a shower by myself or not walking in when someone else was in there. Daddy and I did everything together. He was never, ever out of my sight, day or night, always within reach, except when I was a Very Bad Girl and he locked me in the basement, which was almost never.

Being sent to my room or forced to sleep in my own bed, all alone, all night long—those were torture. I needed to be with someone. Not all these people, not go outside and play with the kids (what was play?), I just needed that one person to protect me, keep me warm and safe, make me feel like everything would be okay.

I needed my daddy.

They looked at me funny every time I asked for him. Looked at me even worse, like I was going to make them cry, when I finally answered all their questions about Daddy and what it was like back home. Even then, they never went to get him or brought me back home. So I stopped talking.

Then I got sick all the time. I couldn't ever remember being sick back home with Daddy. The first time, it scared me. I thought I was dying like people on TV. The mommies told me to stop being a baby, it was only a cold. But they still kept taking me to the doctor where Bad Nurses gave me shots if I didn't have a fever, but then a day later, I would have a fever and feel even worse.

Sometimes at night, finally in quiet but all too alone, I'd let myself cry, making myself more miserable because one of Daddy's rules was Baby Girls Don't Cry, and I'd hug myself and pull my fuzzy blanket over my head to block out the rest of the world. I'd try so very hard to pretend it was Daddy holding me tight and keeping me warm and that he'd still be there in the morning when I woke.

The adults all acted like I should thank them, like they were heroes for taking me away from Daddy. Before I met Dr. Helen, a lot of them said it was okay if I was angry and hated Daddy.

How could I ever hate him? He loved me and I loved him. He kept me warm and safe and away from these crazy people and doctors and nurses who stuck me with needles all the time and social workers who wanted me to talk about things they didn't understand and from the new daddies and mommies who got so mad at me (one even hit me!) and the kids who said mean things and tried to take my fuzzy blanket and make me cry but I wouldn't let them.

I was safe at home with Daddy. Even the few times when I was a Very Bad Girl and we'd just see about that and give you some time to think about what you did and how you can be a Good Girl, I never felt scared.

Not really. Well, maybe a little. When I was a Very Bad Girl, Daddy would lock me in the basement with no lights I could reach to turn on and the house would go cold and quiet, so quiet, and I knew he was gone and not coming back until I figured out how to be Good again. I'd drink from the sink near the washer and eat cans of tuna fish he kept down there and sit in the dark and think about how to be a better Baby Girl.

The first time it was scary—not the dark, the being

alone for the first time ever. All my life Daddy was right there, close enough to touch, every second of every single day. I thought I might go crazy that first time left alone.

I cried. I couldn't help it, but then, finally, after a long, long, longest time, the door at the top of the steps opened and the light hurt my eyes but there he was, so big and strong, glowing like the sun and moon, like he was my whole wide world and I ran up and leapt into his arms.

He always came back. Always. And when he did, he always said the magic words, the best words in the whole wide world, the words no one here will ever say, not the way he did, not the way that made my insides glow like a light bulb had been clicked on so bright the light leaked out of me like a song coming straight from my heart.

When Daddy came back, he'd pick me up, give me a hug and say, "I love you, Baby Girl."

No matter how much time has passed, no matter how I know I should feel now that I'm grown and know the truth, how can I ever hate that man?

CHAPTER 11

IT WASN'T LIKE in the movies where stunt drivers were able to miraculously steer flying cars simply by wrenching the wheel and hanging on, jaw clenched. Thankfully, Lucy's memory of the topography had been close enough that she'd sent the Subaru off the side of the hill at an angle that pretty much aimed her where she wanted to go.

The few seconds she was in the air seemed to defy the laws of physics, the concrete wall looming in her windows, filling her vision. But then gravity worked its magic and the car fell back to earth, slamming into the pavement hard enough to send an explosion of pain through Lucy's foot and to jerk her body against her seatbelt, but not enough to make the airbags blow.

Thankful for the SUV's solid suspension that turned the collision into a series of severe bounces, she tapped the brakes and gingerly corrected her steering, wary of skidding into the concrete barrier. The rear fender scraped against the wall but she kept control, maneuvering the vehicle into the center of the wide paved path designed for bicyclists and pedestrians.

The motorcycle—June now clinging to her abductor, eyes wide with fear as he spun it fast and tight around the ramp's final switchback—was about twenty yards in front of Lucy, heading straight for the river.

As soon as Lucy cleared the concrete walls, she saw the river and a motorboat waiting. Now it was a real race, the Forrester and the motorcycle approaching the boat from opposite sides of the landing. Lucy took the straightest path, aiming to intersect the motorcycle and block its route. With limited room to maneuver, she held her course despite the motorcyclist swerving away from the river, obviously trying to steer around her.

He was almost past her, close enough for her to hear June's scream for help over the roar of the two vehicles, when she slammed the brakes, pulled up on the emergency brake, and wrenched the wheel, spinning the Forrester into a controlled skid. The vehicle pivoted, tires protesting, and came to a halt directly in front of the boat, forcing the motorcyclist to also brake hard.

Whoever was manning the boat—a man wearing a Steeler's cap and dark parka—must have decided to cut his losses because even as the motorcyclist was backing his bike up, fighting for room to cut around the Subaru, the boat's engine growled and it sped away.

Lucy flung open her driver's door, aiming her weapon at the motorcyclist. Seth came sprinting down the steps from the plaza above, calling to June. Not exactly the kind of backup she'd hoped for.

"Stop!" Lucy shouted.

The motorcyclist's face was invisible behind the dark

shield of his helmet but his head jerked in what appeared to be a nod. He pushed June off the cycle, sending her sprawling to the pavement, twisted the bike's handlebars, and roared off, heading down the trail. Lucy almost had a shot, but Seth ran right into her line of fire. Thankfully her reflexes were good enough that she released the trigger in time.

"June, are you all right?" Seth fell to his knees beside June, his hands running over her arms, legs, and belly, searching for injuries.

"I'm fine," she gasped. "It all happened so fast."

He pulled her into his arms, but kept his head raised, searching around them for any threat.

Lucy called the details into Pittsburgh law enforcement. "I got a fair look at the guy on the boat," Lucy told the dispatch operator. "Early to mid fifties, Caucasian, brown hair, Steeler cap, sunglasses, black parka, jeans. Nothing distinguishing."

"How about the boat?" he asked.

"One engine, it was good-sized, though." She closed her eyes in thought. She'd approached the boat from behind, surely there was a name? "Name started with K-A-T. Wasn't very long. One word. I couldn't see the rest. Katrina, maybe?"

"We have several other callers from your incident. EMS is also en route. I'll relay that the scene is safe for them to approach."

Lucy hung up and assessed the situation.

"How're Oshiro and Walden?" she asked Seth.

He glanced up the hill, panicked. "I'm not sure."

Seth helped June up onto her feet. Her knees were scraped but no other apparent injuries. "We need to get her out of here. Now." Urgency tightened his voice.

"I'm on it." The Forrester wasn't going to get them up the hill. She slung her bag over her chest, then took her cane and left the Subaru behind. As the three of them trudged up the steps, Lucy keeping her weapon close at hand and watching for any other attackers, she called Taylor. "Can I borrow your car?"

"Sure," he answered absently. "Why not sign out a pool car?"

"Because they have GPS and paper trails, and according to you, our guy is a poetic hacker. And someone just tried to grab June."

"Wait, what? Where are you?"

"Plaza beside the Hofbräuhaus."

"I'm on my way."

She turned to June. "You're sure you're okay? Want to get checked out?"

"No." June rubbed her belly. "She's kicking a bit, but everything feels fine. I didn't hit that hard, it wasn't far to fall."

"Maybe we should take you to a hospital," Seth said, his arm circled around her, keeping her so close their bodies touched as if he could act as a human shield.

"No," June repeated, more firmly. "He found me in a hospital before, remember?"

"How did they find us?" Seth asked, his gaze circling up and down the path.

"Wish I knew," Lucy answered. "But I think we shouldn't stick around here while we figure it out."

They made it to the plaza at the top. Oshiro still lay at the curb, a group of bystanders gathered around trying to help. His face was smeared with blood, one eye puffed and swollen, the skin around it split, and his expression black with rage. Walden knelt on the pavement beside him, holding pressure on Oshiro's arm but only using one hand.

"Son of a bitch," Oshiro said, pushing up to one elbow, grimacing with pain. "June, are you okay?"

She smiled at him. "I'm fine, thanks to Lucy. I'm so sorry—"

He shook her words away. "No. I'm sorry. It's my job to—"

Taylor arrived, screeching to the curb in his yellow MiniCooper, cutting short any more conversation. He jumped out, took in the scene. "Man, I miss all the fun."

The more serious a situation, the more Taylor's warped sense of humor appeared. Usually, it was a good way to diffuse the tension, but Lucy had no time for it now.

"Keys," she ordered.

He dropped them into her hand. Seth was already helping June into the front seat. The car wasn't as spacious as the Forrester or as inconspicuous as Lucy would have liked, but it was the best she could do on short notice.

"Is he going to be all right?" she asked Walden.

"Took a bullet to the arm."

"I'm fine," Oshiro protested. "Leave, go with June."

Walden nodded. He let Taylor take over holding the pressure dressing and started to stand. His knees buckled and he landed on his butt. That's when Lucy saw his left side: blood was streaming from his scalp and his left shoulder was definitely messed up, his arm hanging useless at his side.

"You're not going anywhere," she told him. "Taylor, see that they both get to the hospital," she ordered when both Walden and Oshiro looked as if they might protest. "And that they don't leave until they're both checked out."

She headed to Taylor's car where June and Seth waited. Seth twisted around in his seat, his posture filled with urgency. If Lucy hadn't had the car keys, she was certain he would have sped off without waiting.

"Take good care of her," Oshiro called as she limped around to the driver's side.

The ambulance pulled up, its siren drowning out any further conversation, so Lucy gave him a salute to indicate that she'd heard. Then she dropped into the low-slung car, her ankle protesting as she leaned weight onto it and adjusted the seat to a semi-comfortable position.

Full tank of gas, she noted. Only question was where the hell to go?

CHAPTER 12

LUCY TURNED ONTO Carson Street. "Where are you taking us?" Seth asked.

"Back to the Federal Building. You'll be safe there."

"No way. That's where they followed us from. Too many eyes—anyone could have tipped them off."

Paranoid. But with his wife and child on the line, she understood. Approved, even. It was that kind of thinking that might save him and June.

Instead of going straight toward the Federal Building, she turned left onto the Hot Metal Bridge. Best to make sure they weren't followed before deciding on a destination.

"June, did you recognize either of the men?" she asked.

"No." June stared out the window, her expression empty. Distancing herself from the emotions that came with almost being abducted or killed—Lucy had seen it in other victims. A good defense mechanism for the short term, but she knew Nick would argue that it was better to process trauma sooner rather than later.

"Walk me through it. What did you notice? The man's age, body build—did he speak to you?"

June shuddered and remained silent. Seth leaned forward between the two seats. "Stop badgering her. The guy had a visor; there was no way to see his face. He could have been young or old. with all the padding from his jacket there is no way to know his build. Satisfied?"

Lucy tried another tactic. "You drove up from DC last night. Did you use your own vehicle? Any chance someone followed?"

"No and no," Seth answered, sounding angry and more than a little frightened. "I asked a friend to rent a car for us. We met at a crowded bar where she slipped me the keys—we didn't even talk. June left the apartment building through the service entrance and I picked her up in the alley. It was empty. There was no one watching us and no one followed."

Lucy glanced away from the road long enough to meet his gaze. He was as confused as she was—he'd played it smart but not smart enough.

She dialed Taylor—the one person who might be smarter than their cyberpredators. "How's Oshiro?"

"Took two bullets. One went through the muscles in his arm, the other hit the side of his vest."

"Two?" She only heard one shot. Adrenalin did that, dampened sounds. "He was wearing a vest?" Of course he was—this was Oshiro they were talking about. Good thing, too.

"Are you kidding? He probably sleeps in one. Walden says they're waiting for X-rays to see if he cracked a rib, but he's already talking about leaving the hospital and coming back to work."

Oshiro was a lot like her; the idea of lying on a bed in a hospital while others finished the job was intolerable. "And Walden?"

"Shoulder dislocated, gash on his head that needs stitches. He wanted to leave against medical advice, but I convinced him to stay and let the doctors finish."

"Tell them we don't need walking wounded. Tell them my orders are to stay put until the doctors clear them." Oshiro wouldn't care what she ordered—he was outside her chain of command. But Walden might listen. "Anything from witnesses? Maybe video?"

"The locals are asking but so far nothing useful."

"Ideas on how they found June?" She put him on speaker and let Seth explain about the precautions he and June had taken on the way up from DC.

"What about passive surveillance?" Taylor's voice came through the phone. "RFID chips are so small someone could plant one on your coat and you'd never know it was there."

"Do they have the range needed?" Lucy asked.

"No. You're right. But active RFID would—they're slightly larger, need a power source. Or maybe someone planted code on their phones, activated the GPS?"

"Are you both carrying phones?"

"We have to for when if June goes into labor," Seth answered for both of them. "But I picked up prepaid SIM cards on the way here and swapped out our old ones. Wouldn't that take care of it?"

It was exactly what Lucy would have done, but... "Taylor?"

"This guy is good, boss. His hack with the medical records was like Mozart brilliant. I'd need the phones to analyze, see if he could have—"

"Toss 'em," Lucy commanded.

"No, boss," Taylor interjected. "Don't toss them—I might be able to get some good data off them. Put them on airplane mode or shut them off. Take the batteries out if you can. Seal them into a Faraday bag."

Right, one of the special lined bags the cybertechs used to protect confiscated electronics. "Where the hell am I going to find a Faraday bag?"

"You're in my car, remember? I've a stash in the back along with a kill box that will give you extra protection."

She nodded to Seth in the rearview. He folded down the seat beside him and reached into the back, emerging with a silver-colored padded bag. June dropped her phone into it and so did Seth.

"Okay, their phones are secured. What else could they be using to track us?"

"GPS on the cars—a lot of rentals have them now, but Seth's car is still here and you're in my personal vehicle, so no worries there."

"What else?"

"You're probably good. Except for physical surveillance, of course."

"There's no one. And we're not taking a direct route."

"Can I ask, where are you going?"

She hesitated. Not because she didn't trust Taylor but because, despite his assurances, she didn't trust the technology. "I'll call you when we get there." She hung up.

Seth turned to her. "Then I'll ask. Where are we going?"

Lucy grimaced. It hurt to even think about, the one place she'd been avoiding for fifty-nine days. "My mother's house."

The Girl Who Never Was: Memoirs of a Survivor
by June Unknown

You Can Never Go Home, but Sometimes Home Comes to You

"IT'S BEEN FOUR months and she still won't speak," Social Worker told New Doctor. We're at New Doctor's house, which was all wide, bright windows overlooking a garden filled with color. It looked so peaceful out there I wanted to walk barefoot in the grass. But, of course, I was inside, sitting on the floor drawing pictures of the flowers, listening to the grownups talk about me above my head. They sip coffee and sit on comfy-looking chairs. So different than all the other doctors' offices. "I've finally gotten her to wear clothes— you'd think she was an animal, running wild and naked."

"I suspect that was how she lived before you found her." I liked New Doctor's voice. It was soft and measured; it felt safe. She had said call her Helen, but I don't call anyone anything—why should I? They're here and gone so fast.

"Doesn't make my job any easier. Seventeen placements. Some didn't last more than a night."

"Why not?" New Doctor asked.

She had hair that is more than one color—most of it is dark, dark brown—Sienna, if I used my 128 Crayons to draw it—but there's this streak of white down the front over one side I can't stop staring at. It's like someone painted it. I like the idea. Wonder if I could paint myself—only I wouldn't do it to make people look at me, I'd paint myself to blend in so no one could see me and then I could have peace and quiet without people always wanting things from me.

Social Worker, her red hair tied back in a scarf today, glanced my way but I pretended to ignore her. Her voice lowered, the way it does when grownups want to talk about me but think I can't hear. Just because I had nothing to say to them didn't mean I wasn't listening.

"If there's an adult male in the house, she crawls into bed with them. Naked." Her voice up ticked as if this were a Bad Thing.

It wasn't. It was natural. That's what Daddy said. I couldn't help it if these other, different, new daddies didn't know how to love a Baby Girl the way she should be loved. But at night when it was cold and I was all alone, I needed Daddy. Even if it was a substitute daddy.

"And she touches them," Social Worker finished. "It's most inappropriate."

New Doctor made a noise like she was sad. But she

smiled at me so I knew it wasn't me making her sad. That made me feel good, so I smiled back. "Obviously, she's been taught otherwise. Conditioned over years— it's going to be difficult to retrain her to fit into society."

"That's why I came to you. My supervisor shared your research with me. Said you had pretty much retired? We thought—I mean, there's no money or anything in it, but I could get you approved. And it's better than Western Psych."

"An institution is the last thing this girl needs." New Doctor sounded serious. I realized she was fighting. For me.

I paid more attention. If New Doctor liked me, could I trust her to find Daddy? It had been so long, I couldn't remember his face, barely his voice. I missed him so much. There were too many people here, too much yelling and noise and touching. I didn't want them. I wanted Daddy. I wanted to go home where it's just me and him.

"Any violence?" New Doctor asks. "Acting out besides the hypersexuality?"

Social Worker shook her head, her ponytail bouncing. My hair used to be long enough for a ponytail, but one of the mommies at one of the new places cut it. Said it was gnatted and might give me lice.

"No. She's extremely docile—would sit all day, staring into space, if you didn't tell her to do something. First week she wouldn't even use the toilet or eat without being given permission."

New Doctor nodded. She didn't say anything but she looked at me like she knew every secret I had. It didn't scare me—I have no secrets. I just wanted to go home. To Daddy. Anytime anyone asked me, I told them. Because it was the truth.

"I should warn you, though," Social Worker said, staring at her shiny blue shoes that match her scarf. "According to our testing, she'll always be Special Needs. Her vocabulary is severely limited, she can't read or write, has no math skills, and as best we can assess, limited comprehension. I doubt she'll ever be able to be integrated into a main stream educational program."

New Doctor watched me watching Social Worker and winked at me. "We'll just see about that."

"So you'll do it?" Social Worker was so excited the scarf almost bounces free from her hair.

"It's not up to me," New Doctor said.

"I'll get authorization—"

"No. That's not what I mean." New Doctor left her chair to kneel down in front of me. She didn't touch me except with her gaze. She looked me in the eye and I looked back at her.

"June," she said, her voice soft and gentle like the fuzzy blanket Social Worker gave me that first night. I take it everywhere, wrap myself in it, so much better than the tight, scratchy Dress Up clothes they make me wear every day.

"Would you like to stay here?" New Doctor said. "Just you and me? Here in my home?"

Hope warmed me like fresh-baked cookies still hot from the oven. Here? Where it was so quiet and felt more like home than anything had since Daddy put me in the back of the van that day so long ago? It's not *my* home, but...

"It's up to you, June. Would you like this to be your new home?"

Stay here or go back to noise and confusion and no Daddy? "Yes, please."

CHAPTER 13

LUCY BACKTRACKED ALONG all the hidden, unmarked, and unnamed roads she'd grown up driving on, avoiding going through Latrobe itself or up Route 981, even though that was the most direct route. Part of it was making sure they weren't followed; a lot of it was avoiding the inevitable: going home for the first time since her mom was killed.

She loved driving these twisty, narrow roads, many of them unnamed and unmarked. Loved the way they started out as gentle, rolling farm lanes but then, with a single turn, ended up perched high on a mountain, overlooking the valley sprawling below. The trees were still barren, spring wouldn't have them budding for another month or so, but as the storm front from the west caught up with them, just as the weathermen had promised, the lack of leaves served to open up the vistas even more, providing stunning glimpses of dark, high-stacked anvil cloud formations.

Finally, she circled through the state park, passing the

1950's era dam that towered over the Loyalhanna River to form the lake to the south. The house she'd grown up in, the only home she'd known before leaving for college, was up in the mountains beyond the river, surrounded by forest. The nearest house was almost three miles away. There were two state-owned cabins a mile or so down a logging road, but old, isolated, and in disrepair, they were rarely rented out anymore. Folks preferred the convenience of being near the lake with its recreation area and full-service campgrounds including Wi-Fi and cell reception.

When she pulled off the two-lane road that switchbacked up the mountain and onto the drive that led to her family home, a wave of nostalgia hit her, more like a tsunami crashing down on her, memories of all the hundreds of time she'd driven this way.

Her and Dad returning home with the perfect Christmas tree strapped to the truck; her mom and her coming home from the grocery store, their bags laden with ingredients to create the best Thanksgiving feast imaginable; the rustle of crinolines and smell of fresh flowers from her mother's corsage after Lucy made her first communion; the fear in her mother's eyes when they came home from the hospital that first time her father collapsed and the doctor had told them he had cancer; Megan in her car seat, not even two months old, that first trip up to visit her mom...so many memories of coming home, and for each and every one, Lucy's mom was there to greet her.

Until today. Suddenly, the pain in her leg was nothing compared to the knot of grief that tightened her chest. The gusting wind, driven by the approaching storm, swirled dead leaves across the drive in front of her as if stirring dire dregs in a fortune teller's tea cup. Omens and portents. Or merely the weight of grief. She couldn't tell.

Finally, the house appeared. It was a simple ranch design, nothing fancy about it except the gingerbread her father had hung along the porch eaves and a river rock chimney at one end. Her dad had died when Lucy was twelve, but before the cancer, that's what he did: built houses. Not just houses, he'd say proudly, homes. But now the red bricks, forest green shutters, and cream siding all looked dull and faded compared to Lucy's memory.

She pulled the MiniCooper to a stop in front of the garage and sat there. Seth climbed out of the back, his joints cracking from being folded into the small confines for so long, and helped June out. Still Lucy sat, staring at the front door. Family never used the front door; they went in through the always-open garage, directly into the laundry room and kitchen.

But today, the garage was closed. Today, no one was waiting, anticipating their arrival with a fresh pot of coffee and homemade *pizelles* still warm, the kitchen smelling of anise and cinnamon.

Seth guided June up the walk to the front door, supporting her with an arm around her waist. She stopped and looked back at Lucy, said something to Seth. He left her reluctantly and returned to open Lucy's door for her.

"Is it your leg?" he asked kindly. "I could tell it was hurting—those bumpy roads didn't help, I'm sure." As he spoke, he reached into the back seat and retrieved her cane and bag. He handed her the cane and took her elbow, and before she knew it, he had her out of the car and standing once more. Funny to see a man whose opponents nicknamed him the Hawk capable of such gentle compassion.

Watching him with June, it shouldn't have surprised her, but somehow it still did. As if there were an undercurrent of the aggressive prosecutor hiding beneath his domesticated demeanor.

"Thanks," she said, handing him her keys. "The silver one will open the front door."

He still held on to her arm, his warmth reaching her even through the layers of her clothing. "Walden told me about your mother. What happened. Thank you for this, this gift of shelter. I can't tell you what it means to us."

She looked away, unable to answer, and focused on the small green buds daring to show on the azaleas surrounding the walk. Soon they'd unfold into a riot of scarlet and fuchsia, announcing the arrival of spring. But no one would be here to see them bloom.

Seth squeezed her arm and returned to June. Lucy watched them climb the steps, cross the porch, and open the door as if the house belonged to them. Or they belonged there. She inhaled, the scent of the approaching storm cleansing the air. Then she limped up the path to the house that in her heart would remain forever empty.

———◆———

"MOM'S NOT COMING." Megan didn't bother turning the statement into a question as she slid into the empty passenger seat of her father's SUV when he picked her up from school. She tossed her backpack into the rear and settled in, knees folded, feet pressed against the dash.

"It's her first day back to work." Her father. Always taking Mom's side of things. Like Mom was some kind of superhero out there saving the whole wide world. Megan knew better. Her mom couldn't save anyone, not when it really counted. Her mom was just a mom—and not a very good one at that.

"First day of *light* duty. *Paper* work," she said. Megan caught her father's glare at her sarcastic tone but ignored it. "Do you have any idea what she's doing today, Dad?"

"Yes. I spoke to her at lunch." He paused, his expression a familiar one. His editorial look—the one where he decided how much to tell her and how much to keep a secret.

Megan was tired of people trying to protect her, treating her like a child. She'd been right there with her mom and dad two months ago when that man, that creep, that sonofabitch who murdered her grams. She'd been there—hell, she'd been the one to help bring him down before the cops shot him.

She'd protected both of her parents that day. Not her mom, the one who carried a gun and whose job it was to keep people safe. People like her grams.

If Megan couldn't trust her mom, the woman who'd saved so many innocent victims, who'd stopped so many bad guys, if she couldn't trust her to keep her family safe, then who could she trust?

No one. That's who. She only had herself. Fine. Whatever. She could deal with that.

She tightened her arms wrapped around her knees. "You have no clue what Mom was doing today."

Her father turned to glare at her. "Don't you use that tone of voice with me, young lady."

"I'm just telling you the truth." She straightened her legs and sat up straight. They stopped at a red light and she took the opportunity to pull her phone out. "Look. This is Mom's so-called desk duty. She lied. To both of us."

For a psychologist, her dad had a piss-poor poker face. He watched the video of the crazy motorcycle dude crashing into two men then snatching up a pregnant woman and her mom driving after him—off the side of a hill!

Frustration, fear, and anger all took a turn but finally he just looked sad. Disappointed. The look Megan dreaded ever being on the receiving end of.

"She had no choice," he said, facing forward as the light turned green. "That pregnant girl could have been hurt."

"She always has a choice," Megan interrupted before he could tell her—again—how important Mom's job was, how she did what she did to save lives. What about their lives? What about Mom's? "Isn't that what you're both always telling me? To think things through, make good decisions."

His mouth twisted at that, ring finger drummed against the steering wheel. Wow, he really was pissed off this time. Megan leaned back again, satisfied that her dad finally saw how out of control her mom was.

"Megan, you can't jump to conclusions and get angry at your mom without even—"

"Even hearing her side of things? Explaining why it's okay when she goes risking her life? Maybe getting hurt.

Again. Maybe she has her reasons. Who knows? She's not answering her phone. At least not when I tried." She flounced back in her seat. "Maybe you'll have better luck."

He was silent until they passed Murrysville and got clear of the traffic. That was her dad. He thought things through. Sometimes it drove her nuts—no need to think about what was obvious; you just did it. Of course whenever she said anything like that, he'd tell her she was so very much her mother's daughter. Passionate and compassionate. Whatever the heck that meant.

Right now, being told she was just like her mother was the biggest insult Megan could imagine.

"Your mother is not ignoring you on purpose. I'm disappointed you'd even think that. Even if you don't like her job, she still deserves your respect." He slid his phone free from his inside pocket and handed it to her. "Give her a try. She was probably busy earlier, though, so it won't mean anything if she picks up now. But you two need to start talking. To each other."

Yeah. Right. Megan took the phone. "Dad, you forgot to put it on the charger while you were at work again. It's dead."

CHAPTER 14

LUCY DIRECTED SETH and June to the bath, fresh linens, and a bed for June. She couldn't bear to walk down the hall to her mom's room, see the photos and memories there, then felt guilty when he glanced at her cane, assuming that was the reason she didn't join them. While he helped June get cleaned up, Lucy heated one of the many frozen entrees her mom had left behind, carefully packaged and wrapped in foil. Coletta Guardino did not believe in microwaves.

Eggplant parmigiana, one of her favorites. While it was cooking, Lucy rummaged through the kitchen drawers. First, the "junk" drawer, where she found a map of Pennsylvania and the Mid-Atlantic states, along with an assortment of felt-tip markers. Then the "scrap" drawer where, among the carefully folded pieces of tin foil and wax paper, ready to be reused when needed— Coletta also believed in never wasting anything, especially not when it'd only been used once or three times—she found a ball of assorted pieces of string tied together.

Lucy unfolded the map and spread it over the kitchen table. She'd left her coat on but the heat had finally kicked in and with the oven on, the kitchen was growing warm, so she hung it on the back of a chair as she studied the map. Where to start?

Tentatively, she marked the location of the mall where June was found fourteen years ago. Stood back and stared, letting the map fill her mind, her gaze spiraling out from the landmark. There was a pattern—no matter how desperate subjects were to make their movements appear random, there was always a pattern.

She added the location where Oshiro had arrested Green Elephant Man that night before they knew he had anything to do with June. Then also added his home in a town another thirty miles away. The three points created a vector—the approach Green Elephant Man would have taken from his home to pick up June at the mall. A total of almost fifty miles from point to point.

But it wasn't Green Elephant Man she was interested in. It was Daddy.

Her meal heated through, she paced around the table, looking at the map from all angles. Funny how her ankle didn't bother her as much, not now that she had something to focus on. She ate right out of the tray—Coletta would not have approved, not at all.

Lucy finished eating and had to stop herself before putting the aluminum foil and tray into the dishwasher. No one left to use them again. She crumpled them and tossed them into the trash.

Turning back to the map, she used the string to draw

an arc with a highlighter, about fifty miles away from the mall in the direction opposite the one Green Elephant Man traveled from. Yeah, that felt right. While it would have been clever to overlap his customer's path, it also would have felt risky. When arranging the drop-off for June, it would have been natural to find a place between Daddy's home base and his buyer.

Which meant Daddy lived beyond that highlighted semi-circle. "Only leaves the rest of the whole freakin' country," Lucy muttered as Seth came in from the hallway.

"Coffee?" he asked, sounding weary despite the fact that it was barely four o'clock. It'd been a long couple days for him and June.

"Just finished brewing." He turned, facing the counter and the coffeemaker but the glazed expression said he didn't even register the appliance. Lucy took pity on him, fetched a mug from the cabinet beside the stove and poured him a cup.

"Fridge is empty, so no milk. Plenty of food in the pantry and freezer if you're hungry."

"This will do," he said absently, looking down at her handiwork.

"June okay?"

"Exhausted. She's taking a nap, got her feet up."

There was an awkward silence. She wanted to get back to work, let her mind fall into the pattern she sought, but it was impossible with him standing there watching.

"So it's a girl? Do you have a name yet?" she asked, twirling her highlighter.

"No. Nothing seems right. My mom offered my grandmothers' names, but Bettina and Gertrude…"

He didn't need to mention that of course June had no grandmothers—or any family names to fall back on. She didn't even own her own name; it'd been created for her by a social worker and a calendar.

"Don't worry. You'll know the right one when you find it." Lucy paused, staring at the map but thinking of other patterns. "June's DNA is in the system, right? Mitochondrial as well?"

"Of course. We've never had any hits. It's weird, hoping that someday a tech will call and tell us that they've found a corpse that could be one of her parents or that they've arrested a man who's her father."

"She believes Daddy really is her biological father?" Seemed like most people would want to deny that as long as possible. But then June hadn't been raised like anyone else she'd ever met. What a tangled existence she must lead—it was good she had someone solid and dependable like Seth at her side.

"We both do. Now." She wondered what he meant by that but before she could press, he gestured to her geographic profile. "You're missing the others."

Lucy glanced up. "What others?"

"Walden didn't tell you? Guess he wouldn't—it's only a theory and not like anyone else is actively working the case. At least not until today." He raised his mug, realized his hand was shaking and set it down again. Lucy could understand his bitterness. This was the woman he loved they were talking about.

"What theory?"

Seth slid into the seat at the head of the table and slid the map around so it faced him. "After we identified June and linked her to the Baby Girl images and Daddy,

Walden kept looking for more victims."

"But Daddy never posted any new images."

"Right. Why should he? The Baby Girl collection would have provided plenty of income, not to mention the money he was paid for June."

"Except this was never about money. It's about something more. An offender like Daddy wouldn't have any normal adult relationships. June was his sole companion for years." She tapped her marker against the map over the site of the mall. "His mistake was in letting her live. He wouldn't make the same mistake again."

"He didn't. Walden found a pattern. The first victims are from the same day June was left at the mall. While she sat there waiting for Daddy to return, he was off picking up his next victims—a twenty-two-year-old and her four-month-old baby coming out of a doctor's office not ten miles away. Then, six years later, a girl's body was found not far from where another child—this one a toddler—was taken. And again four years after that."

"The girl's body was the baby taken the same day June was abandoned at the mall?"

He nodded. "Confirmed by DNA. But they never found the mother."

Lucy blinked, the pattern of time and space swirling through her mind, a whirlwind of depravity. "He might have a girl now."

"The last one taken would be almost five now. If she's still alive. If Walden is right and these cases truly are linked."

"Where? I need to know the exact locations. We might be able to get some idea of where he's operating from."

"*If* he doesn't move house with each girl. That was Walden's theory. Figured this guy was too smart and careful to stay in the same place."

Lucy stared at the map, not blinking for so long that tears blurred her vision. "No. He's wrong. This guy, the world revolves around him. His needs, his wants. He's king of his universe. And every king—"

"Has a castle." Seth pursed his lips, also staring at the map. He leaned forward eagerly, both hands fisted on the table. "Do you think we can find him?"

"I hope so." Lucy already had her cell out—there was no landline at the house, hadn't been for years, not since the new cell tower to the south made it easier and less expensive to use a cell phone—and called Walden. "Finding him might be the only way to save that little girl now that he's searching for a replacement."

"Not searching," Seth reminded her in a grim tone. "Found. He wants my baby."

CHAPTER 15

WALDEN LOOKED UP from his phone as a nurse wheeled Oshiro back into his bed space at Three Rivers Medical Center's ER. It was strange to see someone like Oshiro diminished to a mere patient, dressed in a flimsy gown, one arm bandaged and in a sling matching Walden's. Walden averted his gaze from the sight of Oshiro's hairy legs as the nurse helped him climb back onto the bed. Not because he knew the deputy marshal would be embarrassed by being half-naked—Oshiro couldn't care less about modesty and neither did Walden—but because he knew his friend would hate him seeing how vulnerable and weak Oshiro was right now.

"Two cracked ribs," the nurse announced gleefully. "The doctor wants to watch him overnight. We'll get the antibiotics for his arm started down here and they can finish them upstairs once we have a room ready."

Oshiro pressed the control to raise the head of his bed. He was taking short, shallow breaths and his usually tan face was pale with the pain. "Tell him thanks but no thanks. I'm going home."

She frowned down at him, giving him one of those looks that nurses and priests took special classes to master. That "obey me or suffer the consequences" look. Walden hid his smile as he watched Oshiro muster the strength to counter with his own patented "obey me or I'll blow you away, mo'fucker" glare.

Neither backed down but a page overhead caught the nurse's attention. "I'll let the doctor know. It might mean signing out against medical advice."

"Whatever."

"Fine. I'll send in the nursing student to re-start your IV." She turned to leave but looked back over her shoulder. "It's her first day and she needs the practice." The privacy curtain rattled shut behind her and she was gone.

"Give me my pants back," Oshiro ordered. "No way are they gonna turn me into a human pincushion."

"You didn't see the mess that bullet made of your arm," Walden said. It was a through-and-through wound, the best kind, but the bullet track had been filled with pieces of Oshiro's clothing and dead flesh that the doctor had picked out and flushed clean. "Trust me, you want as many antibiotics as you can get."

Oshiro turned his head to look at his right arm wrapped in a bulky bandage. And winced with even that slight movement.

"Maybe some pain meds as well," Walden suggested.

"No. I need to keep my head clear. Bad enough they gave me that stuff while they were cleaning my arm."

Whatever they'd given Oshiro, they must have

under-calculated because it wore off all at once with him jerking away, fists up, ready to fight, pulling out his original IV. Walden had been glad they hadn't tried to give him any of the same medicine. His doctors had used a local anesthetic on the gash in his scalp, which now sprouted an assortment of surgical staples, and his broken collarbone hadn't needed anything more than a special figure-eight wrap and a sling he intended to ditch as soon as they got out of here.

"Where are June and Seth?" Oshiro asked.

"Safe. With Lucy. She's keeping their location off the radar—Taylor's worried this guy has a way to compromise cell phones."

"Seth ditched their SIM cards before they headed here yesterday. Swapped them for prepaid ones. Untraceable."

"Taylor wants to analyze them, but he thinks that's how they were tracked from DC. Worried about some new kind of remote hack that doesn't rely on SIM cards."

"Shit." Oshiro practically whistled the syllable as the implications for law enforcement sank in. If Taylor was right, then almost every phone would be open for hackers to scrounge around in, accessing private financial data, using the cameras to grab intimate photos or videos, recording sensitive calls...privacy would cease to exist anywhere within range of an affected phone.

"Why didn't they drive up with the guys from the protective detail you set them up with?"

"Seth didn't trust that they hadn't been made. Figured if they stayed behind, acted like business as usual, it would give him and June room to escape without detection." Oshiro frowned. "Those guys were the best,

Walden. They're who I'd call if it was my family. But this guy beat them—"

"I know. Lucy has it covered."

"No. You should go. Don't waste your time here. Go help June."

Walden scrutinized his usually inscrutable friend. It wasn't like Oshiro to get so emotionally involved. "How did Seth pay for that security team? Even though they've won all those judgments, it's not like any of the defendants have actually paid out yet."

Oshiro looked away.

"You paid for them yourself."

He looked back, defiant. "I live alone, work sixteen hours a day, what else do I have to spend my money on?"

"A new vest for one thing," Walden said. "You really care about her, don't you?"

Oshiro's glower was dark and threatening. Walden backed off an obviously sensitive subject. "Seth told you. Did he make you promise?"

"You, too?"

Walden nodded. "Said he's dying. Was supposed to be dead already according to the doctors."

"And we have to look after June and the baby once he's gone." Oshiro's tone was solemn. "I gave him my word."

"Me, too."

They sat in silence for a few minutes when Walden's phone rang. "Lucy, what's up?"

"How's Oshiro?"

"Fine. Ornery as ever. Docs want to keep him overnight but he's saying no."

"And you? Did they fix your shoulder?"

"X-rays showed it's a broken collarbone. I can't do much with my left arm, but other than that I'm fine. Where are you? I can head right out if you want."

"What about that crack on the skull you took? Don't the doctors want to watch you as well?"

Yes. But he wasn't going to tell her that. "You know me. Skull's hard as a rock. I'm fine. Ready to get back to work."

She made a noise that said she was skeptical. "I'm building a geographic profile and Seth told me you had some data points to add. Said there were more victims and burial sites." Her tone was neutral, lacking her usual warmth. For Lucy that said a lot.

"I would have told you sooner, but I had the techs analyze those locations and the time line every which way but Thursday. You can't imagine how frustrating it was to know we figured out this guy's pattern just months after he grabbed the last kid."

He blew out his breath and regretted it as pain shot through his shoulder and radiated up into his neck and skull. "I'm telling you, there's nothing there. This guy must have the resources to pick up stakes every few years—and the savvy to cover his tracks."

"The last girl, Missy Barstow? She might still be alive. She's young enough—"

"That he wouldn't have traded her in for a younger model," he said bitterly. "Christ, Lucy, this guy..." He didn't finish. He had no words adequate for the vile evil this guy embodied.

"Give me the dates and places. Let me take another look." Lucy's approach differed from what the analysts at Quantico's NCAVC did. She combined geographic information with behavior, psychology, and—according to several of the cybertechs—voodoo to narrow her search. Even she couldn't explain it totally, but no one could argue with her results. She'd netted one of the country's most notorious serial killers as well as tracking other predators.

Walden was silent. Not because he disagreed with her, but because he was busy cursing himself. He'd been working this case alone for so long that he hadn't even thought to bring Lucy on board before now. He'd let his stubborn pride blind him—he'd wanted to be the one to capture Daddy. Foolish, arrogant, idiot. He might have cost a little kid her life.

"Do it," Oshiro said. "Lucy's the best tracker I've ever worked with."

High praise indeed coming from Oshiro. Also something he'd never say if he wasn't under the influence of strong drugs. Still, he was right.

"Got a pen and paper?" He gave Lucy the data. No need to check his files, he had it memorized. Thought about those poor kids all the time.

"We're sure it's Daddy, not some other predator?"

"No, but the BAU guys said it would fit his profile."

"We don't know enough about him to build a profile," she said. Lucy was not a big fan of the BAU profiles, he knew. They'd led her astray too many times by being either too vague or too specific.

"But the time line and locations fit. It has to be him," Walden argued. "Besides, what else do we have to go on?"

She made a small noise of agreement. "So, we have an adult female with an infant, and two toddlers taken? But no adult bodies? Just the two girls?"

"My thought was he gets rid of the women as soon as he no longer needs them to care for the babies. Worried about the risk, so changed to grabbing toddlers instead."

"They never surfaced? June's mother and the woman he grabbed the day he abandoned her at the mall?"

"No. But the girls—he leaves them where they'll be found. They're washed, no trace evidence at all, wrapped in plastic—not a tarp, more like shrink wrap, like they're dolls or something. Remote locations with no cameras, then anonymous calls, untraceable, to 911."

"He cares about what happens to them."

"Warped as it sounds, yeah." He rubbed his temple; he'd been doing this for too damn long if these scumbags were starting to make sense to him. Maybe it was a good thing he was moving to the bank squad. Time for a transfer to a desk.

After he caught this sonofabitch.

———•———

LUCY FINISHED PLOTTING the other points Walden gave her. Locations where women and children were stolen, locations where the girls' bodies were found. She added a time line on a sheet of parchment paper as well.

Tracing the locations over time, they formed a definite spiral—a bit zigzagged, but that was to be expected. People liked to think they could be truly random, but in reality, their habits always imposed order onto the chaos.

"There's one more point if it helps," Seth said. He'd watched her in silence, drinking his coffee and Lucy had almost forgotten he was there.

"What's that?"

"Washington DC, five months ago."

His tone held more bitterness than the dark brew in his mug. Lucy glanced up. "What happened five months ago?"

"That's the day I met him. June's daddy." He set the mug down. It rattled against the tabletop, his hand shook so bad. But his voice was steady. As was his gaze. "That's the day he killed me."

CHAPTER 16

LUCY STARED AT Seth. He stared right back. Gave her a slow nod as if his head was too heavy to lift. She remembered this morning thinking how gaunt he looked, aged prematurely—he was only thirty.

"Tell me everything."

He raised his mug but set it back down without drinking, using the time to collect himself. "This was before the threat on the judge when we got protection. I was leaving my office on the way to file some motions, when a man called my name. He walked up, shook my hand, and said he'd heard what I was doing and wanted to thank me. Then he was gone again."

"What'd he look like? Where were you—on the street? How about his voice?"

"There were no cameras anywhere around. It was a cold morning, he wore an overcoat with the collar turned up and a scarf, had glasses and a tweed hat. I remember thinking he was a professor—but I think that's just because he looked like the one I had for Constitutional

Law. Brown eyes. Forties, fifties, who knows? Nothing special."

He paused, his lips twisting into a grimace. "Except he wore gloves. And when he shook my hand, I could tell they were really thick. Figured the guy didn't like cold hands, didn't think anything of it until the next day when the funeral flowers came."

"You traced the delivery?"

"Nothing there. Paid with a prepaid credit card, delivery guy took the order over the phone, no way of tracing it. The card said 'Warm thoughts for June after the untimely, early demise of her husband.' Signed with initials."

"You thought it came from him?"

"I thought it came from another crackpot. You have to understand, ever since we started this, I get a dozen death threats a day. Only thing different about this one was that it came in the real world instead of anonymous emails and tweets from Internet trolls."

"How did you finally put it together?"

"Not me, my paralegal—she loves puzzles. The guy signed it HG. That's the chemical symbol for mercury. And the florist's logo is Mercury, the winged messenger. Then our entire office was flooded with spam about some miracle cure involving mercury—all untraceable, of course. She made me go see my doctor and ask him about mercury poisoning. Turns out she was right."

"But that was five months ago? If they found out so fast, why couldn't they do something about it?"

"I think that's why this guy basically told me what he'd done—he knew they couldn't do a damn thing about it. They tried all the standard chelation therapies, but this is a rare form of mercury. One drop absorbed through the skin and you're toast. But the kicker is, you won't see any symptoms for weeks, maybe even months. Then, once they arrive, you have only days before you're dead."

He wrapped both his hands around his coffee mug. "I've lived weeks longer than the experts thought I would. My doctor can't wait to write up the case report—says there was a chemistry professor had the same thing happen to her, by accident, he wants to compare my brain to hers at autopsy."

"June doesn't know?"

"No. She has enough to worry about. After everything she's been through, how can I tell her that she's about to raise our child alone?"

Lucy didn't agree—if it was her, she'd want time to prepare. But she didn't know June and Seth, not well enough to interfere in their marriage. "Oshiro? Walden?"

"I told them. Made them promise to protect her no matter what. And my family—they don't know I'm dying, but they love June. She and the baby will always have a home with them."

She thought about it. Daddy's perfect revenge on the man who dared to fall in love with his Baby Girl and wanted to raise her daughter. God, what a twisted, evil sonofabitch.

"How long do you have?"

"I started to have weird muscle twitches last week. Sometimes my arms or legs, they'll just give out on me. And I'm weak—not just tired, physically weak." He lifted his mug with both hands as if to demonstrate. "Maybe another week. Maybe just a few days. I can tell my brain is foggy, slow to react."

He gave her a sad smile. "Funny thing is that probably saved my life. When that guy pulled his gun and aimed it at me, I wanted to turn and run but instead my leg gave out and I ended up tripping and falling. Bullet went right past me."

And into Oshiro. "You're sure he was aiming at you, not Oshiro?"

Tactically, it would make sense for the shooter to target the greatest threat first—Oshiro. But if Seth was right, he'd aimed first at the man least likely to be able to stop him.

"You don't forget a big, fucking gun aimed right at you. When I fell, Oshiro was moving to intercept the shooter, ended up in the line of fire."

"If Daddy already poisoned you and knows you're dying, why would he want to kill you now?" Did they have two crazy ass factions out there gunning for June and Seth?

"The doctors said I should have been dead a month ago, but they bought me more time with new experimental therapies. Maybe Daddy is upset that I might be around to see my baby born?"

"Maybe he wants you totally out of the picture so he can move on June?"

"Or maybe he's just playing with me."

She jerked her head up at that. "Seth, have you been in contact with Daddy?"

"Yeah. I think. Not sure. But I get these anonymous messages—as soon as I read them, they vanish. I had the computer forensic guys check and they said they can't trace them."

"Maybe Taylor—"

He shook his head. "It's too late. He's here. I can feel it. And he's coming after June. This is our last chance to stop him."

CHAPTER 17

AS THEY PULLED up in front of Gram's house, Megan spotted a familiar car in the driveway.

"Taylor. What's he doing here?" she asked, jumping out of the car before her dad had the parking brake on. She ran past the MiniCooper. She liked Taylor; he didn't treat her like some stupid kid—truth be told, she kinda crushed on him, but he had a girlfriend. Plus he was old, like in his thirties. But cute, very cute.

Wait. She stumbled on the steps leading to the porch. If Taylor was here, did that mean something happened to Mom? A rushing noise filled her head and her mouth tasted of iron. She plowed through the door, fear propelling her feet.

"Taylor?" she shouted.

Her dad was right behind her, steadying her with his hands on her shoulders just as Mom came from the kitchen. Not Taylor. Mom. "Megan, Nick, what are you—"

Fine. Her mom was just fine. Didn't even remember Dad and her were coming. Obviously not happy to see them here either. Of course not. Why would she be happy to see her own daughter? Why would she even be worried about scaring her daughter about to death? Again.

Megan jerked free of her dad and stomped down the hall, not bothering to take her coat off. Her heart was still racing, fear and fury competing for her attention, making her desperate to just feel nothing.

Hard to do here, surrounded by memories of Grams. God, she missed her. Every day.

Megan opened the door to Grams' bedroom and stumbled inside, banging it shut behind her. She let her coat and scarf fall to the floor but then realized there was a woman lying in Gram's bed. The pregnant woman from the video.

"Hello," the woman said. "I'm June."

The Girl Who Never Was: Memoirs of a Survivor
by June Unknown

How I Found My Voice

I'LL NEVER FORGET that first case where Seth had me testify during the sentencing. He said I could have just given him a victim's impact statement and he'd submit it. When he told me that, gave me that out after all the work he'd put into finding me and prepping me, put my needs before his, that's when I knew I couldn't let him down.

By then, I was nineteen; I realized I couldn't live like most people do, but I still had no idea where my place in the world was. Living like a hermit, alone except for my paintings, felt like having a limb amputated.

Living with others—that was being drawn and quartered in front of a crowd, watching, judging my every response.

I wanted a reason to leave my solitude. I needed someone I could be with. Seth gave me both—and so much more.

But that was later. Now I had to survive this first trial.

The guy was already convicted, Seth kept reminding me. "No matter what happens, nothing will change that, so don't worry."

I don't think "worry" came remotely close to how I felt when I walked into that courtroom. Walden came with me since Seth was busy up front with the other lawyer and the defendant, a guy named White.

Is there a state of being beyond panic? When your heart beats so hard and fast that it pushes your being out of your body? That was how I felt: floating, tethered to reality only by the tightness that constricted my chest and made it impossible to swallow. Like my body was an anchor and I wasn't at all sure that I didn't want to cut it free and just drift away.

But then Seth turned to scan the row of seats behind him and he saw me. He looked so proud and happy to see me—no one had ever looked at me that way, not even Daddy. Like I was special. Like I was important.

To hear White's lawyer and friends and boss and church deacon and wife tell it, he was the victim here. Poor, overworked, overstressed shoe store manager, he'd turned to porn to alleviate his tension and accidentally downloaded photos from the wrong site.

Never mind that there were over three thousand of them, all preschool aged girls. White pled for leniency; this wasn't his fault, his family needed him, would be ruined if he was sent to prison.

And the judge kept nodding, like he was buying it. Even smiled at White's wife.

Then it was my turn. Seth introduced me—I was so nervous I didn't hear what he said—and I approached the podium. I smoothed the pages of the statement I'd carefully crafted with Seth's help, my sweaty palms smearing the ink. Didn't matter—I can't read very well anyway, but I'm good at memorizing things I see and hear, so I was going to recite it from memory.

Except then I looked at White. At all the people sitting behind him, supporting him. His fine, upstanding wife. His fine, upstanding deacon. His fine, upstanding paperboy. Whoever these people were, they looked at me like I was some kind of vile, corrupting, ungodly creature sent to seduce fine, upstanding men like White.

To them, I was the one who should be locked away to protect society. To them, it was all my fault.

Heat blazed through me. My hands shook the entire podium, so I closed them into fists and placed them onto the printout of the statement I would never read.

"Are you okay?" Seth whispered from where he sat at the table beside me.

I nodded, still unable to speak. The silence lengthened. People shifted in their seats, whispered behind me. The judge cleared his throat and nodded to me to start.

Still, I was silent. The judge, his patience ended, glared at Seth. "Mr. Bernhart—"

Before he could finish, I opened my mouth and began to speak.

"The first thing I learned when I was little was that girls are to be seen and not heard," I said, focusing my entire being on the judge. Seth had told me that in almost half of child pornography cases, judges would ignore the sentencing guidelines and give defendants less time than even the minimum called for.

Not this time. Not if I had anything to do with it.

"After living the first ten years of my life never being heard, I'd like to thank you for the chance to speak. To add my voice to the ones you've heard today."

I gathered my breath, totally improvising, but the judge was paying attention and that was what mattered. "I lived the first ten years of my life only knowing one other person. That person was my whole world—literally. I lived for him and him alone. When he sent me away, when I grew too big for him, I thought I would die without him.

"Learning how different my childhood was from everyone else's was a shock. I didn't know how to read or write or do math beyond counting. I didn't know how to talk to other people—didn't even know how to play with kids my age. How could I? I'd never met other kids or any other adults. It was years before I could catch up enough to go to school. I managed to graduate high school but left college after a year—I didn't know how to be around people, especially men. Every relationship ended with me feeling ashamed, guilty, and abandoned.

"I live a fragile existence. Unable to trust myself. Unable to trust anyone else. Unable to focus or do so many things normal people do. I can't drive a car. Have never been able to hold down a job—I can tell time on a clock, but have never learned to translate that into anything meaningful. All of which you could blame on those first ten years.

"You probably wonder what Mr. White and his fascination with underage girls has to do with my failures. Why should he be held accountable for my inability to make up for those first ten years? Ten years of my life that he and others like him watch as entertainment with no thought to the fact that the girl on the screen, the girl growing up before their eyes in thousands of images, that girl deserves a life beyond serving their sexual gratification.

"That girl—me—deserves a voice. Deserves a chance to be heard."

I swallowed hard, a feeling of power surging through me—I'd never felt like that before. Every person in the room was listening to me and only me.

"Now that I'm old enough to understand what was taken from me, I'm in constant fear. Fear of someone like Mr. White recognizing me and coming after me. Fear of men like him using those images of my childhood to coerce other victims. Fear of men like Mr. White using my images to recreate that horror for other little girls.

"Fear that because of my stolen childhood, the violence and horror will never end." I paused, trying to figure out how to wrap up. Wished I could remember anything from the statement Seth and I wrote, but it's too late now. "Mr. White may not be the man who stole my innocence or my childhood or my voice, but he's the man who has stolen my dignity, my privacy, and my future. He's the man who paid for it, who made it *profitable* for me to be victimized. He. Paid. Money. For my innocence.

"I've been diagnosed with depression and PTSD and panic attacks and generalized anxiety, but these fears that haunt my every waking moment and that twist my dreams into nightmares, they are not unrealized, vague, neurotic anxieties. You know that, Mr. Bernhart knows that, and Mr. White knows it as well if he's honest with himself.

"These fears are real. They will torment me for the rest of my life. Will knowing that I have one less predator to fear by asking the court to sentence Mr. White to the maximum allowable by law and to request some measure of accountability in the form of financial restitution give me any measure of comfort?" I hoped I'd used the right terms from Seth's coaching.

"For ten years I had no voice," I continued. "Now that I have the power to speak, I can tell you honestly, yes, I will sleep better tonight knowing that justice has been served and that Mr. White will never harm anyone again. Then I will wake up tomorrow, scared and alone and cowering, too afraid to step foot outside, but I will walk outside into a world that for me is filled with danger. Because despite everything taken from me, I have the power to set things right. One thief at a time. One predator at a time."

CHAPTER 18

———∾∾———

"MEGAN," LUCY SHOUTED after her daughter. She spun to go after her, torquing her ankle and releasing a howl of pain.

Nick shook his head. "Give her some space."

"I guess she'd rather it was Taylor here instead of me." Lucy hated the bitterness the words emerged with. Damn, couldn't she do anything right?

She hated even more the fact that clearly she had no remedy for Megan's pain. The trauma counselor said it would take time, to give Megan space if she needed it, but all Lucy seemed to be able to do was to make things worse.

"Would've helped if you answered any of her calls," Nick said as he hung up his coat with measured movements.

"What calls?" Lucy slid her phone free. Three missed calls, all from Megan. "Shit. We took the back way here, past the dam." The state park tried to use their lack of Wi-Fi and cell coverage as an incentive for folks to take a vacation from the stress of the modern world, but it was still damn inconvenient.

"Then maybe you could have called her. Or me. Let us know you were all right."

"I'm all right? Of course I'm all right—" She stopped, realizing he knew about the attack on June and Seth. Damn Internet. She glanced down the hall where Megan had gone, assessing the possibilities.

"She saw you, Lucy. Driving like a maniac, flying over a cliff—"

"It was barely a six foot hill." Well, maybe eight feet. Still, they weren't talking an Evel Knievel stunt. More dangerous for the Subaru than for her. Anyway, that wasn't her main concern. If video had caught the car chase, it might also have caught her face—or some enterprising reporter might have discovered she was there at the scene. No way would any of her people leak it, but...

Seth, his timing impeccable, emerged from the kitchen behind Lucy. "Hi there. Seth Bernhart," he introduced himself. "The pregnant lady Lucy helped is my wife, June. I just want to thank you both for everything you've done. Lucy saved her life—and my baby's."

Nick flushed. Never a good sign—usually he was the one who kept his emotions in check, dealing with them rationally, while Lucy tended to simply let loose and apologize later.

As he took the few stiff steps necessary to meet Seth in the middle of the living room, Lucy realized she wasn't the only one completely off balance. And it wasn't just because of what happened today. This was about more than what happened two months ago. Ever since they'd moved here to Pittsburgh, her job—the promotion that was meant to keep her safe behind a desk and home on time for soccer games and family dinners—had not only endangered Lucy time and again but also their entire family.

And Coletta had paid the price. But she wasn't the only one. Megan could barely look at Lucy or be in the same room with her, and Nick...Nick, he was overwhelmed, playing both mother and father to Megan, therapist and rehab partner for Lucy, cook, cleaner, and house maid, executor of all the legal stuff that went along with Coletta's death, and the safety net holding their entire family together.

Exhausting—for both of them. For Lucy it was just as stressful to watch from the sidelines as it was for Nick to be taking on everything himself.

"Nick Callahan," he said, shaking Seth's hand. His voice held none of the warmth it usually would have. In fact, it was so cold Lucy wished for her coat.

"Nice to meet you, Nick. I'll just go check on June." Seth gave her an encouraging glance before disappearing down the hall.

Lucy stared across the distance separating her from her husband. Nick glared back. He remained on the opposite side of the living room while she waited for him in the archway leading into the kitchen. Neither of them made a move to get closer.

Okay. It was going to be one of those fights.

She shifted her weight, immediately regretting it as pain shot through her ankle. Her cane was behind her in the kitchen, but damn if she was going to retreat to get it.

He took aim first. "The men today. The ones with guns. The ones sent by a vicious sociopathic obsessed pedophile to hurt a pregnant woman. Did you catch them yet?"

"No."

"Then, they're still after her." He held up a hand as she opened her mouth to explain. "I don't need to know why you did what you did. Honestly, I don't really care. Not right this moment. I need to know if our daughter is in danger because you brought those people here."

Lucy flinched at his words. More so at the assumption behind them. As if she hadn't been calculating the risk the moment Megan stepped through the door. If he couldn't trust her judgment, trust her to know what she was doing, trust that she would always put him and Megan before the job...but that was the problem wasn't it? The job. What it did to her. What it did to them.

Silence gathered between them. Usually she loved how in sync she and Nick could be, how they seldom needed words to communicate the important things. One more thing lost since the attack on her and her family two months ago.

Now they couldn't even fight like they usually did. Instead, they both held back as if afraid of hurting the other, damaging the strained threads holding their family together.

As the silence grew, she remembered her father's words "never start a fight, but always finish it." Two months ago those words had given her the strength to survive, now they humbled her with their deeper meaning.

Her glance caught on the photos over the fireplace. Laughing, happy, proud. Family. She focused on her parents' wedding photo and thought of the advice her mother gave her on her own wedding day.

"Just because you love a man doesn't make him a saint," she'd said. "But you found one of the good ones. Don't take him for granted."

Lucy's inhalation shuddered through her and she stepped forward. One step then another, almost within touching distance of Nick. She held his gaze like a lifeline.

Then she said the two words she could live forever and never say often enough. Two words that were the first she thought each morning when she woke and the last before she fell asleep at night.

"Thank you."

He straightened, tilting his head as if he hadn't heard her correctly. She dared one more step, but resisted the urge to touch him and repeated, "Thank you."

She wanted to smile at his startled expression. It wasn't often she was able to surprise Nick—he knew her better than she knew herself—but when she did, it almost always resulted in laughter and tears of joy.

Like the day she'd ended up in the ER, sent there with a minor injury that occurred during an assignment, and Nick rushed to her bedside. They'd only been married a year, neither used to the unique demands her job placed on a marriage, but all that paled when she told him what the doctors had found: she was pregnant.

"Thank me? For what?" he asked, his expression still puzzled. But as he considered her words he relaxed, his hands unclenched, breathing slowing. Her balance wavered as she leaned too much weight on her bad foot.

He steadied her, his palms on her hips.

"For everything. For being here. For staying with me, even when everything goes to shit despite my best intentions."

"Lucy. Are you okay?" He frowned. "Did something happen that you haven't told me about?"

No. No she wasn't. She'd thought she was, thought she was ready, but returning to work had been more about denying everything that had happened two months ago than it was about salvaging her career. Now, being here, smelling her mother's perfume, seeing her everywhere, hearing her ghost in her head, she had to face the truth: she wasn't okay. She wasn't sure if she could ever be again.

"Let's sit. Get you off that leg."

He guided her onto the couch, and she wondered. What if what she was suffering from wasn't simply grief and the trauma of recovering from what had happened two months ago? What if this constant empty feeling was something worse? Something even Nick couldn't treat?

He sat down beside her, wove his fingers between hers, his thumb rubbing her new wedding ring. She'd lost her original one two months ago…had lost so very much that night.

"Do you think I don't know?" he asked.

"Know what?" she said nonchalantly, but she must have tensed enough that he knew he'd hit his target.

"You need to stop it, Lucy. For two months now all you've been doing is running and hiding. Running to rehab, to doctors' appointments, to the damn gun range. Running away from me and Megan, from facing what happened to your mom, from facing your future. And now you're hiding from a predator."

He took her silence as permission for him to continue playing counselor. Give a guy a PhD...of course, she couldn't complain. Not like she ever turned her job off, not fully.

Just look at where they were now.

"I just want..." She paused, frightened to voice what she really wanted. Her words emerged in a child-like whisper. "I just want everything to go back to the way it was."

"Magical thinking," he chided her—her default when she was overwhelmed. It was one of the reasons why she threw herself into her cases; she wished/hoped/believed that if she could save her victims, stop the big bad wolf from hurting them, then maybe she could keep the evil in the world from hurting her family. Build up some good karma or the like.

"No," she told Nick. "I can't think that way, not any more, not after—" She glanced down at her ankle but it was her mother's face that filled her vision.

"But you've thought like that for so long you don't have anything to replace it with. Lucy, don't you see? You never needed it in the first place. You don't need an excuse to be passionate about your job, about the people you help—you wouldn't be the woman I fell in love with if you lost that. There's no reason to feel guilty about that or make up some silly deal with the universe to justify your passion."

"Of course I feel guilty! How can you even say that? Here, of all places."

He squeezed her hand. "You almost died trying to save us—all of us. You chose us over the FBI. You did everything right. Do you really think your mother blames you for not predicting what a psychopath would do?"

She didn't have an answer to that. "I'm not sure I can still do my job. It hurts so much." He knew she wasn't talking about her leg. "Seeing what it does to you and especially Megan." She shrugged. "First day back on the job and look where we are."

"You need to find a middle ground. Some way to keep your need to help people separate from your need to protect your family. Other law enforcement officers do it."

She didn't need to remind him that most of them failed miserably. She could count on three fingers the number of happily married agents she knew—and they all had supervisory positions that kept them out of the field. Divorce was almost the rule among the men and women who did her job.

Never. She'd quit the job before she quit her family. "I don't know how."

"Maybe Greally is right—it's time for you to transition into a position that will let you do both."

She scoffed at that. "I don't think taking a job investigating my co-workers is the answer."

Nick pulled her close and kissed the top of her head. "We don't need to decide now. But we do need to keep talking. All of us, Megan included."

She glanced down the hallway. Wondered what June, Seth, and Megan were talking about. "You know, if there's video of me out there, then you and Megan are safer here than at home. You should stay the night." It was ironic, but since her mother's home was in a trust not associated with Lucy's name, they would be safer here than anywhere else.

His lips tightened but he nodded at that. "All of us?" He meant her.

"Unless something breaks. I don't want to risk asking the locals for help—too easy for word to get out. And we can't offer June official protection. But I'll ask Walden to come up as soon as he's free from the hospital. He can take June and Seth to a safe house and then you won't have to worry."

"Hospital? Was Walden hurt?"

"Broken collarbone. Timmy Oshiro got shot but he was wearing his vest. They'll both be fine."

"Oshiro—the deputy US Marshal? Big guy, the nurses all loved him because he brought them home baked pies and cakes while you were in the hospital?" Baking was Oshiro's stress-reliever, he said he enjoyed the control and the simple pleasure of always knowing everything would come out right if he just played by the rules—something he was famous for not doing on the job. A lot like Lucy that way.

"Yeah, he's friends with Seth and June. Between him and Walden, they should have plenty of protection." Even as she said it, she made a note to herself to ask a few of the other agents in her squad if they'd mind helping out—two walking wounded would work in the short-term, for tonight, but Seth and June needed to prepare for a longer siege. No way was Daddy going to give up on June. And there was no telling how many others were searching for her.

Nick relaxed, trusting her judgment—a gift that meant more to her than she had words to express. He nodded, stood, and lowered a hand to help her.

"We good?" he asked. She hated that he had to—how far gone was she that her husband of fifteen years, a man who used to be able to read an entire day via a twitch of her eyebrow when she walked inside the door, had to ask?

She stood, turned in his embrace, wrapped her arms around his neck, and pulled him down for a kiss. Despised herself that even that intimacy felt distant, as if she was beyond her body, watching herself. Tried her best to sink into it, to let her body communicate her depth of feeling.

And failed. If Nick realized that, he didn't show it as they pulled apart.

But Lucy knew better. Even if she was too damn numb to feel it.

CHAPTER 19

LUCY AND NICK moved back out to the kitchen. She finished her geographic profile while he began dinner. The aroma of ziti and meatballs filled the kitchen. She called Taylor and forwarded her results to him. It was hard to focus with so many childhood memories wafting through her olfactory senses. Her mom would have never approved of feeding company frozen leftovers. She would have made everything fresh, from scratch.

Taylor sounded excited—but then, he always sounded that way. "You narrowed it down to an area in southeast Ohio, western Pennsylvania, and—"

"And a tiny part of West Virginia and Maryland," she finished. "I know it's a lot of ground to cover, not sure if it will be much help."

"No, boss, this is great. Finally something concrete to give me some search parameters."

Nick sat down beside Lucy, making a shopping list while absently stroking her arm with his free hand.

Maybe the fight wasn't over—they definitely hadn't resolved anything, hadn't even begun to discuss her career options—but this detente was nice. It helped her feel not quite as out of step with Nick and her family, hell, the whole damn world.

"I've been thinking," Taylor continued, the sound of his fingers pounding his keyboard echoing through the cell phone. "Why did this guy wait until after he'd already sold June to Green Elephant Man before selling the Baby Girl image collection? I mean, he was sitting on a gold mine, right?"

Lucy had wondered that as well. "Maybe once he found a new victim, he no longer was as emotionally attached to June? Didn't mind her images out there for others to be using?"

Nick tapped her arm and shook his head. In between milk and OJ on his shopping list he'd written: obsessed.

"Or maybe I'm wrong," she conceded. Nick was right. Why would their subject—god, how she despised calling him "Daddy," it defiled every definition of the word, especially here in this house that held the only remaining memories of her own father—why would he still be this obsessed with June now? In her experience, once predators lost interest in their victims, they moved on without looking back again.

"What about money?" Taylor asked. "Maybe he didn't get all the money from Green Elephant guy when the deal went sour. Maybe that left him short on cash and he needed to make some fast?"

"Okay. So emotionally, he's obsessed with June, that's why he starts with such young new victims, he hopes to groom them into being just like June. Does that mean he's still obsessed with her? Even after all these years? And now her being pregnant gives him the perfect chance to bring everything back full circle."

Nick nodded his approval at her theory.

"I don't know about any of that," Taylor said. "I'm just saying that if there's a money trail, we've got something we can maybe follow. And according to Green Elephant Man's case file, he withdrew sums adding up to thirty-two thousand in cash the week before June was found."

"That's a pretty specific number."

"I know. Might mean something. I can throw it into the search algorithm, see what pops."

"Sounds good. Let me know if you find anything." She hung up, staring at the map now filled with her colored tracings. "Every time I start to think I understand this guy, it makes me want to run in the other direction."

Nick squeezed her hand. "He's not the worst you've come up against. You'll get him."

She wished she had his confidence. But this guy, this Daddy, he felt more twisted than any of the others. More than his warped idea of family. Turning his wrath on Seth after June became pregnant. He could have easily assassinated Seth right there in the street when they first met.

But it wasn't enough to kill the only man besides himself that June had ever loved, no, this SOB had to turn it into a sick game, taunting Seth, torturing him with a certain, painful death.

More than that, he wanted Seth to know he'd die, leaving his family unprotected and at Daddy's mercy.

Bile filled her mouth and she left the table, not

bothering with the cane for the short trip down the hall to the bathroom. On her way back to the kitchen, she stopped outside the half-open door to her mom's bedroom.

Inside, she saw what to anyone else would seem like the perfect family. June lying back on the bed, propped up so she could comb Megan's unruly curls, taking care with the tangles. Megan sat beside Seth, and together, they leafed through an old leather-bound photograph album—the one with Coletta's wedding photos.

"That's Grams in high school." Megan pointed proudly. "Doesn't she look like a movie star?" She flipped the page. "Oh, and here's her first date with Grandpap. He took her to a dance. Look at him, wearing a tuxedo to a school dance and it wasn't even the prom." She sighed and looked up at Seth. "I never got to meet him, you know. He died when Mom was twelve. So it was just her and Grams."

Seth's shoulders sagged and he turned away. Lucy pushed the door open to rescue him. "Dinner's about ready," she announced.

Seth helped June up from the bed as Megan replaced the photo album. Outside, lightning cracked through the sky and rain pelted the window. Damn, she'd thought the storm wasn't supposed to hit until later tonight.

Her phone rang. Taylor. "I've got something, boss," he announced breathlessly.

"What is it?"

"Got a call from Pittsburgh Police. They found our motorcyclist-slash-shooter. Dead."

"I'm on my way." He gave her the address and she hung up the phone. Seth and June had left but Megan sat on the floor in front of the bookcase, glaring at Lucy.

"Don't say it," Megan said. "I know what's coming."

First words spoken directly to Lucy in weeks. A clap of thunder boomed beyond the window.

"You know they lose power up here all the time when it storms," Lucy said, ignoring what she couldn't change. "Can you help your dad gather the flashlights, start a fire?"

"Because you have to go. There's some kid out there more important than me, some bad guy more important than Dad." The words didn't come out bitter or angry. More like resigned. Megan pushed up to her feet and turned her back on Lucy.

"Megan—" Lucy stopped. Realized she didn't have an answer. Had she ever? Pain tightened her chest as she wanted so badly to grab Megan in a hug, somehow find the words to make everything right.

At that moment she was glad she'd left the cane behind in the kitchen. She realized now why she truly despised the thing, not because it drew attention to her weakness, but rather because it was a constant reminder that things were different now. And they could never be the same again.

Lucy stepped forward onto her good foot, finally close enough to reach Megan. Using both hands she hugged her from behind, pulling Megan's rigid body against hers, holding tight. "I miss her, too."

Megan's shoulders slumped and she turned to face Lucy, not fighting but also not returning Lucy's hug. But she didn't run away from Lucy's touch, so it was a step in the right direction. So much anger. The counselor said anger was a normal part of the grieving process, but Lucy sensed there was something more beneath Megan's constant fury.

It wasn't until now, standing in her mother's room, inhaling the faint memory of Coletta's perfume that she remembered being a few years younger than Megan—her father had just died, and she'd stood in almost this same spot, lashing out at her own mother.

More than anger. She remembered the emotions that had crashed down on her those first few months after Dad died. Coletta could do nothing right, nothing to break through to Lucy—it was as if after suffering the pain of losing one parent, Lucy felt the need to build a barrier between her heart and her love of her mother, anything to protect her from feeling that anguish again.

Not anger. Fear.

Lucy bowed her head over Megan, allowing her weight to settle on both feet—to hell with the pain—and held on even tighter. "It's okay," she whispered. "It's okay to be afraid."

She wanted to promise Megan that nothing would ever happen to her or Nick, that she had nothing to fear. But Lucy didn't make promises she couldn't keep and after what Megan had seen firsthand two months ago, she'd never believe the empty words.

"I hate you," Megan muttered into Lucy's shoulder, but the words had no bite. "I hate your job. You go and leave us behind and we never know what's happening, if you'll come home, or if you'll—" She choked into silence. Lucy felt tears slide warm against the side of her neck.

"I hate leaving," Lucy said. "But when things get bad, I think of you and Dad. It's what gives me the strength to make it through. All I ever want is to come home to you.

That's what I'm always thinking. Always. Do you understand that?"

Magical thinking. Suddenly Lucy realized she wasn't the only one in this family who used it as an emotional crutch. This was part of why Megan clung to the idea of keeping their home, of never moving away from the house that had become their family's touchstone. More than avoiding change, more than wishing for things to go back to the way they were before.

"Megan, I will always, always fight to come home to you." Lucy kissed the top of Megan's head and released her. "But talk to me if you're upset or afraid. Don't push me away."

Megan didn't look up; she simply wiped her tears with the back of her hand and stared at the floor. At Lucy's injured foot. "You don't blame me?"

"Blame you? For what?"

"Grams. She never would have been there if it wasn't for me. If I was old enough to take care of myself."

And there it was. Sorrow more painful than anything Lucy's broken, twisted nerves could create hit her so hard and fast she nearly lost her balance. She hung onto Megan, the only way she could stay upright. Bowed her head until it touched Megan's, both now sobbing, their bodies swaying in unison.

"No. I don't blame you, Megan." God, the thought, even the suggestion, that it could have been Megan the killer found that night, alone, vulnerable—Lucy refused to let it go to its natural conclusion. Magical thinking or not, she could not, she would not, allow such a vile image fill her mind, tempting fate.

"No one blames you because it wasn't your fault. You

can't ever think it was. Grams would be the first to tell you that." Lucy wished she had better words to offer—that was Nick's department and she fell woefully short. All she could do was speak from her heart. "We love you, Megan. And none of what happened was your fault."

She raised Megan's face to hers. Tears brimmed over in Megan's eyes and snot coated her upper lip. "Do you believe me? Will you remember that?"

Megan nodded. Lucy gave her one last hug and a quick kiss on the forehead. "Okay. Go clean up for dinner."

"You're still leaving?"

"I have to, sweetie. I have to stop the men after June and Seth—not just because it's my job," Lucy hastened to add when bitter disappointment clouded Megan's face. "Because it's the right thing to do." She drew in a breath, terrified of shattering the delicate bridge she and Megan had forged. "If we let men like that get away, then what happened to Grams could happen to someone else."

Megan frowned, shaking her head as if her mother was a lost cause. "Whatever." And she was gone before Lucy could reach her.

———◆———

LUCY DROVE NICK'S Explorer down the mountain, glad she was in the larger SUV and navigating a proper two lane road instead of the twisty, narrow lanes she'd taken past the dam and river and up the backside of the mountain earlier when she was in Taylor's MiniCooper. The storm was a typical Pennsylvania March gale, blizzard-like winds accompanied by sheets of rain. It was slow moving, forecast to last all night, leaving behind flooding and downed power lines and the havoc that came with that.

Despite the weather, she smiled. When she was a little girl, she'd been both terrified and fascinated with storms. Used to sit by her bedroom window and watch the lightning strikes dance above the trees.

"Nice thing about living up here," her dad would say when he came in to check on her and took her in his lap, wrapping her quilt around them both as they watched nature's fury. "We're protected from all that. No need to worry about flooding—if the dam bursts, and it won't, it will flood the lake and valley, but we're above it all. If the power gets knocked out, we've got our wood burner and fireplace and the propane tank to keep the well pumping. And this house, it's built solid, can weather just about anything."

She'd turn in his embrace and look up at him. "But, Daddy, how can you be sure?"

And he'd hug her tight. "Because I built this house to keep you and your mom safe. For always."

She reached the bottom of the mountain and turned on to Route 981. At the first stop light she pulled her phone out. No telling when she'd get another chance to charge it. Nick's phone was already plugged in. She sighed and swapped the phones out. He was constantly doing that, forgetting his phone. She made a note to call Megan if she needed to reach them.

Hopefully with good news. She dialed Walden. "How's Oshiro?"

"Planning a jailbreak. Not even taking the time to seduce any of the very cute nurses at his disposal."

"Did Taylor let you know they found one of our wannabe kidnappers, dead?"

"Yep. Do you want me back at the office or at the scene?"

"Actually, I was going to ask you to head over to my mother's house." She didn't want to say why—despite the fact that her phone was secured with the latest encryption technology, after seeing the way June and Seth had been tracked, she didn't trust it.

Walden was smart enough to fill in the blanks. "Want me to make sure everything is battened down for the storm?"

"If you don't mind."

"No problem. But if you don't want Oshiro going Incredible Hulk on us, you'd better invite him as well."

"They're not keeping him overnight?"

"Nope. Said he needs to take antibiotics and come back in two days for a wound check. He's gonna have a nasty set of scars, but the bullet didn't hit anything vital."

"How much longer will you be?" She was certain the others were safe up at her mother's house, but having Walden take June and Seth to another location would make her feel even better.

"They just need to finish running this antibiotic is all. Bag's half empty already, so not long, I'm guessing. We'll head out as soon as it's done."

"Sounds good. I appreciate you watching over things for me at home. Thanks." She hung up and continued up to Route 22. She'd just hit the turnoff to the Parkway when her phone rang. Taylor. "I'm almost there."

"Got something, boss." He sounded excited, but not in a good way. With Taylor his moods ranged in almost as many shades of excitation as the pain from her ankle.

"What happened?"

"Got a call from Don Burroughs." Burroughs was a detective with Pittsburgh Police's Major Crimes unit. "He caught our homicide. Said the guy was shot, point blank range in the face in the parking garage of an old bottling plant. With the bike from earlier today sitting right beside him."

He paused expectantly. "And?" Lucy nudged.

"And looks like motorcycle guy is tied to five other killings. We might have a serial killer on our hands."

CHAPTER 20

SETH'S STOMACH BURNED so much his vision blurred. They sat at the kitchen table, him, June, Megan, and Lucy's husband. Passing food and chatting as if there was nothing wrong, as if no one had tried to take his wife and child from him just a few hours ago. Outside the storm raged—at least that fit his mood.

As he passed more meatballs to June—pregnancy had turned her into a devout carnivore—he replayed the ambush from earlier in his head. If Lucy hadn't been there, if Oshiro hadn't caught the bullets meant for Seth...a rush of nausea made him shiver.

"Seth, are you okay?" June asked, her fingers tapping the back of his hand. He blinked back to life, wondered how much of the conversation he'd missed.

Rolling his hand over, he intertwined his fingers with hers and squeezed. "Fine, thanks. Just my stomach." He couldn't look her in the eye with the lie—seemed like he was doomed to leave behind a legacy of lies. More than lies. Sins. Sins of commission and sins of omission. So many that some days he looked in the mirror and thought it right and just that he was dying.

But even a dying sinner had the right to protect his family. That single thought kept him going. He pushed back his chair and stood. "I'll be right back."

Nick watched him stumble toward the archway that led to the living room. "I think there might be some antacids in the medicine cabinet."

Seth nodded his thanks and lurched down the hall. Stomach acid played chopsticks racing up and down from his chest to his throat and mouth and back again. But he didn't go to the bathroom at the end of the hall. Instead he went back to the bedroom where they'd been earlier.

He sank onto the bed and buried his head in his hands. Lucy had wondered why Daddy would target him now, when he was already dying. Not fast enough to suit Daddy, obviously. Especially not with Seth closing in on him. A few tattered gasps here, a word or two there, but hopefully it would soon be enough to lead him to Daddy. He just needed a little more time.

But Daddy knew Seth was getting close—was worried Seth might find him before he could end Seth. So he'd set the trap with the ultrasound, knowing Seth would run with June.

They both knew Seth could no longer protect her, was as good as useless—dead or alive. How did the bastard always stay one step ahead of them?

Megan's phone with its bright purple case and rhinestone studded Eiffel Tower beckoned from where it sat on its charger. Maybe he should just ask.

As he reached across the nightstand for it he spotted

something in the partially open drawer below. A gleam of metal. He slid the door open. A revolver.

Seth lifted the gun free. Fully loaded from the weight. Short barrel, not too heavy—good thing because his hands were so weak he could barely grip doorknobs and turn them properly. The symptoms were escalating. If the doctors were right, he didn't have long.

This could be his last chance. He shoved the gun into his jacket pocket. It made the fabric bulge, but that was okay, he wouldn't need to hide it for long.

Couldn't risk getting his phone from the car to see if there were any new messages. Or…a plan began to form. Maybe he could. But not here.

He used Megan's phone to access his cell account online. Nothing new, just the same untraceable message sent via an auto-repeater that hounded him every hour of every day for the past five months.

They're mine and there's nothing you can do to stop it.

The words were burned into Seth's soul.

Hands trembling, he pocketed the cell. This ended tonight.

He returned to the living room. The keys to the car Lucy had driven them in, that silly yellow thing, were on the buffet that stood against the half wall separating the kitchen from the living room. He leaned against it, looking at June as if it was the last time he'd ever see her again.

If he did this right, it would be.

"I'm going to sit on the porch for a few minutes, get some fresh air," he said as his fingers curled around the keys, gripping them tight.

June looked up. "You sure you're okay?"

"I'll be fine. Long day is all."

"If you want me to pick up any medicine or anything when I run to the store, the list is right there," Nick said.

"No thanks, I'm good." He forced a smile for June and was rewarded with one in return. God, she was amazing. She had no earthly idea how strong she was, but he did. She'd be okay. She had to be.

"Go ahead," he said, still smiling. "You can have my meatballs. You know you want them."

"Not me, the baby," she replied as she speared one from his plate. "She's ravenous." She took a bite. "These are so good. Do you think your grams would mind you sharing the recipe with me?" she asked Megan, leaning toward her as if they were conspiring.

"She taught me how to make them. I'll teach you."

"Oh, the baby kicked. Want to feel?" June guided Megan's hand to her belly.

She was going to make such a wonderful mother. Seth blinked hard, pushed away and turned his back on them, crossing the room to grab his coat. They were the most difficult nine steps he'd ever taken.

"Bring some wood in if you don't mind," Nick called.

Seth nodded. He slid into his coat and opened the door. The porch sheltered the house from the brunt of the wind, but beyond it trees bowed, their branches whipping back and forth. It took everything he had not to look around as he closed the door.

He crossed the porch, ignoring the stack of wood at the other end, ran down the steps, and into the storm.

CHAPTER 21

LUCY HAD JUST made it past the Oakland exit when Taylor called back. "Change of plans," he said. He didn't sound like his usual, eager to catch bad guys, self. Instead, his tone was subdued.

"What's wrong?"

"Nothing. Burroughs said the CSU guys were going to be a while and I found something else. Meet me at the office?"

"What did you find?"

"A few things. The geo profile you did is narrowing down potential suspects—well, combined with the nifty little algorithm I created. Don't worry," he hurried to add. "It's only searching data we can access without a court order. I'm not letting this guy walk on a technicality. But...there's something else. I'd rather show you in person."

"On my way." She headed across the river to the Federal Building. The storm wasn't quite as fierce here as it was to the east, but it was still bad enough that the streets were abnormally empty for a Friday night.

She parked in the secured garage and passed through security without needing to go through the scanner, feeling a twinge of vindication. On the elevator ride up to her office, she dry-swallowed another of the anti-inflammatory pills. She wasn't sure if it was the rain or the stress or just the fact that it was a long day, but her ankle was throbbing worse than the thunder outside.

The squad room was empty and dark except for a light on in her office. Taylor had taken over her conference table and had several laptops set up there. He'd also made use of her white boards, mimicking her style of using one board to jot down random questions and facts and the other to plot out a timeline as she addressed them.

Watching him spin back and forth between his beloved computers to the white boards, she couldn't help but feel a sense of pride. He'd turned into a damn fine agent, even if the Bureau in its infinite wisdom had decided to keep him out of the field.

He jumped when she opened the door. Looked more than a little guilty.

"What have you got for me?" she asked, taking a seat and sitting back, giving him the floor.

He shifted his weight, caught between the white boards and his array of computers. Finally, he grabbed a remote and clicked on the large screen monitor on the wall beside him.

"First of all, your geographic profile is working." A map of western Pennsylvania, Ohio, West Virginia, and Maryland appeared. On it winking lights appeared and disappeared again, at first filling most of the screen, then slowly diminishing until only a handful remained.

"I used it as a framework then added filters for age, computer skills, and here's the kicker," he looked more than a little smug, "I added any public reference that would require a significant amount of cash—set the parameters around the amount we know Green Elephant Man withdrew."

"You can do that?"

He scoffed. "Sure. Think of everything that's out there in public records: bail proceedings, property sales, civil suits, foreclosures, tax debt…it's a treasure trove if you know how to set up the search algorithm."

"You're not searching for child porn or any arrests?"

"Our guy is too smart for that. His porn won't be hosted on any computer that we can touch—and he won't have been arrested, not for anything that would flag him as a sexual offender."

Right, because a charge like that would come with severe limitations and monitoring of any computer activity. Their guy, Daddy, he liked his privacy too much to risk arrest.

"Okay, I buy that. But can you really take a population of a million or more men who fit the basic profile and narrow it down accurately?" That was the thing about profiling—too vague and your net was too wide, too specific and you might miss your target all together and end up aiming at an innocent bystander.

"It's a starting point," he conceded. "But at least we'll have someplace to start digging. And, I think I found June's mother. Maybe."

"How did you do that?"

"I ran missing persons from within the highest probability area generated by your geo profile. Centered on the year we think June was born and went back from there. I didn't find any mother-daughter abductions and only a few pregnant women—but they were all found dead, still pregnant."

The screen switched to photos of missing women. So many that they filled the screen and crowded over top of each other. It was the one thing that always saddened Lucy about her job: how many women simply vanished each year, most of them taken against their will to become victims. How many families were left behind without any answers.

"If she was his first," Lucy said, "he wouldn't have risked a mother-daughter abduction. He'd want someone he could easily control."

"Right. So I went back farther in time, expanded the parameters. I discovered these missing girls, aged five to fifteen, eliminated the ones later found, and given June's Nordic looks and blue eyes, eliminated others based on ethnicity and appearance. Which left these."

The photos on the screen dissolved to eight girls. All blond, blue-eyed. But one could have been June's twin. Lucy stood, leaned against the table and used her cane to point. "Tell me about her."

"Casey Hudson. Seven years old. Got off her school bus one day, but never made it home. No signs of her since."

"Where?"

"Just outside of Akron." The screen went back to the map and highlighted the location. He paused and his voice dropped. "Five years before June was born."

Lucy's stomach twisted. Bastard kept her long enough to get her pregnant and start over. With his own damn daughter. "It's her. Can you run June's mitochondrial DNA against Casey's?"

"I put in a request but it will take time—the sample is so old. It was before mitochondrial DNA was standard."

"His first." She considered. "A crime of opportunity? Spontaneous?" She didn't think so but waited to hear Taylor's opinion.

"You sure, boss? This guy is so methodical. I think maybe he stalked her for a long time."

"I agree. Probably enjoyed the anticipation of choosing, preparing. This guy—he's different from most of our subjects. But either way, he either lived or worked not too far from where Casey was taken. Close enough that he was familiar with the traffic and routines of the neighborhood, escape routes, hiding places, dumping grounds if things went wrong. This guy, he would have every variable accounted for."

"Same way as he programs," Taylor muttered. "But there's something else." He cleared his throat, obviously uncomfortable. "Something I found that doesn't make sense. Unless…"

"What is it, Taylor?"

"Is there any way Seth Bernhart could be working with Daddy?" he blurted out. "Because I traced that first threat. The one against the judge and June. It didn't come from an angry pedophile. I traced it back to Seth."

CHAPTER 22

MEGAN CLEARED THE table while Dad went out to help Seth gather wood for a fire. He came back in alone, arms piled high.

"Where's Seth?" June asked.

"He's gone. So's the car." Dad's voice didn't sound worried or upset. It was his calm voice, the one that meant trouble.

Megan glanced at the sideboard. "The keys are gone but so is your shopping list. He probably went to the store." The words were for June's benefit. She didn't want her to worry.

Dad frowned and she knew why: Seth would have no idea where the store was, so why would he leave without asking?

She joined her dad at the fireplace. "Let me. I can build it so it won't smoke."

He held his hands up in surrender and backed away as she opened the flue and arranged the kindling around one of Gram's fire starters: dried pinecones dipped in paraffin.

"My budding control freak," he told June. "Not quite sure if she's going to be a genius or a sociopath. Teenagers, the brain's not done cooking yet."

Megan rolled her eyes as she lit the fire. Grownups always thought just because they were older they were better at everything. "Either way, you have your fire and no room filled with smoke."

"That was just that one time," he protested.

"Does she realize she sounds exactly like her mom?" June said, laughing. "You two are lucky."

Did she mean Megan and Dad were lucky to have Mom? Or that Mom and Dad were lucky to have Megan? She used the poker to adjust the logs. She loved this house, dreamed of living in it someday. Not with Mom and Dad—they had their house and Megan wanted it to stay just like it was. No, when she was older, after college, she wanted to come live here. By herself. Maybe someday with her husband.

Mom and Dad over in Pittsburgh in the house Megan grew up in so she could still visit. While she lived here in Grams' house. And things could go back to almost the way they were. Close to it as she could get.

"Dad, did you call Andrea to take care of Zeke and Boots?" The puppy and cat were Megan's responsibility but no one had planned for them to be here all night.

"Your mom did before she left. They're fine." Dad glanced around. "June, I'm not sure which chair would be easiest for you—want me to move one of the kitchen chairs out near the fire?"

"No thanks, I feel better standing. She," June rubbed

her belly, "gets cramped if I sit too long."

"Okay. Megan, want to help me change the beds for our guests?" Nick moved down the hall. Megan reluctantly followed him; she hated making beds.

When she joined him in Grams' bedroom, he was on his knees rummaging through the nightstand. "When you were in here earlier, did you see Grams' gun?"

"Which one? The shotgun or the pistol?" Growing up with a mom who carried weapons, they'd all learned how to handle them. Megan was almost as good a shot as her mom, better than her dad. Since Grams lived alone, she didn't bother to keep her guns locked up like Mom did. Megan wasn't sure why Mom bothered. Wasn't like she had to worry about Megan doing something stupid.

"The pistol. She kept it in here, but it's gone."

"It was in the bottom drawer earlier. And the shotgun is under the bed."

He sat back on his heels, obviously worried. "The pistol isn't here. Seth must have taken it." He stood up turning to the window, thinking things through. Dad liked to do that, be certain about everything before he made a decision about a person.

What was there to think about? Megan leaned down, grabbed the shotgun and handed it to her dad. "Careful, it's loaded."

She turned to Grams' closet and barely had to stretch to reach the box of shells on the shelf. After a growth spurt last month, her clothes didn't fit anymore, but no one had noticed. Grams would have. Just like she would have remembered that Megan's birthday was in a week and she'd be turning fourteen.

She'd have something fun planned for them, like she

always did when Megan came to visit. Most of her friends griped about being forced to visit their grandparents, but Megan loved it when she got to come up here and stay. Grams and she would work in the garden, take hikes down the mountain, go fishing at Grandpap's secret place on the river—the place where he'd taken Mom when she was a little girl—and Grams would let Megan use Grandpap's fishing rod.

Megan sniffed, clutching the box of shotgun shells. Why couldn't everything just go back to the way it was?

She missed her Grams. So much.

But right now, at this moment, with danger fluttering through her gut, she missed her mom even more. If Lucy were here, she'd keep them safe.

———◆———

"SETH SENT THE threat to the judge?" Lucy asked, not caring that she allowed her dismay bleed into her voice. "Why?" Threatening a judge was a federal offense. Seth would never risk being arrested, forced away from June's side. But, wait. "When did that happen?"

"Four months ago."

Ahh…after Seth was poisoned and learned he was dying. His attempt to get June and his baby under the protection of the US Marshals. Too bad the judge ended the trial so quickly or it might have worked.

"Did he also post the ultrasound?" she asked. No. That wouldn't make sense—those bullets today were real. Seth would never endanger June or the baby merely to get them protection. Besides, he'd already arranged for the best protection money could buy…just not good enough to keep Daddy at bay.

Taylor shook his head. "No. That was Daddy. I'm sure of it."

"How do you know Seth sent that threat to the judge?"

"More than that, he's been surfing the DarkNet, hanging out with pedophiles. I thought maybe Daddy had blackmailed him into betraying June." Taylor looked stricken. "How could he?"

"He didn't." She was glad he didn't ask her to explain how she could be so certain. But after seeing Seth with June, knowing that he would literally die for her...there was no way she'd believe Seth would betray June. "How did you find all this?"

He shuffled his feet, suddenly looking twenty years younger. "When I got back here, I realized Seth's rental was parked downstairs. Along with their stuff. I figured I should check to see if anything was bugged—maybe that was how Daddy traced them up here." He jerked his chin up. "Did you bring me their phones? I really want to analyze them."

"No. They're still in the dead box in the trunk of your car."

"You didn't bring my car back?"

"Driving down a mountain, pouring rain, in a hurry, and Nick's Explorer was more convenient. Don't worry. Nothing is going to happen to your car." Then she realized what he was doing. Deflecting her. "Taylor, you searched their car without permission or a court order? And whose computers are these?"

"I kind of had implicit permission to look for signs of a tracker—and you can put tracking software on a laptop as easily as you can a phone."

"Taylor..." She caught herself using the same tone she used with the puppy at home. Blew out her breath and sank back into the chair. "Show me what you found."

"None of it is admissible."

"Just show me."

He changed the monitor so it mirrored the laptop's screen. "Seth had two laptops with him. One obviously for work and everyday stuff. That one I left alone once I was sure it wasn't bugged—attorney/client privilege and all that."

"And the other?"

"The other is a totally different story. Almost nothing on it except his own Tor access and a VPN—virtual private network. It makes just about anything you do on a computer untraceable. Unless you know what you're looking for. Like me."

"So you found the threat to the judge."

"Yeah. He thought he'd deleted it, but nothing's ever truly deleted from a hard drive unless you overwrite it with scrubber software. And even then, you might find traces."

"And he was visiting porn sites?"

"Yeah. No downloads, no images on the computer. And he couldn't get into a lot of the hardcore sites—they make you go through a validation process before they'll give you access. But he definitely found a couple of guys. He's been building a database of their details, like profile names they use, locations they mention, stuff like that."

"Were these guys maybe working with Daddy? Or threatening June? Seth said they've been getting death threats ever since they began the civil suits."

"It'll take me some time to correlate things. Not like these guys use their real names—although I think Seth might have been able to trace a few of them back to the real world. Hints they left about jobs and where they lived. Give me more time with it."

"Not until we get his permission and a warrant."

"But if these guys are working with Daddy, they might be here, in Pittsburgh. Waiting for the chance to get at June. Just like motorcycle guy."

"Who's now dead. What's up with the idea that he's a serial killer?"

"Well, maybe not serial killer. Probably more like hit man. Burroughs said they found some IDs that belonged to other men and when they ran their names, they're all homicide victims."

"Here? In Pittsburgh?"

"I don't know."

"Maybe we should head over there and find out." She pushed back onto her feet, ignoring the wave of complaints generated by her ankle. "Grab your gear."

He gathered his laptop and shoved it into a messenger bag. The monitor screen switched back to the geographic search program, combing through thousands of potential suspects.

Even if they found Daddy's home base, it wouldn't be anywhere near Pittsburgh. They needed to find the man. Here. Now. It was the only chance to save June. And that little girl, Missy Barstow, his latest victim.

If she was still alive.

CHAPTER 23

"WALDEN AND OSHIRO—that deputy marshal who baked the brownies you liked—they're on their way," Dad said, awkwardly double-checking that the shotgun was loaded. Then he took the shotgun and shells and left.

Okay, so maybe Mom hadn't abandoned them. Megan still wished she were here. She followed her dad back out to the living room. He set the shotgun between the front door and the bay window.

"Figured you wouldn't want this in your bedroom," he said to June when he caught her watching him. Never mind that they hadn't even bothered to change the sheets on the bed. Did he really think June was that dumb?

She wasn't. "Someone tried to kill my husband and kidnap me a few hours ago, Mr. Callahan. Not sure why you think the presence of a weapon would disturb me."

Megan smiled. It wasn't often that anyone called her dad's bluffs. He looked sheepish.

June crossed over to the coatrack beside the front door and grabbed her purse. "I have a pistol if you think it will help."

"You brought a gun into our home?" Dad asked. He always was so sensitive about guns. If he just relaxed and learned to be comfortable around them…but never going to happen. Because her father didn't see a gun, he saw a person. Make that people. On either side of the trigger. Guess when you worked with veterans, helping them through their PTSD, talking about all that death and destruction, it made you see things differently.

June didn't seem taken aback at all. That's why Megan liked her so much; she wasn't that old, yet she seemed so clear on what she needed to do that she didn't care what anyone else thought. "With Seth being on the road so much these past few months, I asked Oshiro to get one for me. He taught me—and of course, got a carry permit pushed through as well."

Pistol-packing mommy-to-be. The image of June shooting filled Megan's vision. Now that was kick-ass.

Dad must have seen something else when he looked at June. "I'm sure Seth will be back soon."

June returned her purse on the coat rack and swiped at her eyes with a knuckled fist. "I wish I believed that. But I know my husband. He'd do anything to protect us. After what happened earlier—I think he decided to take matters into his own hands."

Dad thought about that. From the look on his face, Megan realized it was exactly what he would've done if he'd been in Seth's position. Part of her felt proud that she had a father who would risk everything to keep her safe. Part of her was terrified by the thought.

And Dad was standing right here, safe and sound. Poor June. Megan rushed to her side. "He'll be all right, June." She looked to her dad. "You need to call Mom. Tell her to find Seth and send him back home."

From Dad's expression, he'd be telling Mom more than that—hopefully telling her to come home herself. He patted his pockets, glanced at the sideboard. "Left my phone in the car. Where's yours?"

Megan ran down the hall to Grams' room where she'd left her phone charging. The charger was there but the phone was gone. She returned to the living room. June paced a circle in front of the fire, her hands pressed against her back. She looked so uncomfortable. "It's not there. Seth must have taken it."

"What's wrong with the phone in the kitchen?" June asked, glancing at the old corded phone on the kitchen wall.

"Power and phone lines go down all the time up here," Dad explained. "Coletta switched from the land line to using a cell once the new tower went up." Still, he crossed over to the kitchen and lifted the receiver to his ear. Then he tried to dial 911 and 0. "Nothing."

June stopped, arched her back, and grabbed Megan's shoulder. Tight. Her face twisted in surprise and she looked down at the floor.

"June, what's wrong?"

"My water just broke."

CHAPTER 24

———

TAYLOR SIGNED THEM out a pool vehicle, one of the Bureau's Tahoes. Big, black, tinted windows, it practically screamed government, but that wasn't what concerned Lucy. It was how the hell was she going to climb into the passenger seat without putting all of her weight on her bad leg?

As usual, Taylor's mind had already processed the problem and come up with a solution. He opened her door for her and pushed the seat back as far as it would go. Then he held her elbow as she stepped with her good leg onto the running board and swung her bad one into the passenger compartment. Once she was settled in, he handed up her cane and bag.

God, she felt old. He was only four years younger than she was, but here she sat, a decrepit wreck, not even able to climb into a damn car by herself.

It didn't help when he practically leapt into the driver's seat, obviously eager to get to their crime scene. She wondered if she'd ever been as young as he was.

"I hardly ever get to drive one of these," he said, adjusting the mirrors. He jerked the wheel and sped them out of the garage, barely waiting for the gate to lift. Lucy grabbed onto her door handle, bracing herself as he took the corner onto Carson too fast and the SUV lurched.

"Take it easy," she told him. "The guy's not getting any deader."

"Sorry, boss." He slowed marginally but his herky-jerky steering, if anything, got worse. "I just want to nail this guy. Daddy, I mean. I've never felt so…" He slammed the brakes at a light that had been red since the last block. "Angry isn't the right word. I don't know what is. But this guy, the things he does, the way he just doesn't give a shit about anyone else. I mean, I know we've chased some bad guys, but he, he just makes me—"

"It's okay, Taylor. It's normal to react strongly when faced with someone so aberrant. This guy, he simply doesn't fit into any concept of what the world should be." Lucy almost rolled her eyes—she was channeling Nick, repeating almost word for word what he was always telling her when she got upset about a case.

"Aberrant? Yeah, he's all that and more." His voice dropped. "Lucy, do you believe in evil?"

No need to hesitate, the answer was easy. "Yes. Yes, I do. Absolutely."

"And this guy, he's evil."

"Yes."

"Then—" He dropped the sentence as if it was a hot coal. "I mean, when we catch him, do you ever wish, fantasize, about…just ending it? Not worrying about a trial or him getting off on a technicality. Just taking care of it, then and there? If he's evil, isn't it our job to protect the rest of the world from men like him?"

The rain and wind seemed distant from the darker elements swirling inside the SUV.

"Do I ever wish things were that simple?" Lucy answered, struggling to put the paradoxes that tugged at her psyche every working day into some coherent form. "Yes. But, our job isn't to destroy evil or take the law into our own hands. It's to uphold the law while protecting the innocent."

"But," he persisted, "the law doesn't always work. Is it worth the risk that it might fail? For guys like this. I mean, I'm honestly not even sure he's human. Maybe his DNA is, but his brain sure as hell isn't."

"That's fear talking. Because it would be so much easier to draw a line, decide that he's something other, on the outside of humanity that deserves to be treated equally under the law."

"So there're no exceptions?"

Yes, yes, there were. Lucy was absolutely certain of it. But she was Taylor's supervisor, his mentor, and she couldn't lead him down that path. Every man or woman who carried a badge and gun had to decide for themselves.

Taylor had never killed anyone, had never even fired his weapon in the line of duty. Lucy had. She had killed. Not just with her gun, with her bare hands, face-to-face, blood slicking blood.

She'd done right. She'd saved innocents, saved her family, saved her own life.

That didn't stop the doubts or nightmares. Wouldn't make it any easier the next time she drew her weapon. For her, the world wasn't the black and white, good and evil, clearly demarcated universe that Taylor clearly wished it was. She'd known other cops who could live that way and sleep well at night. She wasn't one of them.

Lucy's world was shades of gray. Her conscience was clear as far as the lives she'd taken; that wasn't what kept her awake at night. It was the fact that she too was only human. What if she made a mistake, let her emotions drive her to taking an innocent life?

"Here's what I know," she finally answered Taylor. "You have to decide what you can live with. You have to be able to look at yourself in the mirror come morning. And one thing that letting justice take its course gives you is time. Time to be one hundred and twenty percent certain. Time to make sure you can live with the consequences of your actions."

His lips twisted, obviously not thrilled with her reply. Neither was she. It felt much too trite when speaking of taking someone else's life...but what else could she tell him?

She touched his arm. "I trust you to do the right thing, Taylor. Remember that if the time comes for you to make a decision."

"Thanks, Lucy." Then his mood lightened. "Maybe it's a good thing the SAC is taking me out of the field. Sitting at a computer all day, you don't have to think about this kind of thing. I don't know how you stand it."

She didn't have the heart to tell him that neither did she.

----◆----

HE WATCHED FROM the van hidden in the alley across

from the abandoned plant's parking garage. Any of three outcomes were acceptable:

The yellow car. GPS systems were so very helpful.

The Fed with the cane. She'd driven the yellow car to its destination and he had ways to access that knowledge if need be.

Or her phone.

Outcomes one and three were preferable. Machines were much more useful and quicker to divulge their secrets than people.

The laptop beside him chimed: a new message from his operative in the field. *Leaving ER, following, tracker in place.*

Option four: the other two Feds gave him what he needed.

Of course the jackpot would be if the tidbits he'd left here with the body led the police to call Bernhart to the scene. Because it was Bernhart he needed silenced.

There was no way Bernhart could lead them back to him, to his home, his real life. Especially as the man had no idea what he knew.

But if Bernhart told the FBI everything—every last detail of what he'd done and who he'd done it to and why…well, that might lead to complications.

He couldn't afford complications. Not now, when everything was coming full circle.

A black SUV drove into sight, slowing before it turned into the parking garage. With the dark and rain and tinted windows it was impossible to see inside. But then both people in the front rolled down their windows to show their credentials to the officer guarding the entrance.

And there she was. Riding in the passenger seat. Made sense. He'd done his homework. Not only had she been injured and needed a cane, she was a supervisor, rated being chauffeured around to crime scenes.

Okay. Two outcomes left.

Outcome one, her phone gave him what he wanted and he left her dead—a service to his community.

Outcome two, her phone was useless and he left her dead after she told him what he needed to know.

He preferred the first. He was vulnerable, exposed here in this city. He needed to end this. Now. Tonight.

Then get rid of the evidence so he could return home and prepare for his reunion with Baby Girl.

A rustling came from the back of the van. He said nothing, merely raised his hand sharply. It stopped.

Silence fell.

CHAPTER 25

———~~~———

LUCY AND TAYLOR rode the rest of the way in silence. Taylor steered the Tahoe into the narrow lane that led from the main road into the abandoned industrial complex that housed the old bottling plant. Empty warehouses and manufacturing facilities lined the drive, dark, ugly, scabs of buildings looming out of the rain and mist to crowd the Tahoe.

At the end of the barely two-lane street sat their destination, a four-story, red brick monolith. The street divided, one direction going around to the loading dock behind the building, the other going to the entrance to the underground parking area.

Taylor made another gut-wrenching—or in Lucy's case, ankle-wrenching—turn toward the parking entrance and then spun the wheel again and hit the brakes as he steered them into the darkened maw. A single patrol car guarded the entrance, its lights providing the only illumination. Taylor rolled down both their windows as a patrol officer used his Maglite to first examine Taylor's credentials then walked around to check Lucy's.

"They're down at the bottom level. Park where you see the others. I'll radio ahead, let them know you're coming."

Taylor gave the officer a nod of thanks and jerked them forward again and into the dark spirals of the parking garage. Tight corkscrew turns led them down until finally they saw the portable halogen work lights of the crime scene crews leaking between the concrete levels. Before they hit the actual crime scene, they turned onto a level filled with official vehicles: two patrol cars, an unmarked Impala, the crime scene investigative unit, and Medical Examiner's van.

Thankful that the nightmare car ride was over and vowing never to let Taylor drive her again, Lucy grabbed her cane and climbed down. She and Taylor walked down the rain and oil-slicked concrete ramp to the lowest level, their crime scene.

Don Burroughs, the Major Crimes detective, met them at the perimeter demarcated by crime scene tape. They gave their names to an officer manning the scene and followed Burroughs down a path that CSU had cleared.

"Glad to see you back on your feet, Guardino," Burroughs said.

"Thanks for sending over the food for Nick and Megan," she replied. "And thanks also for the other." Burroughs had arranged for a specialist to clean her home after the police were done processing her mother's body and the rest of the evidence.

"Kim actually took care of it all. Figured Nick wouldn't have time to cook or shop between trips to the hospital." That first week, Lucy had spent in a fog of drugs while the surgeons took her back for three surgeries to excise the dead tissue and clear up pockets of infection.

"Tell her we all very much appreciate it." Damn, she should have tried to keep track of everyone who'd helped out and sent them thank-you cards or something. That's what her mother would have done. "The boys good?"

"Yep." He beamed proudly. "I helped coach Don Junior's basketball team to the playoffs."

Nick volunteered to coach Megan's soccer team as well. Lucy never had the time—missed more games than she attended.

They reached the lowest level of the garage. More halogen work lights flooded the area, centering on a man's body lying face-up on the concrete. He was dressed the same as the man on the motorcycle who'd grabbed June. A few feet away the bike sat, a helmet dangling from its handlebars.

"How much longer you gonna need that?" Burroughs asked, nodding to her cane.

"Maybe months, maybe forever."

"That sucks."

Taylor stared at the dead man. It wasn't the prettiest of corpses—not with the blood and brains and bone splayed open where the man's face used to be. "Did you get an ID yet?"

"Meet Kerry Gibbons." Burroughs nodded to the corpse.

"Cary like Cary Grant?" Taylor asked, taking notes on his phone.

Burroughs did a double take, frowning as if he had no idea who Taylor was talking about. "If I didn't know you had a girlfriend, I'd be worried about you, Taylor. No, Kerry, like Terry Bradshaw but with a K."

"As opposed to Carrie Bradshaw with a C?" Taylor pushed, egging Burroughs on.

"Jeezit, give me a break. Anyway Kerry—with a K— Gibbons's name fits him more ways than one. Guy was basically a gorilla for hire." Burroughs smirked at Taylor as if daring him to challenge his knowledge of obscure primates.

"Cause of death?"

"You mean other than the shotgun blast to the face? No signs of other trauma. Livescan fingerprints made the ID."

Lucy ignored them to focus on their crime scene. The parking structure made for a perfect killing ground. Secluded, no cameras or security, one way in and one way out. They followed the path cleared to the body and then back again to Burroughs' white Impala.

"They're not going to find anything." She nodded to the crime scene techs scouring for evidence.

Burroughs heaved his shoulders in a sigh. "I know. But that doesn't mean we don't have anything to work with."

His poker face was better than Taylor's but not by much. "Taylor told me you linked five other victims to Gibbons."

He glared at Taylor for spoiling his surprise, then pulled a swath of evidence bags from his overcoat and placed them on the trunk of the sedan like he was dealing cards. "Five drivers' licenses found laid out around

Gibbons' head. Like a halo or crown or something."

"Any local?"

"All out of state." Taylor leaned over them, aiming his phone to take pictures of each license. Lucy didn't bother; she knew Taylor would send them to her cell as well.

"St. Louis, New Orleans, Des Moines, Sacramento, Bakersfield." Lucy frowned at the unfamiliar names belonging to the licenses. All men, ages between mid-twenties and sixty, three Caucasian, one Hispanic, one Asian, different appearances...nothing to show any connection.

She turned back to Burroughs. "NCIC?" The National Crime Information Center was the first step in linking a name to any crime.

He lowered his head as if they were huddled up, fourth and long. "All five dead. All within the past five months. All murdered execution style. Twenty-two to the head. No evidence except for the bullets."

"So Gibbons was a hit man?" Taylor asked, bouncing on his toes. "Maybe he was shot by someone he was supposed to kill himself?"

"Gibbons doesn't exactly have a rep as a mastermind. Can't see him traveling all over the country, setting up on vics, doing a hit, and walking away again without leaving any trace." Burroughs shrugged again. "But maybe I'm wrong."

"First thing, let's check with Homeland on the travel," Lucy said.

"I'll start knocking on doors, see if there's any word on the street. And check for any alibis," Burroughs said. "We're getting warrants on his house."

"Don't forget electronics and data storage," Taylor put in.

"Taylor, reach out to the other jurisdictions, get their files for us," Lucy said. Locals were more apt to quickly respond to a polite, personal phone request from the FBI than any paperwork Burroughs submitted.

The medical examiner's people were getting ready to bundle the body in preparation of moving it. "If Gibbons wasn't behind those five murders, then who killed him? And why leave the drivers' licenses?" Taylor asked.

That wasn't what was bothering Lucy. Didn't even make her top three. "More worrisome is: what's his connection to Daddy? And does Daddy have anything to do with the five dead men?"

"Who's Daddy?" Burroughs asked.

As Taylor filled the city detective in on the threats against June and what happened earlier today, Lucy flipped through the drivers' licenses. New Orleans. St. Louis. Sacramento. Des Moines. Bakersfield. The places bothered her.

"All dead within the past five months?" she asked, interrupting Taylor. "You're sure about the time frame?"

"Yeah. Why, is that important?"

Lucy stiffened, her bad leg spasming with one of the damn electrical shocks that made her muscles quiver. The pain was secondary to a memory: Seth's voice. Telling her that five months ago he'd met the man called Daddy.

What had he said? That was the day Daddy killed him.

CHAPTER 26

"WE'VE GOT TO go," she told Taylor, rapping the floor with her cane.

"You're not holding out on me, are you, Guardino?" Burroughs asked.

"We'll send you anything we find," she assured him. Any facts, she added to herself. Vague speculations…that was another matter. "C'mon, Taylor. We can get more done at the office and I need to put my foot up."

Taylor looked surprised that she'd mention her injury but nodded, even offering her his arm to lean on. She shook it away but limped dramatically as they made their way to the far end of the floor, past the crime scene perimeter, to where the Tahoe waited.

"I'll drive, you work." She took the keys from him.

"I thought we were going back to—" He broke off when he saw her expression, and by the time she'd hauled herself, cane and all, into the Tahoe's driver's seat,

Taylor was hopping into the passenger side. He slammed the door, the resulting vibration making her wince as it jostled her foot. Damn, she really, really needed to take another one of those pills the doctor had given her. And ice, blessed, numbing ice…Ahhh, that sounded like heaven.

"What's up, boss?"

"I'm probably just being paranoid—"

He shook his head vigorously. "You always say, 'Trust no one, assume nothing.' Besides, it's not paranoid when you're almost always right."

"This is one time where I'm hoping I'm not."

"About what?"

She gestured to his laptop. "Pull up Seth Bernhart's court appearances. Go back six months."

"Sure, no problem." A few clicks and he looked at her expectantly. "Okay. Now what?"

"Compare them to the places and dates the five men were murdered."

"No. You can't think Seth—"

"Just do it, Taylor."

It took a little longer, probably because he didn't want to admit the pattern he was seeing. "He was there. In or near all those cities at the time of their murders."

"Doesn't mean he did it," she reminded him—and herself. But the knot in her gut kept twisting tighter and tighter. She grabbed her phone and tried to call Nick. No answer. She'd forgotten; he'd left it in the Ford.

Taylor's expression lightened. "Right. In fact, smart guy like him, no way would he leave a trail this obvious. And why would all their drivers' licenses end up with Gibbons?" Now he smiled, relieved. "Plus, Seth has been with us all day. He couldn't have killed Gibbons or had those drivers' licenses. Someone is trying to frame Seth for those murders. Has to be Daddy."

No, Lucy thought. If Daddy was the killer, he would have framed Seth months ago and reveled in watching the police drag Seth away from June. He would love forcing Seth to leave June unprotected, would delight in his humiliation and disgrace.

But if not Daddy, then who had killed those men? And why?

She dialed again, this time trying Megan. It went to voice mail. "Megan, ask your dad to call me as soon as you get this. It's important."

Taylor hunched over his computer, searching for more data to guide them. "Maybe Daddy hired Gibbons to do the killings for him? Except I still don't get it. I mean, I understand shooting Gibbons—cleaning up loose ends. But why let us know about the other murders?" He slumped back in his seat. "For a guy who stayed hidden for decades, he sure as hell is making waves now."

"Never underestimate the power of obsession." As she spoke, Lucy tried texting Megan. *Call me. Now.*

"Sure, I get that. But—wait." He jerked upright, rocking the SUV. "Maybe this isn't about June. Maybe it's about Seth. I mean, Seth stole June, right? He's the father of her child. And he's helped to make men like Daddy pay dearly."

Lucy had already gotten there, but let him continue. A sick knot of worry twisted her gut. She wanted to protect Seth and June from Daddy, but in doing so, had she left a killer at her home with her family?

"Today, the shooting, it was Seth who was the real

target," Taylor continued. "Oshiro jumped in the way. So, after he couldn't kill Seth, Gibbons took June when the opportunity presented itself. But, think about it, if Seth was out of the picture, Daddy could go after June and her baby any time he wanted. She doesn't qualify for Wit-Sec, and no one can afford the kind of protection needed twenty-four/seven forever. All he has to do is either kill Seth or convince the cops that Seth is a serial killer, then he's got an open field to June whenever he wants."

He turned to Lucy. "Boss, we need to get some protection up to wherever you have Seth and June stashed."

Lucy had arrived at the same conclusion if via a vastly different line of reasoning. Everyone she'd left behind was in danger.

CHAPTER 27

IT TOOK SETH a while to find the right spot for his ambush.

He drove through the deserted recreation area near the lake. There were a few private homes, two boat landings, a small man-made beach and playground, plus the campground that was closed for the season but it had cell coverage and Wi-Fi, making it the perfect starting place.

But where to end it all? Someplace that would do damage, obscure the truth. He parked in the campground and used Megan's phone to scour the online maps of the state park and adjacent recreational area.

There was a trail leading up to a waterfall and the gorge above the dam. If the weather was better, that might work. But there was no way he'd make it up there in the dark and rain. As if to prove his point, a gust of wind made the low-slung car shudder.

He glanced up river. The dam was invisible in the dark, but when they'd driven past it earlier, he remembered being impressed by how big it was. Massive and tall with water being released to bring the spring-swollen river's level down, it had made the earth tremble.

Yes. The dam would do nicely.

Megan's phone chirped with an incoming text. He ignored it just as he had the calls from Lucy earlier. She wouldn't understand—well, maybe she of all people would. But she'd try to stop him.

His head swam, and for a moment, he lost his train of thought. The moments of confusion were becoming harder to fight past. He'd seen autopsy photos of the scientist who died from mercury poisoning. Her brain—atrophied and full of holes—the damage was apparent even to a layman.

That was his brain. All he had to work with. He couldn't risk waiting, letting the poison continue its relentless march to oblivion.

Lightning struck over the lake, the resulting thunder shaking the car. A good night to end this.

A good night to die.

The Girl Who Never Was: Memoirs of a Survivor
by June Unknown

What Color Is Love?

HOW DOES SOMEONE like me fall in love?

Before Seth, anytime I was with a man, it wasn't me—it was simply an older version of Baby Girl. Pleasing, appeasing, basking in the slightest hint of attention whether it was healthy or sick, cruel or kind.

After that first trial when I spoke as myself, for myself, for the first time ever in my life, I felt different. As if there was a spark of power in me, if only I could figure out how to fan it to life. I wanted to live for me, not for someone else.

Yet, I couldn't do it alone. With Seth, I didn't need to. With him, there was no constant vigilance, searching for any hint of pleasure or displeasure. He didn't hold back affection or praise or even pride. When I was with him, I felt real.

I still had no idea who I was, but I could feel myself shedding the facade that was Baby Girl and leaving it behind once and for all.

After that first trial, Seth asked me out to dinner. To celebrate. We went to a fancy restaurant, I wore my nicest dress—the one I'd bought special for Dr. Helen's funeral the previous year—and he ordered sparkling cider instead of champagne for us to toast with since I was still underage.

The menu was a bunch of curly letters I couldn't make sense of, so I asked him to order for me. After the waiter left, we sat in silence. Before this we'd always had something to talk about—the case, Dr. Helen and how she raised me, my painting, his family, his career ambitions.

He was the first and only man I'd ever felt comfortable talking with and now it was as if we'd just run out of words. Was this how it was for everyone? I had no idea.

He didn't seem uncomfortable, not at all. Instead, he was smiling. This strange little smile I had no idea how to interpret. It wasn't lust or passion or attraction— those I could read and encourage all too well. This was something new. And that scared me because I didn't know what to do with it. Anxiety that I might do the wrong thing churned through me, like riding that bright yellow school bus that took me away from the safety of Dr. Helen's house every day when I was a kid.

His smile widened. He laid his hand over mine as if he felt my nervousness. I felt calmer, still on edge, but not ready to mentally bolt. I did that sometimes when things got overwhelming with men. Who am I kidding? I did that *every time* I was with a man. Like my body would go on autopilot, seducing and pleasing, knowing all the steps, and my mind would just run and hide in the dark cellar of my mind, the place Daddy would leave me when I was a Bad Girl.

"Was that true?" Seth finally said. "What you told the judge? Being scared all the time?"

I couldn't look him in the eye. I pulled my hand away and gulped down some water, almost spilling the glass when I set it back down. All around us were couples, leaned forward over candlelight, murmuring. I could almost see the invisible sexual tangos dancing between them.

I knew how to dance that dance. It was practically encoded in my DNA. Usually if a man asked me uncomfortable questions, I'd answer with my body, changing the subject to something more pleasurable for him. It never failed. But I wanted something more with Seth—and that scared me because I had no idea what to do about it.

"I'm not like normal people," I muttered, fascinated by the assortment of silverware laid out around my plate. "Once, when I was little, before I went to Dr. Helen's, some kids chased me out into the street and a truck was coming. I just stood there. Not afraid or anything. It almost hit me. I wasn't afraid, not at all."

The foster mom who was meant to be watching me had gone nuts. Yelled and screamed and spanked me, then locked me in my room so I wouldn't go wandering—which was fine with me. that was what I had wanted in the first place, to be left alone.

"Of course you weren't afraid—you'd never been close to streets or moving vehicles. You had no idea how to judge distance or speed." I still don't, but that's beside the point.

"No, you don't understand. I understood I was in danger. I just wasn't afraid. My heart never raced, I never felt any of the things normal people feel when they're scared." I paused. "A few of the doctors—not Dr. Helen, but some of the others—they said I might be a sociopath. Incapable of feeling anything. Not real emotions. Just whatever I learned to fake."

My face still down, I slanted my eyes up to see his reaction. He wasn't repulsed or disgusted. Thoughtful. He looked thoughtful.

Just like Dr. Helen had all those years ago when she helped me label my feelings. I wasn't very good with words, so we used pictures and sounds and smells to help me sort things out. I had no clue what emotions were—and I rarely ever showed anything I felt inside, not to strangers, not even to Dr. Helen, not for a long time.

Fear was easy, even though I rarely felt it—just about never once I moved to Dr. Helen's house. It was stinky, wet, moldy, blacker than the darkest night, like the cellar where I went when I was a Bad Girl. Alone in the dark.

Joy was just as simple. It was bright, bright light, the way it chisels into the black as the door squeaks open and Daddy stands there, calling for me, and I race up the cellar stairs and leap into his arms.

Pleasure, pain—those were more difficult to sort out. I had no comprehension of some of the bigger emotions: anger, envy, lust, shame, sadness, hate. Those I didn't learn until I left Daddy.

Despair was the color green mixed with the smells

of that food court and the damp of wet panties as I sat and sat and sat, waiting for Mr. Green Elephant.

Contentment was a cup of hot cocoa warming my hands as I snuggled in Daddy's lap and he brushed my hair, making me all pretty.

Betrayal was the smell of doctors and the pinch and lies that came from the nurses who told you it wouldn't hurt a bit and gave you shots.

Love...that one was the easiest one of all. Love was Daddy. His body pressed on top of mine so I almost couldn't breathe, the way he sang to me and I'd stand on his feet and we'd dance and dance and dance until we fell on the floor laughing, the itch of his cheek against my skin when he hadn't shaved. He was everything. Isn't that what love is? When you make someone else your everything?

Dr. Helen thought that was a real breakthrough. Asked me to think about one question, but I never could, kept pushing it away. *If Daddy was my everything, did I really believe I was his?*

I hadn't thought about that in years, but now tonight, sitting in this fancy restaurant with Seth, her words kept hammering at me.

"But you didn't lie to the judge," Seth was saying when I tuned back in. "I could tell. All those things you said about the panic when you walk out the door, or around men, waking up at night...those were true."

I shrugged, tried to steer him to something else. "Like I said, I don't get afraid like other people."

Another long pause. This was not going well. Anxiety crept over me like my old fuzzy blanket I used to hide under, let it filter the light and the world away as I retreated.

"A truck almost killing you doesn't scare you, but...standing up in that courtroom, being here tonight...God, I'm an idiot." He took my hand again, squeezed it, his fingers resting against my fluttering pulse. "Are you okay? How do you feel? Don't panic. We can leave if you want."

I looked up, surprised. No one except Dr. Helen had ever asked me that before. How did I feel?

That hot rush that had given me strength in the courtroom earlier was a distant memory. Until I saw the look on Seth's face.

"I'm so proud of you," he said. "Standing up to your fears—without ever even saying a word to anyone. You just...You are the most incredible, the most brave person I've ever met."

For the first time in years, I had a new emotion to add to Dr. Helen's chart: Pride. This, the way the angles in Seth's face melted, the soft blur of his words, the warm feeling that started in my center and spread out making my fingers and toes tingle. This was pride.

Like an addict, I wanted more. To stand for myself, to feel strong and...necessary.

All my life, I'd been the one who needed, who couldn't survive without someone to please. Suddenly, someone needed me. And all he wanted was for me to just be me—fears and faults and flaws and all.

And that was how we started.

Seth didn't push me as I tried out my newfound independence. The only thing he refused me was sex.

Not because he was playing any kind of game, but because he knew if we were meant to be together, we'd need to learn how to create our own unique intimacy. First on an emotional level, then on a physical one.

The exact opposite of every other man I'd ever known. How could I not fall in love with him?

We had our struggles—I'd fall back on old patterns, he'd get frustrated—but still, he took me home to meet his family. And I fell in love all over again.

A big, boisterous clan, they immediately embraced me as one of their own. It was more than overwhelming, and I'd sometimes feel the need to retreat, but they always made space for me, giving me time and breathing room.

For the first time ever, I had a family.

More important, for the first time ever, I wanted to make a family. Because I knew no matter how screwed up I was, Seth would take care of us. Any baby I brought into the world with him would be cared for and loved and tended to and...safe.

That was the dream come true.

Too bad it didn't quite turn out that way.

CHAPTER 28

"DAD," MEGAN SHOUTED. June's grip on her shoulder tightened as she leaned all her weight on Megan.

Her father came rushing in from the kitchen. "What's wrong?"

"I think the baby's coming," June said.

He took two steps forward then one step back. "Are you having contractions? When did they start? How far apart?"

June took a few deep breaths and relaxed, releasing Megan. "My back's been cramping since last night. I thought it was the long car ride."

"When's your due date?"

"Not for another three weeks." She suddenly looked panicked. "That's too soon, isn't it? Where's Seth? I need him."

Megan squeezed her arm. "It will be okay, June. Just breathe. Think about your beautiful baby." She hoped that was the right thing to say. Her dad gave her a nod and June took a few deep breaths, seemed to calm a bit. "Do you want to sit? Lie down?"

"Feels worse sitting." She took a few steps, leaving Megan. "I'm fine now. Maybe it's a false alarm."

The puddle of fluid on the floor said otherwise. Megan glanced at her dad. "No need to panic," he said. "First time mother, labor can last for hours. Lucy was in labor thirteen hours with Megan."

June's eyes widened at the thought. Way to go, Dad.

"Let me get a mop, wipe this up," Megan said.

"Sorry about the trouble," June said. "I'll go get cleaned up." She moved down to the bathroom as Megan joined her father in the kitchen.

"What are we going to do?" she asked.

"Three weeks early. I think we need to get June to a hospital." No duh—Megan definitely voted for the baby being born in a hospital, not here, anywhere but here. He frowned, staring past her out the window and the storm. "I can't leave you, but it's too dangerous to send you for help."

No way did Megan want to venture out into the storm, everyone depending on her to make it to a phone without getting lost. "I'm not leaving June."

"What do you know about delivering babies?" he asked. At first she thought he was joking but he was serious.

"We saw a movie in health class. It was pretty gross. And they talked about it in my emergency responder class." Part of Megan's preparation for her black belt was taking an advanced first-aid class in addition to performing community service and teaching the younger kids at the dojo.

He nodded grimly. "That's more than me. Plus you can shoot better than I can."

Shoot? Oh yeah. The bad guys after June. "Like you said, she might not even have the baby tonight."

"Maybe we should both just stay here. But what if there are complications? We need to consider the odds of that versus the odds that your mother was wrong and someone might have followed her here. She said Walden was coming, but who knows how long he'll be."

Megan blinked. He was asking her to weigh in on the decision as if she was an adult. She thought hard, trying to put her fear aside and think about what was best for June and the baby. "You should go. You can move faster than I can, get help up here. Besides, either Walden or Seth will probably get here soon."

Seth. Where was he? Was he even planning to come back or was he going to try to stop the bad guys all by himself? If so, then they wouldn't be coming here. That was one good thing.

She grabbed the mop from the laundry room and cleaned up the mess on the living room floor. By the time she'd finished and returned to the kitchen, it was clear her father had made up his mind. He had a pot of water on the stove, scissors and string waiting on the counter nearby. "Just in case."

"So you're staying?" She bit her lip as she looked out to the storm. "I can't go through the woods," she confessed. "I'll get lost. I'll have to take the road and that's miles longer."

He gave her a quick hug. "Sweetheart, it's okay. If it comes to it, I can find my way down the path to the lake. There are phones there at the rec area."

"You're leaving me?" She didn't want that either. She wanted him to stay. Here. Where it was safe. With her.

He looked stricken at the idea. Wrapped his arms around her, pulling her tight. "No, Megan, I'm not. I'm just thinking through all the options. But there is no way I'd ever risk you. I know it sounds awful, but you're *my* baby. You come before anyone else's."

Megan clutched at him, wishing she never had to leave his embrace. "Then why was it so easy for Mom to leave? She had the same choice to make as you do."

"It's not the same and you know it. To start with, she left you with me. She knew I'd take care of you, no matter what. And she had no idea Seth would take the car and your cell phone."

Didn't matter. Mom had still left. And now she and Dad were going to have to do this all alone, deliver a baby.

"I know Mom has to do her job," Megan started before he could tell her to stop being a spoiled brat and grow up—heck, that's what she kept telling herself. But...all the words in the world couldn't change her feelings. "But sometimes I wish there was someone else who could fight the bad guys." She looked down at her feet, hating to chance spying her father's disappointment. "Sometimes I wish she'd choose us."

Dad folded her into a hug that rocked her onto her toes. "Honey, she does choose us. You know that. Just like I know that you're very proud of the work she does, the lives she saves. But it's tough seeing her go, isn't it?"

She nodded into his chest.

"Can I tell you a secret? It is for me, too."

They stood still for a long moment, then he held her at arm's length. "You up for this? Helping June and her baby?"

Excitement pushed her fear away. "Yes, sir."

He didn't look convinced, but gave her another quick hug, kissing the top of her head like she was a baby. "I love you. And I'm so very proud of you. You can handle this, I know you can."

They separated. Dad rubbed his face, deep in thought.

"Do you know where Grams keeps her first-aid kit?" he asked.

"In the bathroom, under the sink."

"When June's done in there, you grab it, set up everything we'll need. Get the lantern and flashlights out, just in case." As he spoke, he grabbed the heavy-duty flashlight from the junk drawer and tested it. "I'm going to get more wood for the fire." He looked around the room, frowning. "Not sure what else we can do."

"Women have been having babies for millions of years. It's going to be fine." She blinked, realizing she sounded just like her mom: confident and in control. If only she actually felt that way inside.

They returned to the living room as June emerged from the bathroom. She'd obviously been crying, her face splotchy and eyes red. "Are you leaving?"

"Just bringing in more wood. Are you doing okay? Do you need anything?"

She held both hands under her belly as if protecting the baby from everything that was going wrong. Took a deep breath. "Okay. It'll be okay." She looked to Megan. "Right?"

Why was she looking to Megan for reassurance? And how could she sound so calm? But then she realized what choice did she have? The baby was coming no matter what, panicking wouldn't solve anything.

She straightened and glanced at the photo of her grams on the mantle. What would she do if she was in Megan's position? That was easy.

"How about a nice cup of tea?"

CHAPTER 29

LUCY TRIED MEGAN one last time and when she couldn't make it through, she called Walden. "How far are you from my house?"

"We're almost there. Got a bit of a late start—"

"Hey, Lucy Mae!" Oshiro's voice rang out. "No way I was gonna miss this party."

Of course not. Mr. Superman wouldn't let a few cracked ribs and a gunshot wound slow him down. And people accused Lucy of pushing herself.

"When you get there, I need to speak to Nick—no one's picking up when I call. And you need to keep an eye on Seth."

"Seth? Why?"

No way was she explaining her wildly unsubstantiated theory over the phone. Besides, Walden and Oshiro were friends of Seth; it wasn't fair to put them in that position until she had facts.

"I need to ask him more about his recent cases. You

know what? It's going to be crowded up there and Taylor wants his car back. Send Nick and Megan back to the city. Less distractions for you two."

Silence for a moment and she knew he was parsing her words, not understanding what was behind them. But Walden being Walden, he didn't ask why she wanted Nick and Megan back with her, away from Seth. One of the reasons she loved working with the man. When it came to dissecting theories for a case, he'd gleefully question her every idea, rip them apart with surgical precision. But he'd never question her judgment when it came to her family.

"Will do," he finally said.

"Thanks. And tell Oshiro to stay out of trouble."

"You kidding? I'm putting in for hazard pay just hanging out with the guy."

Lucy hung up, started the Tahoe, and steered it up through the levels of the empty parking garage. Taylor hunched over his computer, oblivious to anything else.

"Hang on," he said, talking to himself as she left the parking garage and turned down the narrow drive leading back to the street. The rain still pounded steadily but the tall warehouses lining the drive blocked the wind. She turned the wipers up to their highest setting and hit defrost. "Whoa. Hang on. I think my algorithm—" He jerked upright. "What the hell?"

Ahead of them a wall of flames filled the night. A Dumpster had been pushed into the drive and set on fire, Lucy saw between swipes of the wiper blades. Her tactical instincts kicked in and she accelerated.

A layperson would slam on the brakes, try to swerve to turn away from the obstacle. But that meant stopping and becoming vulnerable to an ambush. The best way to handle a barricade like this was the same way her mom had taught her to handle a deer running at a car—basically a modified PIT maneuver. Hit the obstacle at the far corner, using the momentum of your vehicle to pivot it one way while you sped past it in the other direction.

Too slow and the obstacle might spin the entire arc, crashing into the rear of your vehicle. Too fast and you might skid out of control.

Lucy judged the rain-slick pavement, the size and weight of the Dumpster, ignored the fire—it was there to trigger primal fear, wouldn't pose a danger unless the Dumpster tipped over on top of the Tahoe and the fire spilled out—and aimed her driver's side front bumper at the far right hand corner of the Dumpster. There was a little more room between the Dumpster and the brick wall of the warehouse they were passing on that side. If she hit the Dumpster just right—

The headlights caught a figure standing in the rain just past the Dumpster. A little girl, barefoot and soaking wet, wearing nothing but a pink nightgown, her face reflecting the flames.

Taylor saw her as well. "Lucy, look out!"

The Tahoe hit the Dumpster's corner as planned—not hard enough to blow the air bags, just hard enough to spin the Dumpster out of their way. Except now she had no room to maneuver around the little girl in the center of the road. Who wasn't moving. Just stared at Lucy and the SUV rushing toward her, squinting her eyes against the glare of the headlights.

"Move, get out of there!" Taylor shouted to the girl.

Lucy didn't have time for useless words. She jammed on the brakes and yanked the wheel as hard left as possible, spinning the Tahoe to follow the same trajectory that she'd sent the Dumpster in. Not enough, they were still going too fast. She hauled her bad foot up to hit the emergency brake. The smell of burning rubber filled the vehicle.

Her vision tunneled to focus on the little girl who stood frozen. Lucy barely registered the dark van with its rear doors open parked between the girl and the end of the drive or the flames marking the Dumpster's movement as it finished its arc by slamming into the Tahoe's rear driver's side panel.

Taylor pressed his face against his window, watching as they skidded in front of the girl; while Lucy furiously spun the wheel back the opposite way to avoid going a full 180 and risk hitting the girl with the rear of the SUV. Instead, she aimed for the wall of the building opposite them. They'd slowed enough that was the safest course for everyone.

The SUV hit the wall. Taylor's laptop flew past Lucy, careening into the back seat. The airbags deployed, filling the passenger compartment with smoke and powder and swaths of fabric dropping from the ceiling as well as bursting free from the dashboard.

The Dumpster lurched to a stop, bouncing off their rear quarter, in effect swapping positions with the original angle of the SUV that now sat stopped, blocking the road horizontally.

"Can you see her?" Lucy asked Taylor, choking on the smoke. Her seat belt had tightened and wasn't helping; she could barely draw in a breath. Never mind the red-hot blaze of pain racing up her leg. "Did I hit her? Are you okay?"

She raised her head, trying to see through the windshield. A rush of cold air and water hit her from Taylor's side of the vehicle. Still stunned, she swung around to face him, just as he yelled something incomprehensible.

His body was dragged from the vehicle and out into the night.

She blinked, trying to focus, the airbag smoke burning her eyes. A man. A man had Taylor.

It took two tries to get her seatbelt unfastened. She drew her weapon but Taylor and his abductor had moved far enough away that she had no shot—and no cover, not sitting in the vehicle.

Her door opened with a groan of metal. She slid out, forgetting how high the Tahoe was, but her good foot caught the running board in time to save her from a fall. Adrenaline swept away the pain as she landed on the pavement and stumbled around the backside of the SUV, using it as cover. The Dumpster was behind her, only five or six feet away, the heat of the flames rising over its sides warming her back.

She barely noticed. All her focus was on Taylor. The man used him as cover, couldn't be much taller than Taylor's own five-seven. He must have come prepared because he was forcing Taylor to place handcuffs on himself as he dragged them back, a semi-automatic pistol held to Taylor's head. It could have been Taylor's own service weapon.

She aimed her Glock but the girl stood between her and the man. And the man was smart enough to stay behind Taylor, the only part of him exposed was his arm holding the weapon. Taylor snapped the handcuffs shut and raised his head, his expression a mix of shock and fear.

"Stop!" Lucy shouted over the roar of the flames behind her and the sound of the rain. "Federal agents. Put your weapon down."

She wasn't expecting the man to obey—it was clear this was a well-planned attack—but hoped he might stop to answer, giving her a few more precious seconds to find the shot she needed. They were almost to the rear of the van.

Lucy moved forward, her weapon trained on Taylor and the man. She had almost reached the little girl who still wasn't moving, hadn't even turned to watch the commotion behind her. Least of Lucy's worries. If she let Taylor get inside that van...

"You know what I want," the man shouted, raising his head just enough for Lucy to see he wore a ski mask. "Call me when you have it."

They reached the open rear door of the van. Lucy braced herself. There'd be a moment, just a moment, when the abductor would need to show himself as he loaded Taylor inside. That's when she'd take him down.

The abductor swung Taylor around, ready to push him into the van. Lucy forced herself to slow her breathing. Get ready, get ready... In the instant before the abductor would have been exposed, he lowered his weapon.

Just long enough to shoot a puddle standing between him and the girl.

Fire blazed up from the pavement. Lucy blinked

against the sudden light as she realized the attacker had done more than prepare a diversion with a puddle of gasoline. He'd left a trail of it leading to where the girl stood.

Her aim remained on the attacker who waited, his mouth a pale, twisted goblin grin in the light of the fire, the rest of his face concealed by the mask. The fire raced toward the girl.

Taylor met Lucy's gaze. His eyes were wide, his chest heaving, but he gave her a nod. She'd already made her choice, was holstering her weapon even as she spun toward the girl who stood perfectly still, although there was no way she couldn't sense the fire rushing toward her.

As Lucy lurched to reach the girl, her bad leg slowing her, the man threw Taylor into the van and hopped in after him, slamming the door shut. Lucy traced the trajectory of the flames—she was too slow, she wasn't going to reach the girl in time.

The van sped off. Lucy closed the distance, was only a few feet away when the flames hit the puddle where the girl stood waiting. Fire gushed through the air. Lucy pushed off with her good foot and leapt.

She tackled the girl, cradling the girl's head in her arms, and rolled them free from the puddle of gasoline, flames following them as the girl's nightgown caught fire. Lucy rolled them on the wet pavement, once, twice, then stopped as the flames died and they were clear of the blaze.

She pushed up, her elbows scraped, leg crying for mercy, and examined the girl. No injuries except some redness to her feet and ankles, and the bottom of her nightgown was singed.

Running footsteps came up from behind her. The patrolman who'd been guarding the entrance to their crime scene. He had his weapon drawn and was yelling into his radio. Lucy glanced down the drive just in time to see the van career onto the main road and vanish from sight.

"I need an ambulance and road blocks—they took Taylor!" she shouted over the rushing in her head.

She knew she needed to slow down, but the adrenalin flooding her system was in control of the moment. She sat on the filthy pavement, water splashing around her, fire in front of her and behind her, and couldn't tell if her face was wet with rain or tears as she hugged the girl to her chest.

"What took you so long?" she asked the patrolman as he bent to see if either she or the girl were injured.

"You kidding?" he replied, his voice coming in a staccato as he heaved in one breath after another. "Broke my record for the forty. It all happened so fast."

Sirens and lights filled the street behind her as Burroughs and the other cops arrived. The Dumpster and Tahoe blocked their path, stymieing any attempt at pursuit. Burroughs jumped out of his Impala and ran over to her. "Lucy, what happened?"

She squeezed her eyes and looked away. "Taylor. He took Taylor."

CHAPTER 30

LUCY SOMEHOW MANAGED to get a call into the on-duty agent at the federal building to send the alert of Taylor's abduction and set up a trap on her cell phone as well as Taylor's. That would track any incoming or outgoing calls as well as activate the GPS locators. When she finished, she stared at her phone and couldn't remember if she'd actually made the call or had only imagined it.

The girl cradled in her lap hadn't said a word, hadn't moved. "It's okay," Lucy murmured, stroking her hair and bending over her to shield her from the chaos surrounding them. "You're safe now."

The girl didn't even blink. She stared at the spot where the van had been.

"Do you know your name?" Lucy asked. Missy Barstow had been only ten months old when she'd been abducted. She couldn't be one hundred percent certain this girl was Missy, but she bore a strong resemblance to her parents' pictures from the case file.

The girl's face went blank as she considered the question. She didn't look at Lucy as she answered. "Girl."

The single word was heart wrenching. Lucy buried

her face in the shoulder of her parka, wiping away water and hiding her expression. Bastard, she thought, rage drowning out any thought of professionalism. There was no hell, no torture heinous enough for the man who called himself Daddy.

"Your name, your real name," Lucy told the girl once she composed herself, "is Missy Barstow. Your mommy and daddy—your real daddy—have been looking for you for a long, long time. They miss you very much and will be so happy to have you back."

The girl's face remained blank but she clenched both fists and drew them up to her chest as if warding off an attack. "I want Daddy. I was a good girl. He said to stand still and I did, no matter what, I did. Where's Daddy?"

Lucy had no strength left to answer, so she simply hugged the girl tighter. Burroughs finished delegating tasks to the officers and joined them. He crouched down and gave the girl a warm smile. "Hi, sweetie. Let's get you out of this rain."

He lifted her from Lucy's arms and transferred her into the shelter of the wrecked Tahoe while they waited for the ambulance. She didn't resist, wouldn't even look Burroughs in the eye, just kept turning her head to stare in the direction the van had taken.

Lucy trudged after them, rain battering her from all directions, yet she felt nothing.

"Guess we know why he planted those drivers' licenses," Burroughs said, standing outside and leaning against the open rear door of the Tahoe, shielding Lucy and the silent girl from the weather. "It was a trap. This guy's got balls, I'll say that for him. No way after what happened down at the waterfront today would you resist coming to see the actor who tried to grab that girl. But why target you? Thought you said he was after June Unknown and her husband."

The ambulance arrived, sparing Lucy the need to answer. Good thing since she had no answers, just an idea that scared the crap out of her. Had she told Taylor where June and Seth were? She couldn't remember.

"Lend me your phone," she asked Burroughs. She didn't want to tie hers up in case Taylor's abductor tried to call. Burroughs stood, looming over her as she dialed Walden, obviously intent on listening in. But the paramedics moved him aside as they transferred the girl to their stretcher.

"You need checked out, ma'am?" one of them asked, nodding to Lucy's scrapes along her palms and arms.

She was waiting for Walden to pick up and spared the paramedic only a cursory shake of her head before closing the door on him, Burroughs, and the chaos of the scene.

"Yeah, Boss," Walden answered. "Just heard about Taylor. We'll turn around."

"No," she ordered. "You need to get to the house and evacuate everyone. Take them someplace safe. Don't tell me where, not until this is all finished."

Oshiro's voice came through. "You think he took Taylor to get intel on June's location?"

Not June's, Seth's. If her theory was correct, Daddy needed to know if one of the dead men had given him up. But it was still just a theory, so she didn't waste energy on words. As soon as she knew Nick and Megan were clear of the situation, she would confront Seth herself. "Keep my family safe, Timmy."

"Yes, ma'am. They're in good hands."

"How close are you?"

"Pulling into the drive now," Walden replied. "Sorry it took us so long—there was a wreck on 22."

"Didn't you say Taylor's banana-mobile was here?" Oshiro asked. "I don't see it."

That would explain a lot. "Walden, call me once you're inside and secure."

She hung up and tried Megan's number again. "Seth. We need to talk. I know about the men. About Sacramento, DesMoines, Bakersfield, New Orleans, St. Louis. Daddy took Taylor. He might be going after June and my family next. Call me. I know you want to do this alone, but you'll get a good man killed. You need to let me help."

A knock at the window startled her. She glanced up to see John Greally standing there, his expression a professional mask studded with cracks chiseled by worry and anger. She unlocked the door and he opened it, sliding in beside her, and closing it once more.

"Tell me everything," he commanded.

She did, leaving out only her suspicions about Seth. No proof and no relevance to any official strategies to rescue Taylor.

"The fire was headed toward the girl," she finished. "Our subject stood, watching. He knew I had no time to take the shot and save Taylor, he knew I had to choose. So did Taylor." Her voice dropped but still sounded much too loud in the hollow confines of the SUV. "I let him take Taylor."

They sat in silence for a long moment, then Greally the ASAC morphed into Greally her friend and wrapped an arm around her shoulders. She was glad for the tinted glass giving them privacy.

"Taylor knows you had no choice," Greally said. "Even if you did, he would have wanted you to save the girl."

"I'm so sick and tired of being backed into a corner. Of doing the right thing yet still losing."

"It's not a game, Lucy."

"Tell that to the guys at OPR when they play Monday morning quarterback and dissect my every move. I allowed a serial killer with no conscience to abduct one of my men. Take him right in front of me while I had a weapon trained on him. I'm finished, Greally. This is it."

He moved his arm away from her and turned in his seat to face her, his expression stern. "Is that self-pity I'm hearing, Special Agent?"

She shook her head. It took everything she had to meet his gaze. "No, sir. It's a warning. You might want to distance yourself. Because I will get Taylor back. And I will stop this subject. Whatever it takes."

———◆———

ONCE HE WAS ready, Seth pulled his and June's cell phones out of the special bag and box and turned them on. It was a short hike to the dam and he wanted Daddy to follow him every step of the way.

Unlike Seth's previous quarries, Daddy would be expecting a trap. Fine with Seth. He wasn't planning to get away with murder, not this time. All he needed was to close the distance enough to get a few well-placed shots off.

He was betting on the fact that after trying to have Seth killed earlier today, Daddy wouldn't be able to resist finishing the job face-to-face.

Megan's phone sounded again. Lucy. Again. He'd listened to her messages, felt bad about Taylor, but really what more could he do besides what he was already doing? He sat in the driver's seat, staring at the phone. He should be moving, but his body was suddenly sapped of energy and it was all he could do to keep from dropping the phone.

He'd left a message for June in the glove compartment, but there was a chance no one would find it. It was too late for Lucy to stop his plan, so he answered.

"I'm going to finish this," he said by way of greeting.

"I know. But Taylor shouldn't pay the price. That's not what you're about, not why you killed those men."

He didn't have an answer for that and almost hung up, when she said, "I checked the police reports. Each of them had images from the Baby Girl collection in their possession. Images that we've never seen before. The autopsies say those men were tortured, water boarded, before they died. I know that wasn't for fun. Not even for revenge."

"I needed information and it was the fastest way. Don't you think for one moment that I enjoyed it—"

"Of course not. Those men were stalking you and June, threatening your family."

"He told them to. Sent them after us. Gave them special access to his private collection. Sick, twisted bastard. He's not getting away with it. Not again."

"You turned your phones back on. He'll know it's a trap."

"Even without Taylor, sounds like you're getting along just fine."

"Not really. He left his computer behind."

"He was tracking our phones?"

"Yes. I can be at your location in forty minutes. Will you wait for me? Or at least let me negotiate something with Daddy to save Taylor?"

"Negotiate? No such thing. Not with him. He takes what he wants and doesn't give a shit about the rest of the world."

"Know how he got Taylor?" Her voice snagged as if she was in pain. "I was lining up a shot to take down Daddy and save Taylor when Daddy lit his latest victim, little Missy Barstow, on fire. I had to make a choice, Seth. And Taylor knew—he watched me choose Missy. I abandoned my man, Seth. You have to give me a chance to get him back."

He closed his eyes and pressed his free hand against his face, trying to block out the image she described. "Is she okay? The little girl?"

"She's alive. I don't know if she'll ever be okay."

Seth's chest tightened as he held his breath. Lucy waited on the other end of the line. Finally, he could take it no longer. He blew his breath out and with it his last hope.

"What did you have in mind?"

CHAPTER 31

HE HAD NO idea why the Feds left the ER, hell left the entire city behind, to drive up a mountain near Latrobe. But if it led him to his payoff, he'd keep following.

To avoid being spotted on the deserted rural roads, he had to stay far behind them once they turned off the main highway, but the tracker was doing its job, so he was only about twelve minutes out when they finally came to a stop. Finding a hiding place for the SUV while he performed his recon was more difficult, but the storm helped as did a muddy logging road about a quarter of a mile down the mountain from his target.

The rain didn't bother him—it made for better concealment. He secured his weapons so they'd stay as dry as possible but still be accessible. A Desert Eagle in a holster strapped to his thigh, three magazines in one of his cargo pockets, two folding knives, one concealed fixed blade, and a fully-automatic MAC-10 he'd customized with a muzzle suppressor and night scope. Locked and loaded and ready for action.

As he climbed up to the house, mud and dead leaves squished beneath his boots; he grinned. This was more like it. So much better than the job had been until now: basically stalking the pregnant woman and her husband.

Not that he minded the hunt. But part of what he'd been paid for was to also let the targets, especially the husband, know he was there, watching. Damned unprofessional, in his opinion, but he wasn't in a position to say no to Daddy. Even though they shared some of the same tastes, at least he didn't turn his own kids into fodder for other men's jerk-off sessions.

Daddy might be a master geek, hacking into his computer and holding it for ransom until this job was done, but he had some ideas on how to turn the tables on the SOB.

The tree line ended in a clearing around the lonely house. Using his scope, he surveyed the location. One car in the driveway—the Feds' gray Taurus. Both Feds inside the front room along with another man, obviously a civilian. A teenaged girl and the pregnant woman paced back and forth, moving in and out of sight. The pregnant woman held the girl's arm and looked to be in pain.

Crouching low, below the level of the windows, he made his way across the yard with its straggly shrubs and flowerbeds. A few tiny purple and yellow irises bloomed beneath the window beside the porch. He crushed them beneath his boots as he strained to hear the conversation.

One of the Feds was talking on his cell phone and then handed it to the civilian.

He peered inside, spotted a shotgun near the door. Despite their injuries—the big one had his right arm bandaged and moved slowly, the other wasn't moving his left arm—the Feds were also armed. So that was at least three shooters—he could probably count out the girl and pregnant woman. Good odds, he'd had worse and come out ahead of the game, but he couldn't risk the pregnant woman getting hit. She was worth some serious change to the fetish-freaks. Not to mention the bounty Daddy would pay.

There was no sign of the real target: the husband. Daddy wanted him, bad. Fast. Which made him wonder what the guy knew—obviously something worth money.

Flashing lights coming down the drive made him tense, but the porch above him provided good cover. Not cops. An ambulance.

For the pregnant woman. He considered his options, a plan forming. It would piss Daddy off, but it would be leverage to force a face to face with the porno king. Only one of them would be leaving that meeting alive.

Best of all worlds. He whistled through his teeth, watching as two paramedics laden with gear wheeled a stretcher up to the house, leaving the ambulance doors wide open and unguarded.

Easier than stealing candy from a baby.

———•———

THE VAN LURCHED from side to side so harshly Taylor feared he'd be sick. He never did very well in cars, not without something to distract him from the movement. Kneeling, his hands cuffed to an U-bolt welded to the floor, unable to see where they were going, his imagination soaring with ideas of just how badly tonight might end…a wave of bile forced his jaw to clench shut as he swallowed it down, praying it wouldn't come right back up again.

Focus, he told himself. What would Lucy do? Hostage situations are all about connection, she'd say. Figure out what they want, make them think they're going to get it, and work from there.

"I'm Special Agent Zach Taylor," he said when he was certain he could keep his voice steady and not throw up. "What are you hoping to accomplish here? Maybe I can help."

At first he thought the driver would simply ignore him. The man had said nothing to him since he'd thrown Taylor onto the floor of the van, snapped the second pair of cuffs waiting and already attached to the U-bolt around the chain of the ones that secured Taylor, slammed the van door shut, tightened Taylor's cuffs, emptied his pockets, then hopped into the driver's seat. And now they were heading lord only knew where.

Taylor forced the myriad of gruesome visions of blood and torture away and tried again. "What do you want?"

"Sure as hell wasn't you," the man snapped. His accent was not Pittsburgh, not enough hills and valleys to it. More flatlander. Midwest. "Supposed to be that bitch cop in the passenger seat. Then we'd be done already."

"Maybe I can help you. If you tell me what you wanted from Lucy. We work together."

"You mean you're her driver." He yanked the wheel and they changed lanes. Despite the rain, they were going pretty fast. The Parkway, Taylor guessed. Heading east. "Right about here is where I lost them. Tell me where she took them and I'll let you go."

"Them? You mean June and Seth?"

"I mean my girls and that worthless piece of trash who keeps sticking his nose in my business. Where are they?"

Taylor had no clue. Lucy hadn't told him. Not that this guy would believe him. What would a man willing to burn a little girl alive as a diversion do to Taylor to get the info he wanted?

His stomach rebelled at the images his mind conjured. Connect. He had to connect with this guy.

"I loved your hack on the medical database," Taylor said. "Man, that was epic. A real thing of beauty."

"You found that?" The man's tone was one of surprise and for the first time he met Taylor's gaze in the rearview mirror.

"Took me a few hours, but yeah. It's what I do."

The man made a grunting noise of acknowledgment. They drove on in silence for a while, turning off the Parkway onto a road that had stops and starts. No tollbooth, Taylor thought, creating their journey in his mind, must be 22. Lucy's mom had lived off of 22, just north of Latrobe. Could she have taken June and Seth there for safekeeping?

He immediately wished he hadn't thought of that—it was easier to not know something than to know it and hide it.

The van made an abrupt turn, sending Taylor sprawling as his legs slid out from under him, wrenching his wrists against the too-tight cuffs. They bumped over a curb, another sharp turn, and then came to a stop.

"Great thing about a dark van on a dark and stormy

night, sitting behind a dark, out-of-business furniture store in the middle of an empty strip mall? No one's gonna notice anything that happens here."

The man spun from the driver's seat and entered the rear of the van where Taylor scrambled to get back on his knees. No way in hell was he going to face this guy lying on his belly. He braced his weight on one leg, thinking he could get a kick or two in, maybe.

The man crouched down and raised Taylor's phone. He snapped a few pictures of Taylor, the flash blinding. By the time Taylor could focus again, the man was back in his seat, hunched over a laptop he'd opened up on the passenger seat.

"How convenient. Lucy's number is right here. Once I hide my code in this photo of you looking especially terrified, she won't think twice about opening it. And I'll have my way in, can track her, see who she calls, hear everything she hears."

"Is that how you tracked Seth and June here from DC?" Taylor asked, stalling for time.

The man didn't seem to mind. "No. Met Seth in person. Fool had no idea. Swapped his phone for one I'd cloned, so I already controlled it. Planted a GPS tracker in with the battery as well. Once I had his phone, it was easy to infiltrate the girl's. All she had to do was open a text with a photo from her dear hubby after I intercepted the original and modified it."

Easy? He was talking about software that could be worth millions on the DarkNet—and almost as much to legitimate companies so they could develop a protection against it. Taylor fumed in silence, wondering how long he had to live once the man accessed Lucy's phone.

There had to be someway out of this, someway to warn her.

The man stopped typing and sat back. "Huh." He sounded surprised but not upset. "Might not need your Lucy after all. Looks like June and her man are back on line. At a," he leaned forward, peering at the screen, "campground outside of Latrobe."

Latrobe? That was near Lucy's mother's house. But why would June or Seth turn their phones back on? It was suicide.

The man stared silently at the computer then abruptly swiveled back to face Taylor. "It's a trap, of course. No way would she not have confiscated their phones, right?"

He spoke as if he was used to talking to himself and not getting an answer. Taylor debated remaining silent but then decided he couldn't engage the man unless he turned his monologues into a conversation.

"Right," he answered. "I keep Faraday bags in my car. That's why you lost the signal after Lucy took their phones."

Then it occurred to him—if Lucy turned the phones on, she'd have done it to signal Seth and June's presumed location to Daddy. But how had she gotten to Latrobe so quickly? Helicopter? He envisioned Lucy and the SWAT team preparing his rescue and felt better. A little better, any way.

"And here's the invitation to her party," the man said, squinted at Taylor's phone. "Guess you're worth something after all. She wants a hostage exchange." He stared at Taylor for a long time, assessing him.

"Is your Lucy that smart?" the man asked. "Smart

enough to think she can double-cross me? I googled her after what happened on the river this afternoon, sounds like she might be." His grin showed his teeth. "Well, now, I doubt she's as smart as me. I might just have my own trap. With you as the bait."

CHAPTER 32

~~~

OF COURSE GREALLY didn't walk away—not even after
Lucy told him her idea to rescue Taylor. Once Daddy
replied with his conditions and instructions, he dove in
with both feet, marshaling the field office's SWAT team,
coordinating a helicopter, clearing things with the locals.
So typical of him, putting his people before his career.

Her idea was simple: an old-fashioned hostage
exchange. She wasn't surprised that Seth had agreed to
cooperate. After all, it got him exactly what he wanted:
face time with Daddy.

What happened after that, well, as long as she got
Taylor back safe and sound, she figured her conscience
could live with the consequences, even if her career
wouldn't.

Pittsburgh Police cleared an LZ for the Bell Ranger
carrying the FBI SWAT team. Walden called on
Burroughs' phone just as Lucy spotted the helicopter
approaching.

"Everyone safe?" she asked.

"Yes, but Seth isn't here. He took Taylor's car and Megan's cell phone. Plus he's armed with your mother's pistol."

Pretty much what she anticipated. "I'm taking care of Seth. Just get my family out of there and send June to a safe house."

"One problem. June's in labor. We called for an ambulance."

The sound of the helicopter almost drowned him out. Before she could reply Nick came on the line. "Lucy, are you okay?"

"I'm fine. I have to go, won't be in contact. You and Megan go with Walden and Oshiro and I'll catch up later." She had to shout the last as the helicopter hovered then descended. "I love you!"

His response was buried in the noise. She tossed the phone back to Burroughs. Greally escorted her to the helicopter, one hand steadying her elbow. She had to leave her cane behind—needed both hands free if she was going into an active shooter situation. As long as she looked down at where she planted her feet and didn't try to pivot or run, she'd be fine. Even her pain had quieted down, smothered by adrenalin.

"Got everything you need?" he asked, nodding to Taylor's messenger bag strapped across her chest.

"I'm good."

"I'll update you in the air if we learn anything." They ducked beneath the blades and he helped her up into the passenger area where the eight-man SWAT team waited, looking formidable with their MP5s and tactical gear.

The team leader, Hambly, handed her a headset

once she was strapped in. "Got your ballistic vest," he said, nodding to a bundle folded beside her seat. "We were just reviewing tactical options."

He held a tablet out in the center of the space. It revealed a topographical image of the recreational area where Seth waited for them. "We'll place snipers on the ridge here and here." Hambly pointed. "Sierra one, you're the south position, Sierra two, you're on the north." He glanced at Lucy. "You know the terrain. Any chance of getting a position across the lake?"

"The winds down the gorge are too erratic. It will make any shot across the water difficult."

"Okay, we stick with mid-range positions. Between the beach area and the campground, I'd prefer the beach. Less cover, less options for escape. We should be able to pin him down."

Lucy nodded. "I'll steer him there when he calls for the final instructions."

Her radio beeped as the pilot keyed in. "Got a call for you, Guardino."

Greally's voice came through. "Taylor's phone just came back on line."

"Where?"

"He's already at the lake. West side, near the dam." He gave her the coordinates and signed off.

The position was on the shore opposite the campground. "He's got the high ground there. Wants to control where the exchange takes place," Lucy told Hambly.

"Worse than that, there's no LZ on that side. And snipers are going to have a hard time of it with the thick foliage." Their specialized scopes would pick out the humans but they wouldn't be able to accurately tell which human was their target. Not unless Lucy persuaded Daddy to leave the cover of the trees.

As she stared at the terrain on the tablet she suddenly understood exactly what Daddy had planned. "He's going to use the dam."

Hambly scowled and nodded. "He's going old school, Cold War, Checkpoint Charlie style."

"The dam is fifty some feet high, and since he's already there, he has control of all the sight lines. There won't be any sneaking up on him."

"There is if we can rope out the snipers here and here." He pointed on the map.

Lucy shook her head. She'd grown up tramping over both sides of the gorge, knew how the acoustics worked, how steep the sides were. "He'll hear you coming. Plus the angle's too steep, they won't have a sightline."

As if on cue, the pilot clicked through again. "Guardino, another call being relayed. This one from our subject."

The techs back at the High Tech Computer Crimes squad were routing all calls through both Lucy and Taylor's phones via their computers.

"Is this Lucy?" a man's voice came through the line. "And the world-renowned FBI Hostage Rescue Team? Taylor would say hi but he's a bit tied up."

Lucy forced herself to be cordial. Hardest acting job she ever had to do. "What can I do for you? I'm sorry, I'm not sure what to call you."

"Daddy will do. As for what you can do for me, you can land on the east side of the dam, down at the beach. Then I want you and Seth to walk up to the dam.

There's a lock on the gate, but I'm sure you can manage that. We'll do the exchange on top, at the midpoint. Just you, Lucy. No guns. No men in black. Any of them leave the helicopter and your friend here is dead."

CHAPTER 33

———— ∿ ————

PAIN FLOODED THROUGH June. Every instinct screamed at her to flee, escape to that quiet place in her mind that she'd carved out as a safe haven when she was little.

No. This was too big. She had to stay alert. She couldn't let Seth down, let anything happen to their daughter just because she was too cowardly to face reality.

The sound of a car driving up to the house sent the men scrambling into defensive positions at the windows and door. June ignored them, pacing a route that took her from the living room, into the kitchen, around the table, back out and down the hall, then back again to the fireplace. She tried to count the steps but pain kept interrupting her.

Megan matched her step by step, giving her a hand to squeeze when a contraction hit, coaxing her to breathe. June wished it were Seth. Felt near tears at the thought of doing this alone, without him.

Not just the labor. What came after. What would she

do if he didn't come back to her? How could she ever do this alone? She had no idea what a mother was supposed to do…no idea what normal was.

Another contraction ripped through her, this one stronger than the last. She buckled with the pain. Megan held her up. "It's okay, June. The ambulance is here."

The door opened and two paramedics entered. The men gathered and talked as she and Megan continued their pacing. Then one of the medics approached her. "Are you okay to walk to the ambulance, ma'am? If so, we'll get you strapped in and do our assessment on the way to the hospital. Don't want to keep this baby waiting, do we?"

He took one elbow and Megan the other. As they walked past the coat rack, Megan grabbed June's coat and purse. They continued outside; the wind had died down although the rain was still steady. The other medic had stowed their gear and waited at the open door to the rear of the ambulance. Together they helped June climb inside and onto their stretcher.

Megan jumped in to tuck June's coat and purse between her and the wall of medical supplies carefully stored in glass cabinets. The first medic, the driver, left again. June heard his voice and the other men beyond the back doors of the ambulance. She had the feeling Oshiro had been asking to ride along with her and the medic was arguing with him.

"Come on, Megan," Nick called from where he stood outside in the rain. "They need to go now."

Megan nodded and gave June a quick hug. "I'll see you at the hospital. Everything will be fine, I just know it."

June glanced up from the gurney and waved good-bye as the paramedic still inside with her closed the doors, blocking her view of anyone outside. "First, I'm going to start an IV, just a precaution, then we'll be on our way and I'll get the monitors on you."

With practiced motions, he quickly inserted the needle into June's left arm. She barely felt it against the cramp of another contraction. The paramedic sat back and frowned at the still empty driver's seat. The driver's door was open but there was no sign of him.

"C'mon, Joe, we're good to roll," he called out.

An unseen man jumped into the front of the ambulance and slammed the door shut. They sped off, the vehicle rocking as they accelerated down the winding drive to the main road.

"Hey, lead foot," the medic yelled. "Slow it down, will ya?"

Instead of slowing, the driver sped up, then suddenly braked hard. June grabbed the stretcher's bars as they lurched into a hard right hand turn. The medic with her was tossed off of his seat and caught himself against the cabinets.

"What the hell? Joe, where you going? The hospital is down the mountain. Left, you idiot." Bracing himself with one hand against both sides of the vehicle, he moved forward to lean into the driver's compartment. There was a loud noise and the medic staggered back then slumped to the ground.

June knew that noise. A gunshot. She twisted against the belts holding her in place to glance over her shoulder. All she could see of the medic was one hand stretched out against the floor and his face, a blackened, bloodied hole where his eye should be.

It never occurred to her to scream. Not even when they took another sharp turn and bumped to a stop. Not even when she heard the man driving unbuckle his seat belt and step into the rear compartment.

Instead she clutched her purse and bag to her chest as if they were the fuzzy blanket she used to hide under. The man loomed over her from behind. She looked into his face.

"You're not him," she said in shock. She'd been so certain it was Daddy come for her. "Who are you?"

He tapped the muzzle of his pistol against her belly. "He sent me for you, Baby Girl. But I've decided to change the plan. Behave yourself and you and your baby both live. Give me any trouble and..." The muzzle ground into her flesh.

"Please, don't hurt my baby. I beg you."

He ignored her to glance out the rear window. "Good, they're heading down the mountain, never even saw that we went the wrong way. As soon as they're gone, we can backtrack out of here."

As he spoke, she slid her hand from her purse, concealed by her coat gathered over her. He turned around, pistol lowered to his side, a gleam in his eyes as if already collecting his reward.

June shot him, pulling the trigger over and over and over until the revolver was out of bullets. The sound echoed, thunder booming inside the small space long after the man's body hit the floor, leaving a trail of blood and brains on the door behind him.

CHAPTER 34

AS SOON AS the helicopter landed, Lucy called Seth and told him about the change of plans. While he made his way over from the campground, she put her vest on under her parka and exchanged her headset for a hands-free earpiece.

"There's almost no cell reception past the dam," she told Greally, who was monitoring things from the office.

"The radio should do the trick," Hambly assured her from where he also listened in. "As soon as you make contact and have his attention, we'll deploy."

He didn't sound too happy and Lucy understood why: their best weapon, the sniper teams, would have no way to gain the high ground without Daddy spotting them. Which meant setting up for an upwind, uphill, near-impossible shot over the lake to the top of the dam.

He read the worry on her face. "We're gonna get him, Guardino. I don't care if we need to climb a freakin' tree to get the shot, this SOB is not getting away."

"You going in armed?" Greally asked over the radio.

"Just until we get in sight of him, then I'll leave it. A subject like this, he'll enjoy taking control, watching me obey him."

Hambly shook his head. "I don't know how you do it, getting into the head of these sick, twisted freaks."

She shrugged. Seth drove up in Taylor's car and honked the horn. They'd drive up the service road to the dam, go the rest of the way on foot.

"What did this guy do that he's got a target on his back?" Hambly asked.

"Fell in love with the wrong woman," Lucy answered.

Hambly chuckled. "Story of my life." He clapped her on the shoulder. "You need anything, just holler and we'll be there."

She climbed down from the helicopter, taking care to balance her weight on her good leg. A burning sensation ran down her spine as she crossed to the car, as if she could feel Daddy's sights on her. Once she was inside and Seth pulled away, she told him, "We've got back-up listening in via my radio. They can hear everything we say."

He glanced at her, then nodded his understanding. No more confessions of murder, not with half the office listening in. "I left our phones behind after you called, so we don't have to worry about him." He meant Daddy. "Have you heard from June?"

"She's with Walden and Oshiro. On her way to the hospital."

"The hospital?"

"She's in labor. The baby is coming tonight."

The car stuttered to a stop as he clenched the wheel

and bowed his head forward over it. His shoulders shook, then he drew in a breath, and straightened once more. "Then this ends tonight. For June. For our baby."

He glanced at her and shifted in his seat so she could see the revolver snugged into his waistband at the small of his back. "Promise me that, Lucy. No matter what, June won't ever need to worry about him again."

Lucy never made promises she couldn't keep. But this one was easy. One way or the other, between her and Hambly's team or even Seth himself if it came to that, Daddy was as good as dead.

"I promise."

———◆———

MEGAN SAT IN the back seat of Walden's car with her dad. They were a few minutes behind the ambulance—had to douse the fire and turn off all the lights and everything at Grams' first. Oshiro was in the front seat beside Walden, leaning forward, peering through the rain.

"Where are they? We should have caught up with them by now."

Walden said nothing, but Megan felt their speed increase even as they rounded another curve. Even with only one good hand, Walden drove like her mother, faster was always better. Then, suddenly, he jammed on the brakes.

"What is it?" Dad asked.

"Look. Down the mountain." Walden opened his door and got out of the car, peering over the guardrail. They were on the outside edge of one of the many switchbacks that circled the mountain, and from here, could see all the way down to the lights of the homes in the valley below.

Megan didn't understand why Walden sounded so worried and from his frown, neither did Dad. But Oshiro got it. "Shit. Turn this thing around."

Walden got back into the driver's seat and quickly spun them into a U-turn. Oshiro leaned over the seat to talk to her dad. "Where else does this road lead?"

"Nowhere. Just down to 981."

"I mean, what's up the mountain? If we'd gone right instead of left at the end of the drive."

Then Megan got it. It was only March; there were no leaves on the trees yet. They could see the road all the way down the mountain and there'd been no cars—definitely no flashing lights from an ambulance.

"Someone took June?" she asked. "Who? The paramedics?"

"Maybe they weren't really paramedics. Or maybe they were ambushed. Who knows?" Walden was steering them around the curves so fast Megan grabbed for her door handle.

"Where does the road lead?" Oshiro asked.

"It dead ends about a half mile up the road from Coletta's," Dad answered. "There are a few logging roads along the way. That's it."

They reached the turnoff for Grams' drive. "Stop here," Oshiro ordered. Walden slowed, then backed into the driveway, the front of the car pointing out like they might need a quick escape. He turned the lights off but didn't turn the engine off.

"You two stay here," Walden said. He reached up to switch the dome light off then opened his door. Oshiro got out as well and they met at the trunk. Megan turned in her seat and tried to see what they were doing.

Dad was smarter. He got out of the car and slid into Walden's seat. She craned her head and spotted the two men in the rearview mirror. Walden was strapping his bulletproof vest on, fastening the Velcro one-handed, while Oshiro held a shotgun.

Then the sound of a gunshot cracked through the night. Not very loud, but quickly followed by others. Walden left at a jog, Oshiro following close behind.

"Should we get the shotgun from inside the house?" Megan whispered to her dad. She had no idea why she was whispering, but it seemed the right thing to do.

"No. Stay here with me. If they're not back in a few minutes, we'll go for help." He slowly inched the car forward so they had a good view of the road up the mountain.

Megan gripped the edge of the seat back, barely risking a breath. She tried to remember what her Kempo instructor said about releasing fear and controlling her breathing—same thing her mom always told her when they went shooting. But right here, right now, sitting in the dark with no idea what was happening, breathing was the last thing she could think about.

Lights flashed on the street above them. The ambulance's headlights. A man's figure was silhouetted in front of it—no mistaking Oshiro's build—waving them an all clear sign. Dad put the car back in gear and drove up the mountain until they were parked across from where the ambulance sat on the side of the road.

"What happened?" he asked Oshiro, rolling down his window as if he wasn't sure if he should get out of the car.

Megan was sure. She needed to check on June. She hopped out and ran over to the ambulance's rear. The doors were open—one of the windows was shattered and there was blood everywhere. Walden was dragging a dead body out of the way, his body twisted since he could only use one arm.

When he saw her, he spun to block Megan's view of the dead man, but it was too late. Megan stared at the man who was dressed like a soldier or hunter. She knew she should feel something—a man, a person, was dead—but all she could think of was June. "Are you okay?"

June nodded even as she clutched the rails of the stretcher she was strapped to, her face contorted in pain.

"She isn't hurt." Walden assured her. Her dad and Oshiro arrived behind her.

"Who's that man? Did you shoot him?" Megan asked Walden.

"No. June did." With Oshiro's help, Walden gave the man's body a final heave, rolling it out of the ambulance, giving them room to get to the medical equipment.

"The baby's coming," June gasped. Megan jumped inside the ambulance, almost slipping on the blood-covered floor, and skidded onto the bench seat beside June, grabbing her hand.

"Breathe, June. Like this," Megan demonstrated the panting she remembered from their health class video. "Dad, you know how. Can't you help her?"

Dad climbed into the now crowded ambulance and scooted past Megan to sit closer to June's head. "That's right, June. You can do this."

Walden finally found a kit labeled OB. He opened it and looked at the equipment: two yellow plastic clips, a bulb syringe, scissors, clamps, pads, sutures wrapped in tiny foil packets with illustrations of wickedly pointed curved needles on the front.

"I have no clue what half of this is." He looked to Oshiro. "You're a combat medic, right?"

"Yeah. I can use a tourniquet and chest tube—maybe amputate a limb if you need it, but this…"

Megan pointed to the yellow thing that looked like a hair barrette. "That's an umbilical clip, you put two on and cut between them. But first you suction the baby's mouth and nose with that." She pointed to the bulb.

"You know about this stuff?" Walden asked.

She nodded. "A little."

June cried out with another contraction, clawing at Dad's arm. Megan swallowed, her mouth suddenly dry. "Walden, set up that oxygen and put it on June's face."

Walden glanced past Megan to her dad. Anger sparked through her fear—just because she was a kid, didn't mean she didn't know what to do. After all, this baby was coming whether they were ready or not. "Dad, I've got this. Really."

"Trust her, she'll be fine." Nick answered Walden's silent question.

Megan wasn't sure if he meant her or June, but that was okay. She closed her eyes, took in a deep breath, and tried to remember everything she could from her first-aid course and the health class. Thank God she'd stayed awake for the whole thing.

"Oshiro, help June hold her legs back so I can take a look." Ugh. This was the disgusting part. But the men looked a ton more afraid than Megan. She took comfort in that. "June, I'm just going to check, see how far along you are." As if she knew—well, if she saw a baby's head poking out, guess she could figure that out.

Instead of relaxing, June lunged up and grabbed Megan's arm. "Promise me, Megan," she said, ignoring the men, focusing on Megan alone. As if Megan was the one in charge, the one who could promise anything. "Whatever happens to me, promise me that my baby will grow up in a home like yours. Surrounded by love. I want her to be strong, to never surrender, despite whatever happens to her."

"Like you," Megan whispered. Another contraction. June squeezed Megan's wrist so tight she felt the bones crunch.

"No," June gasped. "Not like me. Not a victim. A hero. Like your mom."

"My mom?" Megan was too scared and exhausted to control her surge of anger. "My mom got my grams killed. She's no hero."

She felt more than saw Dad's grimace at that. Who cared? It was the truth and he knew it. So did Mom— that's why she acted so distant and moody all the time. Just because they'd started talking again didn't change the facts.

June fell back, panting. She raised her palm to caress Megan's cheek. "She is a hero, Megan. She did what she did to save you. I want my baby to grow up with a mother like that."

Now it was Megan's turn to clutch at June. "She will. You'll be a great mother, June. I just know it."

There was a hiss as Walden finally figured out how to connect the oxygen. He gently adjusted the prongs beneath June's nose.

June's face shadowed with something more than pain. "I'm afraid," she whispered. "I think I should give her up, maybe. Find a better family for her. The family she deserves."

"No. June. No."

Behind her, she felt Oshiro shift and knew he felt the same way. He reached down and stroked June's arm, but said nothing.

June's answer was cut short as a powerful contraction rocked her body. She screamed in pain then began panting. "I have to push. She's coming. Megan. She's coming."

CHAPTER 35

———— ⌇ ————

BY THE TIME they reached the dam, the rain had slowed to a drizzle. Lucy had Seth turn off all the lights, interior and exterior, before they got out. She circled around to the rear of the car, opened the trunk and retrieved a short tire iron.

"What's that for?" Seth asked, leaning against the car. He was moving more slowly and unsteadily than she was.

"He said there was a lock on the gate."

"He thought of everything, didn't he?"

"Are you okay?" she asked.

He pushed off the car, a strange smile shining through the dim light. "Yeah. I'm going to be a father. Hell, maybe I already am."

She couldn't argue with that perspective on things. Lord knew it was the thought of her own family that had gotten her through worse situations. At least they were safe.

They linked arms and hauled each other up the slope

to the gate at the end of the dam. The spillways were open, rushing water pouring through, echoing through the gorge and leaving the ground with the slightest tremor. Lucy didn't like it—she had a hard enough time making sure her bad foot was planted firmly as it was.

She handed Seth her Maglite and he needed both hands to hold it steady while she dealt with the padlock. She didn't bother trying to unlock it—the hasp was thick and sturdy, unlike the cheap chain link that held it in place and snapped with judicious leverage from the tire iron.

"You going to be able to fire that gun?"

"Got six bullets, only need one to do the job." His tone was nonchalant and his posture open as if he'd left all his worries far behind.

"Okay, then." She hauled the chain-link gate open and they stepped onto the dam. It was only about eight feet across here at the top, the walkway interrupted by several hoists positioned to manually raise the floodgates if necessary.

"Stop there!" a man's voice came from in front of them. "Inside the gate there's a radio."

Seth waved the light around until it fell on a small Motorola walkie talkie. Lucy retrieved the unit and clicked it on. "We're here. Let me see Taylor."

"Did you really think we'd be making the exchange here out in the open where your snipers can watch and wait? There's an access hatch below the first hoist. Open it and climb down to the catwalk. Taylor's waiting."

Lucy wasn't too surprised by the change in venue— like she'd told Hambly earlier, Daddy thrived on control. But that meant she had a greater weapon: chaos.

In the form of a dying man with nothing to live for and everything to die for. Chaos as in an FBI agent who tonight had seen her career go up in flames—literally.

Chaos as in the other items she'd taken from Taylor's trunk: two roadside flares. One for her and one for Seth.

———•———

"WHAT'S HER NAME?" Megan asked June as Walden drove them down the mountain in the ambulance. She marveled at the small creature suckling at June's breast, eager for her first meal. A surge of pride washed through Megan. June did most of the work and her father and Oshiro helped, but she'd just delivered a baby!

"I don't know. I was so scared I wouldn't ever get to see her that I couldn't think of a name. It felt like tempting fate."

Sounded like something her mother would say.

"Your birthday is in June?"

"I don't know when my birthday is," June said. "But the day I was born was in June. The day they found me, saved me. Not that I understood that then." She shifted her weight and the baby made a cooing, sucking noise that made Megan smile and yet feel close to tears. "March—not such a good name. Not for a fighter like her."

"Julia?" Megan suggested. "Like Julius Caesar?"

"Beware the ides of March? Isn't that when they killed him?"

They hadn't gotten that far yet in English class. "Oh. Guess not, then."

"How about Lucille? After your mother? I would

have never lived this long, wouldn't have her without your mom."

"Lucy isn't short for Lucille. Her real name is Lucia. She hates it."

Their eyes met and both of them laughed, the noise swirling through the ambulance and chasing the shadows and fears away. Megan had the sudden feeling that someone was resting their hand on her shoulder, giving her an encouraging squeeze.

"Your grandmother, then?" June asked. "She must have been a very special lady to have raised your mom alone. To make such a wonderful home. What was her name?"

Megan smiled—not at the request but at the warm memories that flowed through her. She touched her hand to her shoulder, could swear she felt another hand slip away, followed by the brush of lips against the top of her head. "Her name was Coletta. And I think she'd like that very much."

CHAPTER 36

IT TOOK BOTH of them to open the service hatch, mainly because Lucy couldn't plant her weight on her left foot. The heavy steel protested with a screech barely heard over the roar of the rushing water below. It fell open, clanging against the concrete, releasing a damp, yet pleasant, scent, not unlike the smell of the woods after a lightning storm.

Ozone from the water, Lucy guessed as she led the way down the ladder into the belly of the dam. It was slow going as she had to hoist herself down every other step to save her bad leg, but she couldn't risk it going out from under her now. Seth's pace was almost as bad, his balance wobbly, several times pausing to steady himself.

The interior passage was rhomboid shaped with the narrow end forming the ceiling. Two strings of incandescent light bulbs hung from wires suspended from the ceiling. The concrete walls angled away from them, leaving wide-open space on either side of the metal catwalk. Below, the gush of water sent ripples of light across the walls and the vibrations ran from the metal into Lucy's bones.

The catwalk had iron railings along both sides except where there were intersecting catwalks leading out to the floodgate mechanisms. Lucy dared to look down, clutching the railing tight, and immediately regretted it. Usually she had no problem with heights, but trapped inside tons of concrete with invisible, hungry waters rushing eagerly below, made her head swim. Daddy had chosen his tomb well.

"Ready?" she asked Seth. She could barely hear herself but he nodded. She positioned herself as a shield in front of him as they slowly moved past the first hoist area into a stretch of uninterrupted catwalk. There was a good thirty feet before the next hoist mechanism and the shadows gathered around it.

"We're here," she shouted into the radio, wondering if it would work down here.

"I said no weapons," Daddy chided.

Lucy pocketed the radio and held her jacket open, making a show of slowly removing her service weapon and placing it at her feet. She still had her backup weapon concealed at the small of her back, but he didn't ask her to take her parka off.

"Good girl."

"Show me Taylor."

"Say the magic word."

"Please. I need to see that he's unharmed."

A few moments later, two figures appeared in front of the hoist mechanism. Taylor, his hands cuffed in front of him but appearing uninjured, and the man known as

Daddy.

———◆———

"HERE'S HOW THIS is going to work," Daddy said, pressing his gun against Taylor's head with enough force that Taylor had to bend his neck. He spoke into a hands-free microphone, as if by making Lucy use a handheld radio he would gain the upper hand.

The guy obviously didn't know Lucy, was all Taylor could focus on. He couldn't believe how relieved he was when she appeared—and how guilty he felt about Seth being there. Seth was innocent, a civilian. It wasn't his job to risk himself.

"Taylor and Bernhart will walk toward the middle, pass each other, and continue until we each have what we want."

"What's the catch?" Lucy's voice came over the radio. She was buying time, Taylor was certain—as was Daddy.

"No catch. You and Taylor are free to go after that. On my count."

Taylor almost took a step forward, he was so eager to get away, but Daddy hoisted him back and spun him against the steel plate of the hoist mechanism so they were face-to-face.

"You didn't think I'd let you off that easy, did you, Taylor?" Daddy said. He held Taylor in place with the flat of his hand and his weight pressed against Taylor's throat. Before Taylor could raise his cuffed hands to fight back, Daddy flipped the pistol to hold it by its barrel and swung it in an arc against Taylor's left side.

The blow landed with such force that Taylor would

have collapsed to the ground if Daddy hadn't been holding him upright. He tried to gasp—would have screamed with the pain—but Daddy's hand clamped tight against his throat until his vision swam red.

"Hey!" Lucy yelled. "Stop that!"

Daddy didn't turn around but he did turn his radio back on so Lucy could hear. "That blow just fractured Taylor's spleen. He'll die of internal injuries if you don't get him to a surgeon within twenty minutes or so." Daddy's smile was inches from Taylor's eyes, filling his vision. "Like I told you, I know I'll win because I control all the parameters. The players, the playing field, and now the clock."

He released Taylor, hooking one arm under his before he could fall. The pain was unlike any Taylor had ever felt before—not even when he'd taken his close-quarter combat training and the instructor had gotten below his guard and landed a kick to his solar plexus.

"Move," Daddy commanded. "Now."

Taylor stumbled forward, barely able to raise his head high enough to see Seth approaching from the other direction. Behind him Lucy waited, her hands in fists at her sides, body angled forward, tense, a sprinter waiting for the starting gun.

The pain grew with every step until he was forced to bend over and grab hold of the handrail to keep him upright. Just a little farther.

Seth stared past Taylor, concentrating on Daddy. They were almost at the midpoint where their paths would cross.

"I'm sorry," Taylor murmured, hoping Seth would hear him above the roar of the water below.

Seth's gait faltered and he glanced at Taylor. Then he did the strangest thing. He smiled. As if there wasn't anything to be worried about.

One more step and he was behind Taylor. In front of him, Lucy's fists opened and closed as if counting the seconds. Taylor tried his best to shuffle forward faster. But then he realized it wasn't him she was staring at: it was Seth.

Of course she had a plan—Lucy always had a plan. Taylor relaxed. It was going to be okay, he was certain.

"Lucy," Daddy called out in a jovial tone. "I did forget one little catch. You might want to tell your HRT boys to clear off the dam and get back to their helo."

Taylor faltered and glanced back to see Daddy waving a smart phone in triumph. He'd spent time scouting the dam and surrounding area before letting Taylor out of the van—must have planted cameras. Damn spytech. It was making it so the bad guys had nicer toys than the good guys.

"I've rigged the dam to explode. No one leaves here until after I'm good and gone. I see your friends step off that helo again or if you try to open the hatch before I radio back that it's clear and it all blows."

Chapter 37

LUCY WAS FAIRLY certain Daddy was lying about the explosives. There was no way he'd have time to plant them—and why would he have access to explosives in the first place? He was bluffing. Had to be.

How many lives was she willing to risk on "fairly" was the question.

Taylor collapsed, one arm slung over the railing, still ten feet short of her position. But he was almost within reach of her service weapon. If he was in any condition to shoot, it would be one more advantage. Seth kept moving toward Daddy, marching down the center of the catwalk.

"Tell them, Lucy!" Daddy yelled, obviously assuming she was the greater threat. "Tell those SWAT boys to clear out, now."

Lucy shuffled forward, ostensibly to help Taylor but really to get closer to her weapon, which lay a few feet to his right. She watched Seth carefully, knowing he'd make his move soon.

"Stop right there," Daddy shouted at Seth, dividing

his focus long enough for Taylor to slide his hand to within a few inches of her weapon. Good. She let her parka fluff around her, clearing her path to her backup weapon. Movement from in front of her caught her eye. Seth, reaching back to draw his revolver.

A shot reverberated against the hollow concrete walls, followed by another, both coming from Seth. Lucy grabbed her backup Glock and hobbled forward as fast as her bad leg would carry her. Seth had braced himself against the railing, needing both hands to steady his aim. Daddy clutched at his arm, his gun on the catwalk at his feet.

"Drop it, Seth," Lucy said.

"Can't do it, Lucy."

Damn it, she had to stop him. "We need him alive."

"You know damn well there're no bombs. He's bluffing."

"I don't give a shit about him. I'm thinking of you." Remembering that others were listening in, she grabbed her earpiece and tossed it over the railing.

"Do as she says," Daddy screamed the words. "You can't shoot me. I'm unarmed. I surrender."

Seth hesitated for a fatal moment. Long enough for Daddy to charge him, both men grappling against the railing so Lucy couldn't get a clear shot. Seth's gun clattered to the ground and skidded past her.

"Do it, Lucy," Seth shouted. "Go ahead, shoot."

Despite his wound, Daddy got the upper hand, pinning Seth sideways against the railing, his back bent as he fought against falling. Seth still stood between her and a clear shot at Daddy. A shot rang out from behind her, sparking against the railing mere inches from Daddy.

Taylor, who from his position at the railing had a better angle.

She searched for a shot of her own, when Daddy suddenly released Seth. He raised his hands in surrender, turning to her.

"They can't shoot me," he told Seth. "It's against the rules. You of all people should know that, Mr. Assistant US Attorney."

Seth slumped against the railing, obviously spent. "Step away," Lucy told Daddy. "Keep those hands where I can see them."

"Aren't you going to arrest him as well, Special Agent?" Daddy mocked her. "After all, he tortured and killed five innocent men."

Seth made a noise like a wild animal. He lunged forward, pulling the road flare from his overcoat pocket. The flare had a short spike at the bottom, designed to anchor it into the ground. Seth plunged it like a spear into Daddy's neck.

Then he yanked off the cap, igniting it. Daddy staggered back, hit the railing, and toppled over it, bright red and orange sparks coloring his scream as he fell.

"They weren't innocent, you bastard," Seth called after him. He clung to the railing with both hands, his knees buckling. Lucy drew close, bending to grab her mother's revolver and pocketing it, keeping her own weapon in her hand.

"Step away from the edge, Seth."

His eyes were wide as he shook his head. "No. I can't."

"Seth, I need your help. Taylor needs your help. He's injured and I can't get him out of here by myself. Please, step away."

He turned, his gaze riveted to the dancing light from the water below.

Lucy tried another tactic. "Think of June. Of your baby."

"I am." The words were choked with tears. "June's safe now." He turned, straightened with an effort, and finally looked her in the eye. "She's safe. That's all that matters."

He backed up against the railing, arms held wide, leaning back precariously far over the abyss.

"Either take the shot or let me go," he pleaded. "Either way, I can't stand the idea of her finding out what I did. Please. Let me die a hero in her eyes."

"You'll always be her hero, Seth. Nothing could ever change that." Despite her words, Lucy's aim didn't waver. "But don't you think June deserves the truth? After all she's been through?"

He shook his head, denying her words. "She deserves more than that. She deserves peace of mind. She deserves to feel safe inside her own home. She deserves a future."

"She does. You dying doesn't give her any of that."

"No. Because before the poison kills me, they'll drag me through courts, the press. That can never happen. They'll never leave her in peace. They'll keep hounding her. And they'll have won. Daddy, the others like him. I can't let that happen."

Before she could stop him, he twisted his body and threw himself over the railing, plunging into the darkness. Lucy darted forward, hit the safety rail so hard it knocked her breath away.

A splash came from below. And then there was silence.

CHAPTER 38

SEVERAL OF THE SWAT guys stayed behind so there was room for Taylor, Lucy, and their combat medic in the helicopter. Once at the hospital, the surgeons whisked Taylor away—in mid-sentence, asking for his laptop, of course—leaving Lucy behind in the ER.

"Ma'am, you might want to get yourself checked out," one of the ER nurses told Lucy.

Lucy glanced at her, the world suddenly tilting as her ankle totally surrendered. She wobbled and fell against the wall. "Maybe you're right. But first, could I use your phone?"

The nurse ignored her request—as Lucy had learned nurses were prone to do—bundling her into a wheelchair, propping her leg up, removing Lucy's shoe, brace, and sock to reveal blood oozing from the top of her foot. Not to mention the ankle swollen to almost twice its normal size, leaving indentations from where the brace had constricted it, and bruises in various shades of red and purple.

Damn. Her surgeon was going to be pissed off.

Not as much as Nick was once she called him and he came down from the maternity ward. His grin was a match for the one she'd seen the day Megan was born—until he saw her ankle.

"It's not as bad as it looks," she said. "I walked in here without my cane."

He closed his eyes for a brief moment. She knew that look all too well—his "searching for Zen, Lord give me patience, what the hell" look. "And you think that was a good idea? Ditching your cane?"

No way could she have climbed into the dam or gotten across that catwalk with it, but she just looked sheepish and said, "Maybe not."

He sighed and sank onto the side of her stretcher—she was waiting for an X-ray of her ankle, but the doctor said he thought it was just a surgical pin working itself loose after the trauma of the night.

"Megan delivered June's baby," Nick said.

"What? Why?" She jolted upright, jostling her ankle and releasing a new wave of pain. "Is she okay?"

"You should have seen her. She was incredible." Lucy hadn't seen Nick beam so proudly since the day Megan was born.

"Of course she was. How's June? And the baby?" Sooner or later, she'd have to tell June about Seth. She was glad she was stuck down here; it gave her time to decide exactly what to say.

"They're gorgeous, beautiful." He wove the fingers of his left hand between hers, their wedding rings sliding together. "I cried."

Laughter burst free, rattling the narrow stretcher. "Tell me all about it."

By the time he'd finished, she wasn't laughing—not after hearing how June had to kill a man or that Megan was there to see the aftermath.

If she had any doubts about her future—about their future—they all evaporated.

Walden stuck his head through the privacy curtain. "You decent? Up for a visitor?"

"Sure, come on in."

He pulled the curtain aside and held it for Megan, who bounded in, wearing a set of hospital scrubs and looking much too grown up in them. When had her little girl blossomed into an almost-grown woman?

Megan rushed over and gave Lucy a hug. "Did you hear? I delivered a baby."

"I heard. I'm very proud of you."

"Oshiro cried," she said. "So did Walden, but he won't admit it."

"I was up front driving," Walden protested. "You didn't see any tears coming from me."

"Liar."

"That's my story and I'm sticking to it."

"Where's Oshiro?" Lucy asked.

"Won't leave June's side," Walden answered. Typical over-protective Oshiro.

"Have you heard anything about Taylor?"

"He's getting a CAT scan, but the surgeons said there's a good chance they won't have to operate."

Relief washed over Lucy. Ignoring the stupid oxygen monitor that she didn't need, she wrapped her free arm around Megan. "That's good."

"Guess I'll go check on him, see if they've decided." Walden gave her a nod and left.

"I need to talk to you two," Lucy started. "How would you feel if I wasn't an FBI agent?"

Nick said nothing, he seemed to understand this was about Megan more than anything. Despite the trauma of the night—or maybe because of it—she was finally talking to Lucy, seemed almost her old self. Lucy didn't want to do anything that might jeopardize that.

"I don't want you to quit your job, not because of me," Megan answered.

"Not because of you. For you. For me and Dad and our family." Lucy held Megan close, her mouth near the top of Megan's dark curls. "I think we need time to heal. A chance for a fresh start."

"But what will you do? You're not really good at anything else."

Ouch. Out of the mouth of babes. "For starters, I'll be at your next Kempo tournament and all your soccer games and we can find Grams' secret recipe for that awesome chocolate ganache cake you love and make it for your birthday."

Megan, pressed against Lucy's chest, nodded. "I think she'd like that."

"I do, too."

"And you know, Mom," Megan continued, a glint in her eye. "You don't need to carry a badge to be a hero."

Smart, smart girl. Lucy kissed the top of Megan's head just like she used to do when Megan was a baby. She used to inhale that delightful baby scent as if it were nectar from the gods, ambrosia that could sustain her as she left her family to face the evil out in the world.

But the more she fought, the more evil there was and the less she could protect her family from it. Maybe that wasn't what she should have been focused on all these years. Maybe life was more about standing together than standing behind a defender.

Maybe Nick and Megan—and her mom—never needed her to protect them. Maybe all they needed was Lucy to be *with* them.

Well, she was here now. And nothing was going to tear them apart. Not ever again.

Family first, Coletta's voice echoed through her mind.

Family always.

———◆———

AFTER SHE WAS cleared by the doctors—no new broken bones and the old ones looked nicely healed, but definitely a new ankle sprain and she hadn't done the damaged nerves and muscles any favors—Lucy gave her new cane a test drive and made her way up to Taylor's room.

He was pale, too pale, but awake and sitting up, working on his laptop. "Hey, boss. They said I have to stay in bed for a few days, but I get to keep my spleen. Never knew I wanted it in the first place, but figured it might come in handy some day, so that's a good thing, right?"

"What kind of drugs do they have you on?" she asked, pulling up a chair to sit beside him.

"Very, very good ones." He grinned up at her. "I highly recommend them."

Maybe this wasn't the best time, but she wanted to

see June and the baby, then head home with her family. "About what happened tonight. At the end—"

"I know what Seth did," he said, suddenly sober. "I know you were trying to protect him. I heard the SWAT guys saying you told them Daddy and he went over together while Seth was struggling to keep Daddy from shooting us."

She held her breath, waited. Taylor searched her face for a long moment. "I can live with that. Face myself in the mirror."

"Thanks."

"What I can't live with is that you didn't tell me. You knew he'd killed those men and you said nothing."

"I didn't know. I suspected. No evidence. Just a wild-assed theory." He stared her down—so unlike the usual Taylor. "Okay, more than just a theory. But he paid for what he did."

"On his terms. That's not justice. If he'd lived, would you have let him get away with it?" He waved his hand at his laptop, swinging the IV tubing with it. "I've put together most of the pieces. All of those men were threatening June. Daddy paid them to do it. But Seth tortured them, Lucy. Why didn't he come to us instead? Let us handle it? It's our job."

"Because he was already facing a death sentence." She explained about the mercury poisoning. "He thought those men could lead him to Daddy—not like we'd been able to find the man in all these years. And he knew he was running out of time." Taylor opened his mouth but she continued, "I don't condone what he did. If he hadn't died down there beneath the dam, I would have arrested him myself."

He shook his head. "No, you wouldn't have. You would have let him see his baby, say good-bye to June, and die on his own terms."

She thought about it. "Maybe. Probably. But we failed him, Taylor. And it was the only way he could protect his family."

"See, that's where you're wrong. Because my guys found him."

"Who?"

"Daddy. Your geographic profile along with my search algorithm hit the jackpot. His real name was Oren Imus and he lived outside of Akron, Ohio. Fourteen years ago, he was fired from his job as a software engineer and tried to sue the company for wrongful termination, saying the child pornography they found in his company computer was planted there because they wanted to steal his ideas. He lost and had to pay court costs and attorney fees."

"Thirty-two thousand dollars' worth," Lucy filled in the blanks. "So he sold June and when that didn't pay off, he sold the Baby Girl images."

Taylor nodded. "Point is, all we needed was more data and a little time. If Seth had come to us, those five men might still be alive."

She'd seen the police reports on those five men. What they'd found on their computers—and in two cases, they'd also found live victims. Without Seth's intervention, what might have happened to them?

Taylor saw her look of doubt. "You're just like him, Lucy. You don't see it, but you are."

"I'm no vigilante." Although there had been times in her career when she'd been tempted. But what cop doing the job she did could say otherwise?

"No. But you trust your instincts more than your team. How many times in the past two years have you left Walden and me in the dark?"

"I was trying to protect you."

His stare and silence said it all. She pushed to her feet. "You're going to be a great squad leader, Taylor."

"They'll never let me back in the field again, not after this." He frowned, then looked up at her. "But I'm okay with that. Does that make me a coward?"

"No. It makes you the right man for your job. Enjoy it. Catch tons of bad guys. And never forget why you do it. You'll be just fine."

She'd almost made it to the door when he called her back. "Lucy…Are you going to be okay?"

She turned around slowly, using the cane to pivot her weight. God, she felt so old, ancient. "I'll be fine. Can still face myself in the mirror."

The Girl Who Never Was: Memoirs of a Survivor
by June Unknown

EPILOGUE

WISE MEN AND poets are always asking why? Why is there pain and suffering? Why is there evil? Why are we here?

As I hold my baby, her skin pressed against my skin, feel her breath burble from her cheeks, smell her sweetness, I think the answer is so very simple and so very hard. We are here to learn how to love.

Not just how to give love blindly as I did with Daddy.

More than learning how to accept and cherish the love offered to us as Seth taught me.

Rather, how to *live* it. Every day. With every beat of our hearts.

Seth's final gift to me came in the form of a letter. He didn't try to explain, he left that to others. I think there, at the end, he knew and understood love better than anyone on the planet ever has or ever will.

To my dearest, beautiful, brave, and amazing wife and daughter:

You are my everything.

If you don't remember anything else, please remember those four words and cherish them as a truth larger than any man could ever speak.

I want to be there with you both so badly that it breaks my heart. If there was any other path, know I would have taken it no matter how painful.

In my mind I am there with you. My arms wrap around both of you, holding you so tight, so that we three, together, our beating hearts echo into eternity with a force strong enough to power the universe.

That is how much I love you both.

I don't regret it—not any of it, not one single moment—so please remember that when shadows fall over your own memories. Know that what we had, what we two created, was beautiful, strong, enduring. Our love, our life together, our baby is absolute proof of what God intended when he started all this; that yes, there is light, there will always be light, and with light comes hope and strength and triumph.

You will have doubts, my beautiful, amazing, courageous, and yet blind, wife. Fear will creep in and you will worry you are not strong enough. Know that you are. You will be the best mother a child could have. I only wish I could be there by your side to watch our beautiful, strong, and amazing daughter grow.

Know that I will always be with you both. Know that you are loved, deeply and completely. Know that you are not alone.

Be happy.
Your loving husband.

As I read Seth's farewell, holding our baby as she slept, surrounded by his family, our friends, and knowing that they were all now my family, I knew he was right.

I don't know my real birthday; I still don't know my real name. Although I now know who my mother and father were, I only have the birthday and name that were given to me by strangers.

But I know when my life began. And it was the day two strangers knocked on my door and entered my empty life. The day I found a reason to enter the world, a reason to believe there was something worth fighting for, something worth living for.

The day I met Seth and became the girl who is June Unknown. The girl who does more than endure or survive, but who has learned how to speak up against evil.

The girl who has learned how to live. And, finally, how to love.

CHAPTER 39

MONDAY MORNING AT 9:04, Lucy marched—well, okay, hobbled, but in her mind she felt as if she were marching—into the Assistant Special Agent in Charge's office. John Greally was already behind his desk, peering into his computer monitor, a cup of coffee down to its dregs beside his elbow.

Lucy slid the piece of paper she'd spent all night working on across his desk to him, then stood at attention, using the cane to keep her upright. As soon as this was finished, she planned on going home, collapsing, treating herself to an hour-long soak in the whirlpool at the rehab clinic, collapsing again, then scheduling an appointment with her surgeon to let him yell at her for jeopardizing his precious creation—aka her ankle and foot—and probably returning to another hell-month of physical therapy and rehab.

She was looking forward to it. For the first time in two months, she felt in control of her life.

Greally glanced at the letter on his desk but not at her. He closed down his monitor, changed to his reading glasses, picked up her letter, and stood to read it. His face remained expressionless as he scanned it once, then again. Finally, he strode over to the credenza lining the wall beside him and slid her carefully crafted resignation letter into the shredder.

Then he turned to face her, brushing his hands together and giving her the same look she'd seen him give his teenager when she acted out. "What the hell was that?"

"My answer. You asked what I wanted. I'll print you another copy."

He shook his head and sank into his seat—his administrator's chair behind the desk, not the chair beside her. "Sit down."

"I'd rather stand. Sir."

He glared up at her. "That's an order, Special Agent Guardino."

Lucy squinted at him, then shuffled to the seat beside her and lowered herself onto it. "You can't refuse my resignation. Sir."

"I can and I will. Because you're not resigning." She opened her mouth to protest but he silenced her with a raised hand. "You're separating from the Federal Bureau of Investigation on a medical pension. There's a big difference. Trust me, Lucy, all these years behind a desk have taught me how to navigate this maze of red tape. Folks like Ms. Carroll want you to get angry and resign because it saves them time and money."

"Carroll can go—"

"Now, now. People like her can be useful. You just

have to understand the game." He turned to his computer and clicked a few keys. "I see here that you have twenty-six days of unused vacation time. We can't even begin the separation process until that's used up. And then we'll have to get another complete medical evaluation, documentation of the degree of disability, Carroll will need to have it signed off by DC, then there will be the separation interviews and final paperwork...all told, we should have you free and clear by the end of May."

"May?" she protested. "What the hell am I supposed to do until May?"

He raised an eyebrow. "Did you miss the part about vacation?"

"Carroll will never—"

"You let me handle Carroll and her winged monkeys. As for how you fill all those empty days..." He opened his desk drawer and removed a stack of paper clipped pink message forms. Leaning forward, he dealt them out like poker cards. "These came while you were gone the past two months." He snapped down one group of messages. "Requests for interviews, book deals, and speaking gigs."

Lucy leafed through them. Major network TV, New York agents and publishers, a famous true crime author. "What the—"

"These," Greally dealt her another stack of pink paper, "are teaching positions, honorary degrees, non-profit board positions, and these," a third stack, "are private consulting and security firms."

"You've got to be kidding." Lucy looked up, stunned. He smiled back.

"Face it, Lucy. As many enemies as you've made in the Bureau, you're the public's ideal of a kick-ass FBI agent. Of course people are going to want you to be the face of their company or non-profit or guest commentator. And they'll pay good money for it."

"I'd basically be a paid shill. No way, we don't need the money that bad."

He slid another smaller stack of messages out from the desk drawer. Dealt them one at a time in front of her. "I saved the best for last. These are non-profits that don't want you as just another name on their letterhead; they want you to join them. Full-time advisor, part-time private consultant, whatever you want. But they're out there, boots on the ground, getting the job done when local law enforcement doesn't have the resources and we can't make it a priority."

She scanned them more carefully than the previous slips. National Center for Missing and Exploited Children. The Polaris Project. NAMUS. She'd worked with all of them. While not certified law enforcement agencies and with no arrest powers, they did good work—more than the public knew, since they shared all their investigative results with law enforcement and it was the cops who got all the credit.

But these guys, this was where the real work was being done. They saved lives every day, even though they didn't carry badges or guns.

"Who's this one?" she asked. "The Beacon Group?"

He leaned back in his chair looking smug. "They're relatively new, but their funding is solid and so are the people behind them. They're looking to build a high-quality staff of investigators. Their focus is cold cases, missing persons."

She nodded. Pretty much where her talents lay—and her interests.

"As of today, you are officially on vacation. Once those twenty-six days are up, I'll start the medical pension paperwork. Should give you plenty of time to investigate your possibilities, talk with Nick and Megan, decide where you go from here."

Lucy was still staring at the slip of paper. Beacon Group. She liked the name, the idea behind it. Lord knew, after the past several years of working sex crimes, she could use some light to steer her clear of the abyss she'd found herself lost in.

She pushed to her feet with her cane, pocketed the pink slips of paper, then reached across the desk to take Greally's hand.

"Thanks, John." She never called him by his first name, not here at work.

He clasped her hand. "Thank you, Supervisory Special Agent Guardino. The Bureau is grateful for your years of service and dedication. You will be missed."

As soon as she cleared his door, she slid out her cell phone.

"How'd it go?" Nick said when he answered.

"They're going to force me to take vacation," she answered with a mock groan. "Twenty-six days. Can you believe it?"

"Cruel and unusual punishment. But perfect timing. Next week Megan's school is out for spring break—"

"And it's her birthday. Let's get out of town, go someplace warm and sunny." She stopped, turned to the wall, hiding her face from any prying eyes. After months of feeling numb, pushing away her emotions, she suddenly had a hard time stopping tears. How crazy was that? "Someplace where we can be a family."

"Any thoughts about what you want to do after this so-called vacation?"

"I think Megan had it right. I don't have to carry a badge to do the job I want to do."

There was a pause. "And you're okay with that?"

"Yes."

His voice dropped, low and intimate. "We good?"

This time she didn't dodge the question. She stood straight, trying in vain to pour the depth of her feelings into the cell phone. Tears warmed her cheeks but she didn't turn away from a stray secretary who passed, staring at her with a disdainful arched eyebrow.

She finally had an answer for Nick. Without him she never would have survived any of this. "We're good. We're on our way to being great."

And she meant every damn word.

Dear Reader,

Thanks so much for joining in on Lucy's fifth adventure! If you haven't read her first stories, they are: SNAKE SKIN, BLOOD STAINED, KILL ZONE, and AFTER SHOCK.

The Lucy Guardino Thrillers are the only series I know of that come with a warning—and there's good reason for it. Most of the crimes and bad guys depicted in these stories come from real life and HARD FALL is no exception.

The criminal Lucy is chasing in HARD FALL is the most vile and twisted individual I've ever written about. Yet, I didn't invent him. I read about similar criminals in a *USA Today* news story, and it made me sick to think of people like them walking among us.

Instead of depicting his crimes (far too horrid for me to ever actually portray on the page), I wanted to shed some light on this dark stain of humanity and wrote of the girl who survived. She is a product of my imagination but, as you'll see, also inspired by true events.

I hope you find her story and Lucy's journey in HARD FALL empowering and inspiring.

Lucy's adventures will continue in LAST LIGHT, available May, 2016.

As always, thanks for reading!

CJ

EDGY READS

www.EdgyReads.com

CPSIA information can be obtained at www.ICGtesting.com
Printed in the USA
BVOW08s0336050216

435609BV00003B/4/P